IRIT walked in from the kitchen carrying a tray of crackers and cheese and saw Slaight with his head resting on the sofa. "What's happening, Ry? I have a right to know. This whole thing is destroying you. And it's destroying us. Tell me. You've got to tell me."

Slaight raised his head and looked at her. She was remarkably beautiful. He was tired and she was right. The whole thing was eating him alive. He knew he would need her help to see it through.

"Irit, it's a long story. I'm going to tell you all I know. I want a glass of bourbon on the rocks, tall. Then I'm gonna start at the beginning and tell you every goddam thing I know about that dead cadet."

Lucian K. Truscott IV,

a third-generation graduate of West Point, is the first writer to explore the hidden world behind the gray walls on the banks of the Hudson. Turn the page and read the rave reviews for this utterly candid look at the United States Military Academy.

DRESS GRAY

DRESS GRAY

"A frightening novel about 'a secret cult head-quartered on the Hudson behind a stone facade' . . . the author mounts an attack on his alma mater with brilliance and fury. It doesn't look like the United States Military Academy will stand a chance against Lucian K. Truscott IV. . . . His prose is muscular, strong and free-swinging. . . . Up on the Hudson, behind the gray walls, they can't be too happy about the publication of DRESS GRAY. It ought to be required reading for high school seniors with West Point in their plans."

—*Newsday*

"THE LONG GRAY LINE IS GOING TO BE SPUTTERING ON THIS ONE. . . . "
—*Middletown Times-Herald Record*

"Absorbing . . . Mr. Truscott effectively drama-tizes the social upheavals of the 1960's: the change from the World War II to the Vietnam way of seeing things, and the effect that change worked on American soldiers and civilians. . . . DRESS GRAY succeeds as a compelling portrait of the Military Academy."

—*New York Times*

Lucian K. Truscott IV

DRESS GRAY

FAWCETT CREST • NEW YORK

DRESS GRAY

Published by Fawcett Crest Books, a unit of CBS Publications, the Consumer Publishing Division of CBS Inc., by arrangement with Doubleday and Company, Inc.

ISBN: O-449-24158-0

THIS BOOK CONTAINS THE COMPLETE TEXT OF THE ORIGINAL HARDCOVER EDITION.

Dual Selection of the Literary Guild

Printed in the United States of America

First Fawcett Crest printing: January 1980

10 9 8 7 6 5 4 3 2 1

For Carol Troy

BOOK I

May 25, 1968

1

Ry Slaight was walking punishment tours on Central Area when they told him. Each cadet told another as they passed, marching at attention, M-14 rifles upon their shoulders. Area regulations required silence, so the news swept across the area like a hot wind, a ripple of whispered air, until it reached Slaight, who was marching in and out of a tiny piece of shade down at the western end of the area, near the stoops on either side of the First Class Sally Port, a vaulted passageway through the barracks.

"They found a body up in Lake Popolopen this morning," said a voice. The cadet talked out of the side of his mouth, eyes straight to the front. It was hard to tell who spoke.

"They know who it is?" asked Slaight, who had about-faced and was marching alongside the guy who had whispered the news.

"Some plebe," said the cadet matter-of-factly. "Don't know his name."

"When. What happened," said Slaight. It was a command, not a question, and his head swiveled sharply toward the other cadet as he spoke. The cadet glanced at Slaight, then focused again on the pavement in front of him. It was the way on the area: straight to the front at all times. The sun was bright, and it caught Slaight's black patent-leather visor, reflecting a white spot of light on the stone wall of the stoops ahead. The cadet could not see Slaight's eyes, but he could see Slaight's left hand, clenched tightly in a fist. They halted, executed a slow, simultaneous about-face, taking their time. It was a leisure due them because they were cows. Juniors. Upperclassmen. Even walking punishment tours on the area, cows were cool. They marched north across the area.

"Found him this morning, floating," the cadet whispered. "Don't know what time. Early, I think. They say it was an accident." Slaight marched a few steps, about-faced on the iron storm drain at mid-area, and marched south. He wanted to be alone.

This was Slaight's third month of May spent walking punishment tours on the area in as many years. It wasn't that he was a dullard. Slaight just seemed to attract unwanted attention from the officers who ran the Tactical Department the way the cadet uniform attracted stares on the street in New York City. The Tactical Department was West Point's expanded Dean of Students, an elaborate system of command which supervised every aspect of cadet life outside the classroom. It began with the tactical officers, thirty-two of them, majors, each of whom commanded a company of 160 cadets. Then there were four regimental commanders, colonels, each of whom commanded eight cadet companies. At the top was the commandant of cadets, a brigadier general, a position which was traditionally a key step on the ladder of army success. Many former commandants went on to become Chief of Staff, top dog at the Pentagon.

It seemed odd to him, but Slaight had always felt a peculiar sense of comfort, of well-being, when dealing with the Tactical Department, despite the fact that three times his encounters with officer superiors had landed him with slugs, assignments of twenty or more punishment tours on the area. The TD was both a father and a mother to the Corps of Cadets. It scolded and punished cadets, guiding them through four years of academy life with Pavlovian precision. Slaight often mused that if he had gone to a civilian college, he'd have been kicked out by now. At West Point, breaking the rules was expected of cadets. It was part of *playing the game,* the eternal struggle between cadet and academy, the artificial give-and-take of the system which defined one's identity at the United States Military Academy.

Slaight knew the area. It was punishment as punishment should be, and he hated it. But after some fifty hours walking the area, Slaight had come to admire the

11

concept of walking the area. It was time meant to be wasted, good time, weekend time, and it was time lost to the cadet punished. Gone. Forever. Slaight derived no small amount of satisfaction from the private notion that he used the area. It was like reading a book, he decided. Only thing was, what you read on the area had to be your own mind.

Slaight walked alone in and out of his small piece of shade, his eyes adjusting and readjusting to the hot late-May sun beating down on the area, turning the fifty-by-hundred-yard rectangle of concrete between the barracks into a stone oven. There were many styles for walking the area. Some guys walked in little informal groups, a few yards apart, as if the company of others afforded quiet solace. Some guys walked slowly, trying to cover as little ground as possible in each three-hour stint on the concrete. Others rushed from one side of the barracks to the other, as if their speed would hurry the clock along. Some guys cruised the area, covering every inch of the hot rectangle, like they were establishing territorial imperative over the ground they walked. Slaight always walked the same strip of ground, down near the sally port, loosely following a series of cracks in the concrete which had been patched with tar in a pattern he found . . . interesting . . . nonlinear. And so he always walked a slightly crooked path, stepping to the left and right of the tarred cracks, but never on them. Slaight's area style had nothing to do with his politics, which were conservative, and everything to do with his sense of himself, which struggled somewhere in the mucky, ill-defined area inhabited by twenty-one-year-olds.

The barracks hummed, crackled with Saturday afternoon cadet life. Stereos clashed from window to window. Up on the rooftops, sun bathers peered over stone battlements and called encouragement to guys they knew on the area. Down in the sinks, the basement shower rooms and locker rooms, electric shavers purred and water splashed, and a lonely, echoed voice could be heard from the 13th Division, singing a song by The Association. Through the sally port, the cadet mess hall clanked and chugged, and

12

Spanish voices of waiters yelled across the massive, gymnasium-sized south wing as tables were set for the evening meal. Veal cutlets. Slaight could smell it. Three years had trained his nose. Veal cutlets and lima beans and mashed potatoes.

Slaight knew it wouldn't take long for the name of the dead cadet to emerge from the ooze which was the eternal undercurrent of rumor, speculation, and false hope just beneath the surface of the United States Military Academy. Death was part of the undertow, infrequently discussed but forever back there in the rear of the mind, among the theorems and axioms of applied science, the chaotic patchwork of textures of military tactics and strategy. Knowledge of death was not learned but absorbed in such a way that it was part of the unspoken tongue, the code among cadets. It was one of those shared things which set them apart, death was. They imagined they faced it every day, and in a way, they did. Vietnam waited. It would not go away.

Perversely, they did not want it to, not a war, not *the* war, the only shooting war since Korea, not the year before Slaight and his classmates graduated. West Point in the spring of 1968 was probably the only place in America where the war in Vietnam was a "good deal," the accelerator pedal of army success, the escalator of army promotions. The war had kicked everything at the academy into high gear, put an edge on the experience of being a cadet which had been missing three years previously when Slaight entered West Point as a plebe. The war made the air at West Point dry with tension. It was like the centerfold in *Playboy*. The academy opened naturally to the page which sold the place. War was the reason West Point existed. Everything else was filler.

They liked to think that war was their reward, the currency they were paid, cadets did. War was the object of their ambition, the thing they were supposed to lust after the way Harvard and Yale guys were supposed to lust after jobs with big corporations, admissions to law schools, graduate degrees. War was said to be the final measure of the man. Officers at the academy frequently likened the

13

war to sex. As intercourse was necessary to propagate the species, war was necessary to thin it out. Hell, as long as there had been men, there had been wars. Two thousand years of recorded history couldn't be wrong. Military Academy doctrine decreed that war cleared the senses of civilization, established those who *counted,* brought things like "politics" and "international relations" to a head. Peace, if followed, was merely afterglow. This was a vision of the world with which cadets were comfortable because they were not yet acquainted with dead bodies.

"Guy's name is David Hand," a voice reported. "Drowned. Been dead a couple a days. Grim scene, they say."

Slaight stopped marching the area, removed his hat, and with the coarse wool sleeve of his dress coat, wiped his forehead. He knew David Hand.

He had come to West Point from New Orleans the year before like he had nothing to lose. There was something about the kid that said he had the place figured out. This was not the way plebes were supposed to act. Slaight, who had been his squad leader during the first month of Beast Barracks, knew it. David Hand knew it. Slaight knew that David Hand knew. It brought them close together.

In any military unit, especially one as small and tightly knit as a squad—eleven men—there exists a glue between men so tight, so intimate, so intense, it has traditionally remained unknown outside the confines of military life. The language has had difficulty expanding to contain the unmentionable. In recent years, an intellectual term has been in use to describe such behavior: male bonding. But the language of West Point barracks life has always been far more succinct. For years, West Pointers have referred to their roommates as wives. Slaight thought the term . . . wives . . . had its roots in the shared experience of plebes. Being a plebe, he thought, was like being a woman for a year.

Plebe year at West Point has often been compared unfairly to pledging a college fraternity. True, there is something of the atmosphere of a fraternity about the whole of

14

West Point life—jocularity, playfulness, hilarity in the face of shared hardship. But to be a West Point plebe is to capitulate oneself to a system so foreign, so completely absorbing, and so totally dominating that the similarity between plebe and pledge ends with the letter "p." Plebe year was the thing which ultimately drew the distinction between West Pointer and all others. For plebe year imbued in the cadet heart an incendiary mix of pride and shame which each man would hold forever secret by a tacit pact as old as the academy itself.

David Hand had been inordinately skilled at the thousand little details of plebe life. No one could shine shoes better than he. His uniforms fit as if they had been custom-tailored, while most plebes looked like Cadet Sad Sacks. He could "spout poop," recite the myriad memorizations of plebe knowledge with an ease of delivery which skirted the edges of boredom. He was always on time, while his classmates fumbled through each day as if blindfolded. David Hand had seemed comfortable as a plebe. He retained an odd aloofness, when all the unwritten rules said he should have been soaked in humility.

Slaight, the squad leader, noticed there had always been something David Hand kept to himself, some private place neither Slaight nor the plebe system could reach. Slaight had admired him secretly for preserving a portion of himself which the academy would never touch. Slaight decided it took courage. For to withhold from West Point that which West Point considered it rightfully owned—namely oneself—violated the academy's most sacred rule. In return for receiving the secret gift the academy had to offer, a special knowledge of the inner workings of power among men, one had to first surrender himself and become powerless. David Hand had refused to do this, and now he was dead.

Ry Slaight placed his hat on his head, lifted his rifle from his right shoulder to his left, and walked the area. He looked over at the west face of the four-sided clock in the middle of the area. It was almost 5 P.M. His fifty-third hour on the area was almost over. He had seven hours left to walk. He studied the stone barracks surrounding

15

him. Most of them had been built in 1850, in a style now called Military Gothic—basement, stoop, four stories, four rooms to a floor, toilets in the hall, flat roofs edged with battlements. They looked like tenements.

He was trying not to think of David Hand. It was the fourth time in his life he had considered death up close. Each time it seemed to get worse. There was too much he knew about David Hand, the plebe. More intriguingly, there was too much he didn't know about him for Slaight to simply forget David Hand. Now he was dead, and Slaight knew there were things he'd never know about the guy. It bothered him, gnawed at him, being so curious about a dead man. So Slaight, walking the area from one side of Central Area to the other and back again and again, resolved to look into meditation, which he imagined was about the business of not thinking. Maybe he'd order a book about it, the next time there was a Marboro ad in the New York *Times*. That was what he usually did when he was curious about something: order a book. But he'd have to do a little digging to satisfy his curiosity about David Hand, dead by drowning at nineteen.

2

Across Thayer Road from Central Area, in a high-ceilinged office on the third floor of the Academic Headquarters Building, Major General Axel W. Rylander, superintendent of the Military Academy, picked up a telephone and punched a button:

"Get me Hedges," he said, referring to Brigadier General Charles Sherrill Hedges, the commandant of cadets. His secretary dialed the four-digit number for the commandant's office, located about one hundred yards away across the street in the Brigade Headquarters Building, at the southeast corner of Central Area. The call was answered by the commandant's secretary. The two women,

16

as intermediaries for their respective bosses, spoke to each other frequently. They chatted for a moment before they put the call through. Then Hedges' secretary punched a button:

"General, it's the supe on line two." Hedges replaced a pair of binoculars in its black leather case, straightened his uniform jacket, and mentally counted to ten. He picked up the phone.

"General Hedges," he said, knowing the voice on the other end of the phone would be that of the superintendent's secretary, Mrs. Moore.

"One moment, General," said Mrs. Moore.

Hedges winced at the sound of the woman's voice. He had no patience for the formalities of secretaries and intercoms and buzzers and *waiting*. That was why he purposefully omitted the word "sir" when he picked up the phone. *General Hedges*. He liked the sound of it. It was like saying *yeah?*, thumbing his nose at the waiting, the wasted time. Hedges had a thing about wasted time. Back in Nam, up in his C & C ship, his command and control helicopter, when he grabbed the mike and punched into the battalion radio net on the ground, he wanted to be talking to the lieutenant or captain in command of that unit he was looking down on. It wasn't just policy, it was the gospel. His commanders *never* used their RTOs, radio-telephone operators, to relay messages.

Once he had relieved a platoon leader because the lieutenant had not personally responded on the radio to the C & C ship. He told the lieutenant's RTO to put the platoon sergeant on. He told the sergeant to tell the eltee he was finished. He didn't want to see him back at base camp. He didn't want to see him *anywhere*. That eltee better hie himself on down to Division and start looking for a desk to hide behind . . . the sergeant was *yessir—yessir—yessiring* up a storm, breaking radio procedure, but he didn't give a good goddamn, he was too pissed at that lieutenant to go wasting any more time on the sergeant. . . .

And now Hedges was waiting again. Waiting for the superintendent to come on the line. Seemed like he spent half his time waiting for the superintendent on the telephone. He wondered what in hell Rylander had done on the radio in Nam when he was a division commander. He tapped the eraser end of a pencil on the desk. The telephone seemed to burn his ear with silence. He was on hold.

What was he doing wondering what Rylander had done in Nam? He'd heard enough about the almighty 1st Cavalry Division to know what kind of commander Rylander had been in Nam. He was old-school, one of those grandstanding SOBs who never got the hang of the fact that Vietnam wasn't Normandy and the gooks weren't Nazis. He'd been up there in II Corps with his almighty cav troopers, making huge sweeps, divisional maneuvers so grandiose every VC worth his rice knew a week in advance what the 1st Cav was doing, where they'd strike next. But he was all over the television, even made the cover of *Life*. Big color picture of Rylander with a gold scarf around his neck and a pair of mirrored sunglasses on, looking out across a bunch of hills that were probably crawling with VC and NVA regulars. And all kinds of quotes from Rylander about the "new enemy," turning the 1st Cav into a "new concept" of a "fighting unit." He sounded like one of those eggheads in the Pentagon, spewing garbage out of some field manual.

Hedges had shown how it was done with his brigade in the Big Red One, the First Infantry Division. He demanded the toughest area of operations in the Iron Triangle, and he nailed down that AO like he was fencing in his own back yard. There wasn't a gook within fifty miles who didn't know Hedges' Hellions were holding that piece of real estate. They kept their distance, that was for sure. Once an ambush captured a VC province infrastructure leader, and they interrogated him, scared the hell out of the little yellow coward. When he'd had enough, he said the VC had a name for Brigade Commander Hedges. It was some gook word—never could remember it right, but it translated to "Red Devil."

"Charlie, Charlie?" The voice of General Rylander broke the silence. "Charlie, what about this plebe they found up in Popolopen this morning? You got anything

18

more for me? I'm going to need a report before close of business today, you know."

"I've got Terry King on it right now, sir, and I should be hearing from him any minute," said Hedges, referring to his Third Regimental commander, Colonel Phineas Terrance King, with whom he'd served in the Big Red One. They had been battalion commanders together, before Hedges got his brigade—Hedges' Hellions, Terry and the Pirates . . . those were the days . . . his mind was wandering again. He thumped the eraser on his desk and blinked.

"Terry's the best man we've got, sir. He'll have the whole ball of wax wrapped up for us. I've got complete confidence in him, sir. We've got the lid screwed on tight, and it's going to stay that way."

"Goddammit, Charlie, the lid better be on tight. June Week starts the day after tomorrow, and we're going to be overrun with weight from Washington. The Chief of Staff's going to be up here. You know that. And if there are any questions about this business . . ."

"There won't be, sir," Hedges broke in, clipping his words crew cut short. He knew how to deal with Rylander. Reassure the old bastard, reassure him again, then cut him off and let him go back to wondering what pasture he was going to graze in, when his time was up as supe. It worked every time.

"Yeah. Okay," said the superintendent. "Give me a call, will you, Charlie, when Terry comes in with that report? I want to know what went on."

"Will do," said Hedges, again purposefully omitting "sir." He dropped the phone in its cradle as soon as he heard the click on the other end. Talking with the superintendent of the Military Academy was like going shopping with the wife. Hedges reached for his binoculars. Sitting around waiting. Waiting. Waiting in one of those Fifth Avenue stores while she tries on this dress and that dress, saying *yes, dear,* reassuring the old bitch, then cutting her off, opening the wallet, flipping the credit card at her with a wordless glare. Worked every time.

Christ, it was a pathetic state of affairs when the supe

19

reminded you of your wife. Jesus! The army was in sad shape when a lily-livered old relic like Rylander could creak his way through the machinery and plop! There he is! Supe! Well, Rylander was just lucky as hell his classmates, that crowd from the class of '40, were in all the key slots down in the Pentagon right now. Every stud worth the price of his pants down in Washington knew the DCSPER, the deputy chief of staff for personnel, had been Rylander's roommate when they were cadets. And everybody in the CIA knew Rylander's *Life* magazine "victories" were just so much smoke Westmoreland and LBJ were blowing in the face of the country and the Congress. Everybody in the Agency knew Rylander and the 1st Cav had been just running around up there in II Corps blowing away a lot of bush and wasting a lot of brass and lead. Hell, Johnson had been screaming at Westmoreland for another face, another symbol, another set of starched fatigues he could put on the tube every night and show off, like generals standing around in front of TV cameras meant wars were being won. Rylander had gotten the nod.

Now it was all over. Vietnam was finished. Hedges knew it. Just a few days before, he'd been talking about how the war was messing everything up with Colonel Addison Thompson, head of the Social Science Department at the academy. They talked frequently. Hedges had been a protégé of Thompson's when he was a cadet, and Thompson had followed—some even said helped—the young general's career ever since. Thompson was as politically plugged in as any officer in the army. His connections were older, and reached deeper, and were tethered to more debts than anyone Hedges knew. Thompson had powerful friends in both political parties, but more importantly, he had helped to place, over the years, career bureaucrats in every key agency in the federal government. Right now, at this very moment, Hedges knew, close friends of Thompson's were in policy-making positions in the State Department, the CIA, the ultrasecret National Security Agency, not to mention the West Pointers he had sprinkled liberally through every echelon

20

of the Department of Defense. Colonel Addison Thompson, in short, was a man of considerable power. And the truly astonishing thing about the man was that no one suspected the silver-haired old social science chief up at West Point of anything more than occasional pointy-headedness. He was known all over the army as West Point's most liberal academician.

It had been Thompson who told Hedges about Bobby Kennedy. Only days before the California primary, Kennedy was chasing Hubert Humphrey right off the map. The thing that rankled Thompson was the fact Kennedy was using the war to do it to Humphrey. Hell, it had been his brother, JFK, who started the war. And according to Thompson, Bobby Kennedy had goosed the war along while he was Attorney General. Thompson had found out about Bobby Kennedy and his meddling ways from his friends in the CIA. He was always sticking his nose in the Agency's business when he was Attorney General. It was like JFK had given him some kind of family credit card to play around with the world. Both Kennedys, but especially Bobby, were constantly meddling in the affairs of the Agency. And Vietnam was the mechanism for the meddling. They had wanted to know everything that was happening in that godforsaken little country. They had pressed the CIA into operations its own experts warned against. Then JFK had committed troops—they were called "advisers," but everyone knew they were just the opening wedge.

And now Bobby Kennedy was using what had been his own personal little war to clobber Humphrey. He was successfully stealing the war issue from McCarthy, and nobody—*nobody*—knew the real truth about Bobby Kennedy and the CIA and the war in Vietnam. Nobody but Colonel Addison Thompson and a few others. And Hedges knew. He remembered the time back in '62 Bobby Kennedy had worn a green beret as he had helicoptered around, on a secret mission for his brother the President. Hedges had been his escort officer. The memory settled inside him like a good hot meal. Hedges was satisfied.

He'd gotten his, over in Vietnam: two tours of duty, one in '62–'63 as one of Kennedy's "advisers," the kind of job where you could drop out of sight for a year and really get your feet wet, really get a handle on what was happening over there. That was when he first found out about Bobby Kennedy and his toy green beret and his unusual affection for things military. Then '66–'67, his battalion command, a field promotion from lieutenant colonel to brigadier general (skipping the rank colonel altogether), and his brigade in the Big Red One.

He watched his flanks over there. He nailed down his little piece of real estate and he stayed put. He collected his basic load of medals, even pulled down a little publicity himself, the night his battalion had been overrun by an NVA regiment, and they hadn't suffered a single KIA. Blew away two hundred gooks that night. Vietnam had had its glamour, but now anybody could see that careerwise, the war was finished. Addison Thompson had been predicting as much for two years. And so Hedges was already lining up his ducks for his next move. The first duck in line was the superintendent.

Brigadier General Hedges had always thought of himself as a kind of dues collector, the man you pay. In 1948, the year they graduated from the Point, his roommate told him he should have studied accounting, not tactics. It seemed like Charlie Hedges was always tallying things up, counting. Naturally, his roommate missed the point. Charlie Hedges never counted. He measured. He was one of those rare individuals with a nearly animalistic sense of smell for other men. He didn't need to count the odds. He just knew, just like he now *knew* that the war had peaked, careerwise. It was indeed no mistake that Charles Sherrill Hedges was the first man in the class of 1948 to be promoted to brigadier general, two years ahead of his class 5 per cent list, the select group promoted ahead of schedule.

General Hedges could smell the fear coming off the superintendent's words over the phone. He could *see* it. It was like . . . steam, rising out of those vents along Thayer Road, hot mist rising and disappearing into the air. Everybody tended to ignore fear, especially when they sensed it might be coming from their superiors. But not Hedges. He used fear, used his nose for the weaknesses of men to maneuver them into positions most advantageous to him, Hedges. In his mind's eye, he pictured the superintendent of the Military Academy, pacing the carpet in front of his desk, switching the phone from ear to ear, staring out his windows overlooking the Hudson, staring out there, waiting. Men like him were always waiting. Waiting and worrying. Rylander was a worrier. Every moment in the life of the Rylanders of the world was that moment in Nam when somebody yelled *"Incoming!"* and you ducked and ran for cover. Rylander was always ducking and running, and he didn't even know it.

Hedges prided himself not for his courage—for which he had been amply decorated—but for his sense of timing. What good was courage if you didn't know when to exercise it? What good was an act of bravery if no one noticed? And so General Hedges honed his sense of timing, worked on it, polished it . . . labored over it the way Rylander probably worked on his golf strokes. Hedges knew one day his sense of timing would really pay off. And he knew that day was fast approaching.

Hedges leaned back in his leather reclining desk chair and ran his stubby fingers through his thinning hair. At 5'9" tall, forty-two years of age, he cut a figure of extraordinary military bearing. He weighed a perfect, trim 155. His face had the ruddy good looks of a young Jimmy Cagney, helped along by five minutes each morning in front of a sun lamp, which he kept in the lower right-hand drawer of his desk. The eighteen custom-embroidered ribbons on the breast of his uniform jacket were arranged in seven rows: two rows of four, two rows of three, two rows of two, topped with the Distinguished Service Cross, the nation's second highest award for heroism in the face of the enemy. He got that one the morning after the NVA regiment had tried to run over his battalion. A miniaturized Combat Infantryman's Badge was poised over the DSC, between the edge of his lapel and the seam of his jacket sleeve, giving his uniform breast an uncrowded, yet massively impressive display of official decorative color. For this reason, Hedges did not often remove his uniform jacket, preferring to wear it even when he felt a bit uncomfortable. But he would remove his jacket and hang it on one of those standing valet hangers next to his desk—the breast of the jacket still visible to anyone in the office—to achieve the appearance of informality, if seeming a little loose served his interests. In fact, it could be said accurately that General Hedges wasted little time with matters which did not in some direct way serve his interests. Leisure time, he reasoned, was wasted time. And so when he played squash during his lunch hour, he played for two reasons: One, to win. Two, to stay fit. The game, squash, was good for his image.

Having disposed of the superintendent and his niggling, time-wasting telephoning, Hedges was indulging in a little image-building. Patton had his pistols, MacArthur had his dark glasses. Hedges had his binoculars. He was sitting in his wood-paneled, forest-green carpeted office in the Brigade Headquarters at the southeast corner of Central Area, and through his Nikon binocs (which he had bought on sale at the Ton Sun Hout Air Force Base PX while waiting for his R & R flight to Hawaii) he was watching the two dozen or so cadets marching Central Area below him. Hedges kept the binocs in their shiny black leather case at the upper right-hand corner of his desk expressly for this purpose. Anyone walking in his office would see the binoculars case, nicked and scraped from hanging around his neck in combat, one of the many mementos of his career strewn around his office: the six unit plaques on the wall behind him gleaming brass and enamel and polished walnut reproductions of regimental crests; a relief map of the Iron Triangle on the wall above a three-cushion brown leather sofa; a pair of chromed, crossed bayonets mounted on a VC flag next to the map; on his desktop, a 1:25 scale model of a Huey Model D, outfitted with miniature M-60 machine guns on its door, a toy version of his C & C ship back in Nam.

Hedges held the binoculars to his eyes and with his
24

right index finger focused each eyepiece. He could see the mouths of the cadets marching the area. He watched them passing each other on the area, one heading north, the other south. General Hedges shifted his vision from cadet to cadet until he identified what he believed to be a continuous conversation between two cadets whispering to each other as they passed on the area. Then he picked up the telephone and called the Cadet Guard Room, located immediately beneath his office in the Headquarters. But he didn't pick up just any phone. He picked up a battery-operated army field telephone, directly connected to a similar unit in the Guard Room. Hedges turned the crank on the side of the field telephone and listened to the pleasant whirr of the little generator which would ring a bell on the field telephone downstairs.

"Yessir!" came an excited voice over the field phone. "Cadet Guard Room, sir!"

"Give me the area sergeant. This is the commandant speaking," said Hedges. When the area sergeant, the cadet in charge of the punishment tour detail, came on the line, Hedges told the cadet to report to him. Within thirty seconds, the area sergeant was at his side. Hedges pointed out the offending cadets and ordered their names be brought to his desk.

The area sergeant returned with the cadets' names, General Hedges pulled from his center desk drawer a pad of two-dash-ones, Disciplinary Report Forms, and in his neat, tutored hand, wrote up the cadets for talking on the area. Eight more hours walking the area. In his nine months as commandant of cadets, General Hedges had become known for his binocular-fed pad of 2-1's. In fact, it was so extraordinary for a man of his rank and stature—a *general*, the *commandant of cadets*—to take time out of his day to write up cadets for minor infractions of regulations, that the general had become known among cadets as "Two-Dash Hedges," a sneering reference to the pad of 2-1's he kept close at hand. But still cadets talked on the area.

This was a source of some discomfort to the general, for when he began his campaign to control talking on the

25

area, he figured it would take only a few slugs to bring the practice to an abrupt halt. Nine months later, he found himself on the lookout for repeat offenders. If the commandant observed the same cadet or cadets talking again, even several weeks after he had first reported them, he would whip out his 2-1's again, adding to his disciplinary report the words "Gross lack of judgment." This wording escalated the punishment to twenty hours. There was one cadet walking punishment tours on the area who had been out there every weekend for nine months, having been caught repeatedly talking on the area by the commandant. In all that time, it had never occurred to General Hedges to order the man up to his office to answer the obvious question: Why? So the cadet walked and the general watched, and the eternal game went on. As he watched the cadets marching back and forth across the area, as he zeroed in on their lips with his Nikon binoculars on this afternoon in late May, Brigadier General Charles Sherrill Hedges knew that today, anyway, he had accomplished his mission. In the time-honored way of the Military Academy, cadets were being taught a lesson. They were being punished.

3

"General? General?" Thirty-five-year-old Althea Shanks peered around the door leading into Hedges' office. "General, Colonel King is here to see you. Should I show him in?" Hedges placed his binoculars on his desk and looked up.

"I'll see him now," he said. The door opened, and Colonel Phineas Terrance King, a lanky six-foot-tall Oklahoman who walked with a slight limp, a shrapnel wound received in Vietnam, stood in the doorway.

"Terry! Come on in! What have you got for me?" Hedges rose from his chair and walked around his desk, tugging at the front of his uniform jacket. Phineas Terrance "Terry" King was his personal emissary to the rest of the world, his right-hand man, his most trusted subordinate. And he was more than that. He was a buffer zone between Hedges and everyone below him in the chain of command. Though the office of the commandant was fully staffed—deputy commandant, S-1, S-2, S-3, and S-4, several special assistants, cadet activities officer, a normal quota of noncommissioned officers including a brigade sergeant major—Terry King was Hedges' man. He was present at all sensitive policy meetings. He was taken into the confidence of the commandant on matters considered to be of importance to the academy, the army, and the nation. But most importantly, he was used by the commandant as a kind of major-domo executive assistant, given secret extra duties which he understood were of special sensitivity. It was Hedges' sly way of stepping slightly outside the direct strictures of the chain of command to pick the man in whom he would place the burden of his trust. He picked his Third Regimental commander, one of four colonels who served in that capacity for each of the four respective cadet regiments. But Terry King was Big Red One. He was Terry and the Pirates. He was . . . *combat*. King understood this. He appreciated the fact Hedges had chosen him. He knew it meant that Hedges would look out for him. Hedges was going places. Therefore, King was going places, too.

Colonel King walked twelve steps forward to the spot where Hedges stood waiting for him, exactly opposite the middle cushion of the leather sofa. King's garrison cap was clamped tightly under his left elbow. Hedges held out his right hand. It was one of their signals. King did not have to salute Hedges, as did all other officers who reported to the office of the commandant of cadets, no matter their rank, position, or relationship to General Hedges (with the sole exception of the supe, of course). The two men shook hands. Hedges sat on the middle cushion of the leather sofa, where he always sat. King sat on the edge of an armchair across from the general, where he always sat.

27

On his lap he held a manila folder containing the report on the dead cadet.

"It doesn't look good, sir," said King. "You want to just read it for yourself, sir?" Despite the informality of their greeting, King was careful to preserve the deferential "sir," with which he either began or ended his sentences. The word carried more than respect. It meant thanks.

"No, come on, Terry, you know me better than that. What do you think I put you on this thing for? Exercise? Give it to me straight. What's up with this business? The supe's been on my back all day. I've got to have something for him before he goes down to that dinner for the local civilian biggies at the Bear Mountain Inn tonight. He's champing at the bit."

"Looks like this kid . . . let me see . . . here it is . . . David Hand . . . Company F-4 . . . looks like he might have been killed, General, sir."

"What in hell! Come again with that."

"There's a pretty strong possibility the kid was murdered, sir. I've been on this thing since you called me at home this morning. They found him about 0530. You called me about 0545. I was up there by 0615, on the scene at 0630.

"Good. What did you find out?"

"Well, sir, one of the companies found him on a reveille run. Somebody spotted the body floating about ten feet off shore in Popolopen. At first they thought it was a parachute. Looked white. You know, back up, just a shiny white surface, like a piece of nylon in the water. The skydiving team is always jumping into Popolopen in wet suits, so they thought it was one of the team chutes. Then one of the upperclassmen took off his boots and waded in. Water was about chest-deep. He reached out and touched it, and it was the kid's back. Dead a couple of days. Bloated. White as this piece of paper. They say the guy puked, right there in the lake."

"Really?"

"Yessir. So another cadet waded in, and they hauled him up on shore. He was in one of the other companies. Nobody knew him. They didn't even know if he was a

28

cadet. Thought he might be one of the kids from the post, a high school kid. Fishing accident. So they left him where they found him, ran back to the barracks at Camp Buckner, and reported the body to the duty officer. They still hadn't identified him by the time I got there. His face was totally misshapen by the water, the whole thing was pretty ugly."

"Yeah. Go on."

"Sir, first thing I did was to get rid of all the cadets who were hanging around. I got hold of Lieutenant Colonel Evans Fitzgerald, the provost marshal—he's class of '58—and got him up there. He brought his MPs and put them on a search for personal effects around the general area where the body was found. I kept Fitzgerald with me. I told him right off to keep this thing tight. He was very co-operative. We both figured we had a dead cadet on our hands, even though there was no way of telling, not at 0630 in half light, anyway. And the kid was nude. Not a stitch."

"The body was nude? Completely naked?"

"Yessir. We covered the body with a tarp from Fitzgerald's jeep, put him on a stretcher, and hauled the kid out of the area quick. No sense in too many cadets getting a look. You know how these things get around."

"I certainly do. I've been hearing about it all afternoon."

"Yessir. I got back to Headquarters Building at Buckner, got all the upper-class company commanders together, and ordered a check of morning reports. Nothing. Then I told them to have everybody form up for a normal breakfast formation and to take extra care with the reports. No counts. Name by name. Ten minutes later we had our man. Hand. David. Home town: New Orleans. Company F-4. Sixth Training Company at Buckner. The plebes had only been up there at Buckner for two days, and the kid had simply gotten lost in the shuffle. He drowned the first night they were up there, moving in. And with a thousand plebes moving all their summer gear into those crowded quonsets and tents, nobody assigned to their regular squads or platoons from the regular academic year, all the companies in the roster order they'll be in for July, when summer training starts for the plebes . . . well, sir, the kid got lost, and nobody missed him. That's all."

"Well, somebody's head's gonna roll for that. Terry, I want the man who's responsible in here this afternoon. I want him standing tall in front of this desk. I want some ass kicked, and I want it kicked today."

"I'm not so sure you will when you hear the rest of it, sir."

"What's that you say?"

"Sir, I said I'm not so sure you'll want to move right away when you hear the rest of it, sir. I think, if I might respectfully make a suggestion, sir, that the best thing for us to do at this point is to keep this whole thing as low-key as possible. If we go dealing out a huge slug to some cadet company commander because Hand dropped out of sight and nobody missed him, the whole corps is going to be buzzing. They're going to know something's up, and they're going to want to know what it is."

"Okay, okay. I see what you mean. Get on with it. The supe's going to be on the horn any minute."

"Yessir. Anyway, Evans Fitzgerald and I stuck pretty close together all day. We got the body down to the hospital early, and Fitzgerald got in touch with one of the doctors he deals with all the time on auto accidents, that kind of thing. Somebody named George Consor, major, class of '59. Fitz says we can trust him. Consor did the autopsy. Sure enough, he'd been in the water almost two days—about thirty-six hours, to be exact. That means he drowned about 2100, night before last, the first night the plebes were up at Buckner for their June Week orientation."

"So where'd they find the body? You never said."

"Sorry sir. Slipped by me. Let me see . . . here it is. They found him down at the far end of Flirtation Walk, down near Class Rock, you know, that huge boulder the plebes paint with the class numerals every spring. Seventy-one. The numbers are already up there. Apparently, they'd painted them on the rock that afternoon—the afternoon before he died. But I had Fitz check it out quietly with the kid's company. Hand wasn't on the rock-painting detail. Wasn't his kind of thing. Closest anyone can recall, he spent the whole afternoon in his bunk, reading."

"Go on. What did the autopsy show?"

"Death by drowning. No signs of struggle. Water in the lungs. No internal injuries. No sign of heart seizure, or any other . . . what the hell did that doc call it . . . of yeah, no sign of any other trauma which might have caused death. Fitz checked with the Office of Physical Education. The OPE guys say he was an excellent swimmer, took Advanced, scored a 2.8 out of a possible 3.0, received a Red Cross Life Saving badge, the whole works. Kid was a fish."

"So what makes you figure the kid might have been killed? Any sign of drugs, alcohol?"

"None. The doc ran a complete autopsy. I wasn't in the room, of course. I had a lot of running around to do, but I left Fitzgerald at the hospital to make sure nobody got in on the autopsy. The doc did the whole thing himself. No nurses, no aides. I figured the best way to handle it, to keep the lid on, like you said, was to limit access to sensitive data to grads."

"Good move, Terry. Outstanding. But get to it. What else?"

"The doc found out the kid had sex almost immediately before he drowned."

"Sex? You mean he got laid? How'd he know that?"

"Semen in the urinary tract. The major, Consor, says there are always traces of semen in the urinary canal after sex, unless you urinate right afterward. Well, apparently the kid didn't piss. Normally, the doc says, the relaxation of the muscular system upon death would have caused the bladder to partially empty. But apparently the temperature of the water caused the kid's penis to shrink up so much it was damn near up inside his crotch. The bladder never got a chance to release any urine. So the semen was still in there. The fact is this, according to the doc: The kid was fucking just before he drowned."

"Maybe he masturbated, then went for a swim. Then

31

he just waded in and killed himself. Maybe he was the only guilt-ridden wanker we got here. Christ, anything could have happened. What makes you so sure it was murder?"

"Fitzgerald. He's damned sharp for an M.P., you know. He ran Checkpoint Charlie in Berlin during the crisis. And he investigated one hell of a lot of murders over there in Germany committed by whores, pimps, or both. A lot of GIs got it in the back in Krautland, General. I'm sure you know that."

"Yeah, I remember. I had one in my company. In '54, in Stuttgart. Some German bitch ran a knife up under the guy's ribs right in bed. Hellish scene over there."

"Yessir. Well, Fitzgerald says there are two dead giveaways. One: The kid was stark naked. The kid probably wouldn't have stripped naked to jerk off. Two: Fitzgerald's MPs found the kid's uniform up in a rock formation not far from the scene—about a hundred fifty feet up the side of the hill, over the edge of a little rocky outcropping with a flat top. His uniform was neatly folded, his shoes aligned, socks tucked neatly into his shoes. Nothing missing. Wallet, money, ID, everything intact. The whole area was rocky, and the top of the outcropping was heavily carpeted with leafy mulch. No footprints, nothing they could pick up, anyway. But Fitzgerald went over the scene like a pro. He must have spent about two hours up there alone, poking around. He says there were two people up there, and the other person was not a young lady."

"How's he so sure about that?"

"This." Colonel King reached into his jacket pocket and pulled out a cadet summer dress shirt epaulet, a gray wool-covered rectangle, pointed at one end, squared off at the other. The epaulet King held in his right hand was distinctive for two reasons: It was emblazoned by a light gray cadet crest, the color assigned to the cadet junior class, second-classmen, cows. The epaulet also had a stripe of thin gold braid running along its squared-off edge, the insignia of a cadet corporal, a rank reserved for cadet second-class squad leaders. The colonel held the epaulet in his hand and both men stared at it.

"Didn't belong to Hand," said Hedges.

"Nosir," said King. "Both his epaulets were on his dress shirt. Whoever was up there with Hand lost his epaulet, and he was a cow."

"Any way of telling who it belongs to?"

"Fitzgerald had it printed. Negative. Brass on the crest freshly shined. And there's no regulation requiring the cadets to mark the damn things with their names, because they're passed from one class to another."

"You sure it couldn't have been left up there from before, by somebody who might have been up there last week?"

"Fitzgerald doesn't think so, sir. It rained the night before the kid died. This epaulet doesn't show any signs of dampness. The other thing was where it was found."

"Where was that?"

"Right under the kid's trousers. Fitzgerald says whoever was up there with Hand lost the epaulet, looked around for it, but it was dark, and he just didn't find it."

"That's it?" The two men continued to stare at the cadet epaulet in disbelief.

"Well, sir, here is the scene, as reconstructed by Fitzgerald. This Hand kid goes down to the end of Flirtation Walk after dark with this . . . upperclassman. Whoever. Obviously, they don't want to be found out. They climb this rock formation, not an easy climb. Hand disrobes. The . . . perpetrator probably does the same, judging by the fact that he loses his epaulet. There is sex. Anyway, Hand comes. They decide to go skinny-dipping. Hand is pushed underwater by someone stronger than him and held there until he drowns. Or he is surprised by someone not stronger than him. Take your pick. The kid's an excellent swimmer in good health. He didn't paddle out there and start drinking Popolopen until he sank."

"So maybe he cramped up. Who knows?"

"The doc says the chances are slim. He says in such cases there are normally signs of internal muscular contractions, even after death. With Hand . . . negative. The doc says he figures Hand was surprised from behind, in water over his head, and held under. He sucked in a good volume of water, an indication that he wasn't tired or out of breath, the doc says. And he didn't find any skin under Hand's fingernails, so if he struggled, all he did was flail around. The doc says he was surprised from behind. Fitzgerald agrees."

"All right. This Hand was probably killed. Then what?"

"The killer goes back to the hill, climbs up the rocks, dresses, cleans up the area, leaves Hand's clothes as he left them, making it look like a solitary swim and accidental drowning. Exits scene. Fitzgerald says most probably the guy didn't realize he'd lost his epaulet until he got back to the barracks. Cadets are losing the damn things all the time and not noticing they're missing. I must have personally written up three or four cadets in the past week, since they went into the summer white dress shirt, for missing epaulets."

"That sounds plausible."

"Yessir. The whole damn thing is plausible. Almost too plausible. You know what Fitzgerald said, sir? He said what he'd like to think is we've got some civilian psycho prowling the woods, surprised Hand and killed him. But that's so goddamn unlikely . . . ignores the semen, lack of struggle, and the goddamn cow epaulet." King held the thing in his hand as if it were alive.

"Fitzgerald says this was a neat job, sir. He says this is murder premeditated. He says whoever killed Hand knew him, had his trust, probably had sex with him . . . at least watched him. General, it looks very strongly like we've got a homosexual cadet murder on our hands, and we have no suspects. Zero. Nobody saw Hand go up Flirtation Walk that night. Afterward, his absence went unnoticed for thirty-six hours. Nobody saw nothing. We've got problems."

Hedges straightened the bottom of his uniform jacket and looked across the room at his trusted deputy, Phineas Terrance King. He knew King had done a good job. An exhaustive job. He sensed King was right. He smelled it.

34

Every nerve ending in his body tingled with that crazy mix of fear and excitement that comes when adrenaline fires the system. Hedges ran his fingers through his hair, felt the dampness forming imperceptibly on his forehead. His lips wore a thin smile. He knew about the smile. It was something he couldn't control. He knew about it from seeing his face in photos taken up in the C & C ship in combat in Nam. The thin smile was always there. By the time they landed, back at base, it went away. He'd never seen the smile in a mirror. It was as if his mind wouldn't allow his face to show itself what it looked like under stress. Hedges felt secretly embarrassed. The thin smile hid from everything but the camera. King broke the silence.

"Sir, what are we going to do about this thing?"

"How many copies of that report have been made?"

"This is the only one, sir."

"Fitzgerald know I called you this morning? He know you came up here to see me this afternoon?"

"Nosir. He thought I was post duty officer—something like that. He assumed I was there on official duty. Never asked any different. Good man, Fitz. I've always liked the hell out of him."

"Roger. Anybody else? I mean, anybody else know you're up here reporting to me?"

"Your secretary, sir."

"Besides her. The doctor. This man, Consor. He know?"

"Nosir. We left him at the hospital hours ago and told him to go about his duties normally, as if nothing had happened."

"You have a driver drop you here in an official sedan?"

"Nosir. I used my POV all day. You said you smelled trouble this morning when you first called me, and I took you at your word, General. I remember what used to happen back in Nam when you smelled trouble. Jesus."

Hedges felt his thin smile turn into a grin. He leaned back on the leather sofa, ran his fingers along the creases on his trouser legs.

"Damn fine job, Terry. Damn fine. I'll see that the supe

knows what a hell of a job you've done for us on this. Now, here's what we're going to do. You give me the report. Give me the epaulet. I guess it's evidence, and the supe's certainly going to want to look at it. I'll get over to the supe's right away. You get back to Fitzgerald. Tell him this thing is hot. Tell him it's going all the way to the top, and he's not to speak to anyone. You have him talk to the doctor, the major, and have him tell the doc the same thing. Nobody talks. And any MPs Fitzgerald had sniffing around with him . . ."

"The MPs, sir. You were saying?"

"Yeah. The MPs. How many were actually involved in the investigation, on the scene? How many got a look at the body, the evidence?"

"Fitzgerald handled it mostly himself. I think one or two MPs were up there with him at one point."

"Tell Fitzgerald to have them transferred. Korea. Germany. Someplace out of the country. I do not want those men available. Tell him the word came from the top. Do not specify me or the supe. Let him draw his own conclusions. I don't care if he thinks the chief is involved. Just tell him to get those MPs off this post by tomorrow, and on their way overseas by next week, understand?"

"Yessir. I don't think there will be any problem. Fitz is very well connected with MP personnel branch down at the Pentagon. He'll get the job done."

"Terry, give me the report and the epaulet." King handed them over. "Now, you let me handle the supe. He's got one hell of a lot on his mind with June Week coming up. I think you know I've got good instincts when it comes to dealing with crises like this."

"Roger that, sir. I remember that time in Nam . . ."

"Now listen-up, Terry," Hedges cut him off. "I want this kept ultra-quiet. It is an accident. The kid was skinny-dipping and he drowned, right? I want the death announced in the mess hall the way they announced those two firsties who killed themselves in that goddamn Corvette last week. Accident. Tragedy for all concerned. The Corps of Cadets sends its condolences. A moment of prayer. Whatever you think is best, understand?"

"Yessir. I've got a copy."

"For the next two weeks, I want you to do some quiet sniffing around. I want to know about this kid, Hand. I want to know who his friends were, who his enemies were, who his squad leaders were, who he came into regular contact with in extracurricular activities, if any. I want you to run a thorough check on this kid. I want it in writing. Take two weeks. When you figure you've got the kid nailed down, I want details. Names. Dates. 2-1's. Roommates. Trips away from the academy. Cadet aptitude reports. Anything you can get from the academic side of the street. I want Cadet David Hand in this office, like he was standing in front of me with his heels locked and his chin in. I want his life, Terry, every last breath the bastard took. I want to *smell* him, Terry. You got me?"

"General, sir, you know you can depend on me."

"Okay. But keep this on the QT. If you start a thing where the cadets think 'the word is coming down' on Hand, all hell will break loose. So be careful and take your time. Get back to me as soon as you're ready."

"Yessir."

"Now, I've got to get over to the supe's office before he loses his lunch. Keep in touch. Let me know if there's anything I can do."

Colonel Phineas Terrance King stood up and saluted. Hedges didn't even notice. He was studying the toes of his shoes, which were highly polished but in need of a final buffing before making the trip across the street to the supe's office. It was a short walk, but Hedges had a lot of thinking to do and a short time in which to do it. He felt good. Time was beginning to compress, to shrink, and though he acted quickly, he felt as if he were moving in slow motion. It was a feeling he knew well, as if he were moving in motor oil instead of air . . . the compression of mental time, psychological time, while "real time" raced ahead . . . it was what had made him a good combat commander. He created time for himself when situations refused to yield it. Hedges felt the thin smile on his lips again. Pressure. He smelled it. He breathed tension the way other men breathed a woman's perfume. It was like

37

being a little drunk . . . high . . . your hands tingled and your mind felt supercharged, above it all. Charles Sherrill Hedges reached in his pocket and felt the gray wool of the cadet's epaulet. He walked across Thayer Road. He had been born to be a general. He thrived on the army, ate it and drank it and breathed it and slept with it. . . .

Walking through the sally port into the courtyard inside the Academic Headquarters Building, Hedges remembered an old sergeant he'd had as a squad leader when he was a lieutenant. It had been his first command. They were in the field on maneuvers somewhere in the red clay of Georgia, and the sergeant was drunk. Lieutenant Hedges was momentarily perplexed. He didn't know whether to punish him, indulge him, scold him like a child, put him to bed . . . he didn't know what the hell to do. He wished he was older. He was green. He knew it. The old sergeant, a buck sergeant who had been busted up and down the stripes three or four times in the twenty-some years he'd been in the army . . . the old sergeant wrapped his arm around the young lieutenant's shoulder and whispered to him:

This army's like a woman, sir. A cunt. You can smell her. Just remember: If you're not fucking her, she's fucking you.

4

"Heeeeaauh! Slaight!" The sound was a nasal bark, like a seal's. Slaight heard it as he walked down the long, wide hall of second floor, New South Barracks, heading for Room 226, in the corner, overlooking the hospital.

"Heeeeaauh! Fuckin' Slaight!" It was his roommate, Leroy Buck. The sound was their signal, a ridiculous noise one of them had started back when they were plebes. They weren't allowed to talk with one another when they passed in the area of barracks, which meant anywhere outside their own rooms, so they barked: a low, nasal directionless sound. Nobody could figure out where it was coming from, or what it meant. It didn't mean a thing. And three years later, they were still doing it.

"Heeeeaauh!" barked Slaight. "Jesus fuckin' Christ, I'm tired from that area. My feet feel like hamburger patties. My goddamn shoulder feels like somebody's been pounding on it all day with a telephone pole. Goddamn fuckin' area."

"You're not going to believe what's come down from fuckin' dingo Grimshaw, Slaight," said Buck, his thick southern drawl dragging his words from his mouth like the blade of a plow through bottomland. Buck was from Burning Tree, Indiana, a town of about forty near the south end of the state on the Wabash River. He was born so far out in the dirt farm boonies, he considered even Slaight came from a city. Slaight was from Leavenworth, Kansas, a metropolis of about twenty thousand.

Buck's father worked a piece of land near Burning Tree as a tenant farmer, the modern term for sharecropper. His father planted and harvested another man's land with his own equipment, realizing three fifths of the crops' profits. His people were of the land, of the dirt, and they were dirt poor. It was 1957 before Leroy Buck knew that houses were heated with anything besides potbelly stoves. All his life he had slept under a pile of his mother's hand-stitched quilts. When he arrived at West Point in 1965, the distinctive cadet black, gray, and gold wool blanket became his most treasured possession. He still took the blanket home with him on leaves.

"Yeah, Buck, well, you're not gonna believe what I heard out on the fuckin' area. You're just not gonna believe it."

"Well, goddamn-goddamn," said Buck. When he was hard-pressed for words, which was often, for he spoke slowly and his voice could not keep pace with his mind, he repeated the word "goddamn."

"You remember that plebe from Beast last year? That real smart son of a bitch from New Orleans?"

"Well, goddamn-goddamn. You mean beanhead Hand.

39

That . . . goddamn smack we fuckin' nailed the last week of first Beast? Now . . . how in *hell* you think I'd ever forget the memorable smack Hand?"

"I didn't."

"So c'mon. What about the little creep? He leading a beanhead revolution over there in the . . . goddamn . . . Fourth Regiment?"

"No. He's dead. . . . They found him this morning up in Popolopen. Floating. Drowned two days ago. Somebody out in the area said they found him stark naked. Grim scene, they say. It was all over the area. Beanhead Hand, our star plebe. Fini."

"Goddamn-goddamn." Leroy Buck leaned back on his bunk, surrounded by pages from the New York *Times*. He had been reading the financial section all afternoon. The stereo was playing a Merle Haggard tune. Leroy Buck's accent, his pigeon-toed half-stumble way of walking, his penchant for cowboy boots off-duty, and the little sprout of blond hair that stuck up like a feather at the back of his head . . . the whole scene, him sitting there in the middle of a roomful of newspapers and magazines and dirty laundry, all of it spelled one word: hick. He was anything but.

Glancing around the room, Slaight figured immediately what Buck was up to. He was getting ready to hit the computer center down in the basement of Thayer Hall, the main academic building, where he would throw in a complex program he had written for the IBM 360 which accomplished a rudimentary projection of stock trends for the few issues he held, based on their thirty-day performance. Slaight had noticed the year before that Buck rarely bothered to write programs before he sat down at the key punch and started banging out the cards, which fed into the maw of the computer, would spew answers to work/study problems they had in thermodynamics, mechanics of solids, mechanics of fluids, nuclear engineering, electrical engineering, all the applied sciences they took as cows. Leroy Buck was the only person Slaight had ever met who had a grasp for both higher math and the English language. He consumed books, magazines, newspapers, and other printed matter like a data disposal. He was a plowshares-to-swords genius.

"What else you hear about Hand?" asked Buck, obviously stunned. He had stopped his compulsive consumption of the stock market data in the *Times*. Slaight stood in the door, pulling off his white cotton gloves, his M-14 clamped between his knees. Sweat was dripping off his chin, hitting the rear sight assembly, and dribbling down the stock of the rifle.

"Nothing. They say it was an accident. All the Fourth Regiment guys were talking about it, down at their end of the area in their little group. There was so much bullshitting going on out there, the area sergeant had to come down and warn them about Two-Dash Hedges. He was doing his fuckin' number up there in his office. You know. Watching us with his binocs."

"Fuckin' Hedges. That dimbo couldn't squint and spit at the same time. Hear anything else?"

"Nope. Hey, help me out of these goddamn shoes, will you, you worthless, lazy, no-good-for-nothing dufus rack hound. I can't even bend fuckin' over."

The two cadets talked to one another like a couple of sergeants. It was a habit they'd picked up during summer training, out in the field, when there was nothing better to do than stand around with the sergeants and listen to them tell lies. After a couple of summers spent training with "the real army," what had passed for slang among cadets seemed limp. Pale. So they picked up the jargon of sergeants, a cut, jab, and hammerlock way of talking with all the earmarks of the American outsider. It was a blue-collar tongue, sprinkled with acid put-downs and a strangely backhand authoritarianism. Sergeant talk was fueled by cigar smoke and mess hall coffee, greasy fatigues and scuffed boots, afternoons spent ghosting at the motor pool, and an instinctive, almost magical feel for the manipulation of subordinates whom "the real world," society, might class as smarter, or better than the sergeants themselves. It was underdog lingo, full of aphorisms and clichés discarded by others, which took on new life and meaning in the coarse texture of a sergeant's timing and delivery

The way army sergeants talked reminded Buck of the men his father hired to help with the harvest, workers who drifted in and out of the Indiana bottomland around Burning Tree with the seasons. Sergeants reminded Slaight of the guys he'd known in downtown Leavenworth, the old man who ran Snooker Poolhall, the night manager at the Apco service station, where Slaight hung out in junior high, and a black dude in Slaight's high school class who was the generally acknowledged leader of a gang down near the Missouri River on the east side of town. For both cadets, there was a romance to the way sergeants talked. Cadets were supposed to be gentlemen. Sergeants talked dirty. It was sexy.

"C'mon, man, help me with my fuckin' feet." Slaight was lying on his bunk with his feet propped up on his Brown Boy, the tan cotton quilt every cadet slept with like a Linus blanket, a postadolescent teddy bear. Buck untied Slaight's shoes. His feet had swollen an inch. The laces on his shoes would barely tie. Slaight groaned as Buck pulled each shoe off. He wiggled his toes. They were numb. Buck peeled the cotton socks from Slaight's feet. They were caked with blood, like somebody had taken an electric belt sander to them, bloody and raw. Blisters had turned into open sores and oozed a mixture of blood and clear fluid. Three hours a day walking concrete, five days in a row, had taken an ugly toll. Slaight studied his feet with mild disgust. He'd seen them in worse shape, the year before, when a similar stint on the area had almost hospitalized him. The thing that pissed him off was the fact that his tactical officer, Major Nathan E. Grimshaw, had decreed that no one in his company could be medically excused from walking the area. He had threatened that anyone with a medical excuse from the area would walk an extra day of punishment tours for every day he had been excused.

Thus did Rysam Parker Slaight III find himself in Room 226 of New South Barracks, studying a pair of feet which indeed resembled hamburger. Later, he would go on emergency sick call over to the dispensary and get the duty doctor to work on his feet, put them in a salt bath, patch them with moleskin, maybe give him some Darvons and a handful of codeine pills for the pain. Pills were necessary for serious area walking, and everyone in Grimshaw's company kept a neat stockpile of painkillers in case they were sentenced to pounding the concrete.

Buck was poking fun at Slaight, remarking that his feet were evidence of what happens to a "city boy" when he's got to do some walking. Slaight said he'd like to see Buck spitshine his bare feet with black polish and try to pass the area inspection.

"Only way you'd make it through three fuckin' hours out there, Buck. Barefoot. I wanna see that plowboy gait of yours out there someday, you fuckin' cracker thwacker." Buck laughed and wet a towel in the sink to wipe the blood off Slaight's feet.

"So . . . whatdaya figure is up with fuckin' Hand gettin' himself dead, Slaight? Suicide? You figure the little bastard just decided to cash his check? That'd be his style. Dramatic-like. A fuckin' floater. Beanhead Hand. Jesus."

"Man, I just don't know. Can't figure it. But something big was happening over at Brigade Headquarters this afternoon, I'll tell you that much."

"Yeah? What?"

"Fuckin'-A, Buck. Wished you'd have been there. Just as they were forming us up to dismiss the area formation, just before this little dipshit firstie sergeant says, "Aaaeeeereeeaa Squuaaaaaad, Diiiismissed!" just before he squeaked it out, up drives this blue Chevy, and out jumps our fuckin' number one favorite colonel, Third Regimental Commander Phineas T. King. Old Phineas T. had a big folder in his hand, and he was humpin' and galumpin' and limpin'—close as he could come to running—into the building. His shoes were all dusty and cruddy, his cap was on crooked, and he was unshaven. You could see his whiskers all the way across the fuckin' area. I bet he's been on that Hand thing all day."

"Why King?" asked Buck, genuinely perplexed. "He's
43

not Hand's Regimental C.O. Hand ended up in the Fourth Regiment, right?"

"Yeah. Fourth. But you know the story on old Phineas T. He's fuckin' Two-Dash Hedges' fuckin' A-number-one hit man. Does everything but wipe his goddamn ass for him."

"Yeah . . . they were Big Red One buddies, right? Over in Nam?"

"You got it. Well, I checked out old Phineas T. humping his ass into the H.Q., and I figured something's up. So I bopped into the Guard Room acting like I was checking out the area schedule for Monday. Then I walked through the rear exit, the one that leads to Brewerton Road, right there where the ramp leads to New South. As I scooted through the main entrance to the H.Q., this secretary comes down the stairs. I've seen her around there before—works in the S-1 office. So I stopped her, asked her if Colonel King had found the general's office okay—you know, teasing her, like King had never been in the building before. She laughed. She said, yeah, he's up there with the general right now."

"So fuckin' Hedges has got his best buddy, Phineas T., on the Hand thing, huh?" Leroy Buck was sitting upright now, straightening the *Times* and a sheaf of notes he had taken off the stock pages.

"We can't be sure about that. I don't know what he had in that folder. Maybe he was delivering Hedges' copy of *Playboy*. Who knows? But you know what I think we've got here? I think we got a scene just like what happened with the infamous Magnificent Seven last year. You remember."

"Yea . . . the Mag-7. Jeez, I almost forgot about them."

"Phineas T. was up to his fuckin' skinny neck in the Mag-7 thing. They caught that yearling smoking dope up at Camp Buckner last summer, so they discharged him on medical or something. Covered it up. But old Phineas T. wasn't satisfied. He swoops down on the seven guys who shared the squad bay with the dope smoker, and inside of

44

a week, they got their leave time pulled, and they were restricted to barracks for the whole year."

"I remember now. That one kid who was one of the Mag-7, used to be in our company, he came and told us about it. They didn't even know the fucker was smoking. The guy they caught even admitted to Phineas T. he had been going up behind the mess hall at Buckner and doing the stuff by himself, in that little clump of three trees back here, at night. So Phineas T. holds a little 'court-martial,' with himself as prosecutor, judge, and jury. He didn't have a shred of evidence those guys even knew about the dope smoker. Next thing they know, their shit is packaged up, their leave time is yanked, and they're confined to barracks. Christ . . . those guys got bottled up so fast, they didn't even feel the lid coming down." Buck finished shuffling his stock market notes and whistled softly to himself.

"Hey, Buck. You know the Mag-7 were never even written up. There wasn't a single piece of paperwork on the whole business."

"How'd you find that out?"

"C'mon, Buck. Your memory's fading on you. Remember that day we talked to Sergeant Major Eldridge up in Building 720, the Regimental H.Q., don't you?"

"Oh, yeah. The crusty old critter was stomping around the halls like a caged opossum. I got you."

"Well, he said the book was closed on the Mag-7. Hell, he said the damn book was never open. Said the supe didn't know what in hell had gone on out there at Buckner, didn't know fuckall. Sergeant Major said Hedges was behind the whole thing. He said Hedges used King to bring down the hammer on those guys the same way he used to bring it down in Vietnam. One day a guy would be there, the next day he wouldn't. Nobody'd know a fuckin' thing about what happened, and nobody asked questions. Sergeant Major was in a state of shock. Hedges was pulling the same shit at West Point he was pulling in Nam."

"Yeah," said Buck. "I recall that day now. Old Sergeant Major Eldridge was really shook up about the whole thing."

"Damn straight. He was really loyal to Hedges. He served as Hedges' sergeant major the whole year they were together in Nam back in '66–'67. Then Hedges brought him up here to Woo Poo when they made him commandant. Hedges put the sergeant major over here in the Third Regiment, so he could keep an eye on his friend, Phineas T., I'd guess. That's all over with now."

"What . . . do you mean by that . . . Slaight?" asked Buck.

"You know what the story is on old Eldridge, don't you?"

"Negative. Give me the poop."

"Heard it just the other day from one of the cadets up in Building 720. Hedges is giving him the heave-ho right after June Week. Has to do with trouble Eldridge had with his son. The kid got bounced out of basic training down at Fort Dix with a bad discharge because they claimed to have found some dope taped under his wall locker. Eldridge says his son swears it wasn't his. He said some other guy fucked him, because the whole platoon knew his old man was a famous lifer noncom. Thing was, they never even brought the kid up on charges. Never court-martialed him. They just processed him out administratively, so the kid never got a chance to defend himself. Got an undesirable discharge. Broke old fuckin' Eldridge's heart. He wanted the kid to go through basic and AIT, then get into the prep school down at Belvoir and try for an army appointment to West Point. Christ, it's a real tragedy. A classic."

"And Hedges didn't do anything for him?"

"Are you kidding? The sergeant major went up to see him about his kid, see if Hedges could pull a couple of strings for the kid, at least get the bastards down at Dix to charge the kid with possession, and let him defend himself. What does Hedges do? He takes a fuckin' walk. In the opposite direction. Know what he said to Eldridge? He said, 'I don't want to hear about it.' That was it. 'I don't want to hear about it.' You believe that?"

Buck whistled that low whistle between his teeth and stared at the floor.

"Jesus H. fuckin' Christ," Buck stuttered. "The sergeant major was a legend. Hell, everybody in the fuckin' army knew he was Audie Murphy's platoon sergeant in the Third Division during the war. He's got the . . . fuckin' . . . Medal of fuckin' . . . *Honor,* for crying out loud. He was the dude who was feeding fifty-caliber rounds to Audie Murphy when he shot up that German battalion. You seen the goddamn movie. They even let old Eldridge wear his blue and white stripe Third Division patch on his right shoulder still, you know. Most of 'em wear their Vietnam unit patches. Not fuckin' Eldridge. He still wears the Third."

"Last time I saw Eldridge, walking along Brewerton Road, he looked like a truck had just run over him. Said they were retiring him. Big ceremony. Giving him the Legion of Merit, like he needs another ribbon or something. But the whole thing is happening after June Week, when none of the cadets from the regiment will be around to pay their respects. Most of the officers will be on leave, too. Christ. Thirty years in the goddamn army, and Hedges is pushing the sergeant major out the back door. I don't think he's too big on old Two-Dash Hedges any more. Nosir. I'd be willing to bet you my cow stripes old Eldridge would give anything to carve off a piece of Hedges before he leaves. I'll bet you Eldridge is chewing on his hat brim up here in 720 to keep himself under control. That clerk I talked to said the sergeant major had fuckin' blood in his eyes, he was so pissed."

"Think we can get anything out of the sergeant major about what Phineas T. was doing up in Hedges' office this afternoon?"

"You fuckin'-A right I think we can get Eldridge to feed us the poop on what King was up to. What's he got to lose? His Legion of Merit? He's out of here, out of the army in two weeks. I never thought I'd see a hard-core, brown-shoe army sergeant with a short-timer's attitude, but old Eldridge had it written all over him when I saw him shuffling along Brewerton Road. Fuckin' Hedges

47

stepped on his dick when he turned his back on Eldridge. He took the sergeant major for granted, figured loyalty was a prerogative of rank. He couldn't have made a worse mistake. When Eldridge got the cold shoulder, he wrote off Hedges for good. I wouldn't be surprised if he didn't put trash all over Hedges on the old-sergeant-grapevine. You know how those old fuckers stick together. One of 'em can't fart in Korea without the rest of 'em hearing the echo. And Sergeant Major Eldridge has always been one of the heaviest of the heavies. If he trashes Hedges, his bullshit isn't going to be worth fuckall when it comes to senior NCOs."

"So what do we do about Eldridge?"

"Give me a clean pair of socks out of my drawer, will you, Buck? I'm finished messing with these damn feet." Buck got up and handed Slaight a neatly folded pair of black cotton socks. Slaight grimaced as he pulled the socks over his swollen feet.

"I'll tell you exactly what we do about Eldridge. We put a bug in his ear, that's what we do. Let him know we're interested. Colonel King probably had him galavanting all over the goddamn place today, anyway. I'm sure he knows the shit's astir. And we ask him to keep an eye peeled for any relevant poop-sheets which come to his attention. He's always feeding us poop-sheets, anyway. Half the shit we've got filed away in this room came through Sergeant Major Eldridge during the past year. He is one goddamn fountain of poop-sheets. Good stuff, too. Remember back in January, when he fed us that poop-sheet that said they were doing away with reveille, two weeks before it happened? We won about three hundred bucks betting on the demise of reveille."

"Poop-sheets." Buck whistled again and gazed around the room. Two-twenty-six looked like the final resting place for all academy paper officialdom. A paperwork graveyard. The room was madly organized chaos, like a political campaign headquarters in the final throes of the last week before the election. Buck remembered when his father was running for county Democratic chairman back in Burning Tree. The family living room looked just like his room at West Point. Papers and books piled on the window ledge, overflowing the bookshelves, stacked on both gray metal desks. A metal typewriter table had been imported to hold a stack of magazines, two rows, eighteen inches deep. Two olive-drab file cabinets—the kind with five legal-width drawers—lined the walls behind both desks, to the left and right of the window overlooking New South Area. The file cabinets contained thousands of poop-sheets, army slang for official documents of every description, relating to matters as banal as trash pick-up schedules, as momentous as first-generation photo copies of the minutes of meetings of the Academy Board of Visitors, the closest thing West Point had to a board of trustees.

Neither Buck nor Slaight could recall why they had decided to start collecting poop-sheets. They probably hadn't decided—sometime in the past, the flow had simply begun, and now after three years, it couldn't be stopped. One poop-sheet after another found its way to Room 226, via a circuitous route of cadets and NCOs with chain-of-command positions through which streamed a steady flow of official memoranda, records, orders, bulletins, disposition forms, and just plain extraneous make-work military gibberish. Their room had become a corps-wide repository for poop-sheets. Buck read them, and Slaight filed them. Buck filtered out useless data and fed relevant information to Slaight on a nightly basis, when they took their showers just after taps. Between them, they probably knew more about what transpired at the United States Military Academy than the brigade S-1, the adjutant, the officer with responsibility for the generation and flow of all academy paperwork. They were fascinated by the swamp of paperwork upon which the army seemed to float, for within its murky depths, they surmised, could be found more than a few of the secrets about what made the wheels go round.

"So here's the plan, Buck. Tonight, I'm going up to Eldridge's quarters. I'll wait until he's had a few beers, then I'll put the bug in his ear. I'll fill him in about Hand from last summer. The kid was not without his share of enemies, you recall. Then I'll let him know that it would not go unappreciated if he passed along any relevant poop-sheets coming to his attention about the death of Cadet David Hand. I give the sergeant major three days, max. If there's a lid down, he'll uncork the fucker. Nothing gets past an old sergeant major like Eldridge who decides to call in his debts. Nothing. If Hedges so much as burps over his tuna salad sandwich, Eldridge will get a report on what key he burped in. All we've got to do is sit back and wait."

"Slaight . . . you wily-ass SOB, I think you done got it nailed," said Buck, grinning widely, making his already youthful face look positively pubescent. "Now, I suggest you haul your ass over to the hospital and let that doctor over there have a look at those feet. He's probably going to recommend you for a medical discharge, this time."

"Shit. I just want my basic load of Darvon and codeine. Seven more fuckin' hours and I'm finished, Buck. Seven goddamn hours. Give me a half-dozen Darvon and a couple of those big horsepill codeine caps, and I'll hump my fanny from here to New York. Jesus. That it should come to this. Darvon, codeine, and fuckin' moleskin."

"At least you're not up there floating in Popolopen, polluting the lake," said Buck, digging into his papers again.

"Yeah. Christ. Hand's dead. Guy told me on the area today, I just about dropped my gun. Drowned. It just doesn't . . . fuckin' *fit*, you know, Leroy?"

"Yeah."

"So what is it you got for me, Buck? Let's have a look."

"Aw, just another goddamn DF from Grimshaw. More total wisdom from the tactical officer, bless his khaki ass. But this one's a goody." Buck handed Slaight the memo. It had been run off on DD Form 314s, official Department of Defense DFs, Disposition Forms. DFs like it came down from Grimshaw on a daily basis.

DISPOSITION FORM

SUBJECT: Marriage

DISPOSITION: 1 ea. 1º & 2º Cadet Rooms

CLASSIFICATION: None

1. You gentlemen are no doubt aware that June Week is nearly upon us. I have before me a list of 1º cadets who intend to marry, subsequent to June Week festivities and Graduation. It has come to my attention that several 2º cadets have become "engaged." I would remind all you gentlemen of the following:

2. Pick yourself a good Army Wife. This is not a matter to be taken lightly. A good Army Wife is necessary for your Career. Many of you have heard me expound upon the fact that I had to turn in my first wife for a New Model. Gentlemen, my first wife did not cut the mustard. She had to go. My present mate fills the bill. She is All-Army and Gung-Ho. In fact, I have affectionately dubbed her "Rangerette Grimshaw." As cadets, you will not—repeat, *not*—address her by this nickname.

3. Do not be fooled by Clever Packaging. (I think we all know what is meant by *this*.)

4. Do not let June Week get the "best of you." You all know what I used to tell my troops in the old Triple-Deuce in Nam. Keep it in your pants, and it'll stay between your legs. Good advice, gentlemen. You may chuckle now, but someday you will know the accuracy of my words.

GRIM

Nathan E. Grimshaw
Maj/Inf
Tac Off Co. D-3

"Fuckin' Grimshaw. You can't beat him, can you?" asked Slaight with mock amazement.

"Nope. Not old Nathan E.," said Leroy Buck, his nose deep in the financial pages of the *Times* again. "Now,

51

drive your ass over to the dispensary, you lazy dimbo. That poop-sheet ain't doing your feet any good. Now, get."

5

Axel W. Rylander, Major General, United States Army, had been a turnback. He had flunked mathematics his third-class year at West Point, and after summer tutoring, had passed a make-up examination in mathematics and been readmitted to the corps of cadets with the class behind him, repeating his third-class year. The phenomenon of the turnback was at once West Point's way of punishing a man for not trying hard enough and yet hanging on to promising young cadets whom the army would have missed had they simply been flunked out altogether. So General Rylander, class of 1940, should have been class of 1939. Among generals, Rylander was a running joke. He had, in effect, two sets of classmates—those with whom he had been admitted as a cadet and those with whom he had graduated. Rylander, however, thought the joke was on everyone else. He had twice as many classmates as his contemporaries. Therefore, he had twice as many friends in high places, looking out for his interests.

Having been a turnback, Rylander hardly shone in academics, graduating in the deep confines of the bottom quarter of the class of 1940. His academic standing did little to hold him back. He was captain of the army football team and first captain, the highest ranking cadet, brigade commander of the cadet corps. When he graduated, he married the daughter of the owner of a large brewery in northern New Jersey. She was "horsy," which meant she was well placed in that stratum of the social scene in the New York metropolitan area who considered horseback riding somewhere between cleanliness and godliness. It had not hurt the career of young Lieutenant Ry-

52

lander when his wife's father was chosen by President Roosevelt to become the deputy Secretary of War in charge of production in 1941. Much could be said—was said—about Axel W. Rylander and his Washington connections during the war years. But truth was, he had taken his duty assignments as they had come to him, and in 1945 was still commanding the same company he'd had for the past year and a half. His father-in-law's War Department position had been, if anything, a nuisance, for the suspicion that somewhere behind the scenes strings were being pulled for him followed Rylander throughout the war. And it pissed him off but good. He was an infantry combat commander. The only thing his father-in-law ever did for him was to send him a pair of boots from L. L. Bean during the winter of '43 in a War Department pouch that had gone to the Fifth Army Headquarters. That was it.

General Rylander paced the sky-blue carpet of his office overlooking the Hudson. The great room had a twenty-foot-high ceiling with exposed wood beams that had to be sixteen inches across. The walls were oak-paneled, and sliding doors opened along one wall onto the wide stone stairwell which led into the courtyard of the Academic Headquarters. He figured the office had once been a conference room before some superintendent had come along and decided to expand, to move from the cramped corner office which had served superintendents for nearly a hundred years. He wasn't particularly happy with the new arrangement. The big office seemed . . . hollow. There was too much air in the place. A man couldn't get in there and light up a cigar and get some smoke going and muddy up the light, create a little cocoon around himself in which a man could *think*.

In his two years as superintendent, Rylander had done little to his office. Same desk. Same chair. Same dull gray drapes. Same leather sofa. Same small conference table and chairs over at one end of the room. Same portrait of Sylvanus Thayer, class of 1808, the fifth superintendent of the academy and so-called Father of West Point, the man who founded the academic system still used at the academy in 1968, small classes, testing and grading of students every day, emphasis on the applied sciences and engineering. Old Thayer just sat up there on the wall, staring, glaring at everyone who walked into the supe's office. It was like he still owned the place, like he knew, up there in heaven or wherever he was, that the academy was virtually unchanged from his day. He had the eyes of a psychopath, thought Rylander. Or maybe he had a tiff with the man who did the portrait, and the artist had painted in that crazed glint, that cast to his eyes which meant they never looked the same. Rylander continued to pace. There was little else in the big room to catch his eye. His office was completely devoid of what he called "garbage," the standard collection of mementos of one's career. The year before, when Army beat Navy, they'd tried to present him with the "game ball," which had been mounted on a walnut stand and was flanked on either side with brass castings of football players in action. He told them to put the thing in a glass case over in the gym, "where the paying customers can see it." So the presentation Army-Navy game ball was sitting in a glass case next to the Army Athletic Association ticket window, as per the supe's instructions.

Major General Rylander was pacing the sky-blue (infantry color) carpet in his office because he was bothered by this business with the dead cadet they found up in Popolopen early that morning. He heard about it around 9 A.M. from his aide, who burst into his office with a telephone message from the duty officer up at Camp Buckner, where the plebes were stashed during June Week, preparing for their summer training. The duty officer had called about fifteen minutes before Rylander reached his office, and the aide just found the message, buried in some papers on his desk, taken by the Academic Headquarters Duty NCO, who went off at 8:30 A.M. Rylander expected the normal flap would begin any moment— phone calls, messengers, military police, and emissaries from the Tactical Department running all over the place. He waited. Nothing happened.

At 10:30 A.M., an hour and a half after he first received word of the dead cadet, he received a call from the deputy commandant of cadets, Colonel Theodore Reed, class of '50, who reported that General Hedges, the commandant, had wanted to personally make a report to the supe, but he was at that moment on his way out to Buckner. Or someplace. The colonel wasn't sure. He had received a cryptic message from the com to call the supe and "let him know what's going on." The dead cadet's name was Hand, David, class of 1971. He drowned in Lake Popolopen. That was all he knew.

Rylander was busy preparing for June Week. That was why he worked a full day on Saturday. Seemed like every year there was more to do. This was just what he needed: a dead plebe. He spent most of the day on the phone to Washington. It was the Chief of Staff's thirtieth class reunion (he was class of '38), so there were additional preparations to be made, a private reception at the supe's quarters for the chief's classmates, an address to the class of '38 on "The Military Academy of the Future," a special picnic up at Round Pond honoring the chief and his wife. June Week was normally a hellish time for the academy superintendent, and now *this*. A dead plebe laid at his feet three days before the whole thing was due to begin. Just what he needed. Rylander felt his stomach grumble and remembered that he had forgotten to take his Maalox at lunch. He reached into the top drawer of his desk, pulled out a sterling silver flask, and took a quick swig. Blaaah! The stuff tasted the same, no matter what you drank it from.

Rylander had waited all day for a follow-up report on the dead cadet from the commandant. When by 5 P.M. he had heard nothing, he called Hedges. He hated to call Hedges. They worked only a hundred yards away from each other, and it seemed like there should be some better way of doing business than the telephone. He thought about putting on his cap and just walking over to Hedges' office and asking what the hell was up with the dead cadet, but then he thought again. Hedges was the one who was supposed to report to *him,* the supe. Hedges should be hot-footing it over to the other side of Thayer

Road about twice a day—once in the morning, once in the afternoon—for a face-to-face with the man he worked for. Rylander made a note to himself. *Daily meetings w/Hedges here. AM—PM.*

The phone call to Hedges had produced nothing but hot air and a promise for a report before close of business, an hour away. He never got anything out of Hedges over the phone. He always had this feeling Hedges was using the phone as a weapon, wielding it in a circular fashion, like a sling. He had this image of Hedges whipping the phone around and around his head . . . then letting it go . . . the phone sailing through the air like a mortar round . . . black and slow and deadly. Rylander *heard* his stomach this time, grinding and crunching like gravel beneath a truck's tires. He reached again for the Maalox. June Week was going to get the best of him again this year. He could tell.

Everything had to be perfect for June Week. It was the high point of the year at the academy. In the crisp, early summer mornings, West Point was fresh, lime-green, *young* in some odd, indefinable way. Thayer Road, the area of barracks, the Plain, the cliffs overlooking the Hudson River Valley, all would be crowded with "old grads," wandering around the grounds, checking to see that the academy, though it changed perceptibly from year to year, carried on the grand traditions of the Long Gray Line. Maybe that was why West Point seemed young during June Week. Because every year the old grads who returned seemed older.

The men who would walk the grounds of the academy during June Week *were* the Long Gray Line. The traditions preserved by West Point were their traditions. At least, the old grads thought the traditions were theirs. June Week was time of high emotion, a time when the academy stood at attention to be inspected by those of the Corps who had come before. June Week celebrated the past, held it aloft and worshiped it, for in the past was to be found the path to the future.

June Week was West Point with shoulders back and head high, West Point in its most public incarnation, in full-dress uniform, handsome, cinematic, regal, the military way of life carried to its most elegant conclusion. June Week was a grand parade of perfection. Every year the New York *Times* and the *Daily News* and the wire services and the three television networks sent reporters to the academy. The news media made its annual pilgrimage, it seemed, to reassure the world that at least here among the great gray stone buildings of the academy, here among the cadets with the close-cropped hair and the impeccable manners, here among the medal-bedecked officer corps—here at *West Point* life went on, unperturbed by events outside. The news stories emanating from June Week would chorus: At West Point they still *believed*.

Everything had to be so perfect for June Week that the entire plebe class was moved, en masse, to Camp Buckner, the summer training installation ten miles away from the main academy grounds where later that summer they would undergo two months of intensive field exercises. Technically, in May, the plebe class was of West Point, but they were not yet West Pointers. They had not been "recognized," the formal ceremony following graduation parade when each plebe would shake hands with each upperclassman in his company. Plebes were thus not yet fit for public consumption. They would spend June Week by themselves, getting ready for summer training. It was a carefree, unhindered week for the plebes, the first time all year when they were not under the constant gun of the upper classes. Lake Popolopen offered swimming, canoeing, sailing, water skiing, fishing, and for the first time since they had entered the academy, access to Camp Buckner's own version of West Point's famous "Flirtation Walk," along which amorous adventures with those of the opposite sex could take place.

Now this plebe, Hand, had been found floating in Popolopen down at the end of Flirtation Walk. The deputy com had said it looked like an accident. Accidental cadet deaths were all too common during June Week, though rarely, if ever, did one receive public exposure. Every year, one or two cadets would do themselves in. This year it had already happened. Two first-classmen
57

had killed themselves in a Corvette, making a last-minute dash back to the academy from Snuffy's Bar, a little roadhouse located precisely fifteen miles from the academy gate, the closest bar where cadets were permitted to drink. Their deaths went unreported in the press. The year before, Rylander recalled, a drunken cadet had run over a child in Highland Falls, the small town just off post. The cadet had been charged with manslaughter and was later exonerated. The whole business was hush-hush. Many cadets never found out the "accidental" killing of the child had occurred.

Where was Hedges? Why in hell is it taking him so long to get that report to me?

Brigadier General Charles Sherrill Hedges had been commandant of cadets for nine months; Rylander had been superintendent for two years. The two men did not get along. The superintendent sat down behind his large oak desk and scratched his crew-cut head. He was beefy and tall—6'1", 220 pounds, only a bit over his playing weight when he had captained the army football team. His face was soft, unlined, almost youthful-looking, despite his fifty years and combat experience in three wars. He had the offhanded bearing of one who had been brought up to think he was better than everyone else. This had not been true of Axel Rylander. He was a Wisconsin farm boy and had worked his father's small dairy before he entered the Military Academy in the summer of 1935. The Depression had killed his mother, and an appointment to West Point the year of her death had seemed at once a blessing and a cop-out, leaving his father and kid sister alone to run the dairy . . . it had bothered him when he was a cadet. In retrospect, he thought the guilt he felt leaving his family behind was probably the reason he was a turnback. He could never keep his mind on his studies, so he took out his frustrations on the football field, where because of his size and his anger, he excelled.

His career had been a normal one—command time, staff time, combat, all the army schools, a graduate degree in foreign relations from George Washington University, gotten at night when he was stationed at the Pentagon as a lieutenant colonel in the '50s. If there was anything that set him apart, it was his command of the 1st Cav back '65–'66, when the war was being won. Everything seemed to go right for him that year. The 1st Cav made headlines almost every day. The press needed something to focus on, something to hold up as evidence that, indeed, a war was being fought over there in Vietnam, ten thousand miles away from the nearest American Main Street. The correspondents who were covering the war, Cronkite and some of the older ones anyway, remembered Rylander from World War II. They remembered Bastogne, the refusal of the greatly outnumbered 101st Airborne troopers to surrender. Rylander had been there. No doubt about it, Bastogne brought back a lot of memories . . . and the memories of another battle, another war . . . the memories gave Rylander credibility.

Now they wanted another war, and he gave them one—the kind of war he remembered: great division-strength operations sweeping across huge pieces of the II Corps highlands, rushing to the Laotian border and back again. Rylander deployed more troops in the field on actual combat maneuvers than any unit commander in Vietnam. The 1st Cav would go two months before a "stand-down," a return to the rear area for a brief respite from life in the jungle. Rylander's division was the army the way the American people remembered their army from service in World War II, Korea . . . from the late movie on television. Rylander commanded a division that got out there and *got the job done.*

That the job which was getting done had little bearing on the political realities underlying an elusive military situation went completely unnoticed by press, politicians, and public. In '65–'66 the war in Vietnam was being won. The 1st Cavalry Division was the most visible symbol of this uncontested fact. General Rylander was a symbol. He symbolized the military man of history textbooks and Hollywood motion pictures. He symbolized the military man *Life* had celebrated on so many covers over the years. Rylander went on the cover of *Life.* Not long afterward, the President showed up at his division headquarters, in the company of a phalanx of public relations types from Saigon. There were TV crews all over the place. The President looked around the headquarters, went outside, and shook some hands. Rylander recalled thinking that he looked like he was campaigning somewhere in Texas—it was all dusty and he was hot, sweat straining his armpits and the back of his white shirt. Then he walked up to Rylander and asked if he could take a ride in a helicopter. Just like that. Rylander had been dumbfounded. The President sounded like a kid asking a parent if he could ride the roller coaster. It was in the tone of his voice. Through the famous Texas drawl, Rylander detected that touch of fascination and fear and awe only a kid would experience just before his first ride on a roller coaster. So they climbed in the chopper and went up for a ride. One of the PR types from Saigon took Rylander aside and told him not to take the President anyplace. "Just ride him around a bit. You know," the man had said. The cameras rolled. That night, all across America, it would look like the President of the United States was taking off on a combat mission, really getting up there on the front lines and mixing it up with the troops. Truth was, Rylander rarely if ever used the helicopter which sat next to the division headquarters bunker. He preferred to look at things on the ground, see the terrain the way the foot soldier would see it, walk around and get a feel of the goddamn land.

Now, three years later, the same President he'd taken for a ride in his helicopter had abdicated. The war in Vietnam had not been won with a few crack Airborne units and a Marine division or two, as the Pentagon and the politicians had hoped. Now the "brushfire war" was called a "protracted struggle." Official United States Army language had adopted the political slang of Chairman Mao to describe the war which just seemed to ooze from day to day with no end in sight. Slowly, the country was being weaned from its historical fascination with the military. Men like Axel W. Rylander had become, almost overnight, obsolete. And he knew it.

In one year, at the end of his tour of duty as superintendent of the Military Academy, his career would be over. Rylander leaned back in his chair and stared at the lush green hills across the Hudson. In one year, he'd be cashiered with a third star and shuffled off to a harmless duty assignment where he could serve out his final years in the army with quiet dignity. It was the army way. The pay-off. An active-duty pension. The pasture.

Rylander knew that the army of 1968 had changed in quantum leaps from the army of just three years ago. Right now, down in the Pentagon, they were looking for some young buck, some up-and-comer to push on the public as an image for the New Army General. What bothered Rylander about his commandant of cadets was the fact that Hedges was just the man they were looking for. He was young. He was hot. He had combat experience. And something—some gut instinct deep down inside Rylander—told him Hedges was well connected politically. The army general of the future, he surmised, was going to be a political animal. Hedges was such an animal. He was moving ahead with unreal speed, and he was toeing the current Pentagon line, prattling to the cadets in his lectures on the war about "the airmobile concept" and the "body count." Hell, his old unit was now called the 1st Cavalry Division (Airmobile) in deference to helicopter tactics, the new doctrine which was coming out of the Pentagon in a desperate attempt to find some kind of formula with which the Vietcong could be effectively dealt a crushing military and political blow. The magical ingredient, the key to instant success, was the body count. Helicopters and body counts. Rylander scratched his crew cut again and laughed out loud.

Hell, he'd fought in North Africa, Sicily, Italy, the Battle of the Bulge, and finally in Germany itself. He had walked his way through most of World War II. Now they were flying around over in Vietnam in helicopters . . . all Hedges could talk about when he was telling war stories at cocktail parties was his "C & C ship." It was like he was talking about some temple, some place he went to worship, the way he talked about his C & C ship. So they flew

61

around in helicopters, and they spent the night on cots in places they called base camps, and they counted bodies. This was winning the war. Well . . . if it wasn't winning the war, it sure was promoting those who flew the most missions and counted the most bodies.

Hedges almost glowed when he talked about body counts. In his unit, they stacked the enemy dead like cordwood, took pictures of them, and put the photos on the wire services and television. Often, Hedges would have a big plywood crest of his unit leaning against the bodies, so everyone would know which unit had scored the victory. One night at a reception Rylander had given for the Board of Trustees of Boston College, Hedges pulled from his Dress Blues jacket pocket a color photograph of a particularly large stack of Vietcong dead, with his unit crest prominently displayed in front of the pile. The Boston College trustees were horrified. It wasn't just a color photo Hedges was showing them. It was his family Christmas card. The photo had been duplicated and run off on a white background, with the words "Season's Greetings" and "Peace to the World" ringing the photo of the dead VC bodies. One of the trustees from Boston College approached Rylander and asked him if the commandant was trying to make some kind of sick joke. Rylander walked across the room and asked to see the card. Hedges showed it to him, explaining that he and his wife had just sent out two hundred to their entire Christmas card list. It wasn't a sick joke. It was Charles Sherrill Hedges, Brigadier General, United States Army. An up-and-comer.

Counting bodies was a crime. An enemy was an enemy, and he deserved respect. Counting his dead, and photographing their bodies, violated Rylander's notion of the nature of war. Every soldier knew that wars were fought over land, territory, *dirt*. You deployed your forces, executed maneuvers, killed enemy soldiers, and you occupied land you took away from them. When you had occupied and controlled all of the land, as the Allies had done in World War II, as had been done in World War I, as had been done in the Civil War, as had been done by Napoleon, and by Caesar, and by Alexander the Great . . . then you *won*. The fact that II Corps, the area of operations over which he had command, was now completely controlled by the Vietcong, meant that in three years of war in II Corps, the United States Army had lost.

Sitting in his office waiting for Hedges to show up with his report on the dead plebe, General Rylander was disgusted. But he would hide his disgust. For in truth, his disgust was turning slowly to shame, and generals were not supposed to feel shame. And he, Axel W. Rylander, was certainly not going to feel shame in the presence of his manipulative, political commandant of cadets, Charles Sherrill Hedges. Rylander sat up straight in his chair. He swiveled around and gazed across the Hudson. West Point, he resolved, was not going to go the way of the Charles Sherrill Hedgeses of the world. Not while he was superintendent, it wasn't. He swore softly under his breath. After twenty-eight years in the army, he was resigned to protecting the United States Military Academy like it was a piece of turf in some gang war in the Bronx. If the nation had any idea what was happening to its sacred West Point . . .

6

"General, the commandant is in the outer office." It was Mrs. Moore, Rylander's secretary. The superintendent swiveled his chair around so it faced his oak desk, nodded his head in a signal to his secretary, and took a pad of yellow legal paper from his lower left-hand desk drawer. He chose a sharp pencil from a row of pencils to his left, next to the phone. The door opened. Hedges strode into the supe's office. He reached a spot immediately in front of a chair located slightly to the left of the desk and about two feet away from its corner. It was a subtle gesture, and Rylander took note. According to protocol, the commandant should have placed himself squarely in front of the supe's desk, about four feet distant, and reported his presence in a military fashion, waiting for a signal from the supe to walk over to the chair and sit down. Instead, Hedges was poised, ready to sit down as he spoke:

"General, I've got that report from Terry King we've been waiting for. He just stopped by my office and gave it to me. I got over here as soon as I could." Rylander looked at Hedges. He was not carrying a brief case, a manila folder, the distinctive light blue Top Secret container for sensitive information, a sheaf of papers . . . he wasn't carrying anything. Rylander waited a mental four-count before speaking:

"Where is it?"

"I am prepared to give you the facts, verbally, sir. You seemed in a hurry when I spoke to you on the telephone. I figured you just wanted to get the facts and be on your way down to Bear Mountain for the dinner." Rylander didn't move a muscle. He did not want to give Hedges the slightest indication that he was being invited to be seated. Let him stand there and stew a minute. Nothing in writing. *You seemed in a hurry.*

"General Hedges, I will determine when I am, as you put it, 'in a hurry,' and when I am not 'in a hurry.' " Rylander let the sarcasm of his words sink in. "It so happens that right now, at this moment, I am not 'in a hurry.' Do you understand me, General?"

"Yessir . . . I just thought . . ."

"General Hedges, I do not expect you to sit in the commandant's office all day and 'just think.' " Again, the sarcasm. "Today, I expected you to get that report on the dead plebe to me. It so happens that all day I have been, as you put it, 'in a hurry.' There is much I must do in preparation for June Week. You are aware of this. The plain fact is, I did not hear word one from you until 1700, exactly forty-five minutes ago, when I had my secretary place a call to your office, and we spoke. You have not exactly been very solicitous of my time, if you are indeed, as you say, aware of the fact that I have been 'in a hurry.' Now, where, may I ask, is the report?"

64

"Back in my office, sir." Hedges' words were curt, and edged with the realization that he was getting a grilling. He drew himself to his full 5'9", and pulled at the bottom of his uniform jacket. Rylander noticed it was a nervous habit Hedges had, the constant straightening of his uniform, as if every crease had to be in precise alignment in order for Hedges to function properly. He often thought of Hedges as a machine, so perhaps it was true. Machines need to be aligned, balanced, in order to run. So, obviously, did Hedges.

"You will get the report to me at 1300 tomorrow?" asked Rylander. The inflection in his voice was that of a question, but clearly it was a command.

"Yessir, 1300 it is, sir," replied Hedges, looking Rylander in the eye. Hedges felt blood moving inexorably into his face, and he knew that by now, he had reddened. The knowledge angered him, and sped the reddening of his face. Soon, he knew from past experience, he would be crimson.

"Well," Rylander paused again for a count. "Sit down. Let me know what you've got. I want it all. Every detail King gave you." Hedges eased himself into the chair at the edge of Rylander's desk, pulling on the bottom of his jacket, running his hands along its front seams, making sure they overlapped properly. Rylander watched Hedges with detached amusement, as he aligned and tugged, putting himself together. Hedges' face was the color of a ripe tomato. That it has come down to this—a store mannequin soldier in custom-tailored greens, pulling and yanking on himself like one of those dolls his daughters used to have, with strings you pulled, and they talked, or made a squeaky noise that passed for talk. And now this . . . machine . . . Hedges . . . was pulling on himself, straightening his tie, running his fingers down his buttons, making sure they're all buttoned and straight, nothing out of alignment . . . any minute the puppeteer was going to let loose and Hedges would collapse in a heap of cloth and papier-mâché . . . the soldier of the future. Rylander shuddered, deep in his gut, picked up his pencil, and sat ready to take note on Hedges' report.

"Sir, what we've got here . . ." Hedges' eyes drifted to the right, out over the river, then focused quickly back on the superintendent. "Sir, what we've got here is a clear-cut case, a tragic case, an accidental drowning which apparently occurred, sir, when the individual, Hand, David, Company F-4, nineteen years of age, was skinny-dipping down at the end of Lake Popolopen by himself. Violated every regulation on the books. Swimming alone. Off limits, making use of Flirtation Walk and vicinity after dusk . . . swimming in the nude. I could go on. I'm sure you see the pattern, sir. The young man was a problem plebe, an accident looking for a place to happen. Looks like he found it. Or we found him. Depends on the point of view, sir. If you get what I mean." Hedges smiled a strange, thin smile Rylander had seen before. The smile was completely out of place. There was nothing humorous about the death of a cadet, accidental or otherwise. Hedges' smile seemed to mask something within him . . . something strange, and inhuman. Rylander was seized with the realization that Charles Sherrill Hedges did not know the smile was on his lips, *The man has lost control of himself.*

"Go on," he said. "Let's hear the rest of it."

"That's it, General," said Hedges. "A tragic accident. I think we should notify the parents ASAP. They're going to want to make funeral arrangements, and we can't let this thing get in the way of June Week. . . ."

"You let me worry about what does and what does not get in the way of June Week, do you understand me, General Hedges?"

"Yessir. Roger that." The smile had become self-satisfied now. Rylander caught Hedges' casual usage of radio talk—*roger that*—and it disgusted him.

"You're sure that's it?" asked Rylander, drilling his eyes into Hedges' thinly smiling face. "That's all Terry King had for you?"

"Yessir."

"Well. Get that report to me tomorrow by 1300. I want to take a look at it in writing before I notify the next of kin. You can go now. You are dismissed, General." Rylander did not look up from his notes.

Hedges rose sharply and executed a snappy salute.

"Good evening, sir. And you and Mrs. Rylander have a nice time at the Bear Mountain Inn." Hedges turned neatly on his heel and walked quickly out the door.

Rylander swiveled his chair and looked out over the Hudson. The sun was low, and the river had a greenish-blue tint, picked up from the sky and the reflection of the wooded hills on the other side of the river. The river never changed. Looked the same way it did when he was a cadet. *Hedges.* They had a phrase describing men like Hedges, when he was a cadet. Guys like him thought they were "all over it."

I'll show him who's all over it. He folded his notes and stuck them into an inside pocket in his uniform jacket. Picking up his gold-braided cap, he walked through the sliding doors, down the stone steps, through the courtyard, across Thayer Road, through Central Area, down Diagonal Walk, across the Plain. He enjoyed the walk. It took five minutes, and he was home.

7

Six-thirty P.M. A telephone call.

"Colonel King speaking, sir."

"Terry? Hedges. I'm at the office. Get over here as soon as you can. Forget dinner. I've just seen the supe, and he's hopping mad about this business with the dead plebe. He gave me explicit instructions that we're to clean it up. ASAP."

"Anything I can bring with me, sir?" Silence on the line. King can hear Hedges flipping through some papers.

"This report you gave me this afternoon . . . is this the only copy of the autopsy done on the kid?"

"Yessir. You've got the whole thing. I made sure Fitzgerald turned over all his paper work to me. I personally collected the autopsy report and all copies from Consor, the doc. Destroyed the copies this morning, sir."

"Well, get yourself on down here, Terry. We've got some work to do. The supe went crazy, started throwing his arms around, says he wants this thing sanitized, squeaky-clean. Says he wants to be able to use it for a shaving mirror, it's so shiny. And he wants it on his desk by 1300 tomorrow."

"Sir?"

"Yeah, Terry, what is it?"

"Sir, what exactly does the supe mean by 'sanitized'?"

"He means he wants Hand's death reported as an accident, a regrettable, tragic accident. You know what he said when I told him the kid was probably a fag, and probably murdered by another cadet? He said—and these are his exact words, Terry, I swear to God—he said, 'I don't want to hear about it.' You should have seen the look on his face. His skin was green."

"So we've got to rewrite the report, sir? The whole thing?"

"That's right. And we're going to need a new autopsy. The supe isn't going to want to see anything about murder or semen in there. So you'd better do some thinking about how we're going to come up with a brand-new autopsy report."

"No problem, sir. Got it covered."

"What's that?"

"No problem, sir. When Consor handed me the autopsy this morning, I told him I wanted all his copies. I found some blank forms, along with his copies. Got 'em up in my desk."

"Stop by your office on your way down, Terry. I want those forms. And what about this man, Consor? Can we trust him? Should we call him over and tell him our problem, give him the word straight from the supe?"

"I don't thnk so, sir. He's a grad . . . but you know these doctors, sir. They're not combat arms. I think we can handle the autopsy. We'll just excise what we don't want in Consor's report, retype it and run it through the photocopier over his signature. Look good as new. That's all anybody gets their hands on nowadays, anyway. Photocopies. The supe'll never notice. No problem, sir. Got you covered."

"Damn fine, Terry. Damn fine. I'll see you down here in . . . let's say . . . half an hour, roger?"

"Roger that, sir."

"Terry?"

"Yessir?"

"Don't let the little woman know what's up. Tell her you've got officer's call or something. See you in three-zero."

"King out."

Brigadier General Hedges cradled the phone. He ran his right index finger down the front of his uniform jacket, touching each brass button, feeling instinctively for the wings of the little embossed eagles, straightening a button if its wings were not horizontal. He sharpened a pencil. The electric pencil sharpener whirred softly, sounding like a generator back in Nam, bunkered out behind the hootch, sandbagged in so you could barely hear it hum. He thumped the eraser end of the pencil on his desktop, waiting.

The whole thing was like a duck shoot back in Maryland on the Chesapeake, when he grew up. They'd sit out on the edge of the bay on little stools in a blind, waiting. Waiting for those damned ducks. Ducks would come by, they'd stand up and shoot them. First, the father. Then Harry, the oldest son, Hedges' brother. Then little Charlie with his .410 gauge single-shot. He'd stand up and bang away, reloading as fast as his little fingers could fumble another shell into the breach of the shotgun. It always pissed him off that he was last, that the rest of them called him "Little Charlie," because he was always the youngest, the littlest. Now he was the commandant, things were different.

He was going duck shooting again. The feeling was the same. Sitting there in his office, waiting. Always waiting. But this time he was going to get off the first round. And there was only one duck: the superintendent of the United States Military Academy. Hedges thumped the eraser faster, dropped the pencil, straightened the bottom of his uniform jacket, touched the knot of his tie, felt the sterling-silver clasp he used to pinch together the points of his collar, custom-tailored Dacron and cotton khaki he'd ordered from some outfit over in Nam. He ran his fingers through his hair, back to the collar of his shirt, starched stiff against his rough, tanned neck.

Never in the recent history of the Military Academy had a commandant of cadets superseded a superintendent. Traditionally, each position was considered an important step in a general's career. Commandants usually left West Point with a promotion to major general and a division command. Superintendents usually received a promotion to lieutenant general and moved into a key slot in the Pentagon, or took a deputy command slot over in NATO Headquarters. Commandants and superintendents moved up and away from West Point.

Hedges considered the situation. No matter who won the election in November, the war was going to start winding down. Addison Thompson said it was coming. Sentiment in the Congress was turning. It wouldn't be long before a coalition of antiwar senators could bottle up a defense appropriations bill and demand White House concessions on the war to let it out—concessions like troop force reductions, cutbacks in air strikes against the North, reduced military aid to the South Vietnamese regime. As he had done many times in the past, the head of West Point's Social Science Department was watching over the careers of his protégés. Hedges knew he was at the top of Thompson's list, and that Thompson was right: No matter what happened in November, Vietnam combat command was no longer the thing for army generals with an eyeball on their futures.

Hedges made up his mind. He'd use the murder of Cadet David Hand to knock off the supe. That prissy SOB with his society wife, sitting over there in his office, playing around with his telephones and his secretaries and his social plans for June Week . . . what the hell did he know about what was going on at West Point? Nothing. Rylander was so obsessed with his formalities, with the

70

pomp and circumstance of power, he had no idea of the essence of *real* power, the control of the life of one man by another. He'd never suspect a thing.

That bunch of half-assed flunkies over in Headquarters would keep him insulated . . . that gaggle of desk jockies, always running around wheezing and flapping and all for what? For the greater glory of Axel W. Rylander, that's what. He figured he could get away with rapping his knuckles on the head of Charles Sherrill Hedges, he had another think coming.

Hedges turned the notion over in his mind, flipping it from side to side, examining the plan for rough spots, nicks, scratches in the metal . . . it really was like shooting ducks! The idea of knocking off Rylander, moving from com right up to supe, taking that walk across the street for the last time . . . Hedges felt like he was holding a rifle, rubbing linseed oil into the stock, tightening the sights, working the rifle's action, the bolt sliding over and back and forward and over and locking and over and back and forward and locking again . . . the notion felt warm and sticky and smooth . . . elegant. It wouldn't be an easy shot, but it was the thing he'd been training for all his life. Hang Rylander with a phony report on the murdered cadet, then sit back and watch him cook when the heat was turned up . . . watch the son of a bitch buckle and twitch and fry when the scent of scandal began wafting along the Hudson . . . Rylander sitting there in his office with his telephones ringing, not knowing what to do. . . . Hedges thumped the eraser on his desk, making mental notes, plans . . . time compressing again . . . that familiar, comfortable sensation of floating, slow-motion, above the ground, like he was in his C & C ship, strapped in, left hand on the mike, right hand gripping his web gear, floating up there above the action, yelling above the roar of the rotor blades into the mike, calling in fire, shooting ducks. . . .

8

At 6:30 P.M. Ry Slaight was sitting neck deep in 105°
water in one of the Jacuzzi whirlpools in the physical
therapy room of the West Point Hospital. He had decided
to skip supper, a privilege enjoyable only on Saturday
nights. The nurses' aides in the PT room had left one of
the whirlpools full for Slaight when they went off-duty.
He had arranged the deal on Monday and had spent an
hour soaking in the whirlpool every day after walking the
area. It was privilege. It was cow.

Slaight just stripped, eased himself down into the stain-
less-steel tub and sat on the wooden bench on the bottom,
dialed 105 on the thermostat, flipped the Jacuzzi switch,
leaned his head back on a rolled towel, and blew out a long
breath of hot, stinky air, area air, air full of sweat and
gritty concrete dust and the rank stench of his sweaty
fuckin' gray wool dress coat, barracks air, West Point air.
The hot swirling water pounded him like a soggy jackham-
mer, going to work on his legs first, down there at the
spot where the jet nozzle stuck into the tank. Then he felt
the water at the base of his back, rooting around in his
muscles, tugging on the knots of tension he brought over
with him from the area, pulling that goddamn M-14 off
his shoulder, floating those eight pounds of steel and wood
and leather up over the edge of the tank and away. Then
he felt his neck let go. It was a slobbery, lazy feeling, like
somebody had landed a good one on him in plebe boxing,
and he had brushed the edges of consciousness, swimming
around out there in that gray area where your legs are
rubbery and your balance lurches in and out of contact
like a New York subway pulling away from a station platform—*wham! clank!*—the cars banging together as the
train picks up speed . . . balance slipping and swaying
and rushing away. . . .

He felt good. He'd stay in the whirlpool until his toes 'elt like they were growing together, they were so water-'ogged, then he'd wrap a towel around himself and pad down the hall to the duty doctor's office for his nightly 'oot-doctoring.

The hospital at West Point was like another world, completely separate from the academy. Inside its walls, the rules changed: It was doctors and patients, not officers and cadets. Of course, the academy did what it could to limit the breakdown in discipline perceived inside the hospital. The presence of the hospital commander on the Academic Board, the academy board of governors, saw to that.

Cadets who were hospitalized, for example, were required to mop the areas around their bunks and make their own beds every morning, except when their temperatures exceeded 100°. It seemed like a little thing, mopping your area, making your bed. But when Slaight had pneumonia as a plebe, had spent twenty-eight days up in Ward Two, staggering around his bed every morning, slopping the mop, soaking his cotton slippers with ammonia suds, yanking on the sheets to square his bed corners for ward inspection at 7:30 A.M., it was just like being back in the barracks. The significance of his duties in the hospital ward had not been lost upon him. He was sicker than he'd ever been in his life, but he knew that back in the barracks, the Tactical Department had targeted the hospital—the doctors, the nurses, the aides—all of them were the goddamn enemy.

The enemy! Jesus! The fuckin' VC were supposed to be the enemy! Every day they screamed and yelled about the fuckin' VC, little commie dinks, fuckin' yellow slopes, all they heard about from the tacs and the rest of the fuckers who'd been to Nam was VC–VC–V-fuckin'-C. But they weren't the only enemy, the VC. There were enemies all over the goddamn place. You listened to the tacs, every dude in the Academic Department was the enemy. You listened to the gorillas over in OPE, anybody who couldn't do more than ten pull-ups was the goddamn enemy. You listened to the Juice P's, the Fluids P's, the

73

Solids P's—the professors in all the applied sciences—anybody downstairs in English or Social Science was the fuckin' enemy. And you listened to any grad any goddamn place in any goddamn department doing any goddamn thing from teaching nuclear physics to picking his teeth . . . listen to a grad, and anybody who wasn't a grad was the goddamn enemy. Listen to Infantry dudes, and the Artillery was the enemy. Listen to Armor, and Signal was the enemy. Listen to the ribbon-wearing combat arms officers, and anybody pushing pencils in any of the noncombat arms was the chickenshit enemy.

Christ! If you really listened-up at West Point, if you believed all the bullshit they shoved at you every day, really *believed* it, you'd flip out paranoid-schitz for sure! Slaight shifted position on the wood bench so the jet nozzle shot a stream of bubbles right up his backbone. It was a damn good thing guys didn't get to do time in the whirlpool every day like this. If they did, inside of a month there'd be nobody left at West Point. Whole goddamn Corps would up and resign. Old Woo Poo had it all figured out. They take your life for four goddamn years and they cram every day full of formations and classes and parades and inspections and reports and studies and problems and they leave you with zero time to think. Too much thinking softens the brain. That was the West Point attitude. Tac was always saying: *Nobody's payin' you to think mister they're payin' you to act you got that straight?* Funny thing was, the dumb bastard was right.

"Well, well, well. Mr. Slaight. Imagine finding you here." The voice came from somewhere behind him, and Slaight turned around on the bench in the whirlpool to see who it was.

"Using your Saturday evenings profitably these days, I see," said the voice. It was Consor, the doctor Slaight had had when he was a plebe, twenty-eight days with this guy thumping his chest and peering down his throat and shooting his fanny full of antibiotics. Twenty-eight days under the supervision of a doctor, and the goddamn guy had to be a grad. Now he's the Saturday duty doctor.

Slaight cursed his luck. He'd never get any codeine out of Consor. Grad docs were too hip to cadet scams.

"How's it going, Major Consor?" asked Slaight. "Long time no see."

"Maybe long time no see for you, Mr. Slaight, but I've picked up your scent over here occasionally. It seems your chest colds and flus dovetail nicely with the schedule of midterm exams, I've noticed, Mr. Slaight. Let's see. How many days of bed rest have you pulled down over the past year, Slaight? Ten? Twenty?"

"Been keeping an eye on me, have you, sir?"

"You bet, Slaight. You may cough your way past these young captains we've got over here, but the first time you draw me on sick call, I'll shove so many needles full of distilled water in your ass, you won't be able to sit down for a week."

"Come on, sir, you know I wouldn't try to pull anything on sick call. Only time I've been over here this year was when I got the flu. They gave me the basic load of pills and sent me to bed for a few days, that's all. I was sick. For real."

"How many days, Slaight? How many days of bed rest you rack up this year? Tell me. I'm curious."

"Eight, sir. Four pairs. I never pulled down a whole week. There's guys in my company who talk their way into a week of bed rest all the time. Not me, sir. I just come in for a couple of days' rack when I get worn out, that's all. Nothing outrageous."

"Indeed. What are you doing over here tonight, Slaight? Working on your muscle tone for summer leave?" The major was standing next to the whirlpool tank in his khakis and white coat, grinning like he'd caught Slaight breaking some minor regulation, which he had. Technically, the whirlpool was a prescription therapy, and cadets needed a doctor's signature on a "sick slip" to use it. Slaight's deal with the orderlies in the physical therapy room had been strictly off the books. He traded a week of whirlpool for a stack of back-issue *Playboys*.

"Nosir. I've been on the area all week. I've got an

Emergency Sick Call slip to come over and have somebody take a look at my feet. Are you the duty doctor tonight, sir?"

"You guessed it, Slaight. What seems to be the problem with your tootsies?" The major grinned widely and leaned on the tank. Slaight lifted one of his legs and propped his foot on the edge of the steel tank. The whirlpool had softened the skin around the edges of the broken blisters, and the bleeding had stopped. But his feet still looked like Salisbury steak, raw. The major whistled.

"Christ, Slaight, why haven't you been over here before this? Your goddamn feet are a crime."

"I've been coming over every day after area formation, sir, getting them worked on. I just peeled off all the moleskin and bandages. That's why they look sorry." He had both feet on the edge of the whirlpool now, and the quiet purr of the Jacuzzi vibrated his toes slightly.

"You mean you've been over here every day this week, and nobody has issued you a medical excuse slip from the area formation?" The major looked incredulous as he poked at Slaight's raw toes.

"I've been coming every day, yessir, and one or two of the docs who've seen me have tried to issue me a medical excuse, but I don't want one, sir. Can't take one. Got to walk my hours and get them over with. I've only got seven left to walk, then I'm finished. I'll be off on Thursday."

"What do you mean you can't take a medical excuse, young man? If a doctor issues you a medical excuse from the area, you take it, and that's that."

"No can do, sir. My tac, Major Grimshaw, won't let anybody in the company be excused from the area for any reason. We had guys walking hours this winter with hundred-degree fevers. Grimshaw says if you take a medical, he'll give you double hours for every hour you get excused from. Nobody wants to walk those extra hours, sir. Guys in the Company will crawl the area rather than have Grimshaw come down on them like that. Last year, one of the firsties decided to take a medical excuse from the area in May, and Grimshaw had him walking seven hours

76

a day all through June Week, soon as his excuse ran out. Guy walked up until the night before graduation. He was so worn out, he didn't even bother going to the graduation ball. Family didn't even come up for June Week. He was broken. Everybody in the company saw him go, day by day, just fading away out there on the area. He had hemorrhoids, shin splints, I think the guy even had bursitis by the time he was finished with the area. Grimshaw put him out there for eight days, seven hours a day, fifty-six hours in all. It was incredible. I'm not about to lock horns with Grimshaw after that."

Major Consor shook his head slowly from side to side, poking a wood tongue depressor softly into the flesh of Slaight's right foot. He reached over and shut off the Jacuzzi.

"Get yourself out of there, dry off, and come down to my office. We'll take a look at those feet of yours." The doctor turned and walked out of the PT room as Slaight pulled himself slowly from the steaming tub. Old Consor wasn't such a bad dude after all. He pulled on his summer-weight gray trousers, stuck his feet in a pair of cotton hospital slippers he'd gotten from one of the nurses' aides, and shuffled down the hall. He found Consor sitting at his desk in a small room near the dispensary, right where he'd been two years ago. Prints, line drawings, and posters of ski scenes decorated the tiny windowless room. His M.D. and Internal Medicine Specialist certificates were mounted over his desk, along with framed diplomas from Airborne and Ranger schools.

Major George Consor was a small man, 5'6" tall, the absolute minimum required height for admission to West Point. At thirty-two, he was already balding, a shiny spot forming at the crown of his head. His face was all angles, rights and lefts and ups and downs, handsome in a broken, Picasso-like way. Slaight had been up to his house for dinner a couple of times when he was a yearling, after Consor had him as a patient the year before. He remembered that Consor had a good-looking dark-haired wife and three little kids who always seemed to be running around in pajamas with feet on them, fuzzy little outfits,

77

pale blue and pink, real little-kid-looking. Once after dinner when they were having coffee in the living room, and the kids were off in bed, Consor's wife said that Slaight and her husband looked a lot alike. The remark made the two of them nervous, because they did look something alike, like brothers ten years apart maybe. Slaight's nose had been broken twice when he was a kid and had a perceptible bend to the left, and a bulge, a knot of extra cartilage right on the bridge below his eyes. His cheekbones were pronounced. The hollows formed in his cheeks and tapered to a pointed chin. Looking at Consor's face again, a year later, well, they did look alike, which probably explained the gentle tension between them, the constant verbal jabbing and ducking and joking that went on whenever they met in the stands at a football game or in the lobby after a movie. Slaight hadn't been invited up for dinner after that night. Consor's wife had made one of those observations women sometimes noticed which seemed to . . . get in the way . . . interrupt the flow of things between Slaight and her husband. Slaight remembered the subtle tension in the room after Mrs. Consor had said they looked alike. It was sexual.

"Have a seat, Mr. Slaight," said the major. "Put your feet up on that stool." Slaight did as he was told. The major worked silently, quickly, surely, swabbing each foot with some kind of antiseptic solution, drying them with sterile gauze. Then he took a roll of what looked like thick white tape from a cabinet next to his desk.

"This is some new stuff we just got in," he explained, as he began cutting away with a pair of scissors. "It's padded moleskin, a quarter inch of high-density foam with an adhesive backing. Better than the old cotton stuff. They developed it for Vietnam, but they found it just absorbed moisture and jungle rot over there, so they shipped it all back to the States. Now we've got it." He applied the thick moleskin to Slaight's feet with gentle skill, ringing the raw areas with open circles of padding, leaving a hole in the middle for the raw skin to breathe. When he was finished, Slaight's feet looked like something out of Walt Disney . . . or the space program. White stuff in a weird, arty pattern all over the place . . . Slaight stood up. They felt good. He'd been so mesmerized watching Consor work on his feet, he'd forgotten what a good doctor the guy was.

"What else have they been doing for you over here this week?" asked the major, with genuine concern.

"They've been giving me Darvon 65's and codeine, sir," said Slaight. The doctor reached in a desk drawer and pulled out two yellow manila envelopes and handed them to Slaight. Each contained about a dozen capsules, Darvon and codeine.

"Now. Let's see. Anything else we can do for you? Morphine?" The doctor laughed that dry crackle of his and pushed his chair back against his desk. Slaight was surprised. Consor was known as a lifer, one of the rare army doctors who intended to make it a career. He'd figured Consor would balk at codeine. Slaight grinned.

"You know, sir, there is one thing you could do for me."

"Sit down, Mr. Slaight," said the major, indicating the same chair with his forefinger. He always addressed cadets as "mister" the proper way, avoiding the first-name familiarity preferred by many young officers. Consor's manner made Slaight feel . . . *respected*. That was it. With Consor, there was no illusion of equality, that bullshit *all us men together* nonsense you got from some officers. Instead, you got this steady feeling the man respected you as a cadet, as a subordinate. It made Slaight feel comfortable, but hardly at ease. The difference was subtle but sure. Consor knew what it was all about.

"What have you got on your mind, young man?" asked the major. "You want me to see what I can do about your tac, Grimshaw? I think what he's doing with your company is reprehensible . . ."

"Nosir," Slaight cut in. "Nosir. That's the one thing I don't want you doing. I'm the only guy in the company on the area right now, and if you so much as squeaked, he'd know where it was coming from. He'd put my stuff
79

in a sling and hang it there for the rest of my days. I don't want to spend firstie year pounding ground."

"I see what you mean," said Consor. "What is it, then? What do you want to talk about?"

"You're the duty doc today, sir. You hear anything about this plebe they found up in Popolopen this morning, drowned? His name was David Hand. He was in my squad last year during first Beast detail. I heard he was dead out on the area, but nobody seems to know anything more than that."

"Sure. I know all about the deceased cadet. I did the autopsy on the body this morning at 0900. Very peculiar case. Very peculiar case, indeed. I started cutting on the body at 0900, finished with him about an hour later. Some colonel from Brigade Headquarters came into my office here and demanded all copies of my report. I told him this was very irregular, but the provost marshall was with him, Fitzgerald, with whom I work all the time on these things. They use me for autopsies because of my internal medicine specialty. Fitzgerald indicated that it was okay to turn the whole thing over to the colonel. Peculiar, nevertheless."

"So? Did you give him your report, sir?"

"Well. You *are* curious about this, aren't you, Slaight?"

"Yessir. I knew the kid pretty well. He was from New Orleans. Had a sister at Vassar. I used to date her when I was a plebe. In fact, she was the girl who used to come and visit me when I was down with pneumonia. Maybe you remember her."

"Indeed I do. The rather tall girl with auburn hair? Quite attractive?"

"That's the one."

"Well. I see your interest has some basis other than aimless curiosity. I guess I can tell you about the deceased Mr. Hand. But I don't know . . . you're going to have to keep this pretty close to your chest, you understand? An autopsy is a sensitive medical matter. And this one seemed particularly sensitive, given the circumstances of the young man's death. The colonel and the provost marshal seemed highly agitated about the whole business."

"Yessir. I understand, sir." Slaight leaned forward eagerly.

"Well." Consor had a Jack Benny way with the word "well," pausing after he said it, waiting for a modicum of suspense to build before going on.

"Well." He paused again, straightening the little pair of Ben Franklin glasses which were always perched on his nose like they were about to fall off. "I gave them my report, of course. I'd just finished typing it myself. You know they don't give us any clerical backup over here. All the clerks and jerks are over in the Tactical Department or down in Thayer Hall. They asked for the whole thing . . . all the copies. I handed them over. It wasn't until they had left that I remembered my handwritten draft." Consor tapped a pile of papers on his desk. Slaight glanced at the pile and looked Consor in the eye.

"So what did you determine, sir? What was the cause of death?"

"I'm not sure I should be telling you anything about my autopsy, Slaight. Under normal circumstances, such a report is to be considered confidential until I'm officially notified otherwise."

"Come on, sir. I knew the kid. Knew him pretty well, in fact. I'm not just curious. I'm . . . *involved.*" The word popped from Slaight's mouth involuntarily and hung in the air between them like smoke.

"Well . . ." Consor paused again, pushing his glasses up on his nose. The glasses were not army issue. Nor was the white jacket he wore, a Dacron and cotton loose-fitting garment he must have picked up in medical school. What set the white jacket apart from those worn by other academy doctors was that Consor's was not starched. In fact, there was nothing starched about Dr. Consor. In some way Slaight had never been able to put his finger on, Consor didn't fit. He was the academy's only doctor who was also a grad, a distinction of absolutely no merit where other West Pointers were concerned. To have dropped out of the sacred combat arms and embraced the discipline of medicine put Consor in a class of one at West Point in 1968. He wasn't just different. He was what

81

the tacs liked to call "a strange bird." It was a pejorative description, and it wasn't meant to be funny. Consor must have sensed this, for he flaunted the extent to which he was different from West Pointers of his grade. He chose to live off-post, though he was eligible for government-sponsored housing. He never made the Officers Club "Happy Hour" scene. He was known as something of a loner. The granny glasses Consor wore symbolized his breakaway stance as a grad, but Slaight sensed Consor's ambivalence about West Point ran deeper than his image suggested.

From precocious personal experience, rooted in his life on the unpredictable, dingy, rotten streets of Leavenworth, Slaight knew that one's image was composed of both myth and reality. Myth served as a shield to protect reality. Construction and maintenance of one's image was necessary, Slaight had learned at an early age, for in myth could be found power reality often lacked. Slaight had detected in Consor this carefully balanced equation which comprised his image as "a strange bird," an oddball West Pointer, a loner on the verge of being an outcast. But Consor had never, *ever* let Slaight get away with anything, even the tiniest con. He played the game—doctor/patient, officer/cadet—and he played it straight. This part of him was real, believable. The rest of it, the granny glasses and all, Slaight guessed was myth, at least in part. Consor used this portion of his image to mask emotions with which Consor had not come to grips.

Slaight watched the doctor. He didn't know whether Consor would reveal his findings. The doctor shifted from side to side in his chair. He was staring out the door, down the hall, as if expecting a visitor to enter at any moment. He wasn't nervous. Nor was he two-faced, a "schizo," as cadets liked to call officers who played buddy-buddy one minute and wrote you up for insubordination the next. Consor was acting the way he always acted. Every motion of his body, every move of his eyes, the way he kept his hands folded, fingers interlocking, in his lap—everything was planned and executed with precision. Slaight figured Dr. Consor needed his planned, precise behavior for the same reason he had created a two-dimensional image for himself. Slaight figured Consor loved West Point, but couldn't bring himself to admit it. Consor had probably suffered an obscene, grim, and, worst of all, lonely plebe year because he was Jewish. In those days, the late 1950s, cadets literally tortured Jewish plebes. It was a part of the academy's heritage everyone had forgotten except its victims. Consor signaled his individuality as a doctor, as a grad, and as a man, for he had been victorious. He had persevered. And for reasons unknown to Slaight, Dr. Consor had drawn an odd but clearly visible strength from his experience. He had a look in his eyes, magnified by his frameless granny glasses, that was impossible to ignore. Consor's eyes were gentle, pale blue, droopy at the edges. When focused and fixed with a glare, they telegraphed: *Don't fuck with me.*

"Well . . ." said Consor again, drawing in a deep breath. Slaight leaped into the gap.

"Out on the area, they said it was an accident, Hand drowning. The word's out. They're gonna announce it in the mess hall at supper."

"That's peculiar," said Consor, studying his fingernails absent-mindedly.

"Why so, sir?"

"I would have thought by now they'd have an academy-wide search going full force. I thought they would demand anyone with knowledge of Hand's death to come forward immediately."

"No search, sir. No demands." Slaight baited him.

"He drowned, of course."

"Yessir."

"But I don't believe it was an accident, and my autopsy report reflects my findings."

"It wasn't an accident?" Slaight stuttered the words in a failed attempt to contain his excitement.

"I believe he was murdered, Mr. Slaight. Hand's lungs were so engorged with water, he could not possibly have drowned from exhaustion. No. I've examined such drownings before. I believe he was overpowered by another person, stronger than himself, and held under water until death."

"You're joking, sir. Right?"

"Negative. The young man was murdered. And there was additional evidence indicating murder, and possible motive, strong evidence. I am shocked that the academy has not moved to find the killer."

"They're not moving, sir. It's so quiet out there, you'd think the entire Tactical Department has gone on leave." Slaight waited. He knew Consor would get around to explaining himself at his own speed. Consor fidgeted, glancing down the hall. He reached with his foot and kicked the door shut.

"Well. I'm not at all sure I should be telling you this, Slaight."

"Come on, sir. If what you say is true, about Hand being murdered, they'll probably nail the killer somehow, and it will all come out in the wash, anyway. If Hand was murdered, you're going to be up on the stand, and no army court-martial is going to take pity on Hand, his family, or anybody else. What harm could you do, telling me now?"

"Mr. Slaight, I see exactly what you're driving at, but the nature of my findings is so sensitive that I omitted a portion of them from the typescript of my report, in deference to the family. It would serve no one's interest to cause the family any more grief than they already must endure. Though my findings were germane to concluding that Hand was murdered, they indicated motive, not cause of death, so I left them out of my report. I informed Colonel King verbally of my findings, however. He knows everything."

"What is it, sir? What are you so reluctant to tell me? I knew the kid. I went with his sister for two years. I want to *know*, sir, you know what I mean?"

Consor turned his head, found Slaight's eyes, and fixed him with that glare.

"Yes, I do, young man. I also know if I reveal my autopsy findings to you, I will be in violation of certain army regulations."

84

Slaight held his breath, waiting. Consor rested his hand atop the handwritten notes on his desk. His glasses slipped to the tip of his nose. Automatically, he pushed them back in place. He leaned back in his gray metal chair and crossed his legs.

"How do your feet feel now, mister?"

"Fine, sir."

"You're still determined to walk tours tomorrow?"

"Yessir. Got to. You understand."

"Yes," said Consor. He paused. Things weren't much different when he was a cadet. West Point had changed, but not much.

"Yes, I do understand, mister. But you will walk the area against my medical advice and best judgment. Is that understood?"

"Yessir."

"As long as . . ."

"What about Hand, sir?" Slaight interrupted.

"You are a persistent bastard, you know that, Slaight?"

"Yessir."

Dr. Consor laughed.

"Okay. This entire matter is being handled in such an unorthodox way, I don't imagine it would do any harm to tell you why I believe Hand was murdered. I based my conclusion on three pieces of physical evidence. You listening, mister?"

"Yessir." Of course he was listening. Consor's question was part of his style, a pro forma exercise in establishing, at once, rapport with and distance from the cadet. It was leadership.

"One. Water in lungs. Evidence Hand drowned. Unusually large volume indicated a struggle, presence of a second person. Two. Semen in the urinary tract. Hand had sex immediately before death. Three. Signs of irritation in the area of the anus, engorged musculature, hemorrhoid-like growth, inflammation of lower colon, high white-corpuscle blood count in the area, indicating a prolonged low-grade infection . . ." Consor paused, thumbing through his notes.

"All the signs, in short, that Hand was getting fucked

in the ass. Including a large quantity of semen in the rectum. Is that clear enough for you, Mr. Slaight? Your man Hand was a homosexual. Did you know that?"

"Nosir." Slaight stared at his taped feet sheepishly. The tiny office was quiet. Down the hall, an industrial dishwasher in the hospital mess hall could be heard chugging into gear.

"Major Consor? Can I ask you something?"

"Shoot, mister."

"Did you put all that stuff in your formal autopsy report?"

"No, I didn't. I wanted to spare the family . . . well . . . I told you. But I did spell out to Colonel King my conclusion that Hand was murdered. Clearly, the man with whom Hand had sex probably murdered him."

"Yessir."

"That's why I find it surprising they haven't launched a Corps-wide search for the killer."

"Yessir. Major Consor, this is going to sound presumptive, but I think you should hang on to your notes, sir. I think the shit's going to hit the fan, if you'll pardon the expression, sir. Somebody's neck is going on the line right now, if my guess is correct. Your notes will ensure the neck that goes isn't yours."

"I see what you mean, Slaight. I didn't like Colonel King's attitude this morning. He marched in here like the autopsy room was a little piece of his fiefdom, told my orderlies to leave the room, then stood around outside until I was finished, as if he was the ward chief. He kept opening the door and telling me to hurry up. Hurry up. I don't know what the rush was. The kid had been dead for thirty-six hours. Wasn't my fault they didn't find him until this morning."

"Colonel King was in charge, I mean, he was the one you gave your typed report to?"

"Yes. Tall man. Infantry. With a limp. You know him?"

"He's my regimental commander, sir. He's the one who put me on the area. Grimshaw, my tac, takes all his clues from King. King came through the barracks one morning

86

last month. I was taking a nap between classes. He walked in, wrote me up for 'failure to assume the position of attention in the presence of an officer' and 'out of uniform during duty hours.' I was in my drawers, between the sheets, fast asleep. Two-dash-one came down with a fifteen and twenty. Fifteen demerits, twenty hours of tours. Most I figured I'd get was an eight and eight. Jesus. Old Grimshaw had a field day with my 2-1. He sent down a memo saying nobody could take naps any more, any time."

"So that's why we're getting all these sick calls asking for medical permissions to take bed rest between classes! I was on sick-call duty last week, and we must have had a half dozen of them. I didn't notice they were all from the same company."

"They probably weren't. Everybody in the regiment is trying to protect themselves with medical permission to get rack during the day, our free time. That won't last past the summer. By next fall, old King will have something figured out to beat the medical excuses. He'll require that they be renewed on a daily basis, something like that. Make it impossible for guys to get a new sick slip every day. Man, you can't let your guard down for an instant in King's regiment. I'd watch it dealing with him if I were you, sir. I'm not trying to give you any unsolicited advice or anything, but . . ."

"Mr. Slaight. I understand what you're getting at. I'll watch myself with him. Are you certain you don't want me to do anything about this Grimshaw character? As a doctor, it's my duty to tell you that you most assuredly should not be walking the area with your feet in such poor condition. There's a strong possibility you could do permanent damage to the sensitive skin on the instep of your foot. I see no reason . . ."

"Sir, I've got seven hours left. I'll make out okay. And I wouldn't pay any attention to Grimshaw. Colonel King's the man you're going to have to watch out for. He's like some kind of human jackal."

"Slaight. I won't have you maligning your superiors in my presence. Save that kind of talk for the barracks."

"Yessir."

"Come back and see me about your feet next week. Let me see . . . you'll walk three hours Monday, three Tuesday, and one Wednesday. Drop in anytime. I'll be here every day."

"Yessir."

"And don't abuse the painkillers."

"Yessir."

"I'll see you next week then."

"Yessir. Good evening, sir."

Slaight walked back to the physical therapy room. He dressed quickly, walked out the basement door of the hospital, up some metal stairs, and into New South Area. The clock on the barracks said it was 7:30 P.M. Buck would be back from supper. He took the stairs to the second floor by twos, and his feet hardly bothered him. He burst in the door of Room 226 to find Buck sprawled on his bunk in the company of *The Wall Street Journal,* several copies of Burning Tree *Weekly Gazette,* the latest issue of *National Livestock Producer,* and what looked to be a three-inch stack of computer printout. Obviously, Leroy Buck had made a stop at the computer center on his way back from supper.

"Slaight, they went and did it tonight in the mess hall. Announced the news about beanhead Hand. Adjutant got up there and gave the poop. Accidental drowning . . . regrets to announce . . . Hand, F-4 . . . Corps of Cadets will send its condolences . . . tragedy . . . then a goddamn lecture about swimming alone during fuckin' summer leave. You wouldn't have believed it."

"Yes, I would. But you're not going to believe what I just heard."

"What's that, Slaight, you son of a—"

"I got the autopsy report on Hand. You won't believe it. The doc who did the autopsy report told me all about it. Wasn't an accident. David Hand was murdered. And the doc says Hand was a faggot, got himself banged in the ass just before he drowned. Doc says: Whoever fucked him, killed him."

"Any suspects?"

"Suspects? Are you kidding? Not even the provost marshal has heard about this. The doc left the fag stuff out of his official report, but he told King all about it. What we figured about old Phineas T. King earlier? Right on target. He was all over that doc who did the autopsy today, took every copy of the official report with him when he left. The doc told me he wrote in his official report that in his opinion Hand was murdered. So tonight they announce it was an accident, huh?"

"Say yeah."

"Buck, this ain't the Magnificent Seven all over again. This is a whole new ball game. Phineas T. is up to his skinny neck in this shit, and he's reporting straight to fuckin' Two-Dash Hedges, so he's in on it, too. We better keep this quiet till we figure out what's going on. Maybe they're just putting out the accident story until they can nail the killer."

"I doubt it, Ry."

"Why's that?"

"If they were looking for a killer, the word would be all over the Corps by now. Place would be crawling with TD fuckers. They'd have the whole goddamn Corps restricted to barracks. Give a listen out there. So quiet, you can hear the fuckin' juke box down in Grant Hall. Slaight, those fuckers are sitting on this Hand thing, sure as shit. They got the lid screwed on again. You going up to see Sergeant Major Eldridge tonight, like you said?"

"Nope. I've heard enough for one day. I'll stop by and see him Monday, before area formation. We've got plenty of time to touch him for his contacts. Besides, I want to give my feet a rest. I got two hurtin' cowboys for feet, let me tell you." Slaight flopped on his bunk and propped his slipper-clad feet on his Brown Boy. Buck had a Waylon Jennings album on the stereo. He was singing something about women, lonesome, and, if you listened closely, mean. Buck was reading *The Wall Street Journal*. Slaight heard him whistling softly between his teeth. It was funny, the way Leroy Buck whistled to himself like that. Often the noise he made sounded like the way he said "wisht." He was always saying stuff like "I wisht I was back home

89

right now. Yellow squash is comin' in." Or, "I wisht they'd goddamn leave us alone, goddamn-goddamn."

"I finish clocking my stocks, Slaight, let's you and me go on over to the late movie, how 'bout it? They're showing one of those Clint Eastwood pictures. One of those Westerns."

"Okay," said Slaight, closing his eyes, letting Waylon Jennings' voice close the space around him. "Let's do it."

9

Seven-thirty P.M. A telephone call.

"Duty Officer Major Consor speaking, sir."

"Major, this is Colonel King."

"Yessir. Something I can do for you, sir?"

"Matter of fact, Major, there is. You can keep absolutely quiet about this plebe we found up in Popolopen this morning. Do you understand me? You may consider your involvement in this matter classified Top Secret. This comes from the highest authority. Am I making myself clear?"

"Yessir."

"We have a very, very sensitive case on our hands here, as I am sure you are aware. It is absolutely imperative that none of the details of this case go beyond where we left them today. If we are to bring this matter to a satisfactory conclusion, there must be absolute confidentiality. Total. You are to report to no one but me on this matter, is that clear?"

"Yessir."

"Now, I am in possession of all copies of your official autopsy report, am I not? I have before me a four-page typewritten report on a DD Form 220, in triplicate. This is what you gave me this morning, is it not?"

"That's it, sir. DD Form 220. That's the official autopsy report form. Autopsies are the only medical operations reported on the Form 220. There's a regulation somewhere ..."

"I'm not interested in the regulation, Major. I am simply reaffirming that what I have in hand is your official report on the death of Cadet David Hand."

"That's it, sir. That's the official report. You've got all my DD 220s. The body was bagged, and at 1400 the funeral home from Highland Falls arrived to pick it up, just as you said it would. I supervised the transfer of the body myself."

"Good. That's damn fine work, Consor. Damn fine. Now, just remember this. We've got a sensitive, potentially explosive case on our hands here. We've got to keep it in the family. Do you understand?"

"Yessir. In the family. I understand, sir."

"Excellent. Consor, don't do anything else, don't talk to anybody from this moment on, don't generate any more reports, don't do *anything* without consulting me first. Got that?"

"Yessir."

"Outstanding, Major. Damn fine work."

"Thank you, sir."

"King out."

The phone went dead in Major Consor's hand. He looked at the clock on his desk. It was 7:35 P.M. He thanked the Lord King hadn't asked him if he'd talked to anyone about the case during the day. Cadet Slaight had left his office not ten minutes ago. He wondered about Slaight, whether it had been a good idea to confide in him. Slaight was an odd case, a cadet who seemed somehow out of place at West Point, and yet he possessed all the qualities of a textbook military leader: poise, bearing, guts, intelligence, and a massive, nearly impenetrable ego. If there was some thing about Slaight, if there was one thing which was going to be his downfall, it was his ego. An ego like his, at age twenty-one, almost completely negated any chance for the young man to really develop a sense of himself, nurture the germ of self-knowledge which after a few years would yield the revealing vulnerabilities of adulthood. Slaight had mastered the great confidence game of youth, the trap-door situation where he'd suck you in with innocent curiosity, then as soon as you'd opened up and let the cat out of the bag, he'd close the trap and squeeze out the rest of what he wanted with a mix of guile, cunning, and plain old-fashioned tit-for-tat trade-off, dealing.

Major Consor remembered the first day he'd met Slaight, three years ago. He was in Ward Two with double lower-lobe pneumonia. Because he had been a plebe, he had been discouraged from going on sick call, and went untreated until he collapsed in the barracks. For the first six days he was in the ward, he was in a semi-coma, fed intravenously, conscious for only a few moments a day, and even then he was dazed and confused.

On the seventh day, his fever dropped to 102°, from a one-time high of 105°, when they'd had to pack him in ice to bring the fever under control. Slaight, a very, very sick plebe, woke up and noticing the doctor leaning nervously over him, rapped out a coarse expletive:

"Fuck. This place looks like a good deal. How long have I been here?" When told he'd been in the hospital a week, he then asked how much longer he could expect to be confined to the hospital ward. Told that pneumonia like his sometimes took as long as a month to heal properly, he thought for a moment and said:

"Hey! I'm gonna miss sixteen parades!"

Consor chuckled at the memory. As a cadet, he'd indulged in the same parade-dodging skulduggery. It was part of the game. Maybe Slaight wasn't so odd, after all. Maybe he was just plain U.S. grade Choice cadet, a red-blooded American boy. Any way he looked at it, he was going to have to trust Rysam Parker Slaight III, he decided.

Better Slaight than King. *King out.* My God, what was this army coming to?

BOOK II

June 26, 1968

10

Wednesday morning, New York City.

Water woke Ry Slaight, splashing against the tub on the other side of the wall directly behind his head. He propped himself on one elbow and peered through the semi-darkness. A clock radio glowed on the bedside table. It was 9 A.M. Heavy curtains blotted out the morning sun. Four weeks to the day since he'd gotten off the area. Over the past three weeks, he'd been to six army posts in six states, on a junket called the First Class Trip, supposedly an introduction to what West Point seniors could expect from the six combat arms when they graduated a year later.

It had been one long six-thousand-mile waste of time and taxpayers' dollars. The firsties knew it. The army knew it. West Point knew it. By mutual agreement, the trip was an excuse for six army posts to throw six formal balls for the cadet first class, which the cadets were required to attend with arbitrarily assigned blind dates, officers' daughters getting their own introduction to what they might expect to find as army wives with army husbands. Now the first class was back, and this was the first morning of Slaight's summer leave, thirty days of free time he planned on spending right here, in this bed, in this apartment in this city with this woman. Her name was Irit Dov, and Slaight was twenty-one-year-old-awestruck-head-over-heels in love with her. They'd met when Slaight was a yearling. After a year of weekends, trips, and leaves, Slaight found himself pretty much under the spell of the strange dark woman in the shower behind his head.

He gazed around the familiar bedroom. Against one wall was a desk stacked with letters and unopened bills and family photographs and old magazines and used airline ticket envelopes. A blond Art Deco dressing table with a huge circular mirror was clean, save for a hairbrush, silver with natural bristles, and matching hand mirror. Atop the night stand on the opposite side of the queen-size bed was a glass of water and two aspirins. Hanging on the cut-glass doorknob was a nightgown, ankle-length pale gray silk with hand-embroidered lace around a square neckline, low-cut. On the floor, partially obscured by the nightgown, was a white telephone. A long twisted white cord snaked through the door and disappeared down a hall. Above him, yards and yards of steel-gray satin were gathered into a tent, peaking at the center, draped to the ceiling above the corners of the bed, falling to its edge in four perfect fabric columns. A cathedral of gray satin. Outside, the street snarled with the impatient sounds of Madison Avenue traffic.

"Ry? Ry? Are you awake? Are you up?" Her voice was high, strident—a morning voice. The shower had stopped its insistent beat against the tiles, and he could hear her padding around, out in the hall. It was a long hall, leading from the living room to the bath, bedroom on the left, a long row of closets and built-in storage to the right. The closets were mirrored, full-length, and fit tightly together so the hall appeared to have a wall which was one huge mirror. Behind every mirror—opening at the touch of a finger on the left edge—was a vertical stack of drawers, notched, of white Formica, shiny, like they'd been hand-lacquered. A thick white carpet ran from one end of the hall to the other, parquet flooring showing on either side. The ceiling was high, maybe twelve feet originally, but dropped a foot and inset with spotlights which could be controlled with a rheostat. Somebody had done one hell of a job on that hallway, Slaight remembered thinking when he first saw it.

"Yeah. I'm awake," he said. "Still in bed. Man, I'm worn out. Beat."

"Stay there," she commanded. He did. The bed felt good, a damn sight better than the web-seating of the C-141 Starlifter Air Force cargo plane he'd flown in the day before, on the way back from Fort Bliss, Texas. No air conditioning, stuffy, smelly, guys sleeping with heads leaning forward against duffel bags between their legs: Nightmare.

"What will you have for breakfast?" she asked from the hall. "I have . . . for you, I have toast and coffee. Will that suit you?"

"Fine," he said, flopping back against a pile of pillows, trying to remember what had happened when he came in late the night before. He couldn't focus, mind slipping and sliding back and forth in and out of fatigue-induced semi-consciousness. His eyes drifted. Between the pillows next to him was the small pillow. As she slept, she clung to it, a six-by-six-inch square of fine linen, flat, almost completely empty of feather stuffing. He remembered watching her before she fell asleep one night . . . it seemed like a long time ago. She cuddled the little pillow. The sight of her would have been pathetic, he remembered, but she was so content, the square of linen against her bosom, a thin bandage of a smile on her lips. She had been unashamed, explaining she never slept without it. He touched the little pillow, picked it up, held it against the stubble on his cheek. It was soft. He tossed it on the bed and closed his eyes, hoping to nap. The small linen pillow was only one of the things he couldn't figure about Irit Dov. Never could. Made him feel . . . nervous. He scratched around his ankles, pulling the gray satin quilt up around his shoulders. She heard him.

"I said stay where you are." She bit off the words like biscuits, her voice reaching toward that peculiar lilt, almost British but not quite. Slaight drew the quilt around his shoulders, warding off the chill from the air-conditioner, purring away behind one of the curtains. His underarms stank, an odor like swamp gas, the body's mix of fatigue and sex. It smelled good. He inhaled deeply. Decomposing pits. He chuckled.

Summer leave. Fuck. Am I ever gonna chow-down for a month. Slaight's eyes drooped closed, and his mind drifted again. . . .

Most of the time at West Point, you were so goddamn lonely you lived in your own head in a fantasy world constructed of safe racktime and dangerous dreams. But you didn't live up in your head really. You lived down in your belly, down there inside you where all your reactions come from. It was . . . necessary.

All day, every goddamn day at West Point, everything was *hit . . . react . . . hit . . . react,* a hell of a lot like boxing, an endless series of blows to the solar plexus, the face, the neck, the stomach, with no time-out to back off and relax. Breathe, reach out, and grab air. Absorb. *Never relax.*

They used to scream it, yell it like marching cadence in plebe boxing. *Hit. React. Hit. React.* Some little OPE bastard named Malloy; with a face like a river rat and a body like cast-iron sewer pipe, he was about sixty-five years old; and he'd stand there in those black pants with gold stripes down the legs and shiny black leather ripple-sole coaches' shoes and his T-shirt with "OPE" and the academy crest over the left tit, he'd stand there with his face coming just under the top rope of the boxing ring and he'd scream at the top of his bloody Irish lungs: *Hit. React. Hit. React.* You never forgot that face or those words and it never ended.

The closest you ever came to leaving that little spot down in your belly, the closest you ever came to relaxing, *really* relaxing, was fucking. Even then, it was only half-release. Parole instead of freedom. For this reason, because they wanted it so much, because they needed it so goddamn much, cadets were really good at fucking. It came natural, like taking a leak after a reveille run and feeling that cold shiver run up your spine, fucking was just something you did because you knew you needed to fuck the way you knew you needed to piss. Release. Let it fuckin' *go.*

Cadets fucked for fun, fucked for love, fucked for sport, fucked to satisfy the humid animal lust of goddamn barracks life all week long, fucked for money even, like male hookers, betting their bodies and their hard-ons against the streets of New York City on a five-dollar weekend they'd find a body and a bed before the bars closed. Most of the time it was charged with tension,

97

quick and hot and sweaty and tinged with a smoldering, smoky smell, like you seared the hairs on the back of your hands getting too close to a heat stove on a cold night in the field, sex so fast and hot it *burned*. Getting laid by a cadet, Slaight used to guess, must have been for a girl what a wet dream was like for a guy: You couldn't remember what had happened when it was over, but you knew it felt good.

Girls were kind of . . . functional. They fit into the machine like an idler wheel, taking up the slack and keeping everything running more or less smoothly, and when somebody put the hammer down, they were always there to . . . flex . . . absorb . . . take the shit when the guys just plain couldn't take it any more. They were different, like another species—like cats, maybe. Soft where guys weren't soft . . . bony, angular, where guys were muscled, hard . . . wide, padded with extras, where guys were stripped down like hot rods, efficient. They looked different and they acted different and they talked different. More . . . grown-up.

Cadets were always punching each other in the upper arms and saying stuff like . . . *heey, say hey, big fella, c'mon let's toss a couple down on the Plain . . . say wha? . . . say, fuckit man, let's get us some rack . . . when them plebes spose't come round for SI, anyways . . . getting fuckin' tired of those zit-faced little pingers . . . oughtta bottle 'em up and ship 'em out with the Japanese fuckin' current. . . .* Cadets talked like high school football coaches with perpetual hangovers. Girls talked nice all the time, like they understood what a shitball place West Point was and all they wanted to do was make you feel better. Used to piss a lot of guys off, all that *niceness,* because it was hard to figure where it was coming from, and at West Point, you were taught the ancient male dogma that if you couldn't figure where something was coming from, best to duck and wait and listen and watch before assuming it was friendly.

So girls had their function, but they didn't . . . *fit* exactly right, like a pair of socks too small, always sliding down into the heel of your shoes, having to stop, reach

98

down, yank up the socks, looking and feeling like some kind of dufus fool couldn't afford to buy himself a good pair of socks. That was the way a lot of cadets felt around girls, like they didn't quite fit together right, because they just weren't used to them, they were never around, and when they were, it was always awkward and strained. . . .

They felt the same way about weekends. Weekends were longed for, always too late to arrive, too quick to leave . . . there was an equation in the minds of cadets between girls and weekends. Weekends meant freedom . . . or parole anyway . . . but a weekend always ended, Sunday night at 1800, dinner formation: a lot of shuffling and horsing around and goosing and yelling at one another across the area . . . guys would stand around and clap their hands together . . . *clap clap* . . . *clap clap* . . . not because there was anything to applaud, anything to celebrate, but because there was nothing else to do at dinner formation on Sunday night. You clapped your hands together the way a football or baseball or basketball coach is always clapping his hands on the sidelines . . . *clap clap* . . . *clap clap* . . . nervous, frustrated, because he's standing there, just standing around, and there's nothing he can *do*.

So weekends ended, parole ended, and so did girls. They weren't *all present and accounted for*, SIR, at the Sunday dinner formation. They were temporary. What it amounted to was the plain fact that they were gone for another week. Cadets wrote letters to girls, lots of letters to lots of different girls, maybe a half-dozen letters to a half-dozen girls at a time. It was a form of contact with the outside world. At West Point, the feeling of writing a letter was just as good as the feeling of receiving one. Guys would labor over letters, work on them, etching each word carefully, like it was evidence they existed or something. You were reaching out with a letter, reaching out and touching someone . . . you could feel it there in that little spot in your belly as the words went down on paper, a warm sensation, molecules stirring, brushing up against one another down there in the place where you lived. Letters went out from zip code 10996 to all different kinds of cadet girl friends.

There was the Girl Back Home. Some guys entered West Point going with the girl back home, and it never changed, they'd write her damn near every night for four long years, and they'd marry her the day they graduated, and nobody ribbed them. There was a special place in the cadet heart for the girl back home. Just about everybody had one, sometime.

There were the Irish and Italian Princesses from the Catholic girls' schools which surrounded West Point like outposts around a night defensive perimeter. It seemed like cadets couldn't move in or out of the place without noticing, or being noticed by, one of those precious little things from Ladycliff, Seton Hall, Marymount—the list went on. It was like a conspiracy hatched somewhere in the bowels of the Vatican to wed the cream of American Catholicism to the cream of the American military.

There were those snobby, snappish liberals from Vassar, the West Point of the Seven Sisters—arrogant, elitist, they were as bad-assed as goddamn cadets. It was probably because they were so much alike that more cadets didn't go with Vassar girls, being as they were only a few miles away across the Hudson in a little town called Poughkeepsie. But Vassar just sat over there, a feeding trough for Ivy League preppies. Cadets were advised by upperclassmen from the time they were plebes to keep their distance from Vassar girls.

There were College Girls, which is to say, girls cadets would meet at "away" football games at mixers and post-game parties. These girls tended toward sororities. If an upperclassman in a company was going with a Delta Gamma from Northwestern, it wouldn't be long before a plebe in his company would be going with a freshman rushee from the same sorority at the same school. Sometimes college girls were traded around, used as currency within the social structure of the academy . . . *fix you up with this fox my girl friend knows, man, if you'll take my guard duty next week . . . gotta poly sci paper due, man, c'mon, I'll even throw in a fin for the weekend. . . .*

Then there were the Working Girls. They were usually from New York City, and they ranged from the East Side (stewardesses and the occasional Playboy bunny) to the West Side (secretaries and receptionists) to the Village (downtown ladies of questionable means). To a certain breed of cadet, in whose ranks Rysam Parker Slaight III found himself, the working girl was found treasure for any number of good reasons.

She did not attend college and was thus not subject to dormitory hours and rules. Nor did the working girl indulge in the penny-ante social game playing which so thickly permeated cadet and college life in the 1960s. Working girls were capitalists, past masters at the you-scratch-my-back-I'll-scratch-yours school of emotional algebra.

She often had an apartment, sometimes one of her very own without roommates (such a girl was Irit Dov), thus removing one thorny expense on weekend leaves: the hotel room. She might even cook. This was a truly rare find. Most working girls were bachelorettes with refrigerators containing the obligatory quarter pound of butter, two eggs, a two-week-old container of raspberry yogurt, the 55¢ size jar of instant coffee, and one can of beer.

She did not raise a fuss about sex. While still a delicate matter, sex was something for which the working girl was often prepared, with birth-control devices, right there in her purse or medicine cabinet. Bye-bye, rubbers! Good evening, diaphragm, pill!

The working girl was usually lonely. This was a character trait attractive to cadets for the simple reason that loneliness was like a permanent flu at West Point. There you were, surrounded on all sides by all these guys, all these friends, and they were always slapping you on the back and asking to borrow toothpaste and trading two skin mags for one stroke book and helping you decipher yesterday's nuke problems . . . and yet walking along Thayer Road back to the barracks from the library just before taps, you could feel like the last person on earth. Working girls must have experienced much the same feeling on the subway on the way home from work. The lonely attract the lonely. This did not often make for profound relationships, but it made for convenient ones.

There was of course a certain cross-pollination between the apples of cadet eyes. Some guys had a girl back home, who was visited on long leaves during the summer and at Christmas, and a working girl in the city, who was visited more frequently, for shorter periods of time. Weekends. The former was treated with care, the latter with precision. Cadets could be counted on. They were efficient. They arrived on time. They were nearly perfectly predictable. Early on, there would be sex. And sometimes they were even cordial, gentlemanly. Sometimes.

This was Ry Slaight's act for the first couple of years he was at West Point. He had a girl friend back in Leavenworth, Kansas, a colonel's daughter, Betty Jane Soah. And he was going out with David Hand's sister, Samantha Hand, who was in his class year at Vassar and was . . . handy. But there always came a time when somebody wised-up . . . one of the girl friends, or maybe both of them at once, sometimes even the cadet. It happened to Slaight all at once, in May of 1967.

He was just getting off the area after three hours of punishment tours. He was walking down Thayer Road, holding his rifle in his left hand, when he noticed a commotion up ahead. In front of Grant Hall, a public gathering place where cadets met their dates, a group of girls were passing out daisies and antiwar leaflets. It was a demonstration. Slaight walked faster, eager to see what was happening. When he reached the gaggle of demonstrators and onlookers, he thought he recognized a couple of the girls. They were from Vassar.

He was tired and hot from walking the area and was about to turn the corner into New South Area, when Samantha Hand stepped in front of him and gave him a mimeographed sheet of paper. He glanced at the piece of paper in his hand. Across the top of the page in large hand-printed letters he recognized as hers were the words:

DESERT! QUIT THE WAR MACHINE!

Slaight stared at her disbelievingly. She thrust forward the daisy, smiling.

"I tried to call you and tell you, Ry, but they said you were out walking the area, being punished. See what I mean, Ry? It's all wrong. You should just give up." Slaight took the flower from her with his free hand, stuck it in his mouth, and began chewing it. He swallowed. He handed the leaflet back to Samantha Hand.

"Stick it up your fucking ass," said Slaight, turning away, walking back toward the barracks. If she only knew, he thought. If she only fuckin' *knew*. Slaight had his doubts about the war, about the academy—about everything. Most cadets did. Nobody was completely immune from the urge to second-guess the cadet experience, digging around, trying to figure out what was bullshit and what wasn't. He'd even thought about resigning. Walking the goddamn area—hot, depressed, all kinds of doubts rattling around in his head like a bunch of BBs in a tin can . . . and his second year at the academy, yearling year, was coming quickly to an end. New army regulations said if you resigned from the academy after the end of your second year, you were subject to five years' active duty as an enlisted man, a GI, a clean-sleeve grunt trooper. He was out there walking the area thinking about resigning the next goddamn week, just before the cutoff, and now *this*—Jesus—humiliated by his own girl friend in front of other cadets, some of them his classmates. He climbed the ramp back up to New South Area, flopped on his bunk, and made up his mind. He couldn't resign now. He would graduate if it was the last fuckin' thing he did on earth. Next weekend he walked his last hour off his slug. Weekend after that, he took off for New York City and met Irit Dov.

Now he was lying in her bed and Jesus, all that was over a year ago, and man, time does get by, doesn't it? Little over a year ago, Samantha Hand's trying to lay on that tired-assed trip about the war, next thing Slaight knows, her brother's in his squad in Beast Barracks, and now he's dead, a faggot, killed up there in Lake Popolopen by somebody who'd just stuck it up his ass . . .

Jesus . . . who'd have guessed that day they were handing out daisies in May of '67 what would happen a year later, almost to the day? Seemed like nothing made sense any more. Nothing . . . added up . . . it was all . . . coming apart, splattering in every goddamn direction at once. West Point was like this piece of granite, a national anchor, but even West Point was pulling loose now. . . .

Feet shuffling in the hall, just whispering across the carpet . . . Slaight whipped his head around, startled. Irit Dov's footsteps faded in the direction of the kitchen, all the way across the living room, huge, forty feet by forty feet square. Irit Dov's penthouse, sitting on top of an apartment building at the corner of East Eighty-second Street and Madison, was rather small as such places go—only two rooms, really, living room and bedroom. The kitchen and bath seemed like afterthoughts. But the penthouse had a spacious, airy feeling, high ceilings, windows all around, everything painted in a dull-finish oyster white.

On the north side of the living room was Slaight's favorite spot, a greenhouselike alcove, a sunroom jutting out over an odd extension of the building below, completely enclosed by casement windows. The sunroom was full of plants, palms mostly. They were tinged with brown edges and had been clipped back, an attempt to fight off some New York palm disease. The palms looked like plants with haircuts. The little room reminded Slaight of the screen porch on his parents' place, outside of Leavenworth. It was bright and green and you could sit in there reading, listening to the steady rumble of the city, and it was like you were in the woods, hearing the invisible sounds woods make, rustling and flapping and whispering away, trees talking to each other, squirrels chattering and birds calling, the quiet rattle of the absence of human beings. Up in that penthouse it was like that . . . nobody visible and yet all this life around you . . . humming and grinding away.

The whole place was full of plants—plants and white furniture, low-slung and deeply pillowed in white muslin.

104

Matching tuxedo couches faced each other at right angles to a fireplace on the west side of the living room. Between them a white Formica coffee table sat close to the floor. Chrome frame chairs with dark brown leather seats and arms faced the fireplace at the end of the white table. Overhead lights, similar to those in the hallway, illuminated barren white walls, where they existed at all. Mostly there were windows, waist-high to the ceiling—windows on either side of the sunroom to the north; overlooking the small terrace to the west; along the entire south end of the penthouse, a glass door in the middle, through which you walked out on a wide terrace, shaded by potted ginkgo trees. The bedroom had four windows, facing south and west. The window in the bathroom was a foot wide and six feet high, a narrow glass peek at the world through the end of the tub.

The penthouse came perilously close to looking like it had been done over by a designer, that spare, Sunday *Times Magazine* look, uncluttered with human interference. But crazy little touches rescued the place from hellish perfection, like the phone running down the hall from the living room to the bedroom, white cord getting in the way underfoot. A thin, threadbare Persian rug lay between the couches. It was faded and frayed, not antiquey, just worn-out. Three or four pieces of battered wicker furniture, in dire need of repair, were scattered about—two chairs in the corners of the bedroom, a table in the sunroom, hiding among the plants, another rattan table on the terrace, weather-beaten, ready to collapse.

And everywhere were magazines, stacks of the damn things, fashion magazines, news magazines, piles of old *Esquires* and *New Yorkers,* French magazines, Italian magazines, untouched stacks of old Sunday *Timeses,* evidence of a compulsive collector of printed matter. The piles were neatly, even cleverly hidden—behind furniture, under tables, stacked on deep-set bookshelves. They looked like they belonged. So did Irit Dov.

Slaight had wandered around the place many times over the past year, exploring. It was his way. He poked into corners, opened drawers, peeked in closets, ruffled through stacks of papers and magazines. He examined the penthouse the way he read books: close-up, giving the place his undivided attention. He was fascinated by Irit Dov's penthouse, its deliberate excesses, casual messiness. In the rooms people lived, he knew, could be found all of their obsessions, some of their secrets. Slaight's year-long inspection of Irit Dov's penthouse apartment bordered on fetish. He wasn't nosy. He was a pack rat, gathering pieces of others' lives, storing them away inside himself. He was vaguely aware of what he did, but he had no idea why. All he knew was, Irit Dov's penthouse had captured him and held him tightly. So did she.

He heard her out in the kitchen: comfortable, muffled sounds, plates and cups and saucers and silverware, running water—reminded him of lying in bed when he was a kid, listening to his mother fixing breakfast downstairs, banging around, listening to the weather on the radio. Slaight reached over and flipped on the clock radio. Some FM station was playing the Jimi Hendrix Experience, "Purple Haze," a little heavy at 9 A.M., so he turned it off.

Something was up. West Point was showing its seams, the nearly invisible little side effects of a system which required absolute precision all year long, absolute adherence to the Honor Code, absolute attention to detail in all the science and engineering courses, absolute total memorization of a million little $(f)X = YZ$ proofs you had to keep filed away in your head all the time. West Point was this hermetically sealed society, closed off from the rest of the world, and to the casual observer, it looked like West Point would remain forever unreachable, perfect in its distance from the grubby world outside its gates, forever frozen in the Celluloid of the late show on TV.

But from the inside there was always this subliminal anxiety, just beneath the surface of cadet lives, pent-up frustrations and doubts, imperfections that had to be hidden, contained, controlled, checked and balanced by self-confidence which appeared to come from nowhere, but which really came from West Point itself, from the United States Military Academy, from the final truth that you were a goddamn cadet, and when push came to shove you dropped all your doubts and insecurities and believed all the bullshit. West Point said it was so, and you believed it: You were better than the rest of them, all those fuckers *outside,* everybody who didn't know the definition of *gray,* all the nongrads and the civilians and the politicians, the goddamn enemy.

But now even that last-ditch circling of the wagons, final defensive perimeter belief was breaking down. Slaight could *feel* it go. He'd been watching it happen, little by little, all through his cow year. The death of David Hand was widening the cracks in the system. Slaight didn't know exactly what was going to happen, but he had a few ideas. All the time, cadets were holding back, repressing these doubts and unconscious feelings they weren't supposed to have. The system caused the cadet to be totally confident, on top of it all, in control 100 per cent of the time. But then came weekends, and weekends afforded that brief instant of relief when repressed feelings could bubble to the surface. Up would come the gas you held down in there in that little spot in your belly where you lived, grumbling, ulcerous, vile, everything you didn't want to believe about yourself but you knew, you just fuckin' knew, was true. He'd watched it happen a dozen times, and he knew it would keep happening. Somehow, he knew the David Hand thing fit, but he couldn't figure which way.

Slaight, his roommate, Leroy Buck, every cadet, was sensitive to every comment on the war, the military, the academy. And the comments hit with gale force in '67-'68, raining down from every side. You couldn't dodge it. When cadets would go down to New York City and hang out in the singles bars on the East Side, the operative method for dealing with the inevitable *what do you do for a living?* question was to mumble, *I go to school near here,* like the girl you were talking to should just know where you meant—Princeton, Rutgers, some damn place. Sometimes it worked.

But there was always the haircut, close on the sides, two inches max on top. And the distinctive cadet manner, inbred, almost impossible to conceal: the stiff back . . . the walk, a quick gait executed with crispness . . . the irresistible urge to say "sir" when you were talking to a guy only a few years older than you, like he was an upperclassman or something. And no matter how hard you tried, you couldn't help but slip up, sometime.

Then the hostility, Jesus, the hostility! A chance remark, a comment like, "Oh, I see they just made you get another haircut," anything could set off the time bomb inside cadets, the repressed humiliation, the feeling they were always being watched over like a bunch of children, scolded and punished and sent to the corner—anything could explode that time bomb. When it went, it was circuit-blowing pain, the kind of jolt you never felt in sports, the ache that made a pulled leg muscle seem like a stain on your goddamn pants. Cadets would wheel and snap like Dobermans, not caring who said exactly what or when or where, just so they could tear off a chunk, get that feeling they were tasting blood.

Once, in a bar in north New Jersey, Slaight watched a classmate bite the top of a guy's ear off, a guy from Princeton, when he'd mumbled something like *West Point sucks* under his breath at the bar. The cadet just reached over, grabbed the guy by the hair, hit him a couple of times in the face, and at first sight of blood spewing from the guy's nose, the cadet pulled the guy's head toward him, held it down on the bar, and chomped the tip of his ear off, spit it out right onto the bar, a grisly, incredible scene. The whole bar just ground to a halt, and everybody stood there, staring, the guy clutching at his bleeding ear, the cadet standing there with this grimly satisfied look on his face, then he turned and walked out, and nobody did anything, nobody fucked with him because they all caught the vibe that the guy would *kill,* he was so pissed.

Another time, Slaight saw a guy slap his girl friend halfway across the dance floor down at Snuffy's, then stumble out to the parking lot and lean against a car and start crying like a little kid, just sobbing and dripping snot all over his shirt front, weeping like a baby. Slaight asked him what happened. The girl had yelled something at him when they were dancing, the guy couldn't remember what she'd said, all he could say was . . . *she just don't understand, you see, man? She just don't understand, man, how fucked up things are, you know?* Slaight watched the guy cry for a while, not saying anything to him. There was nothing you could say to a guy who was blubbering like a fool, who'd just about knocked his girl friend's teeth out, and who'd probably do the same to you if you accidentally pressed the wrong psychological button.

Later the next week, he saw the same guy in the mess hall, and the guy said thanks for being there, down at Snuffy's, and Slaight mumbled forget it, man. Then the guy said he and his girl friend had patched things up, checked into a motel down in Stony Point and spent the whole night fucking. The guy started jabbering about belly fucking, ass fucking, tit fucking, elbow fucking, toe sucking, doing it standing up, sitting down, across the motel room dresser, over the edge of the tub . . . on and on until Slaight finally wandered away, leaving the guy standing there in the aisle in the mess hall, talking to himself about what he had planned for *next* weekend.

The year '67–'68 was that kind of scene, blown-out, hanging right there on the edge all the time. Bobby Kennedy had been murdered a week to the day after Slaight got off the area, and he and Leroy Buck stayed up all night watching the live TV coverage. There wasn't any widespread cadet sentiment for Kennedy. In fact, a lot of guys had gone around the next day complaining that Kennedy had picked a hell of a time to get himself blown away. His death was putting off the First Class Trip for two days, because all the Air Force C-141's were being held on alert to airlift troops to Detroit and New York in case there were riots in the ghettos, like there had been when Martin Luther King died, another event which hadn't drawn much cadet sympathy.

But Bobby Kennedy had appeared to Slaight and Buck like a dim beam of bleak hope, symbolizing a glimmer of forward motion in a country which seemed to have come to a halt the day his brother, the President, was killed five years before. Now RFK was dead, too, and the papers were chasing Gene McCarthy around the country like a pack of rabid dogs, trying to force-feed an image of liberal leadership to an electorate that had fallen asleep with a beer in hand in front of the tube watching scenes from the siege of Khesanh flicker across the screen in full color. It was a sorry-ass state of affairs, 1968, a sorry-ass year with sorry-ass campaigns being run by a bunch of sorry-ass lamester politicians running around saying a lot of sorry-ass shit . . . a lot of sorry-ass shit about the war.

It was so pathetic, it was almost funny. Only a couple of years before, in 1966, West Point was still a hook, a sure-thing name-drop for a free drink at a bar, a come-on to a girl sitting next to you on a plane. Now everything had changed. Down in New York, on June 26, 1968, a rock group called the Velvet Underground would play a smoke-filled hole of a club called the Plastic Exploding Inevitable. Fifty miles up the Hudson, West Point was getting ready again for the first day of Beast Barracks, a week away. The two places coexisted in a sphere so close to splitting at the seams, only sex seemed to be holding things together. The press had noticed as much and coined a neat but illusory headline, "The Sexual Revolution," to describe a carnivorousness between men and women which said fucking was okay as an end in itself. No rules, no court-and-spark, no nothing. Just strip and fuck. Anything goes.

Everywhere you looked, order was collapsing into chaos, but that wasn't it, either. Everything was just turning casual, even sex. This was a circumstance greeted by cadets with great enthusiasm. What did they have to lose? Their virginity?

Thank God West Point couldn't touch you while you were on leave. And thank God for fucking.

11

Irit Dov appeared in the door of her bedroom carrying a wicker breakfast tray with toast and coffee for two. She was wearing a light cotton robe, tied at the waist. Her black hair fell past her shoulders, shadowing her face and her breasts in the dim light.

"Ry Slaight! Ry! Open your eyes! Wake up, you lazy thing! It looks like midnight in here. Come. Take this tray from me. I won't hold it forever." She had a mocking, teasing tone in her voice, and she smiled widely as she appeared to berate him for napping while she had been slaving in the kitchen over breakfast. It was this way between them every morning. He wanted to sleep late, imagining he was skipping reveille, getting away with breaking the rules. She wanted ro rush from bed to bath to street, as if they hadn't a moment to lose, the city was getting away from them, the museums were closing, it would all be *over* before she got him out of bed and out of the house. Usually, they compromised, as they had this morning, Irit letting him nap while she washed and fixed breakfast. Then she'd push him out the door and into the park or wherever they were headed for the day.

What they really did was to make deals:

I'll trade you one sleep-in for a visit to the Metropolitan.

Okay, I'll cook dinner tonight if we can go over to the Five Spot and listen to jazz later.

It's a deal.

Theirs was a way of life which a few years later would be called liberated, as if in deal-making there was to be found some measure of freedom for both parties. Irit Dov and Ry Slaight found not freedom but comfort. There was a tension between them, for each was strong-willed, but they worked out part of the tension in their constant bar-

111

tering, trading of experiences and duties. The rest of it they worked off in bed.

"Sit up, you sleepy fool! What do they call guys like you up there? Rackhounds! I remember. Your friend Leroy, he is always calling you a rackhound. Well, sit up, rackhound. Eat your breakfast. Drink your coffee. There is much for us to do today!"

Slaight grabbed the tray, and Irit eased herself onto the bed next to him. He was awake but about one-third functional, still worn out and hung over from three weeks riding around on wooden benches in deuce-and-a-half trucks, eating dust from the column ahead. Day after day they listened to lectures on the wonders and miracles of modern warfare—"the electronic battlefield," they were starting to call it—then they'd mount up in the goddamn deuce-and-a-halfs and road-march out to some godforsaken military reservation and watch firepower demonstrations. Battalion-sized, elaborately staged, fully armed attacks on undefended objectives, all these tracks and tanks and companies of troops firing live ammunition, all tracers, blazing red and yellow around dusk, with flame throwers and mo-gas explosions all over the place, a goddamn firepower demonstration looked like ten Fourth of July's all going off at once. The assembled West Point first class would watch this incredibly expensive fireworks from bleachers on a nearby hillside, then climb back in the deuce-and-a-halfs and eat dust all the way back to the post officers' club, where they'd pretend it had all been for real and get good and stinking drunk.

Three solid weeks of trucks and dust and lectures and C-141s and formal balls and bullets and booze. Slaight felt like someone had blowtorched his ears, then crawled into his mouth and turned the flame down his throat. His tongue felt like a small sandpile. His eyeballs felt like they'd gone 100,000 miles without a lube-job.

"Hey. Thanks." He managed to get the words out before Irit stuffed a piece of buttered toast and jam into his mouth and handed him a steaming cup of black coffee. He munched his toast and sipped his coffee and looked over at the woman sitting next to him on the bed. She sat there

112

watching him like she was making sure he got it all down, he was sick and she was taking care of him. There it was again. All that *niceness*. Like she knew what kind of bullshit oof-goofing-half-stepping nonsense the Firstie Trip had been, but of course she didn't. She was just sitting there eyeballing him possessively. It was the first time they'd been together since before Slaight started walking the area in the beginning of May. Made him nervous, the way she sat there, not eating her breakfast, just watching him like that. Nervous and . . . wanted. Slaight sipped his coffee. Irit Dov waited.

She was tall, about 5'8" in her bare feet. And she was dark, swarthy the way an Arab is dark. Her skin had the tawny permanent tan of Semitic peoples, whose heritage lay in the desert sun where she came from: Israel. She was a *sabra* Israeli, born and raised there, with a family heritage traceable to biblical times, to the Promised Land. It was part of what made Slaight nervous. She had this . . . presence, this . . . confidence Slaight wasn't used to finding in women, not the college girls he'd gone out with, not the East Side foxes he'd met over the last few years. Irit Dov had class. You could see it in her face. Her cheekbones were wide-set like an American Indian's. Her nose was narrow, aquiline, her nostrils thin elegant slits. It was pronounced, a sturdy angular structure around which the rest of her face settled naturally. Her wide dark face was the most prominent feature of Irit Dov's body, which was equally bony and angular. She had the shoulders of a swimmer, the flat tummy of an athlete, and real honest-to-God *bosoms,* full and round, not like the flat chests of stewardesses and models. She had wide padded hips, long legs, tiny feet.

But what was striking about her, striking in a strange foreign way, were her fingers. Her hands were narrow, the width of her wrists, and her fingers were long and skinny, interrupted by knuckles protruding noticeably, like burls. Her fingers were patrician, they said inbreeding somewhere in the distant past. They reminded Slaight of his grandmother's hands and fingers . . . those of an old Virginia gentlewoman. Irit Dov knew about her hands. She

113

kept long elegant fingernails. She painted them in tones of dark red. Burgundy. Her nails drew attention to her eyes, for she was always glancing down at them, and one's eyes naturally followed hers to the nails, then back up to her eyes. Her eyes were black, like her hair, and unflinching. She was an extraordinary good-looking woman. Even in New York City, she stood out in a crowd. Up at West Point, on Ry Slaight's arm, she was just plain famous.

"Ry, let's make love," said Irit Dov as Slaight took his last sip of coffee. He looked at her face. It was dark, hawkish, shrouded in her long black hair.

"Now?" he asked. "I thought you wanted to get me out of here."

"Shut up, you silly boy," she said, taking the breakfast tray and placing it on the floor next to the bed. She was three years older than Slaight, a world-wise twenty-four, and for this reason she often called him "boy." It was a term of endearment, but it made Slaight nervous. His father used to call him "boy" all the time. Now he didn't call him much of anything any more; Ry, when he had to get his attention at home, but most of the time his father was quiet around him. It was like his son wasn't "boy" any more, symbolizing the estrangement of father and son which comes when a boy leaves home and returns a de facto man, though down deep inside, each knew the parameters of "man," and Slaight was still a boy. But Slaight could never bring himself to just walk up and say, hey, Dad, you can go ahead and keep calling me boy if you want . . . it's been like my nickname for years, you know? Just as he couldn't bring himself to ask Irit to stop calling him "boy," it made him nervous and reminded him of this thing with his dad and all.

"Come, you lazy boy. Make love to me." Irit lay back on the bed and pulled him toward her. With her left hand, she reached down and tugged her robe. It fell open. Her body was the color of cedar shakes a couple of years old, a weatherbeaten light brown, special, unique . . . and it was that color all over, from her face to her toes . . . her breasts were that lovely cedar-shake brown, like she'd been sunbathing, in the nude, but she hadn't, it was just

114

her color, it was like something in the air you could breathe, an odor that got you high. She moved nearer to him and waited, coming on, her feet creeping over his, digging at him with her toes, tightening a grip around one of his calves with her ankles under the covers, Slaight still leaning on one elbow watching her . . . amazing fuckin' woman, goddamn amazing woman, tall and raunchy and gutsy and brown and foreign and so fuckin' beautiful, so goddamn sexy.

"You want me to do your breathing and your shoulders?" he asked, leaning over her and staring down at her eyes.

"Yes, Ry. Please. Do my breathing, you do it so nicely. . . ."

She may as well forget about getting out of here before noon. "Doing breathing" was something they did to one another, it had just come along naturally, like kissing, a part of making love necessary because both of them were so goddamn tense all the time, Irit because of her boutique, a little place on Madison specializing in Isracli fashion, most of it her designs, and Slaight . . . well, he was tense pretty much 100 per cent of the time, it was part of being West Point, part of being gray.

Slaight sat up, reached under her arms, and yanked her upright, angling her body across the bed diagonally, feet in one corner, head and shoulders up near the other. He crossed his legs and sat at her head, looking down. She was watching him, her big black eyes staring straight up, a quiet, satisfied smile on her face. It occurred to Slaight that she'd had this in mind all morning, puttering away out there in the kitchen, humming and planning and working up her juices. . . .

He placed his left hand flat in the middle of her bare chest, palm on her breastbone, fingers touching her diaphragm, then he placed his right hand on top of it, interlocking his fingers.

"Breathe," he said. Irit took a deep breath and exhaled. Slaight pressed down with the exhalation of air, letting up when he felt her taking another breath.

"Let me hear you. Breathe," he said again. This time
115

the exhalation came in a rush of air, an audible sigh, and it was deeper, more air was coming out. Slaight pressed down. Let up. Breathe. Press down. Let up. Breathe. Press down. Aaaaahhhhh. Let up. Breathe. Press down. Aaaaahhhh.

"Let me hear you. It's fading," he said as Irit inhaled. She nodded. Aaaaaahhhh! This time the exhalation came . . . looser . . . Slaight felt his hands go down deeper into her chest and he knew she'd released some of the diaphragmatic musculature with which the body actually takes in and holds air inside the lungs. Breathe. Press down. Aaaaaahhhhh! Deeper again, her chest was caving now, curving inward, feeling like a sponge beneath his hands, a wet pliant sponge soaking up air and squeezing it out. Breathe. Press down. Aaaaaaahhhhh! Jesus. There it went. That terminal sigh, a distinctive sound which signaled she'd finally let go, relaxed, crumbled under the pressing and the breathing and the pressing and the breathing . . . a hypnotic wavelike rhythm . . . pressing and breathing and pressing and breathing and finally letting go, limp, noodley, soggy with total release. Her eyes were closed and she was still breathing deeply, regularly, a steady rush of air in and out, in and out . . . her long fingers curled slightly with each breath, an involuntary reaction of the central nervous system Slaight had noticed some time back. Christ, he couldn't even remember when they'd started doing this weird shit. He glanced over at the clock radio. It had been thirty minutes since they started the pressing and breathing, pressing and breathing . . . time just flew, there wasn't any time, really, just this strange hypnotic flow, as trancelike for Slaight as it was for Irit. . . .

He stopped pressing and massaged the muscles of her chest above her breasts, the pectorals. They were tight, knotted. She breathed, Slaight massaged . . . in a moment they relaxed, soggy. He let his hands slide sideways over her arms, under her arms, and lifting slightly, he slipped them beneath her back, placing the forefinger and middle finger of each hand on either side of her backbone. Now he lifted when she exhaled, shoving the air out of her

116

lungs from below. With each breath, he slipped his fingers up her backbone toward her neck, inch by inch. He let his hands come up around the sides of her neck, leaving his fingertips on her backbone, disappearing now into her skull. With his thumbs he massaged the sides of her neck, digging around in the tendons gently, rubbing, rubbing, rubbing until he felt the neck muscles begin to go. Then he slid his hands up to her chin, gripping her head with fingers at the base of her neck, thumbs under her chin, running down along those two strong muscles on either side . . . and he *pulled*, gripping the head tightly, he *pulled* and *pulled* keeping the tension between her head, which he held in his hands, and her body, which resisted the pulling with friction against the sheets . . . he pulled and pulled gently but surely until he saw the neck release and actually elongate slightly, neck muscles letting go, her shoulders slumping as he released her neck and ran his hands down across her clavicle, his fingers up under her back again, pulling up on the shoulders this time, pulling and massaging at once, keeping at it, kneading and pulling and lifting and moving his hands ever so slowly toward her neck again, slipping them under the neck, fingers kneading the edges of her backbone, then holding with the thumbs and the fingers and *pulling* again, pulling the head away from the shoulders, and this time the neck let go immediately, a quick extension, like a turtle easing out of his shell for a look-see . . . and he kept it up, kneading and lifting and pulling, pausing every once in a while when he noticed her breathing begin to fade, pressing down on the chest again to restart the breathing, pressing down, aaaaahhhhh! easing up and pressing down, aaaaaahhhh! and pressing down . . . that rhythm again, just going on forever and ever, the gentle give and take of hands and skin and muscles and bone and tendon and fingers in her hair and the sound of her breath aaaaaahhhhh! coming up at him like a fountain, a fountain of pleasure and release. Jesus.

He was trying to think how this business got started, but the tendency was *not* to think, the tendency was to breathe and listen and breathe and listen and breathe and

117

listen, listen to her, watch her, until finally his own eyes were closed and everything was happening involuntarily and he was listening to his own breath going in and out, in and out.

"Hey. Ry." He opened his eyes. She was staring up at him, naked except for the robe loose at her sides. "Hey. You. I love you. Did you know that?"

"Yeah." He reached under her neck and pulled her to him, kissing. He rolled forward on his right shoulder in a sideways somersault and came up next to her. He threw his right arm across her shoulders and pulled her to him again, pressing his chest against her breasts. They flattened. He kissed her on the neck. It was damp and smelled of soap. He took her lips in his and chewed gently. Her tongue darted in and out of his mouth. It was sharply pointed and rough, like a cat's. He nibbled her tongue, nibbled her lips, thrust his tongue into her mouth, she drank it in like it was fluid, sucking, pulling on his tongue and rubbing that catlike tongue of hers against it. One thing you could say about Irit Dov. Here was a woman who liked to kiss. Jesus, she'd lie here and kiss for goddamn hours, chewing and tonguing and dribbling all over her cheeks and the pillows. . . .

He eased himself up on the bed, rubbing against her body, feeling her breasts hit the hollows beneath his ribs. His stomach tightened, sucking air sharply. She burrowed her head in his chest, licking that soft spot on his throat, below his Adam's apple, licking and sucking on the skin and wetting down his neck from throat to breastbone. He wrapped his arms around her head and buried his face in her hair.

"Irit. You fox. You smell so goddamn good."

She sucked, he felt her breath rushing across his wet throat, cold . . . chilling the place she'd kissed. The sound . . . *phfffffft* . . . the sensation of her breath on his neck sent little jolts of pleasure across his stomach and down his thighs, through nerves just beneath the surface of his skin, his feet stiffening, toes pointing, feeling like some kind of *wind* was going to come blasting out of the bottoms of both feet, blowing away the quilt, rustling the

118

curtains across the room, he felt . . . Jesus . . . so god-damn . . . Christ . . . *fine.* . . . She gasped, threw back her head, and kissed him on the mouth.

"Ry," she whispered.

"Yeah."

"Take off my robe." He pulled it over one shoulder, she rocked to the side, pulled it from the other, and the robe was off. She spread-eagled atop the satin quilt, naked. Sunlight from the living room came down the hall, diffused through the open bedroom door, broke shadows across her bosoms, bathing them in a strange white glow. Slaight rose up on his hands and knees, sank his tongue into her belly button, circling it, jabbing, slurping liquid gulps of air. She jerked, pulling up her knees, holding on to her ankles with both hands, giggling in a hoarse whisper. Slaight tongued away at her belly button, one hand on each breast.

"Stop that, you devil!" she yelled aloud when she couldn't take it any more. "You're tickling me!"

"I know it," he said, leaning back on his haunches grinning.

"Come here," she beckoned. Her nipples were erect with passion.

"Look at those little troopers," said Slaight, pointing. "Standing at attention, hey." He laughed.

"You come here, my American boyfriend," said Irit Dov, feigning seriousness. That was another thing she called him, *my American boyfriend,* like she had them on three continents, which she probably did. Pissed him off. He felt like he filled only part of her life, and he wanted it all. Made him defensive. The grin dropped from his mouth and he crossed his arms, rocking silently from side to side, gazing across the room.

They'd been together a little over a year, as together as West Point would allow, anyway, and he guessed they were in love. Whatever "love" was by June 1968, after the "summer of love" and the "love generation" and all that shit. It seemed to Slaight their life together was frag-ile, a balloon they batted in the air between them, hoping it would not burst. They had never ventured inside the

119

balloon, for that would have meant a commitment. Ry Slaight and Irit Dov were each other's best fans. An invisible distance separated them, over which neither of them seemed to have control.

Like performer and audience, the two were separated by youthful obsessions: words and sex. By 1968, talking and fucking were supposed to be easy. Events had conspired to create an illusion of freedom. Where once had loomed a pile of time-consuming groping and clumsiness, there was now a convenient social short cut, symbolized by the first night they met. They just went home to Irit's bedroom and climbed in bed and fucked. Everything had to happen quickly. It seemed like neither one of them had a thing to lose.

What a bunch of crap! Here was Slaight, threatened by the notion Irit was just toying with him, keeping him as her New York lover as she moved between Tel Aviv, Paris, and the United States. And there she was, this girl who'd been so stung by the fast-paced scene within which she had to move in the fashion business, by the time Slaight met her she was like steel twice tempered. As a kid, he had ruined the blade of a hunting knife one night by heating it in a campfire and plunging it into a canteen cup of water, watching the fast boil and the disappearing red glow of the steel, over and over. The blade never again held an edge. Twice tempered, the steel had lost its hardness. That was the way Irit Dov had been when Slaight met her. She'd been clobbered by somebody. He knew he would have to treat her gently, because nobody else had.

Irit moved, wrapped her arms around his waist, rested her head in his lap, and looked up at him. He looked down, into her eyes, mad because the spell had been broken between them, but glad because he'd made up his mind. He took her head in his hands and pulled her tightly against his stomach.

"Hey, Irit," he said.

"Yes, Ry?" She looked at him, perplexed.

"I love you, you know that?"

"Yes, I know, you silly boy."

120

"Come on. Knock off the *silly boy* crap. I love you, goddammit. You understand what I'm telling you?"

"Of course. You love me. I understand that. You've told me before. This is not the first time we've made love." She smiled. "I love you, too. What is bothering you, Ry?"

"Nothing's bothering me. I just want to get something straight, you know what I mean? I want to tell you . . . for some reason, I just feel this incredible urge to tell you how much . . . how much I fuckin' love you, Irit. It's like this thing I've been bottling up inside me, like something I've been holding back. I love you. I mean, I *love* you. I want to be your guy, you know? I want you to feel like you can count on me, you know . . . depend on me if you need to. Jesus. I feel like some kind of schmuck, gushing like this. I don't want to embarrass you."

"You don't embarrass me, Ry. It's wonderful, what you're saying . . ."

"I don't know, Irit. I guess I'm just scared."

"Scared? Scared of what?"

"Like scared something's going to happen, and you won't . . . *know*. You won't know how I felt. You won't know I really love you. We've been real tight, you and me, Irit. But I don't know . . . right now I just feel extra *close* to you, like there's some invisible connection between us. Listening to your breathing this morning, watching your chest rise and fall . . . Jesus, it's weird, you know."

"Yes, Ry. I think I know."

"I wrote this poem once. I ever tell you about it? Wrote it when I was a plebe, for my roommate. It was his girl friend's birthday, and he wanted something special to send her, he wanted to send her a poem, but he just couldn't write one that said what he wanted it to say. So I told him I'd write one, and I did. So there I was, sitting in my room at West Point, writing a love poem to this imaginary girl I didn't know. It was strange . . . three years ago . . . but I still remember one of the lines. It said, about love I mean, it said, 'I want to . . . give in to its ceaseless attack.' I didn't know the girl, of course. Didn't

121

know what in hell love was either. But that image of it *attacking*, I guess it stuck with me. I've always thought of love as some kind of warfare, something you're always trying to *win*. Know what I mean?" Irit tightened her grip around Slaight's waist, and he could feel her nails dig into his flesh.

"Yes," she whispered softly. "Yes. I know exactly what you mean."

"Well, goddammit. I don't want to win any more. I'm giving up. I surrender. You got that?"

"Yes, I . . ."

"I just want you to drink every goddamn minute we've got together, Irit. I want to feed you. I want to nourish you. I want to love you so goddamn much . . . Jesus, Irit. I don't know what else to say."

"Don't say anything." She pulled Slaight over, her arms wrapped around the small of his back, nails dug into his flesh.

"Just love me. I do need you, Ry. I need you."

Slaight unfolded, and he was on top of her, his penis between her legs, he was inside her, and it was sticky wet warm squshy. A fetid compost of sweat and the juices of the genitalia settled over them like a soft sheet. He moved his buttocks slowly, back and forth, back and forth, feeling his way in her vagina. She looped her arms beneath his, holding him close to her, their heads touched, and each could hear the quick breathing of the other.

Beneath him, she moved from side to side, up and down, up and down, writhing, tightening and loosening her legs, raising her knees, then thrusting both down against the bed with a soft *thump*. They stayed like that for a long time, then rolled over, and she was on top of him. He looked up. She was bolt upright on her knees, rising and falling with her breaths, regular, deep, penetrating the air between them, her breathing almost . . . visible. He took her breasts in his hands and kneaded her nipples gently, squeezing them between his thumb and forefinger, tighter, tighter, rolling the nipples back and forth, pinching and kneading, holding the weight of her

122

body with her breasts as she leaned forward eagerly. He let go. She fell against his chest, grabbing the back of his head, holding tightly.

A moist sucking noise, like the sound of water against the pilings of a pier, could be heard between their wet, sweaty stomachs. The noise quickened the pace. He moved faster, more boldly against her pelvis. She released her grip on his head and flopped to the side, pulling him over on top of her with her knees. He stiffened his arms on the pillow, looking down at her face. It was wide, and her cheekbones were highlighted in the shadows from the open door.

"Ry," she said softly. "Love me." A tiny gasp of passion separated each word. He closed his eyes. An image formed. He could see her face, she was mouthing the words, *Ry . . . love me . . .* soundlessly, in a vacuum. In his mind, it was as if she were yelling the words at him, screaming. But there was no sound, only her breathing, regular and deep and fast. He opened his eyes, working with the motions of her pelvis.

The head of his penis found the top of her vagina and stayed there, moving against a small, uneven area, the size of a half dollar. It was a membrane just beneath her pubic bone, where her hymen had once been. He knew. He'd gone down there and looked around, studying her vaginal area. It was beautiful, and he had told her so, embarrassing her in the shower one morning. The water was beating down on them, and he was on his knees, splitting her labia, peering . . . *inside.* He hated the word clitoris, so he called hers "boodle," an affectionate nickname she thought hilarious when she learned that it was cadet slang for candy. The membrane in her vagina was ultra-sensitive, and he moved back and forth against it with inch-long thrusts. Again he heard her:

"Ry . . . my . . . love . . . I . . ." She stuttered now, her accent thickened, her voice finding a frantic pitch. Her breath came fast against his cheek, and he moved deeper within her, sliding slowly until his pubis reached hers, the fleshy area just above his penis beating against the folds of skin covering her boodle. He clutched her, pounding his body against hers, letting go. She bucked, throwing him forward, her face contorted, wrinkled vertically, tiny folds of skin in a curtain across her forehead, her eyes tightly closed. It flashed through his mind that whatever *it* was, love, *it* was happening, sex, love, whatever . . . the word *love* stuck in his mind stubbornly as he came in several brief, almost painful bursts of pleasure, driving heat to the base of his neck, tightening the muscles in his calves, rattling his toes. She clutched his balls with one hand and pushed her entire torso upward, a back bend from shoulders to feet, shaking, quivering, as they were joined, hinged at the hips. He raised his head. He looked at her. Then he realized. *She hadn't held her breath.* Always before, she'd grimace and hold her breath. Now her breathing came as it had for the past . . . how many minutes . . . for how long had they been at it?

They settled easily into one another's arms and lay silently. With her left hand, Irit reached over and pulled the linen pillow between her breasts, closing her eyes. The bed was a total mess. He straightened the sheet, folding the quilt across their shoulders. He rested, watching Irit Dov, breasts engorged with blood, reddish, nipples still partially erect.

Jesus.

Her breathing sloped into even distant quiescence, and he leaned against the pillow. They would nap for an hour. When they awoke, she'd tease him for "neating up" the bed, straightening it. He'd grab her by her black hair and kiss her on the mouth to shut her up. That was what they did: teasing and jiving and tossing, riding the tension. He glanced over at the clock radio, glowing in the dim light. It was 12:30. They'd been at each other for just over three hours, not unusual, except for the weird rap he blurted. Slaight crossed his hands behind his head. Already asleep beneath the gray canopy of satin, Irit seemed delicate, vulnerable. He watched her. For the first time he was afraid to drop off, afraid he'd roll over, swing an arm, and break her.

Christ! 150 pounds, dripping wet! What fuckin' nonsense is this?

124

But he sensed things would be different now between him and Irit Dov. He smelled it . . . didn't have the slightest notion how things'd change . . . wha's gonna happen . . . he slept.

12

By the summer of 1968, Irit Dov had achieved a measure of success unusual for a woman twice her age. She was a Madison Avenue boutique owner with a growing sideline in fashion design. She was part-owner of a factory in Israel producing two seasons—fall and spring—of ready-to-wear sports clothes for women. The best of her fall line, full skirts and blouse-over tops for evening in desert beiges and Mediterranean pale blues, had recently been featured in a six-page color spread in the American fashion magazine *Vogue*, in a section called "Around the World with *Vogue*." The French magazine *Elle* had in December of 1967 named Irit Dov one of the year's "top new designers on the international scene." The boutique page in *Women's Wear* called her "one of this year's exciting young things—a girl with *verve,* a girl to watch!" She sold most of her designs through two boutiques in Tel Aviv and in her tiny shop on New York's Madison Avenue, but as she picked up publicity, she was beginning to get small orders from stores like Saks, Bloomingdale's, and Neiman-Marcus. Irit Dov was doing a million dollars' gross business in 1968, of which she would personally realize about $100,000. Irit Dov, at twenty-four, was a woman of means.

It figured. It was in her blood . . . and in her bank account. She had been financed four years previously—enough to open her first shop in Tel Aviv—by her grandfather, Shlomo Dov, an Israeli diamond merchant who was one of the Two Hundred, a select group of men who once every month received from the Johannesburg-based De Beers Consolidated Mines Ltd. a small black leather case containing maybe $1 million, maybe $5 million—maybe more, depending on the year—in uncut diamonds. Shlomo Dov had a business on Forty-seventh Street in New York, in a second-floor loft above a block teeming with men in black suits carrying black satchels from one side of the street to the other, an endless stream buying and selling an endless stream of the world's hardest, most secure currency, the diamond. Shlomo Dov bought his diamonds from De Beers at the price asked, without even opening the black leather case. It was the way of the diamond trade. De Beers owned the diamonds, and De Beers owned their pricing.

He dealt some of the diamonds he bought from De Beers in Antwerp, Belgium, on the diamond exchange, uncut. Others he kept for his own business. In Tel Aviv the diamonds were broken down, graded by experts in his employ and Shlomo Dov always had the last word about a stone, no matter how small. The diamonds were cut in a large loft in a warehouse district of Tel Aviv. From Israel, Shlomo Dov's diamonds were hand-carried in black satchels to London, Antwerp, New York. Some ended up on West Forty-seventh Street, where they were sold without the haggling and bickering characteristic of the diamond business. Shlomo Dov's diamonds were purchased at the price asked, because everyone knew he was one of the Two Hundred. He dealt first-quality merchandise, no matter where his diamonds were "pointed" on the grading scale, whether they were "melees," small stones of a carat or less, or "sizes," larger, expensive gems. Shlomo Dov was a man of respect.

His son, Avi, short for Abraham, was a general in the Israeli Army, commander of a tank *ugda* (task force) stationed along the north-south border between Israel and Jordan. As a young man, in 1946, he had joined the Palmach, the guerrilla strike force of the Haganah, the illegal Jewish militia in British-occupied Palestine. After British withdrawal in 1948, Avi Dov had been a platoon commander in the Palmach, which became the commando arm of the Jewish army.

The full-time Israeli Army was small, only about twelve thousand men, not including draftees. By 1968, most of the men who called the army a career had fought together in four major wars: the guerrilla campaigns against the British and Arabs during the years 1946, 1947, and 1948; Israel's War of Independence; the Suez Campaign of 1956; and the Six-Day War of 1967. The Israeli generals knew each other well. Avi Dov was perhaps better known than most. He had been among the founders of the famed "101 Battalion," which during the early 1950s had made antiterrorist raids across the Israel-Jordan border in response to Arab terrorist activities within Israel. There were those among Israel's enemies—and some among Israel's friends—who had accused the 101 Battalion of terrorism. Some of its raids had resulted in documented deaths of Jordanian women and children.

But the 101 Battalion's daring raids had helped to make Avi Dov's reputation. When he transferred in 1956 to Israel's armor branch, he turned himself into an overnight legend when he devised an eerie—some said cruel—initiation rite for young Israeli armor lieutenants. The lieutenant would stand atop an old discarded tank body. The tank would be doused with diesel fuel and set ablaze. The lieutenant would be required to recite his oath of allegiance atop the burning tank before he was allowed to jump through the flames to the ground.

Irit Dov was among those who thought her father cruel. Though she had served her requisite duty as a teen-ager in the Israeli Army, she was one of a growing number of young Israeli citizens who had problems with Israel's reputation in the world as a mini-superpower, obsessed with military might, competing—or so it seemed—with the Great Powers themselves for domination of the Middle East. Although Irit comfortably embraced the socialism of Israel's ruling Labor party, she had accused her father of "imperialism" once or twice when she heard him talking with army friends of their designs on the Jordanian west bank of the Jordan River, and on the Sinai, the great expanse of desert which separated the southern border of Israel from the strategic

127

Suez Canal. Then came June 1967, and all her doubts became academic. The West Bank and the Sinai were now part of Israel.

It came as no surprise to either Avi Dov or his wife, Daphna, when their daughter at age nineteen used money borrowed from her grandfather to open her first boutique on Tel Aviv's busy Deitzengof Street. Nor was it much of a surprise, four years later, when Irit was named in the influential Israeli newspaper *Ha'aretz* as "one of Israel's jet-setters, one of our citizens who has made the world her market place."

Their daughter was a citizen, but as she paid the eight hundred dollars for an exit visa from Israel and boarded planes at Lod Airport a dozen times a year, it was clear to the Dovs that their daughter had become a citizen of the world. She spent more time outside Israel—specifically, in the United States—than she did in the country of her birth. She was *sabra,* but by 1968, it seemed as if a new Jewish history, a new two thousand years, were beginning for people like their daughter. It made them sad. Though General Dov agreed with Moshe Dayan's military doctrine—"to exorcise Jewish cleverness from Israeli strategy and tactics"—he longed for an Israel in which there were no political disputes as he had with his daughter, as he had occasionally with fellow army officers. It was part of General Dov's gut conservatism that he often ended speeches to his troops with the words: "We must not forget that first, we are Jews. Second, we are soldiers."

Irit Dov had two penthouses—the one on Madison and East Eighty-second Street, in New York, and a small studio apartment atop a building on Hayarkon Street, overlooking a stretch of beach between two large Tel Aviv hotels. She called them "my bird nests," because they were both located high above surrounding buildings, and because she thought of herself as a "bird," the slang word from Britian used to describe a new breed of fast-moving international woman, the model Jean Shrimpton, the actress Julie Christie, the singer Marianne Faithful. She liked to think she designed clothes for "birds." They clung loosely to the body, flowing easily as one walked. Her clothes were unlike the tight, tailored, body armor of other contemporary designers. Irit's clothes were soft, feminine, vulnerable like a second skin. Even her fabrics had a birdlike quality. They were featherlight tight-weave cottons and smooth challis wools. It took a special, hip woman to wear Irit's clothes. It took a "bird."

She often visited museums—in Paris, the Louvre; in New York, the Metropolitan—to find inspiration for her designs. She collected lines, the movement of color in a painting, the way a musician collects riffs from old, perhaps forgotten recordings. From sketches made in Paris—the surrealists, cubists, impressionists—and in New York, the Metropolitan's growing collection of Egyptian art, she gathered the notions behind her designs. She watched American television, especially "American Bandstand," and went to rock-and-roll concerts at the Fillmore East, to capture a feel for what had become known as "funk."

It was an arduous process. She would sometimes spend hours standing before a single painting, a single expanse of temple wall transplanted from Egypt and erected within the walls of the Metropolitan, its paintings of prehistoric scenes intact . . . she'd just stand there, staring. Once a director of the Metropolitan interrupted her as she stared at an Egyptian piece late one afternoon, just before closing. He was a tall distinguished man, and he had watched her in the museum before. This day, he asked her if she wanted to have a drink with him across the street at the bar of the Stanhope Hotel, and she accepted. Through him, Irit Dov would gain access to collections of the museum which were not yet open to the public. And on his arm in 1966 and 1967, she would become acquainted with an exciting, glamorous crowd in New York City. The museum director was one of those men who stood atop a unique intersection where the worlds of money, art, and politics met. One night, Irit Dov attended a party, to which she had been invited by the museum director. Ry Slaight read about the party in the New York

Times and crashed. They met. It happened casuallly, quickly, as things seemed to happen in those days.

Slaight felt at loose ends in the swirling laughter and bubble and swell of the party until he found a pool table in a room just off the study. It was a large house on East Seventy-second Street, overlooking the East River. The pool table, scuffed and beat-up looking, seemed as out of place as Slaight. A guy from Brooklyn in a gray fedora was playing all comers and beating them. Slaight, who had spent more than his share of hours in the Snooker Poolhall in downtown Leavenworth, played the man for twenty dollars and won. He played again. Won another twenty. He played double-or-nothing and lost. Then the man said, "Let's play for a yard, kid." Slaight recognized the term from Mickey Spillane novels. It meant a hundred dollars. He didn't have the money, but by now, he knew he could take the man from Brooklyn, and he did. He was counting the tens and twenties, wandering away from the pool table, when he heard a voice.

"Ry Slaight?" the voice asked. He couldn't place the accent.

"Ry Slaight?" the voice asked again. "Is that your name, Ry Slaight? That's a funny name. Is it Jewish?" Slaight turned. The woman with the voice was dressed in black pants, black blouse, black suede heels. Around her neck hung a thin gold chain. It hung over her bosom and dangled at waist level. It was a long, elegant chain, meant to catch the eye. It did. Slaight looked at her face. It was dark, swarthy, beautiful, shrouded in long black hair.

"No. It's not Jewish. It's Kansas," said Slaight. She laughed, unblinking, her eyes not leaving his.

"You're a funny guy," the woman said, placing her arm through his. Slaight's right hand was stuck in his pants pocket. His left hand was covered with baby powder, from shooting pool. He was looking for the bathroom, to wash up. The woman pointed.

"Over there. When you come out, get me a drink. I will have what you are drinking, Ry Slaight." He closed the door and washed-up.

How the fuck does she know my name? He ran hot

130

water. Must have been watching the pool game. She's a weird one. Foreign. Smells . . . musky . . . like the woods. It was a strange odor. Dark, like the woman. When he opened the bathroom door, she was standing where he'd left her. She slipped her hand around his arm. He pulled two beers from a bucket of ice at the bar, opened them, and reached for glasses.

"I will drink mine from the bottle," said the woman. Slaight handed her the beer. It was one of the expensive brands, from Holland. They sipped the beers.

"This place is hot. Or is it just me?" he asked, searching for something to talk about. The woman laughed, a rough, attractive chuckle. He felt wetness at his underarms, sweat running in a slow river down his back. A hundred-dollar game of pool was like . . . well, it was just a bit over his head, when it came right down to it, especially since he didn't have the scratch to cover, if he'd lost. He wondered if the woman could smell him. He probably stank to high heaven.

"What's your name?" he asked.

"My name is Irit Dov," said the woman. She spoke crisply, with that weird accent.

"Is it Jewish, your name?" He smiled, embarrassed. He was reversing his sentences, something he did when he was tired. The woman laughed, sipped her beer, leaving a thin film of dark red lipstick on the green neck of the bottle.

"Yes. I am an Israeli."

"Can't get much more Jewish than that, I guess," said Slaight.

"Are you really from Kansas?" she asked.

"Yeah. From Leavenworth."

"I guess you can't get much more Kansas than that," said the woman. They both laughed and walked over to the window overlooking the river.

"And you are here in New York on business?" Oh-oh, thought Slaight. Here it comes.

"No. I go to school near here." The dodge.

"And where do you go to school?"

"West Point," said Slaight, looking across the river at the lights of Queens.

"Ah," said the woman. "We have a place similar to West Point in my country. In Israel, everyone serves in the army. I am a corporal in the women's reserves." Slaight swiveled and looked at the woman. She smiled, revealing tall straight teeth.

"You were expecting a lecture about your military?" she asked rhetorically. "I am an Israeli. My father is a general, commanding tanks on the border with Jordan. I have no love of the military. In Israel, the army is something with which we all must live. Here . . ." She gestured about the room where the party showed no signs of ebbing at 1 A.M. "Here things are different. But I can see you know this. You do not belong here." She said it matter-of-factly, and Slaight didn't know what to say, so he said nothing.

"You learned to play the game pool in your town in Kansas?"

"Yeah. I used to play a lot. I don't play much any more."

"You play well," she said, touching his arm with her fingers, tipped by nails the color of her lips. It occurred to Slaight that the woman was coming on to him, but he thrust the thought aside.

Jesus, the fuckin' guys in the barracks are never going to believe this one.

"You told the man in the white hat with whom you played pool you were staying in a hotel on Eleventh Street," she said.

"Yeah."

"Come. You needn't stay in this hotel. I have room for you."

They took a cab back to her place, had a drink, climbed in bed, and fucked. It made a strange kind of sense. She was lying there on this incredible bed in the soft yellow light from a lamp across the room, saying . . . *fuck me . . . fuck me . . . fuck me . . . fuck me . . . fuck me . . .* over and over again. And he was up there humping away, just like the code among cadets said you were

132

supposed to, humping and humping and sweating, and he'd copped the ultimate *good deal,* bed, board, and body for a weekend leave, Jesus, there wasn't anything more fuckin' gray-hog than this.

In the early hours of the morning they lay in each other's arms, she was sleeping, but Slaight . . . he couldn't sleep for some goddamn reason. Couldn't get it out of his head that there was something . . . missing . . . something . . . wrong. . . . What she was chanting was right. It wasn't love-making, it was *fucking.* First time he thought about the difference. They'd rushed ahead, reaching desperately for some imaginary edge which just hadn't been there. They coupled like headlights of oncoming cars, passing each other in darkness at speed. The whole thing, the whole night, passed under them like a flat stretch of two-lane blacktop back home, white lines flickering. Gone.

13

The clock radio read 1:30 P.M. when the phone rang.

Jesus. First day of leave, and the day's already half gone.

Irit fumbled on the floor, found the receiver. Her voice was husky, scratchy from sleep and sex.

"Hello? Hello?"

"Mr. Slaight, please. General Hedges is calling." Irit reached over and shook him. Slaight was facing the other direction, trying to ignore the ringing phone.

"Ry, it's for you. Some woman. She says a general is calling for you. Someone called Hedges."

"Jesus. Hedges. Give me the phone." He sat up straight and took the receiver. First day of leave, now *this.* . . .

"Mr. Slaight speaking, sir." The approved cadet telephone procedure. Say "sir" whether it's a woman or not. Never can tell.

133

"Mr. Slaight. Just one moment, please. General Hedges is on the other line. I'll get him." Slaight waited, shifted the receiver to his other ear, covered the mouthpiece.

"Get me a glass of water, will you, Irit? My throat feels like . . ."

"Mr. Slaight. General Hedges. How are you, young man?"

"Fine, sir."

"My secretary traced you through your leave form, on file with your regiment. I hope I'm not disturbing you, Mr. Slaight."

"Nosir. Nosir. No problem, sir." Slaight pulled the quilt over his naked form against the chill from the air-conditioner. Irit handed him the water, and he took a sip.

"Fine. Damn fine, mister. That's what I like to hear. Listen to me now, Mr. Slaight. Can you hear me clearly?"

"Yessir. Clearly, sir."

"Something's come up. I need you up here. Right away. This afternoon. You understand me, Slaight?"

"Yessir."

"We do not normally interfere with a cadet's leave time. You know that, Slaight. But this is different. We have a . . . very serious situation on our hands, Slaight. I need to see you . . . today. Can you make it up here before close of business this afternoon?"

"Yes sir. I believe so, sir." Slaight remembered to say *believe*. He'd been taught never to say, *I think* . . . always to say . . . *I believe*.

"Outstanding. Damn fine, Mr. Slaight. I knew I could depend on you. Oh. Yes. You will be compensated for your lost leave time. I will personally authorize an extra day of leave. Is that understood . . . er . . . agreeable?"

"Yessir." It was funny. The general's voice sounded official, but informal . . . relaxed. There was a note in his voice . . . Slaight couldn't place it.

"What time you think you can be here, Slaight?"

Slaight glanced at the clock radio. It was 1:35. Thirteen thirty-five, military clock lingo.

"Sixteen hundred, sir. I can be there by 1600." Four P.M.

134

"Good enough, young man. One more thing, Slaight. Wear your uniform. Khakis will do. Won't be necessary to get into Sierra." *Sierra*. One day into leave, and Slaight had almost forgotten the word. It meant the cadet summer dress uniform, gray trousers, white dress shirt with epaulets . . . Slaight focused.

"Yessir. Khakis sir."

"Sixteen hundred, then."

"Yessir."

"Good man, Slaight. See you then." The phone clicked and went dead, the long-distance line whizzing into silence. Slaight flopped back on the pillows, his forehead perspiring despite the air-conditioner.

"Who was it, Ry?" asked Irit, looking sleepy and confused.

"The commandant of cadets. General Hedges, that's who. Jesus."

"What did he want?"

"He wants to see me in his office this afternoon up at West Point. I've got to be up there by four. You think we could drive up in your car?"

"Of course. If it's really necessary, Ry."

"Oh. It's necessary, all right. When a goddamn general calls you personally on the telephone and tells you to drive around to his office, it's goddamn necessary. Necessary! Christ. What a grim note."

"What's the matter, Ry? Why does he want to see you?"

"He didn't say. It was all very official, but kind of . . . chatty, almost. He was *telling* me to come up to his office, but he made it sound like he was asking a favor. But he was insistent . . . no doubt it was an order. Strange. A general kind of . . . playing games that way."

"He didn't say why he wanted to see you?"

"No. But I think I know why." Slaight paused, staring across the room. The drapes glowed from the midday sun. Irit touched his arm. Her hand was cold, icy from holding the glass of water.

"Remember that plebe I told you about? The one they found floating up in Lake Popolopen in May, drowned?"

135

"Yes. You had known him."

"He was in my Beast squad last year."

"I remember."

"Well. He was murdered. I found out about the autopsy they did on the kid."

"Murdered! Ry! You never told me that!" She recoiled, grabbing the edge of the quilt. Slaight put his arm around her shoulder.

"Yeah. I know. I was walking the area when I found out, then I went on the Firstie Trip . . . I didn't want to get into a thing with you about it over the phone, Irit." Slaight paused again. That wasn't it, at all. He'd told her this much . . . he was going to have to tell her everything.

"Truth is, Irit . . ." He paused, breathing deeply. "It was like, you know, one of those West Point things, you know?" He watched her face. No sign of recognition.

"What can I tell you? What I mean is . . ." he was fumbling for words. "What I mean is . . . it was between me and Leroy Buck. This major told me about it, a doctor, a guy I've known since I was a plebe. He did the autopsy. He asked me not to talk to anyone about it. Of course I . . . of course I told Leroy. You know. He's my *roommate*." Irit nodded.

"I didn't figure you needed to know. I figured the whole thing would be investigated, and it would all come out, you'd find out . . . soon enough. I should have told you, Irit. Jesus. I'm sorry." Slaight looked down at his feet. There he was . . . holding back . . . always *holding back* . . . seemed like all he did was *hold back* from this woman he loved. Now she'd gotten involved . . . she didn't deserve being treated like this. He was ashamed. He felt her hand on his arm again.

"I understand, Ry." He looked at her. She did, goddamn her!

"So tell me," she said, "why do you think the general—what is his name?—why do you think this commander wants to see you?"

"The commandant. General Hedges. A real cool one, Hedges. Stainless steel, that fuckin' guy. Cold."

136

"General Hedges. Yes?" She was prodding him.

"Well, he probably wants to talk to me about the kid, David Hand. Which means one thing: They got to the doctor."

"What do you mean, 'They got to the doctor'?"

"They *got to him*, that's all. Found out he talked to me. I'm just guessing, Irit. But this is bad news. Let's get up. We've got to hurry. I got to get into my goddamn uniform, and I've got some calls to make before I see Hedges. This is bad news, and it could get to be worse news real quick."

In the office of the commandant of cadets, Brigadier General Charles Sherrill Hedges replaced the telephone on its black cradle, tugged at the knot in his tie, and looked at the man seated across the desk from him.

"Terry, you've done one hell of a job here," he said slowly, leafing through a stack of papers on his desk.

"Thank you, sir," said Colonel Phineas Terrance King, Third Regimental commander.

"One hell of a job, Terry. This is more than I expected. Much more." Hedges was quiet for a few moments as he glanced through the report on David Hand he had requested of Colonel King a month ago. It had taken two weeks longer than expected to arrive, but considering its contents, the extra fourteen days had been worth the wait. Here was the life of Cadet David Hand just as he wanted. He could see the kid, he could feel him breathe, *smell* him. Terry King hadn't been conscientious, he'd been obsessive. He hadn't missed a thread. This kid was laid as bare as the day they fished him out of Popolopen. The report had everything: friends, squad leaders, enemies, Aptitude Reports, 2-1's, contacts with civilians. Only thing would have yielded any more data than this would have been a wiretap on the kid's brain—a direct connection through his temples to his frontal lobe! This was *it*.

"So I've got this man Slaight coming this afternoon," said Hedges, without looking up from the report.

137

"Yessir," said King. "He's in the report a couple of times, I believe."

"Terry." Hedges looked up. "Terry, I can't emphasize to you the sensitivity of this thing. You've done an outstanding job here. Just outstanding. And the job you've done only underscores what a damned sensitive thing we've got here."

"Yessir."

"Cadet Slaight is due at 1600, Terry. I'm going to need the rest of the afternoon to go over this report before he gets here. Won't be necessary for you to be present when he reports."

"Yessir. I understand, sir."

"Now, let's get this thing straight. You've got Fitzgerald, the provost marshal, under control. Is that correct?"

"Yessir. He understands the gravity of our situation here, sir. If this business got into the wrong hands . . . well, we all saw that kind of thing happen once or twice in Nam, sir, with those damn reporters around all the time. Fitzgerald understands, sir. He was in Nam, Checkpoint Charlie . . . Sir, if anyone knows how to handle himself in a situation like this, it's Evans Fitzgerald."

"I'll take your word for it, Terry. But understand this. Fitzgerald is *your* man on this. You are responsible for him."

"Yessir. Got you."

"And this doctor . . . what's his name?"

"Consor, sir. Major. Class of '59."

"Yes, the one who talked to Slaight the day of the autopsy. You've got him straightened out?"

"Yessir. I was as shocked as you, sir, to find we'd had that leakage when we did. I didn't find out about it until yesterday. This man, Consor, took leave after June Week, three weeks. Had to take it then, before preparations for Beast. Just returned from his home-of-record yesterday. I had the post duty officer call me when he signed in from leave."

"Damn fine work, Terry. Damn fine." Hedges leaned back in his chair, tugging the edge of his uniform jacket.

King eased forward to the edge of his chair, preparing to be dismissed.

"Let me see. You figure this Consor talked to Slaight by chance, Terry? Is that your sense of it?"

"Yessir. He was the duty doc that day. Slaight went over there to get his feet bandaged. He was walking off a slug I gave him. A fifteen and twenty. The doc was working on Slaight's feet in his office, and they were shooting the breeze. Slaight was curious. Consor told him he thought the kid had been killed."

"And you got all the copies of the autopsy?"

"Yessir. I made him go through his files. I got all the copies the day he did the autopsy, you remember, sir. The ones we retyped that night."

"Yeah." Hedges paused, gazing across the area of barracks.

"Terry, what in god-hell was Slaight doing getting his feet bandaged at that time of day?"

"Know what you mean, sir. I asked Consor the same thing . . . wish I hadn't, as a matter of fact. He got hopping mad, really red-faced all of a sudden. Said it had something to do with Slaight's tac not allowing the men in his company to be medically excused from the area. He said Slaight's feet were completely wrecked, that he'd have hospitalized him, but Slaight was afraid of reprisals from his tac, and swore the doc to secrecy. Consor said that was the only reason he didn't file a report to his superiors on the tactical officer. This is one place he's really got us, sir. He was angry. I mean mad as hell. You know how these doctors get. . . ."

"Who is Slaight's tac?"

"Grimshaw, sir. That's the strange thing . . . he's one of my best men, sir. I didn't know a damn thing about this order of his. It's obviously illegal. There's no way a tactical officer can keep a man from being medically excused. . . ."

"Goddammit, Terry, I want a piece of Grimshaw's ass! That stupid son of a bitch! Hadn't have been for his thing about medical excuses, Slaight would never have been over there talking with a doctor in the first place."

"I can understand your anger, sir. But I think we'd better hold off on Grimshaw. This is another one of those areas where . . . well, sir, if we come down on Grimshaw about this in the middle of the summer, heads are going to turn, sir. The heads of other tactical officers. They're going to wonder what's up. Grimshaw, for one, will know precisely who was involved. Slaight. Consor. It's just too close to the quick, sir. Too close for right now, anyway."

"See your point, Terry. Indeed." Hedges rocked forward, resting his forearms on his desk. His eyebrows rose, and the thin smile formed on his lips.

"Indeed. Terry, we just might be able to turn this thing to our advantage. Let me give it some thought and have a good look at your report here. Slaight's due in just over two hours." King rose from his chair.

"Yessir."

"I'll let you know what comes of my meeting with this young man, later. Terry, you've done one hell of a job for me. Keep it up. We'll have this thing under control yet."

"Yessir." King watched as Hedges did what he always did to signal dismissal of his closest confidant. He turned his chair sideways to his desk, facing Central Area, his left hand atop the desk, fingering his binoculars. It was like Hedges had entered another world, a little world all his own. The way he stared across the area . . . staring out the window . . . he didn't say "good afternoon," or "good day," or "see you later," or "you're dismissed" . . . any of the conventional parting words between officers. The general simply went away.

Somewhere out on the West Point golf course, Major General Axel W. Rylander was taking in the June sunshine, beginning his second eighteen holes of the day. He was pleasantly unaware of the conversation between Hedges and Slaight on the telephone, the conversation between Hedges and King in the office of his commandant of cadets. General Rylander was playing golf, his mind at ease. Hedges had been dealt with.

Sunday, May 26, at exactly 1300 hours, Hedges had walked into his office and delivered his report on the

140

death of Cadet David Hand. Death by drowning. Accidental. Autopsy showed water in lungs. No signs of struggle. No other bodily traumas or internal injuries. No signs of drugs or alcohol. One more tragic accidental cadet death, and they all seemed to happen at once, within a couple of weeks of June Week. It was all he had needed.

The cadet's parents had to be notified, of course. The father, a restaurant owner in New Orleans, the mother, some kind of city social butterfly down there, the whole business had been sad and rather unpleasant, especially since the family had been looking forward to seeing their son for the first time since he'd been home for Christmas. It was too bad the kid had to die so close to June Week. The parents had been offered the opportunity to bury their son in the West Point cemetery, but the offer had been made discreetly, through the superintendent's aide, with a kind of . . . institutional frown, intended to discourage them in a gentle, but firm way. It was June Week, after all, old grads all over the place, visiting the gravesites of classmates killed in World War I, World War II, Korea, Vietnam. A funeral for a cadet, a plebe, an accidental death, no matter how tragic, would be, well . . . a funeral would have just upset the flow of things.

It was never stated in so many words, but the father of Cadet David Hand understood. The superintendent's aide had helped him arrange to have his son's body shipped by air to New Orleans. The aide had learned the boy had been interred aboveground in a tomb alongside that of his grandfather. Sad. Very sad. But necessary.

And Hedges. The week following, the superintendent had ordered his commandant to begin reporting twice each day, once in the morning and once in the afternoon, to the building across Thayer Road, walking up those stone steps, through the aide's office and into the huge chamber of the superintendent of West Point. It was symbolic. Hedges was a cocky bastard, and he was obviously going places in the army—up—the man was ambitious. Hungry. But as long as he worked for Axel W. Rylander, he'd damn well *act* like he worked for Axel W. Rylander. After two weeks of twice-daily personal reports from Hedges, the superintendent had worked out a system by which the commandant could leave a Disposition Form with the supe's aide in the outer office, if nothing significant had transpired since his previous report.

Those silences . . . the two generals standing there in the huge office overlooking the Hudson with that huge desk between them, Sylvanus Thayer's portrait staring down at them from the wall . . . those silences, when Hedges really had nothing to report, well, the meetings had become too much for both men. They were getting old, after all. And there were only so many minutes in each day. Rylander felt secure that he'd made his point. Hedges knew he was working for someone besides himself, now. He still made the twice-daily trek across Thayer Road, to drop off the DF and announce his presence, in case the supe had something to say to him, if nothing else.

Rylander lined up his shot on the third tee and squinted into the sun. It was about 2 P.M. In three and a half hours, at 5:30 P.M., Hedges would walk across Thayer Road again and deliver a Disposition Form to the supe's aide. Rylander stroked, satisfied at the resonant *crack* as the head of his driver hit the golf ball, watched it disappear over a low hill in the general direction of the green, northwest, toward Camp Buckner.

14

Ry Slaight and Irit Dov moved silently around her penthouse as they prepared for the drive to West Point. That was the way she wanted it when Slaight finally roused himself from bed: quiet. If he didn't keep his mouth shut, he was snappish, brusque, quite unlike himself. Getting up, getting out of bed, clearly did not agree with him. He wasn't mean . . . he was efficient to the point of compulsion. Even the way he moved was abbreviated, spare. He moved in a truncated trance, with his head lowered slightly, as if he were afraid to raise his eyes and face the day. Irit couldn't imagine how it was to get up in the morning at West Point, 6 A.M., dark at that hour most of the year, cold winds howling up the Hudson all winter as the cadets stood in their barracks areas, waiting to march off to meals. But she knew how it was to get up with Ry Slaight at Eighty-second and Madison. Damned unpleasant. Slaight was machinelike in the morning, and that quality about him—efficiency to the point of seeming inhuman—bothered her. So she kept to herself, stuffing necessary items in her purse, waiting for him to emerge from the bathroom like a bull moose, headed for the door, soundless yet . . . frightening.

Once he told her about the squad leader he'd had when he was a plebe, some guy named Gary Lyons. Every day the plebes had to report to the squad leader's room fifteen minutes before each formation: reveille, breakfast, dinner, and supper. This meant the plebes reported to Lyons at 5:45 A.M., 6:15 A.M., 11:45 A.M., and 5:45 P.M. The function of these four fifteen-minute periods (amounting to a total of one hour each day), he explained with some difficulty, was "Special Inspection," or SI for short. Now, the true purpose of SI was unclear to Irit, but she knew it had something to do with the squad leader checking his plebes before they were permitted to face the rest of the company at formation.

Special Inspection, however, was rarely an inspection at all. It was harassment, pure and simple. Everyone knew it, the plebes, the squad leaders—everyone. Yet it went on every day, four times a day, on and on because it was *driving around*, it was an unreasonable order obeyed without question. It was tradition.

So it's 5:45 A.M., fifteen minutes before reveille, the plebes file into the dark room of the squad leader, Lyons, and arrange themselves against his wall in a line. They are bracing, even in the darkness. Once Lyons had caught one of the plebes with his "neck out," failing to brace, and really reamed him. Lyons could see in the dark. The plebes brace. So there they stand in darkness and silence,

143

as the squad leader and his roommate get in their last few minutes of racktime. Time passes. The plebes fidget and scratch. New-mown haircuts itch. Outside the door, the five-minute bell rings and the plebe minute caller begins his insistent screaming, the Calling of the Minutes . . . SIR THERE ARE FIVE MINUTES UNTIL REVEILLE FORMATION THE UNIFORM IS AS FOR CLASS UNDER SHORT OVERCOATS UNDER DRESS GRAY CAPS THERE ARE FIVE MINUTES SIR! . . . screaming the words in staccato bursts, on down the minutes to the two-minute bell, the last minute the minute caller must scream.

Most of the time, the squad leader, Lyons, slept through the five-minute bell, the four-minute bell, the three-minute bell, old Lyons stayed under the covers in the rack until the two-minute bell had been called and the minute caller's footsteps could be heard disappearing down the hall and down stairs on his way out to formation. Then like a great machine, Lyons threw back his Brown Boy, swung his legs over the side of the bed, stuffed his feet into his shoes (he wore his socks to bed), reached with his right hand for his trousers (draped over the tubular metal head rail of the bed), pulled them over his shoes . . . then shuffling across the room and out the door, stuffed his arms into class shirt and short overcoat (the former already inserted into the latter), slipped his pretied necktie noose over his neck and under the collar of his shirt, rested his cap on the back of his head, gray scarf over one shoulder, and in one fluid motion—a ballet is what it was, shuffling out the door and down the stairs toward the area, composing himself in a slow dance of scarves and buttons and wool—old Lyons zipped his trousers, buttoned his shirt, tightened his tie, wrapped his scarf, buttoned his short overcoat, reached in its pockets for his gloves, everything coming to a neat pile just as Lyons stepped into company ranks to hear the company commander call the assembled cadets to attention. Slaight had told her that often Lyons would complete the entire exercise, from bed to formation, without ever opening his eyes. More than two years later, Slaight was still awed by the total economy of motion and preservation of racktime represented by Cadet Gary Lyons getting himself out of bed.

"Irit? Irit! Where's my garrison cap? I was wearing it when I came in last night. I *know* I was." Slaight's voice was tinged with tension, anxious. He was down on his hands and knees behind one of the sofas when Irit handed him the cap.

"Here it is, Ry. Settle down. How long does it take to drive to West Point? An hour? A few moments more? We have plenty of time to get you there by four."

"Yeah. I know." Slaight took the cap and tucked it under his wcb belt. "I've got to make some calls."

"So sit down and make some calls. The telephone is here, in front of you. Call. Sit still. I cannot stand it when you . . ."

"Yeah. I know. I'm sorry, Irit. It's just . . . you know . . . this General Hedges is no push-ovcr. I'm uptight."

Slaight dialed Leroy Buck's number in Burning Tree, Indiana.

"Yeahello," came Buck's voice, thickly accented over the line, sounding more like "yellow," than "hello."

"Hey, Buck," said Slaight.

"Slaight, goddammit. I just left you at that goddamn bus station in D.C. yesterday. What you doing calling me the next day for?"

"They're digging into my shit on the goddamn Hand thing, Buck."

"Whadayamean?"

"I mean I just got a call here—I'm at Irit's in the city—I just got a call here from fuckin' Hedges. *Hedges.* He wants to see me this afternoon at four o'clock, told me to get up there to his office in my Class A's, my khakis."

"Well goddamn-goddamn. He say what he wanted?"

"Nope. Just told me to come up, that's all. Said I'd be compensated for the lost leave time. You believe that?"

"Shit. That's unbelievable. What do you figure happened?"

"They must have gotten to Consor. You didn't get any weird calls from Woo Poo today, did you?"

145

"Nope. Been home all day, too."

"Well, I'm the only one Consor talked to. That's why I figure they got to him."

"Yeah. I see what you mean. What are you going to do, Slaight, goddamn?"

"I'm going up there to see Hedges. What you think I'm gonna do?"

"Well, goddammit, don't go bitin' my head off. I was just askin'. You gonna talk to that doc, Consor?"

"I was going to call him right after you."

"I bet they got his shit wrapped up tight in a sling, if what you say is right. Old Hedges probably got a fix on his nuts with his binocs, know what I mean? You're not going to get much out of Consor, with fuckin' Hedges vice-gripping his ass."

"Maybe not. But I've got to tell him I'm going to see Hedges. And I want to know what they asked him about ... and how much he told them."

"Yeah. Listen. Slaight, goddammit! I just had an idea. You remember that law 'P' we had last year, that real weird one, kind of roly-poly guy, balding, with the squinty eyes and the glasses with gold frames? I think he was a Harvard guy. Nongrad."

"Yeah, I remember him. Captain T. Clifford Bassett."

"Remember how he was always comin' down in the army's shit, explaining your rights under the UCMJ, and civil judicial rights? Other P's used to call him the commie of the law department."

"Fuckin'-A, Buck. Old Bassett. Sure."

"Yeah. Well, I think you ought to give old T. Clifford a call when you get up there. Stop in and see him after you talk to Hedges. Can't hurt. *He* sure isn't gonna be the one to go rattin' on you."

"Goddamn, Buck. I'll do it. I knew I should call your worthless ass about Hedges. Goddamn, I'm glad I did. I never would have thought of old Bassett, sitting down there in his little cubbyhole in the basement of Thayer Hall in the Law Department. Good fuckin' idea, Buck. Say hey. What are you up to?"

"Nothin'. Loafin'. Got to get on the tractor and do

some plowing next week. Corn's up good. Listenin' to the radio. Same old shit, man. You heard that new one by Loretta Lynn? 'Don't Come Home a-Drinking with Lovin' on Your mind'? Classic."

"Haven't heard it. New York City. No country station. You know that."

"Yeah."

"Hey, Buck. Gotta be going. Have to talk to Consor, then get up to Hedges' office, man. Thanks."

"Slaight. Gimme one minute, goddammit. . . ."

"Shoot."

"First, I seen some real nice black Tony Lama's with a radical boot heel in your size up in Shawneetown yesterday, and I seen some of them Acme rough-outs you been lookin' for. You want me to pick 'em up for you? I got the money to cover you, till you get a check this way."

"Yeah. Jesus. Buy the rough-outs, but hold off on the Tony Lama's—I'd have to see them. They run about seventy dollars, don't they?"

"Yep."

"So get the Acme's. And thanks."

"Slaight. Number two. Don't let that fuckin' Hedges trap you, when you get in there, a-talkin' with him, you hear? Fucker's liable to try to box you into an honor situation, use your honor against you. Be careful. He done it before to a guy, remember hearin' about it?"

"Yeah. Buck, thanks, man. See you."

"You bet. Say howdy to that fox, Irit. See ya."

Slaight hung up. Irit was out on the terrace, watering her ginkgoes. That was something he liked about her . . . she was independent, always seemed to have something to do, some project to chase after, a book she was reading or a design she was working on. And she had this sixth sense for those moments when it would have bothered him if she was just sitting there across from him, staring, while he talked on the phone or read or just sat and thought.

"Hey. Irit. Buck says howdy."

"That's nice. What is he doing? Is he on leave?"

"Yeah. Farming. You know. Indiana."

"It's two-thirty, Ry."

"I know. I just got to make one more call."

He dialed the main number for West Point, got the operator, and asked for Major Consor's quarters . . . that's right . . . C-O-N-S-O-R . . . only one in the book. The line went blank, then he heard a soft electronic connect, and it rang.

"Major Consor's quarters." It was his wife.

"It's Mr. Slaight calling, ma'am. Is the major there?"

"Oh. Hello, Ry. Yes, he's here. Just one moment." Slaight could hear a muffled voice in the background saying, *just a minute*. He was going to another extension.

"How are you, Ry?" said Mrs. Consor, "It's been so long since we've seen you."

"Fine, ma'am." Good. Consor hadn't let on to his wife.

"You'll have to come by for supper sometime, when the academic year begins again."

"Yes, ma'am. I'd like that."

"Oh. Here's George." One phone picked up. Hers went dead.

"Major Consor."

"Sir, it's Mr. Slaight."

"I figured I'd hear from you today, Slaight. Where are you?"

"I'm calling from New York, sir. I'm coming up to the academy this afternoon. General Hedges called me. He wants me in his office at four."

"Aren't you on leave?"

"Yessir. He wants me up there anyway, sir. I kind of thought he might be wanting to talk to me about this David Hand thing, sir. That's why I'm calling."

"Yeah. That's it, all right. Colonel King called me in yesterday. I just returned from leave. He'd been waiting for me for two weeks, apparently. I'm not surprised they've got you coming up today. There seems to be some sort of crash program on."

"What's up, sir? What did Colonel King want?"

"It's the David Hand drowning. He wanted to make sure he had all the copies of the official autopsy, made me check my files. Came over to my office personally. He acted strangely, very . . . nervous. He has a tic, he flares

one nostril, wrinkling his nose and his brow. He was doing it over and over, the whole time he was in my office."

"Yessir. I've noticed the same thing."

"I went through my files. He insisted on watching me.
Anyway, when he was satisfied that nothing existed in
writing on the matter of Cadet David Hand, he asked if
I'd spoken to anyone about the autopsy. I told him I had.
I gave him your name. He asked for it. I didn't want to
. . . I considered doctor-patient confidentiality for a mo-
ment . . . but obviously, Slaight, the Hand matter had
nothing to do with your feet. I had to tell him."

"I understand, sir."

"He was extremely agitated. Very worked up. He told
me not to discuss my findings with anyone else. Said I
might jeopardize a sensitive situation. He didn't elaborate.
But he did ask me why I was talking to you, and I told
him about your feet, that I was treating you."

"You mention Grimshaw, sir?"

"Yes, I did. He wanted to know why I hadn't medically
excused you from the area, if they were bad enough to require a doctor's attention. I told him your tac wouldn't allow medical excuses. He didn't say anything after that."

"Oh, Jesus . . . I'm sorry, sir."

"I wouldn't worry about Grimshaw, Slaight. I told King
I'd go to the wall with Grimshaw if I ever saw another
pair of feet like yours from his company. Colonel King
just nodded. But he got the message."

"Thanks, sir."

"Slaight . . ."

"Yessir."

"Slaight . . . you would be well advised to, ahh . . .
watch your step when you're in there with General
Hedges. I don't know exactly what's going on here, but it
doesn't . . . *feel* right to me. You understand?"

"I think so, sir."

"The whole business is being handled very queerly. No
pun intended. For instance, I have yet to see Colonel
Fitzgerald, the provost marshal. King was the only person
I saw when I did the autopsy, and he came alone to my
office yesterday. There have been no more questions

149

about the autopsy. From anywhere. Anyone. I have this feeling . . . the whole thing has hit some sort of bottleneck, maybe for reasons of secrecy or security, I don't know. One thing is clear to me now, anyway."

"What's that, sir?"

"You've hit the bottleneck. King obviously reported to Hedges."

"Yessir, I knew about that."

"You did?"

"Yessir. I saw him going into headquarters that day I talked to you after the area. I asked around. He went to see Hedges that afternoon, the day you did the autopsy."

"He did. Goodness. He's a very busy man. And a very nervous man. I almost handed him a combat ration of Valium, he was ticking and twitching up a storm . . . forget I said that, Slaight."

"Yessir." Slaight suppressed a chuckle. Good ole Consor . . .

"Mr. Slaight, do something for me, will you?"

"Yessir."

"Let me know what transpires between you and Hedges. I want to know what's going on. For crying out loud, I don't even know what's happened to my autopsy at this point. And after King's warning, I'm not going asking around. Give me a ring when you're finished. I'll be home all evening."

"Yessir. Will do. Major Consor?"

"Yes?"

"Thanks, sir . . . I mean . . . for telling me this stuff."

"No problem, Slaight. Mister, keep your nose clean in there. And listen-up. Understand?"

"Yessir."

"Speak to you later, then. Good-bye."

"Bye, sir."

Irit was standing behind him now, her hands on his shoulders. He could see her reflection in the window across the room. She'd changed into a bright red silk dress, a mini-dress with a skirt with a million pleats, so it seemed to dance and spin with a life of its own as she walked. Her lipstick matched the color of the dress, and

150

Slaight could see her nails, bright red against the khaki of his uniform shirt. He hung up the phone and looked at her. He was tired. It seemed like they'd been up a long time . . . but only an hour had passed since the call from Hedges.

"What now, Ry?" she asked.

"We're going to goddamn West Point," he said. "Come on. Let's get a move-on."

15

It was always the goddamn same, every goddamn time, no matter which way you went: in the bus, up Route 9W; in a car, up the Palisades Parkway; you could fly in a goddamn helicopter straight up the Hudson, digging the view of the river, a stewardess serving martinis and peanuts, and it'd still be the goddamn same. It was *going back,* up to West Point, those final fifty-five miles between New York City and the gate at the end of Main Street in Highland Falls, a grim, depressing trip no matter which way you cut it. Always gave you that feeling . . . what was it, exactly? . . . that feeling you had as a kid on the first day of school . . . a restless churning of the nerves, down in your gut, you didn't know what to expect, who your teachers were going to be, where your classes were . . . always afraid you wouldn't be *on time* . . . you'd be caught there in the door of the classroom with all the other kids already sitting down and the teacher halfway through the roll, and the teacher would turn and look at you and say, *Well, who have we here?* and you'd slink back to the nearest seat, slide in, and say your name in a hoarse whisper above the general rustling of books and chairs and first-day-of-school bullshit around you. . . .

It was the same every goddamn time, a miracle really, West Point could hit that little anxiety button somewhere along those fifty-five miles of road between New York

City and the academy, hit the button again and again until by the time you reached the gate, your stomach was knotted, gripped with Total Fear . . . total fear of what? Fuck. All you were doing was *going back* to West Point, something you'd done dozens of times by firstie year, maybe hundreds . . . yet there it was, that little knot down there, tying your belly to your backbone, automatic stiffening of the posture, straightening of the neck, assumption of the Proper Cadet Attitude . . . and silence. Always total silence. You could be in a busload of cadets, and West Point could have just beaten Notre Dame in Shea Stadium, and still the bus would be seized with silence, rumbling and bucking its way up those fifty-five miles, every guy in the bus sinking a little lower and lower into that hole inside himself the closer they got, sinking and sinking, looking for some kind of goddamn *protection*, like if you went down there far enough you'd find some little guy inside you, come bouncing out saying, *Hey, fuckstick, buck up, man! Only fuckin' Woo Poo you going back to! Chin up, dullski! You been through this shit before! You be through it again soon enuf! Get yourself together, man! Any chick catch an eyeball on you like this, man, she gonna figure you for some kinda faggot or somethin'! Pull your shit outta that sling, mister! West Point ain't doin' this to you! You be!* . . . You could dig around down there forever and still not find that little guy, and by the time the bus pulled up outside Grant Hall, its doors would disgorge the sorriest lot of stray-dog-looking fuckers, heads up, backs stiff, but their faces! Jesus, the faces! You could see the skin hanging, hanging in folds under the eyes, from the corners of the mouth . . . hanging and drooping and sagging like curtains in a funeral parlor as they grabbed overnight bags and marched silently across Thayer Road, up Brewerton Road, up the ramp to New South Area, marching back to the barracks, back to The Life. Seemed like the longer you stayed there, the worse it got. And the older they looked. Firsties coming back from weekend looked like . . . like veterans . . . old grads . . . tottering along, easing themselves through the door of the Orderly Room to sign in, their signatures a pathetic scrawl of resignation, of the experience, repeated over and over and over again, that they were *going back*. . . .

It was no wonder that most firsties returned to West Point from leaves drunk, having learned the army's first law of personal thermodynamics, *kill the fuckin' pain*. . . .

What Slaight was thinking about, driving out of the garage on East Eighty-second Street, was a drink, a goddamn *drink*. That's what he could use, a drink, *right now*, something cold and clear and full of ice and alcohol, gin preferably, indeed, a gin and tonic would do just fine, icing down his right hand and his head, icing down his belly for the drive back, the goddamn drive back up to West Point. Most of the time, he was drunk when he returned. Not stumbling drunk, but drunk just the same . . . numb . . . numb and quiet, in his mind already standing in supper formation, standing there on the area waiting, standing there waiting and clapping his hands . . . *clap clap* . . . *clap clap* . . . clapping his hands like the rest of the dull bastards around him. . . . Jesus. A drink. That's all he needed, to walk into Hedges' office smelling like the inside of the Officers' Club bar . . .

They were driving Irit's 1962 Mercedes-Benz 190-SL, a low white sports car with classic lines, red leather interior, the feel of a good horse between your legs. That's what Slaight imagined the feel to be, anyway. He'd never ridden a horse in his life, but the elegant *creak* of the leather seats, the soft purr of the Mercedes exhaust note, must be like a horse, because he'd never known a feeling like it in his life. Back home in Leavenworth, in high school, Slaight owned a 1949 Ford, a classic automobile he had hot-rodded tastefully until the little bugger came on like a pedigree . . . lowered an inch all around, nosed-and-decked and painted a deep royal metal-flake blue, floor shifter, engine heads milled, ported, balanced, four-barrel carburetor, dual exhausts . . . the Ford was like a smooth pebble from a creek bottom, round and sleek and clean, slipping and sliding down Kansas black-tops like a little piece of midwestern weather, unpredictable, hot and fast. But the '49 felt like a *car* . . . it was Detroit, U.S.A., iron and rubber and plastic rolling stock, and you could always hear this sucking noise, this soft *woooooooosh*, as the four barrels of the carb ate Kansas air and spat fire out behind the rear bumper onto the pavement into the night. . . .

That's what it was. Cars in Kansas always meant nighttime and driving around and rock and roll on the car radio, the raspy yowls of adolescence filling the passenger compartment, a loud, satisfying sound, rock and roll by bands like the Rolling Stones, dirty boys, nasty wired earsplitting firewater music, hugely purposefully offensive . . . the Ford engine would whine, mixing exhaust and music and wind and somehow it all meant you'd never grow old, that all you could really do was live for right *now*. . . .

Not so this 190-SL. Slaight and Irit were always driving in her elegant little sports car in the middle of the afternoon, whipping out to Montauk Point at the end of Long Island for oysters and lobster rolls and beer, taking in the sights. Forget rock and roll on the radio, not in the 190-SL . . . Slaight felt a bit nostalgic for that Kansas hit of gasoline and noise, but he knew it was finished. By the time they hit the George Washington Bridge on the way to West Point to see Brigadier General Charles Sherrill Hedges, he knew he'd already grown fuckin' old, the music had lied, like everything else.

And as if to prove it, here it came again, one more time, Bronx and Riverdale to the right, up the Hudson, Yonkers next . . . the river stretching away in either direction beneath a low haze of summer heat . . . steam rising from the water, obscuring the West Side Highway and the buildings of midtown, downriver . . . and upriver, up there around the bend, past the Tappan Zee Bridge and past Stony Point and past the Bear Mountain Bridge, another fifty miles now, hot wind in the face, turning onto the Palisades, Irit with a scarf around her black hair, squinting behind oversize shades, looking over the

154

low flat hood of the Mercedes, gazing up the parkway toward West Point, *going back....*

Slaight was guiding the Mercedes gently up the parkway, riding the edge of the speed limit, ever conscious that the State Police had a thing about catching cadets and their girl friends speeding on their way back to West Point, like they had nothing better to do, like cadets were the goddamn enemy or something. With the top down and the wind rushing past his ears, Slaight thought at first that his mind was sucking air like the carb on his Ford . . . *wooooooooosh* . . . his memory slipping into that groove always there, just behind his eyeballs, the West Point groove. What the fuck? He was *going back*, first full day of leave or no first full day of leave. Irit, she understood, she was just sitting there being nice and understanding and providing the car, which was what girls were supposed to do . . . and Slaight, he was just slipping back in that goddamn groove and driving that Mercedes and letting the wind blow oxygen past him, he could use the fuel. . . .

The man he was going to see, General Charles Sherrill Hedges, was a complete mystery to Slaight, though he had been commander of Beast Barracks exactly one year ago, when Slaight had been Hand's squad leader. That month of Beast had seemed like a hot, stuffy trial, over which Hedges presided like a lawn-party host, in his tailored khakis and crisp summer dress whites. He was new to West Point, freshly returned from Vietnam, from the Big Red One, and guys had been shocked—laid out—when they saw this piss elegant . . . *dude* . . . that's what he was, a fuckin' dude in his custom uniforms and hand-embroidered ribbons and patent-leather shoes. By the time he was a cow, Slaight was used to seeing officers coming straight back from Vietnam looking like somebody had tied them behind an armored personnel carrier and dragged them through the whole goddamn Delta . . . they were haggard and worn-out and beaten down and etched with the lines of a war that wasn't so much being fought as it was being held together with baling wire and gaffer's tape and spit and oil and nylon thread sent in

155

CARE packages from home . . . these guys looked like they'd *been there*. Hedges . . . he looked like West Point, flashy perfection.

When he took command of Beast Barracks, he made it clear to the upperclass detail that everything was going to be as perfect as he was. *Everything*. To make his point, General Hedges ordered that all cadets would march with thumbs pointed stiffly toward the ground alongside the index finger, which would be curled, along with all other fingers, precisely and stiffly at the first knuckle. Not the second knuckle, or the third knuckle, and not a half-fist, or a fist . . . but this . . . this *contraption*, held in the karate-chop fashion, unwieldy, awkward, shifting the mind from marching, from the beat of the drum, to the curl of the fingers, the position of the thumb. It was nonsense, ridiculous bullshit, and every upperclassman knew it . . . two and three years they'd been cadets, and nobody had ever made them march like fuckin' Nazis.

But there he was, General Hodges, the new com, attending formation after formation, skipping from company to company, checking the knuckle status of his young charges. With the eye of an eagle (later he would become known for his binoculars) Hedges would pluck from a formation a plebe (less occasionally an upperclassman) to give extra instruction in finger-curl and thumb-point, the proper procedure for shaping the Hedges marching hand. He often instructed a single cadet in front of the entire Beast Barracks formation, fifteen hundred strong, delaying meals and parades and training to do so. The routine went on for a month, General Hedges pacing the sidelines of one formation after another, his yellow cotton gloves clasped tightly in his left hand, striking his left thigh, time and again. In the few moments of quiet at each formation—reveille, breakfast, dinner, supper—when orders were not barked and commands were not echoing between the buildings, you could hear him even if you couldn't see him.

Slap. Slap. Slap. Yellow gloves caressed his thigh.

Click. Click. Click. Oversize taps on the heels of his shoes hit the concrete, resonating through the area.

156

He was everywhere.

Slaight was puzzled by Hedges and had often watched him pace the formations. What was it about a goddamn brigadier general that made him come out and play diddlyshit with the cadets? Hedges had an unnervingly casual way with cadets of the upper classes in a one-on-one meeting, calling many by nicknames he seemed to pick from a bottomless pit of snappy, wisecracky handles. Slaight's turn came. One night he was the recipient of extra instruction in finger-curl and thumb-point after an evening formation. It was late, sometime just before taps, and the Beast detail had just marched the plebes back to the barracks after a lecture in Thayer Hall. Slaight noticed from the general's breath that he'd been drinking. Gambling for the moment that Hedges was just a bit more relaxed than usual, Slaight asked him about his obsession with pointed thumbs and curled fingers, since his own thumbs and fingers were being pointed and curled under the general's close supervision.

"Mr. Sam," said General Hedges, deliberately choosing the last three letters of Rysam Slaight's name as his own personal manner of addressing him, "Mr. Sam, what I'm showing you here is just my way of putting my signature on my unit."

Hedges bent over Slaight's left hand, reaching down with his own to correct the posture of Slaight's thumb, the precise curl of his fingers. Hedges' hands felt clammy, cold in the hot summer night air. Slaight stood there waiting while a brigadier general finished leaning over and touching his hands—first his left, then his right—touching them, manipulating his thumbs and fingers until they met his approval. Slaight was chilled by the notion that Hedges was getting off, touching his hands in the darkness. They stood alone on Brewerton Road behind the barracks, and upstairs, guys could be heard yelling at the plebes, johns were flushing, showers started and stopped. In the distance, the mess hall clanked along, leaving supper, heading for breakfast. Noises surrounded them, but they were alone.

157

"Sir?" Slaight asked, breaking the tension, for Hedges was now standing there, just standing there staring at him.

"Sir, what do you mean, 'put my signature on my unit'? I don't understand."

"You march like I tell you, Mr. Slaight," said Hedges, shifting his body until his face was maybe ten inches from Slaight's. "You march like I tell you, and you are *mine*."

Thumb-point and finger-curl were not the only obsessions of General Hedges. He drilled the cadets in the miracle war being fought in Vietnam, far from the "fields of friendly strife" of West Point. At every juncture of training, Hedges pounded the drum of the "Combat Example" into the hot days and nights of Beast Barracks. Not a single thing happened between men, it seemed, to which the Combat Example did not apply.

"How would you like to depend on that man in *combat*?" came the inevitable question from Hedges at lectures, out on the parade ground, on the training fields during bayonet drill and squad tactics.

"If that man failed the test here at West Point, think of what he might do in *combat*." Hedges' words hung over the heads of cadets like flags at half-mast, skeletal images of doom, a vision of all the world in terms of . . . war. But it was the way he used the word, *combat*, like a bludgeon to beat up on guys who were just messing up, being plebes, doing all the shitball stuff plebes are supposed to do on their way to becoming upperclassmen. He swung it like a club—*combat*—word coming around at you all the time, whistling through the air, landing with a dull *thud* on some poor fucker's head every time Hedges took a notion. He didn't criticize performance or point out ways to improve efficiency or encourage better attitudes. The word *combat* was interchangeable with the word *career*.

Hedges rarely spoke of combat in a strictly military fashion, following Clausewitz' definition of war as the execution of political ends by other means . . . "other" meaning, of course, combat. Hedges preferred to speak of combat as desirable, necessary for a man's career. The interdependence of men in combat became an interdependence of careers. Not only were lives at stake . . . so was rank, prestige, ratings by superiors, success. To Hedges, combat meant something else, something almost *holy,* the way he rattled the numbers around his war stories like change in a collection basket up in the Cadet Chapel. Combat meant *body count,* the measuring stick of victory in Vietnam. Hedges' units in the Big Red One had greater body counts than any other units in Vietnam during the time he was there. He'd been promoted faster than any commander in the history of the war. And now Brigadier General Charles Sherrill Hedges was the commandant of cadets, a soldier's soldier . . . a man's man. The lesson to cadets was clear. The Pentagon had assigned him to the academy as an example for cadets to emulate. He was the kind of man they were supposed to become. He was *army.*

The next time Slaight saw Hedges up close was down at Benning, just two weeks ago. There they were on the First Class Trip, and they'd been road-marched in deuce-and-a-halfs out to some godforsaken little hilltop deep in the Georgia boonies of the Fort Benning military reservation, where they were supposed to witness another firepower demonstration, this one an example of the defense of a battalion-size night defensive perimeter. This was the real shit, the way they did it in Vietnam every night, they'd been told in lectures all day. Now it was growing dark, as they were ushered into dilapidated, collapsing sets of bleachers ringing the crest of the little hilltop. Some major from the Infantry School was out there on a PT platform with a mike and a blackboard showing a map of the hilltop, pointing out before it got completely black how the battalion was dug in all around the cadets. And sure enough, you could see them out there, 750 strong, their helmets poking up out of foxholes just this side of miles and miles of Concertina barbed wire, piled in a huge circle around the hilltop. Scattered around the enclosed circle were a half-dozen armored personnel carriers and several M-60 tanks, dug into defoilades, only their turrets and muzzles showing. Then it got dark and the cadets waited.

Suddenly all hell broke loose, mo-gas explosions going off all over the place outside the wire, the guys in the holes opening up with what must have been a division's load of machine guns, loaded with 100 per cent tracer rounds, the air around the NDP blazing with red and yellow piss-streams of tracers, disappearing into the woods around them. Artillery started coming in, *WHOMP WHOMP WHOMP*, then more mo-gas going off, a dozen flame throwers snaking dribbly hoses of orange flame into the bush . . . a half-dozen F-4 Phantoms made a low pass, dropping napalm about two hundred meters outside the wire, lighting up the hilltop like a Broadway stage . . . then more machine guns and mo-gas and flame throwers, and the 50s on the APCs opening up, the tanks shooting into the woods from their defoilades right next to the bleachers . . . a hellish spectacle . . . no VC in his right mind would ever face such Total Firepower . . . this was *winning the war* . . . man . . . look at all those colors and listen to all that fuckin' *noise*. . . .

As suddenly as it began it ended. All the explosions and firing were obviously cued from a central bunker, wired to every gun that had been shooting. Suddenly, total silence. The cadets just sat there, stunned, ears ringing, eyes blinded from all the fire and light and madness. . . .

Three of the M-60 tanks wheeled their turrets and switched on Xeon spotlights capable of throwing a million candle power of white light a mile. They switched on the spots and focused them on a little piece of ground, a little berm, a pile of dirt surrounding—what was it, anyway?—nobody could tell at first, but every eye swiveled toward the berm, waiting. . . .

Inside the berm could be seen another tank, in total defoilade, nearly buried. It was one of those engineer tanks, with a bulldozer blade across its front slope. Slowly, the blade swung up, up, up toward the vertical, until finally it was straight up in the air, directly over the tank, the surface of the blade horizontal, level with the edge of the berm. . . .

And suddenly there he was. Brigadier General Charles Sherrill Hedges, standing on the tank's bulldozer blade, impeccably starched fatigues, spit-shinned jump-boots, camouflaged steel-pot helmet . . . above his head, he held a pair of binoculars—*his* binoculars—waving them slowly back and forth, a recognition signal in the nearly blinding light of the Xeons. This wasn't just any old infantry general. *This was the commandant*, down at Benning, with the troops. He was wired for sound, and from hidden speakers surrounding the bleachers, his voice boomed:

"GENTLEMEN . . . GENTLEMEN . . . WHAT YOU HAVE JUST WITNESSED WAS AN EXERCISE IN NIGHT TARGET DETECTION. NIGHT VISION . . . GENTLEMEN. THIS IS THE KEY. WITHOUT NIGHT VISION . . . GENTLEMEN . . . THERE WOULD BE NO FIREPOWER. WITHOUT NIGHT VISION . . . GENTLEMEN . . . THERE WOULD BE NO DEFENSVE PERIMETER. IF YOU CANNOT SEE THE ENEMY . . . GENTLEMEN . . . HOW CAN YOU SHOOT AT HIM?" All this time, the general is swinging his pair of Nikon binoculars back and forth above his head. As all cadets knew, binoculars had a way of gathering light at night, magnifying it, enabling the user to see more distinctly, even in near total darkness. And there was Hedges, binoculars in hand, delivering the Infantry School lecture on the one-million-dollar night defensive perimeter firepower demonstration.

"GENTLEMEN . . . WHAT YOU HAVE WIT- NESSED TONIGHT IS A RE-ENACTMENT . . . AN *EXACT* RE-ENACTMENT . . . GENTLEMEN . . . OF THE NIGHT ACTION MY BATTALION WAS EN- GAGED IN WITH A FORCE OF NVA REGULARS . . . A NORTH VIETNAMESE REGIMENT . . . GEN- TLEMEN . . . A FORCE THREE TIMES THE SIZE OF MY BATTALION. AND WITH GOOD NIGHT VISION . . . GENTLEMEN . . . WITH EXPERT TARGET DE- TECTION AND TRAINING AND ESPRIT . . . GEN- TLEMEN . . . WE *DEFEATED* THAT NVA REGI- MENT . . . WE *DROVE* THEM FROM THE IRON TRIANGLE WITH THEIR TAILS BETWEEN THEIR

SKINNY LITTLE PAJAMA-CLAD LEGS . . . GEN-
TLEMEN . . . THE NEXT MORNING WE POLICED
UP 250 BODIES . . . GENTLEMEN . . . A BODY
COUNT OF 250 . . . IT WAS QUITE SOMETHING
TO SEE . . . GENTLEMEN . . . GOOKS AROUND
OUR NDP TWO AND THREE DEEP. NIGHT VISION
. . . GENTLEMEN. REMEMBER IT. AND REMEM-
BER YOUR SIX P'S . . . GENTLEMEN . . . *PRIOR
PREPARATION PREVENTS PISS-POOR PERFORM-
ANCE.* I HOPE YOU'VE LEARNED SOMETHING
HERE TONIGHT . . . GENTLEMEN. BECAUSE IN
COMBAT . . . IN *COMBAT* . . . GENTLEMEN . . .
THERE IS NO TIME TO LEARN. THERE IS ONLY
TIME TO PERFORM. GOOD NIGHT . . . GENTLE-
MEN. I WILL SEE YOU AT THE ACADEMY IN
THE FALL."

Jesus *Christ*, it was eerie. Hedges standing there on the
dozer blade of that tank in the blinding glare of those
Xeons—enough light for a rock concert—standing there
waving his binocs over his head, his voice coming from
everywhere at once, crashing around the cadets' ears like
artillery, babbling on and on about night vision and body
counts and the "Six P's" . . . hadn't heard that bullshit
since plebe math. . . .

Slaight eased the 190-SL into an empty parking space
in the lot across from Grant Hall. West Point was unchar-
acteristically quiet . . . a week to go before the start of
another Beast Barracks, only a few detail upperclassmen
around . . . another long summer over which Hedges
would preside with his gloves and his heel taps and his
binoculars and his thumb-point and finger-curl. Jesus.

Sweat poured down Slaight's back, soaked his khaki
shirt, turning his armpits the color of Kansas mud. He felt
that tightness in his gut, like a rat was down there with a
jaw-lock on his intestines. A shiver—visible to Irit, who
sat next to him, waiting—shook his spine. He remembered Hedges' clammy, cold hands that night a year ago,
down there on Brewerton Road, a hundred yards from

162

where they were sitting in the Mercedes. He remembered the look on his face, the smell of his breath—Manhattans. Slaight was not looking forward to his visit with the commandant of cadets.

"Irit," he said, "you can wait in Grant Hall, or you can wander down to the river, around the Plain . . . you know. I don't know how long I'm gonna be in there."

"I know, Ry. I brought some work. I'll be okay. I'll wait for you in Grant Hall. It's cool in there."

"Yeah. Okay." Efficient woman. Hedges would find his match for his goddamn *Six P's* with this one.

"Ry. It's three fifty-five. You'd better go."

"Sure. Christ. My uniform's a soaking mess. Fuckit. I won't turn my back to him. Maybe he won't notice. . . ."

"I'll see you later in Grant Hall, then, Ry?"

"Yeah. Listen. Give this lawyer a call for me . . . Captain T. Clifford Bassett. He's down in the Law Department, probably be in his office right now. The cadet guard in Grant Hall will get him on the phone for you. Tell him I want to see him after I'm through."

"T. Clifford Bassett. Yes. I copied it in my notebook. Is there anything else you want me to tell him?"

"No. Just tell him it's important. I'd appreciate it if he'd hang around."

"All right, Ry. Take care."

"Thanks, sweetness. I'm off . . . off to see the wizard . . ." Slaight laughed, extracting himself from the Mercedes. It was a joke between them . . . *off to see the wizard* . . . the movie was on the late-late show the night they met. But this was no late show. Slaight tucked his khaki shirt, straightened his belt buckle, and walked across Thayer Road.

16

The thing about going to see the commandant of cadets was that you were supposed to be totally intimidated—shaking in your boots, in a state of terminal flap, *spastic* you were so scared. It was part of playing the game. He was a general, and you were a cadet, a little pip-squeak, just a pimple on the academy's ass, and you were taking up his time. Generals just basically should not have to call cadets on the telephone and tell them to *drive around*, ancient academy slang for come around to my room, smackhead . . . the words dated so far back in the distance, it was hard to figure where they came from, who first started using them. But all down the years, their meaning had remained the same. *Drive around*. Being told to come to someone's room—in this case, to the commandant's office—was etched in the cadet memory, an indelible mark left there by plebe year. You were scared because the guy who told you to drive around to his room had total power over you. *Total*. You might want to be somewhere else—in the library, say, studying. Or taking a shower. Or you might have to take a leak, the call of nature. But when some upperclassman rared back and said *drive around*, mister . . . you fuckin' drove around, that was all. You had to. There were times, every cadet could probably name dozens, when you'd actually be required to be doing something else, like writing a term paper or even reporting to another upperclassman. But fuck the term paper. And the other upperclassman . . . if he was outranked by the dude who said *drive around*, you just forgot him, and you drove yourself around to the dude's room and you knocked on the door three times and you walked in and you reported and you might not have the least idea what to expect . . . what this bastard was going to uncork on your skinny shaking little beanhead ass . . . but you examined your options, which amounted to exactly *one*, and you *drove around*. You played the fuckin' game.

Now here was Slaight, and he's a firstie, and still driving around . . . called off his leave in New York City, stuffed back into his unpressed khakis, bent into a sports car, and here he was, literally, *driving around* to the room of Brigadier General Charles Sherrill Hedges, the office of the commandant of cadets, on the second floor of the Brigade Headquarters Building, overlooking old Central Area. Three years, and still driving around, still playing the game. Strange thing . . . Slaight didn't feel properly intimidated. He wasn't shaking in his boots. He wasn't in a state of terminal flap. He wasn't spastic and scared and verging on the edge of control. He was tired, hot, and maybe just a tiny bit *pissed off*.

He checked himself as he turned off Brewerton Road into Central Area. Can't let the commandant pick it up that you're pissed. Got to Assume the Proper Attitude. Got to play the game. He entered the Headquarters and walked up the stairs to the second floor. He nodded at the commandant's secretary, and he turned to the commandant's aide—some captain who'd been wounded in Vietnam and was supposed to be a hero—he turned to the aide and said:

"I'm Mr. Slaight. I'm here to see the com."

The aide looked Slaight over like he was examining dirty laundry . . . stains . . . wrinkles . . . shoes in need of a good shine . . . obviously in need of a haircut . . . the aide looked Slaight up and down and with his right hand indicated that Slaight should sit down on a wooden chair across from his desk.

"You do not appear prepared to report to the commandant, Mr. Slaight," said the aide. "You look disreputable, in fact."

Slaight paused a moment, collecting his thoughts. This was all he needed. The clock over the aide's head said it was 4 P.M.

"Captain, I'm on my leave right now. The general called me exactly two and one half hours ago and told me to report to him at 1600. I just drove here from New

165

York City. I don't have another uniform, and other shoes. I just got off the Firstie Trip. Now I see that it's 1601 sir, and I want to do as I've been told. I want to see the com."

The aide gazed unblinkingly at Slaight with a look of astonishment. The secretary shuffled papers nervously.

"I'll tell the general you're here," said the aide. He disappeared through a door. He reappeared.

"The general will see you now."

Slaight stood up and walked through the open door. At the far end of a long rectangular room sat the commandant behind a large desk. All over there was military paraphernalia: models and plaques and flags and helmets and old unit coffee cups cluttering up the place like it was some kind of goddamn museum . . . or a playroom, a rec room. That's what it looked like! One of those rooms in the new suburban split-level tract houses . . . people were always cluttering up the paneled rooms with their son's old football jersey and bowling trophies and Junior Chamber of Commerce Citizen of the Year awards, stuff like that. Slaight paused in the door, taking it in. He strode forward until he reached a spot he figured was four feet from the front edge of the general's desk. The general looked up from a pile of papers, peering at Slaight from beneath salt-and-pepper eyebrows. Slaight saluted.

"Sir, Mr. Slaight reports to the commandant of cadets as ordered." He spoke the words with inflection, his hand steady above his right brow. The general paused one beat . . . two . . . Slaight could almost hear him counting . . . three . . . then he zipped his hand from the desk, skittering his fingers across his forehead like a third-base line coach signaling the catcher . . . saluting . . . and he stood up, thrusting forward his hand . . . all in one motion, catching Slaight off-guard. The general wanted to shake hands with him! What was *this* shit? Slaight dropped his salute and took the general's hand.

"Good to see you, Mr. Sam! God *damn!* Good of you to come up here today, young man! I know it was short notice, but you did a fine job! On time! Looking good! Have a seat over here . . ." Hedges pulled Slaight sideways toward a green leather thickly upholstered chair next to his desk. It was a subtle gesture, like the handshake. Slaight would not sit *across* the desk from him. He would be seated next to the desk, with nothing between them. Slaight felt it coming on. A *man-to-man* talk.

"Mr. Sam, how've you been?"

"Fine, sir." Slaight watched Hedges with perverse fascination. The man was a catalogue, a Sears and Roebuck of tricks. Every move he made had meaning. Every last fucking one of them. Hedges leaned back in his chair and crossed his hands behind his head, interlocking his fingers. He crossed his right leg over his left, exposing his gleaming patent-leather shoe with the brogue sole and oversize heel and tap the size of a quarter sliver of a silver dollar. Hedges was wearing his khakis. Above his left pocket were perched his CIB and Airborne Wings. At the top edge of his left sleeve was his orange-and-black Ranger Tab. Hedges was relaxed . . . almost too informal.

"So how's leave going for you, Mr. Sam? We're going to compensate you for this trip up here. I told you that, didn't I?"

"Yessir. Well, sir, this is my first day . . ."

"God *dammit*." Hedges unleashed his right hand and slapped his knee on the *dammit*. "Got to remember this stuff. Of course. Your first day. Well." He smiled. "It's all ahead of you then!"

"Yessir."

"All thirty glorious days."

"Yessir."

"And I'll bet you're gonna eat 'em up. Chew up those days. Eat 'em like popcorn, huh, Mr. Sam?"

"Yessir."

"My secretary tells me a young lady answered the phone when we called earlier today. You're gonna chowdown on this leave time, Mr. Sam. I can tell by the look on your face, you rascal." Slaight had no discernible look on his face. Exhaustion, maybe.

"Yessir."

Hedges unfolded, scooted his chair square with his desk, straightened the papers on his desk. A look of grave

167

concern crossed his face. Then he smiled a thin, peculiar smile.

"Mr. Slaight, I think you know me well enough to realize we wouldn't have pulled you off leave if we weren't faced by a pretty serious situation up here." He paused.

"Yessir."

"You have any idea why I ordered you up here to see me today, Slaight?"

Slaight looked Hedges dead in the eye for the first time.

"I've got an idea, sir." Hedges' eyes shifted quickly back to his papers. It was hard to look the man in the eye. He was everywhere at once.

"And what's your idea, young man?"

"It's about David Hand, sir." Slaight wasn't going to be evasive, but he wasn't volunteering anything, either.

"Right. First time. God *damn* we've got our hands full with this business, Mr. Sam." Familiar again. Dropping the occasional, casual curse word. It was known as *establishing rapport*. They taught it Second Class Summer during Instructor Training Course.

"You see all this paper work I've got on my desk here, Mr. Sam?"

Slaight could hardly miss it. The general's question was pro forma.

"Yessir."

"It's all on this David Hand business. All of it. Every last goddamn page. Must be hundreds of them here. Maybe a thousand. I've been on this business night and day." He paused again, waiting.

"Yessir."

"One of the pieces of information we've got in this pile, Mr. Sam, just one little piece of information, is the reason you're in here. You know what it is?" Time to play dumb.

"Not really, sir."

"It's the fact you talked with Consor about his autopsy on the body of that dead plebe, Hand. You were on emergency sick call that day, am I right, Mr. Sam?"

"Yessir."

"What did you think when you heard what the doc had to say?"

168

"What did I think, sir?"

"Were you shocked?"

"Yessir. I guess so."

"You *guess* so?"

"I was shocked. Yessir."

"You damn straight you were shocked, mister. Anybody'd be." Hedges pushed the papers around his desk aimlessly. Slaight figured he'd better play along . . . closer. Hedges might be known among cadets as a dimbo, but clearly he held all the cards. *Play. Play.* It was all a goddamn *game.*

"You see this little stack right here?" Hedges indicated a slim folder at his right hand.

"Yessir."

"You know what it is?"

"Nosir."

"It's your file, Mr. Sam. And it contains one more interesting piece of information, though it has little bearing on why you're here. You were Hand's first squad leader, during Beast last year. Weren't you?"

"Yessir."

"And you drilled the little bastard with an aptitude rating at the bottom of your squad, didn't you?"

"Yessir."

"Something between you and this Hand?"

"Nosir."

"Why'd you rate him eleven out of eleven? Once the academic year began, he was in the top fifth of his class in aptitude." Hedges peered at Slaight closely. Slaight caught his eye again, held it this time.

"Hand thought he was all-over-it, sir. Thought he was too good to be a plebe. He was like . . . like a drain on the squad . . . sapping everybody's strength, sucking blood from the squad. Hurt morale. Wouldn't co-operate with his roommates. Technically, he was a first-class plebe. But he'd never . . . you know, sir . . . come around. Time came to rate him, I had to put him at the bottom. He caused that squad more grief than all ten of the rest of them combined."

"You hate him, Slaight?" Hedges looked away.

"Nosir. I admired Hand . . . it was weird . . . he just refused to bend, and I had to admire the kid for that. He had guts."

"You figure it takes guts to 'refuse to bend,' as you put it?" There was a sarcastic tone in Hedges' voice.

"In Hand's case it did, sir. I put more pressure on him than any other five guys in the company. Most of the rest of them would have caved in, or quit. Probably quit. Not Hand. He had guts. His kind of guts. I don't know exactly how to describe it, sir. It was a year ago."

"I see what you mean, Mr. Sam." Hedges continued to swim through his papers. Slaight glanced at them, trying to read them sideways, with little success.

"About your conversation with Consor. He told you the kid was a homo. Did he not?"

"He told me he suspected he was, sir."

"He tell you he figured the kid was murdered?"

"Yessir."

"You believe him?"

"I believed that he believed his own suspicions, sir. But I'm no criminal pathologist. I don't know what to think about David Hand any more."

"Well, Mr. Sam, he wasn't necessarily murdered. You understand me?"

"I think so, sir?"

"You *think?*"

"I understand you, sir."

"That's better, goddammit. You're not being paid to *think*, Slaight. You've been here long enough to know that."

"Yessir."

"Now. Let's get back to this autopsy business. I've been on this thing, first priority, since it happened. That's a month now. A *month*. I've seen it all. Every report. The autopsy is just one of them. And this doctor . . . whatshisname . . . Consor. His opinion is just one opinion. You get my drift?"

"Yessir." Hedges was definitely drifting somewhere, but Slaight was finding it difficult to tell exactly where.

"Hand was not necessarily murdered. His death was
170

announced as an accident. Officially, that's where it still stands. We would not issue a false report on a cadet death. You know that, Slaight."

"Yessir." He knew nothing of the sort, but "yessir" was clearly called for under the circumstances.

"So at best, you have only a partial understanding of a small portion of a rather large set of circumstances. Am I correct?"

"Yessir. I guess that's it all right." Play. Play along.

"You talked to Consor. Consor gave you his opinion. You formed an opinion about Consor's opinion. Pretty flimsy when you consider what's at stake. A man's death. Don't you figure?"

"Yessir."

"And your memory of Hand . . . while your opinions are still keenly held, your memory has weakened. You said yourself Beast was a year ago."

"Yessir."

"Do you see what I'm getting at here, Mr. Sam?"

"Not exactly, sir." Hedges wouldn't spell it out, not completely, but Slaight would try to get him to come as close as possible.

"What I'm getting at, my boy, is the severity of the situation we've got on our hands here. We've got a dead cadet. An accidental death, most probably. Accidental officially, anyway. But it's the death of a rather peculiar cadet. A homo. You know this because you talked to Consor. True?"

"Yessir."

"Then you understand the severity of the situation here. This thing . . . this business about David Hand has implications for the academy, for the army, for the nation, Slaight. You understand? We've got a dead cadet, a faggot homo. You know what would happen if this ever got out?" Hedges was grinning.

"Nosir."

"You can imagine, I presume." His grin widened.

"I believe so, sir."

"If this gets out, Slaight, we're going to have all those faggot communist demonstrators out there . . . we're going to have them thinking they've got a piece of the action up here at the academy. He was one of *theirs*, mister. If this gets out, all over the world, they'll be watching us, and they'll figure we just let commie faggots in our Military Academy along with everybody else, and then what good you think our military commitments overseas will be?" Hedges chuckled knowingly. He didn't expect Slaight to buy his line of reasoning. He expected Slaight to take the hint and come *inside*. He watched Slaight, waiting for the sign that the cadet understood the charade. The cadet's face was blank. He showed no emotion.

"Not much, I guess, sir." Slaight almost choked on the words. He knew Hedges was playing out a fantasy, an old, old academy game. *We're special. We're one of a kind.*

"This David Hand business involves national security, Slaight. You understand that?"

"Yessir." Hedges was looking straight at him now, his hands placed firmly on the edge of his desk, leaning slightly in Slaight's direction, knowing smile still painted on his face.

"That's why we can't have this business about David Hand getting out. And that's why you're up here today, Slaight. I want you to keep your mouth shut about David Hand. I don't want you breathing a word about that autopsy outside this room. I believe you're going to have a memory failure. Am I correct in that belief, Slaight?"

"Well, sir . . ."

"Look, mister. I'm not telling you to lie. I'm telling you to forget. You can understand that, can't you?"

"Yessir."

"Now." Hedges reached for Slaight's personnel file. He flipped it open. He thumbed its pages slowly. Slaight caught a glimpse of a "Blue Dart" or two in there—the light blue forms with which one cadet could pillory another by writing a special report as an adjunct to the normal Aptitude Rating System. The Blue Dart needn't be signed by the cadet writing it. The Blue Dart was a classic anonymous stab in the back. Slaight saw a few more. He'd collected his share in three years.

"I've been looking through your file here, Mr. Sam. I've been giving it my very, very close attention. You are a very interesting young man. A man with great potential. *Great* potential. Did you know that, mister?"

"Sir . . ."

"You needn't answer that. Unfair question. Your file reveals you to be a man of great *unrealized* potential, Mr. Sam. That's the key right there. *Unrealized*. I don't think you've ever really lived up to your promise. There's talent here. Lots of it. You're a leader, mister. High marks in Instructor Training. Top of your company in Command Voice. Hell of a job last summer in Beast. *Hell* of a job. You've had your share of problems. I see you've spent some time on the area."

"Yessir."

"Major Consor was apparently quite distressed at the condition of your feet when you saw him, Mr. Sam. I want you to know that I've looked into this . . . ah . . . matter . . . the matter of your feet, that is. I made my discreet inquiries. It's my job, Slaight. I am, after all, the commandant."

"Yessir." Oh-oh. Here it comes.

"I can't afford to have any of my boys jeopardizing their . . . jeopardizing their *careers* out there on the area . . . And I don't give a good goddamn who takes a different point of view. The commandant is responsible. Am I making myself clear?"

"Yessir." He's going after fuckin' Grimshaw.

"Let me put it this way. I will take care of this deplorable . . . ah . . . situation in the fall. This most . . . reprehensible behavior will not be tolerated. This . . . this . . . Grimshaw character . . ." The general paused, his jaws working, grinding his teeth. "This little cocksucker Grimshaw will pay, and there will be no repercussions. I will personally see to that. Understood?"

"Yessir." Jesus. He really *hates* the bastard. Slaight wondered if Grimshaw was already in the sling, on his way out.

"I will *not stand* for such . . . such . . . such contemptible *weakness*." The general was stuttering now, staring out the window, working his jaws. Several moments passed in silence. Slaight fidgeted.

"Now. We come to this matter of your potential. Your *unrealized* potential, Mr. Sam. There's something you probably don't know about me. You have any idea what it is?"

"Nosir." Christ, if this guy asks one more rhetorical question . . .

"I am a man who hates—*hates*—to see another man fail to realize his full worth. I hate it, Slaight. *Hate* it. You understand that? You understand what it is to *hate* something, Slaight?"

"Yessir."

"Well, goddammit, I *hate* it when little shits like this . . . Grimshaw can't lift themselves out of the scum of mediocrity. *Scum*. Every *real* man ought to rise, Slaight. Every *real* man ought to stand up and take his shot, Slaight. Got that?"

"Yessir."

"That's why I'm considering making you a battalion commander, first detail of the academic year. A *battalion*, Slaight. Your very own battalion. I know this probably comes as a shock to you, young man . . . but sometimes we . . . sometimes we commanders get the opportunity to reach out and pick someone and give him a shot at the stars. And if you don't take the opportunity, then you're not functioning as a commander should . . . as a *man* should. I've got this opportunity with you, Slaight. And I'm going to use it. I feel secure, having studied your record, that you are battalion caliber. Easily. Battalion. What do you think, young man?"

"Well, sir . . . that's . . . uh . . . very interesting." Slaight got the words out and paused, staring at the general, stunned. It came to him in a flash, sitting there watching Hedges, listening to him ramble on . . . suddenly Slaight knew: *This is the way it happens*. One minute you're just sitting there, and you're just Ry fuckin' Slaight. The next minute, somebody reaches out, and you're *touched*. You're *chosen*. Slaight couldn't get over it. The sensation was almost physical.

"Well, mister, what do you think? Up to it?"

"Yessir . . . it's just that I . . ."

Hedges chuckled in a knowing way, as if to say: "Listen, kid, one day I was in your shoes. Know exactly how you feel. Bit heavy, huh, kid? You'll get over it. Knuckle down. Dig in. It'll pass."

He leaned back in his chair, folded his hands behind his head, threw one leg over the other, rocking slowly back and forth, back and forth, staring across Central Area. Slaight watched him. He looked . . . Jesus . . . *content*.

"So how's your memory doing, Mr. Sam?"

"Sir?"

Hedges continued to rock, back and forth, back and forth, like he wasn't listening. Slaight held the silence between them like a garbage can lid, a shield against what was coming next. For the first time since he walked in the Headquarters, he felt scared.

The bastard's making a deal with me. He's just sitting in his chair overlooking the area, rocking and rocking like this went down every day here! He's making a deal with me! He's telling me he'll make me a goddamn battalion commander if I'll conveniently forget I ever knew Major Consor, much less talked to him about the autopsy. He knows damn good and well I'm in the third fifth of the class in Aptitude, down there with the platoon sergeants and the file closers and the rest of the firstie dead beats. Got it right in the file, black and white. And Blue. But he's gonna hand me a battalion, a goddamn *battalion*, lock, stock, and barrel, like it happens every day around here . . . Jesus, maybe it *does*! Maybe most of those fuckers walking around with stripes on their arms made deals somewhere along the line . . . who knows? It all happens in little manila file folders and behind closed doors and maybe one guy . . . maybe two . . . know what's really going on . . . and right here sits the commandant, and he sure as hell knows. . . .

Slaight's mind spun like somebody had boxed his ears. Here he was, Ry Slaight, and the commandant was treating him like *one of the guys*. It made Slaight feel

175

special. He found the deal, the idea of being a battalion commander, attractive. The whole thing made him feel *desired*. That was it. *Desired*. It was the first time in his life anybody had sat down across the table from him and just come out and offered a deal. He had this feeling if he didn't move *right now*, the whole thing was going to get away from him. Wait a minute. The feeling was familiar—goddammit, what *was* it? He had the same goddamn warm *thrill* he'd had the night he met Irit, when she just looked at him standing in the middle of that roomful of people and said: Come home with me, Slaight. It was in her eyes. She was making a deal. Come home with me and fuck, and you got a place to stay, boy. Sure, it was subtle and between the lines and unstated, but the truth was right there in her eyes. It was all so goddamn businesslike. That's what bothered him at first about her. Everything she did was businesslike. Even fucking. No wham-bam-thanks-ma'am thing, but it was like . . . abrupt. Before he fell in love with her, he followed her. That was it. She led and he followed. The understanding between them was functional. Neat. Uncluttered. Efficient. Slaight was a cadet and he slipped into the scene like he was putting on his pants in the morning. The one weekend . . . well . . .

Now he was sitting in the office of the commandant of cadets at West Point, and the commandant was rocking in his chair and he was making a deal, just as casual as you please. Slaight felt . . . he felt like he'd been complimented or something. Honored. The whole thing meant he was being drawn *inside,* in there with the gears whirring and the wheels turning, and guys like Hedges standing around with oil cans and wrenches, kicking this wheel, goosing that gear, running the goddamn machine. . . .

But the whole idea of a *deal*, Jesus, he'd been uncomfortable around the idea of deals since he was a senior in high school, selling clothes in a men's shop in downtown Leavenworth. There was another senior working there, an Italian kid named Polozzi, and he just had this nose for deals. He'd lurk in the store, watching this customer go by and that one go by, then he'd make his move, collar some poor bastard who was looking to buy a sport coat and a pair of slacks. Ole Polozzi would crank the poor guy up, turn a hundred-dollar sale into three suits, a topcoat, dozen shirts, six ties, three belts, two pairs of shoes. He'd discount this and that as he went along—on his own initiative, for to do otherwise would have been to drop the flow of things—and before you knew it, Polozzi was standing at the cash register ringing up thirteen hundred dollars' worth of stuff for the guy. Old Mr. Wolfe, who owned the place, would come out and see the Polozzi discounts, and after work he'd chew Polozzi's ass, but at the end of the week, Polozzi would win the store's sales contest . . . and he only worked part-time, like Slaight. Polozzi must have made a deal with his old lady to leave her womb, they used to joke. He knew goddamn deals. Slaight stood around selling shirts and socks and ties and an occasional suit that walked in and sold itself, but he never did get the hang of *making a deal*, that magical area known to guys like Polozzi.

Slaight felt uncomfortable. He couldn't shake it. He'd been sitting there listening to Hedges, trying to clock his every move, gauge his every motive, and old Hedges was bobbing and weaving like the pro he was, a real fighter, a goddamn *warrior*. Slaight was fascinated. *Enchanted.* Watching him. Listening to him. But this thing . . . this off-balance thing . . . it was like somebody had a hand around his neck and was pulling him over backward. Weird nervous creepy little doubt . . . this hand on the neck . . . goddammit . . . Hedges was so, well, so . . . seductive . . . Slaight almost forgot, just sitting there watching and listening like some kind of fool. It popped.

What would my father do?

Landed like a tight bare first in the solar plexus . . . Slaight gasped and sucked air and hoped to hell Hedges wasn't checking out his act because it was definitely fraying at the edges . . . splitting at the seams . . . but old Hedges just rocked and gazed the area. . . .

What would my father do? Right here. Right now.

The hand on the back of his neck, tight as a goddamn C-clamp gluing a joint, coming up out of nowhere and

177

clamping down and holding on and not letting go . . .
pulling and hanging on. . . .

First time in his life anybody ever offered him a deal, a
real goddamn *deal*, and he felt that rush . . . *now I'm
gonna get mine, goddammit, the moment has finally come
and I'm gonna get mine, a goddamn piece* . . . some bitter little notion that'd been sitting around the back of his
brain since days when he was a kid in school and he had
to wear last year's sneakers and everybody else was wearing this year's loafers . . . Jesus . . . the stupid shit it
boiled down to in the end, when you really got down to it
. . . a rooty little bitterness that gave you the reflexes of a
goddamn cobra . . . *this is it, Slaight. Move, you fucker.
Move.*

And goddamn if he hadn't been getting off on it,
watching Hedges dealing out his little chunk of power.
Goddamn if the whole scene hadn't sucked him right in,
inside, in there where you felt warm, part of it, *desired*.
He remembered the crummy little bitterness with Irit,
when they were first going out. Went back to that first
night. Cadets were supposed to feel like conquerors, but
Slaight didn't feel like that, he just felt like he was *finally
getting his*. Didn't matter if she was giving or he was taking. What mattered was *getting*. That was the way it was.
When you got your chance, you reached out and *grabbed*.
It was true with women, and now he knew it was true inside the office of the commandant of cadets.

"Well, Mr. Sam, how about it?" Hedges watched him
closely, Slaight with this fist on his neck, holding him.

The old man.

Slaight knew. He just fuckin' knew. The old man would
never buy this act. Not for nothing would he go for the
stinkbait Hedges was fishing with. It was always the old
man. Every time he came up against something that
rankled him a bit, the old man was there, watching him,
hanging over his shoulder like a grade school teacher, the
kind you could fool . . . but only once. The old man.
You could only fool him once. So Slaight played the game
at West Point, but he played it with a tiny kernel of wisdom inside him. The academy had fooled him, slipped

178

one by him early on. But he never let it happen again. He was sensitive to the nuances of the game. He studied them. The game was *it*. To West Point's rules, he added one of his own. The old man's rule. And he stuck by it.

"Sir, I've got to give this some thought. I mean, a lot of guys are going to wonder what I'm doing wearing stripes, sir. You know? There are hundreds of guys ahead of me in aptitude. There'll be a lot of questions."

"Yes . . . I . . . aahhh . . . see your point." Hedges looked away. "I want to make myself clear, Mr. Slaight. Your conversation with Major Consor. A very, *very* sensitive matter. More sensitive than you know. More than I am at liberty to tell you. Understand? I think it's best that you consider you and Consor never talked."

"You mean that day after the area, sir?"

"Exactly."

"It's Top Secret, or something, sir?"

"You could give it that classification. Yes."

"Does Major Consor know this, sir?"

"You let me handle Consor!" An ever-so-slight flare of temper. "His situation is none of your business, young man. And the less you know, the better off you'll find yourself. Believe me."

"Yessir."

Hedges stood, and Slaight rose with him. Again Slaight found Hedges' eyes and locked them for an instant. Hedges rummaged in his papers. Slaight couldn't be sure . . . maybe he caught the barest glimmer of uneasiness in the general's eyes. A flicker. It made sense. It wasn't . . . *right*, somehow, that a general was sitting around his office making deals with a cadet who under normal circumstances would never, ever, come personally to the attention of the commandant of cadets. Slaight got the same feeling Consor had. Something was going on, something *big*, and they did not know what it was.

Then he knew. He just fuckin' *knew*. He'd made it. He'd avoided the trap. He hadn't said yes, and he hadn't said no. It was a subtle point, but one to which all cadets were attuned. He hadn't let Hedges catch him in that Honor Code trap of . . . committing yourself. What you

179

did was, you wove and you dodged and you played coy and you *did not commit*. It was called *using your honor against you*. If you let an officer commit you one way or the other, then he could hold you there with the Honor Code. It was part of the game, the eternal game. Sure, you lived by the code, but you learned to *use* it, too. . . .

"It was good to see you, Mr. Sam," said Hedges, offering his hand, smiling again. Slaight shook hands.

"I think we understand each other. National security, Mr. Slaight. Remember that." Hedges smiled. An insider smile.

"Yessir."

"Good afternoon, mister."

Slaight stepped back to the spot four feet from the desk and saluted.

"Good afternoon, sir." He about-faced and walked from the room.

17

Slaight found Irit in Grant Hall sitting under General George C. Marshall, one of the two nongrads whose portraits hung in that august chamber. Grant Hall was many years ago the cadet mess hall. Now it was comfortably arranged with leather sofas and armchairs and reading lamps, the way an Ivy League club reading room must look, Slaight imagined. It was used as the public area in the barracks where cadets met their dates.

"That lawyer you wanted to talk to, Ry? Captain Bassett? His secretary said he went on leave last week. He won't be back for a month. She said you can talk to him when you return for academics in the fall."

"Shit," Slaight muttered under his breath. Irit stood up, gathering sketches and note pads, stuffing them into a large canvas bag she often carried.

"Let's get out of this place," said Slaight.

"Wait a minute. I just remembered something," said Slaight. "Sit down for a minute, will you? I want to call someone."

The sergeant major.

Why hadn't he thought of him before? Slaight leafed through the phone book. There it was. Sergeant Major Atkins Eldridge. Slaight jotted down his home number, hoping Eldridge hadn't cleared post after retiring, hoping the army had given an old sergeant a few weeks' grace period to make his final move. He dialed the number. A woman's voice answered.

"Sergeant Major Eldridge's quarters. This is Mrs. Eldridge."

"Ma'am, this is Mr. Slaight. I was in the sergeant major's regiment. Is he there? Can I speak to him?"

"Certainly. We've got the packers today, and the movers are coming tomorrow . . . he's a little busy, but he's here." Slaight waited. Then the voice, authoritative, muscular:

"Sergeant Major Eldridge, *sir*."

"Sergeant Major, it's Mr. Slaight. I'm over at Grant Hall. I'd like to come by and see you. I've got to talk with you. It'll only take a minute."

"Slaight! Damn! How'd you know I was still around?"

"I didn't. I just . . . I just called, that's all."

"Well, come on by, mister. Plenty of time. Plenty. That's one thing I got enough of, nowadays. Time. So come by. You know where my place is, don't you?"

"Sure, Sergeant Major. See you in a few minutes."

Slaight grabbed Irit, explaining on the way out the door they had to see this guy before leaving West Point. He told her briefly who Eldridge was, saying he'd tell her everything later, the meeting with Hedges, all of it.

They drove along Thayer Road, turning off for Washington Gate. Down at the end of a long drive lined with the houses of colonels and lieutenant colonels, old brick army quarters built in the 1930s, were several wood-frame, clapboard structures, no less sturdy, no less elegant

181

than the brick homes. The sergeant majors lived there. Slaight pulled up in front of the second house to find old Eldridge standing at the curb, waiting for them.

"Well, well, well. So this is the famous Irit Dov," said the sergeant major, opening the door of the 190-SL on her side. "This is indeed a pleasure, Miss Dov. I've heard so much about you . . . from Mr. Slaight, of course." Irit smiled. She knew. Slaight and the sergeant major shook hands. He escorted them to a small brick terrace next to the house. There were folding lawn chairs, and Mrs. Eldridge had prepared a large pitcher of iced tea.

"Hey, Sergeant Major. You think I could get a beer? Irit?" Slaight turned to her, opening an imaginary can in the air. She shook her head no. Mrs. Eldridge poured iced tea.

"Sure. I'll get you one," said the sergeant major. "Could use one myself, I'll tell you." He walked inside, and Slaight followed. In the kitchen, the two cracked beers and took long drafts.

"Jesus," said Slaight. "Man, I needed that."

"What's on your mind, Ry?" It was the first time the sergeant major had ever called him by his given name, and it reminded Slaight the old soldier was retired now. Gone from the army. Slaight grabbed him by the arm as the sergeant major started back outside.

"I'd like to stay in here for a minute, Sergeant Major," said Slaight.

"Sure."

"I'm gonna ask you something, Sergeant Major, and I know it's putting you up against the wall, so if you don't want to answer, I'll sure understand."

"Yes. Go ahead." A look of concern crossed the old man's lined face. You could almost see the three wars in his face. It was tired . . . not physically tired . . . just tired. And sad. A man can only see so much, and then . . .

"Sergeant Major, I want to know what you've heard about that plebe they found up in Popolopen, David Hand. Before you answer, I should tell you I've just been to see the com. I'm on leave right now, and they called me up here today, special. There's something big going on, and I want to know what it is. I figured you might have some idea."

The sergeant major studied the face of the young man in his kitchen. Here was young Ry Slaight. He was fond of the kid. Fond of him . . . like a son. Slaight had gotten all worked up over that business with those guys they called the "Magnificent Seven," because he thought they'd been screwed. They had. The sergeant major had to explain to Slaight there were just some things in life you couldn't do anything about. Then had come the news about his own son, and Slaight was up in Building 720 the day he heard, and he told Slaight about it, told him the whole story for some reason. He guessed he just had to explain it to himself all over again, that there were some things in life you just couldn't affect. Slaight listened, nodded, but he knew Slaight didn't believe it for a goddamn minute. Didn't believe that business about *some things in life* . . . Slaight didn't believe it because he, the sergeant major, didn't believe it, either. It was just something you said to younger men, hotheads, young fireballs with a burr up their asses. You said it to cool them off, but you didn't believe it any more than they did. He looked at Slaight's face, red and sweating and young and hot and handsome like a colt . . . he looked at the kid and he knew he'd have to tell him.

"Yeah. I know about this Hand thing. Big goings-on. *Big*, Started the day they found him. Kept up all through June Week. Still going the day I retired . . . lemme see . . . two weeks ago, now. They got you up here, huh?"

"Yes, Sergeant Major." When you addressed a sergeant major, you said, *Yes, sergeant major* to him the way you said *Yessir* to an officer. It was the way.

"Cut that crap. You can call me old Moonface, for all I care. Did you know that's what they used to call me? Old Moonface? It was because I was a platoon sergeant when I was eighteen, so goddamn young I was moonfaced, I guess. You can call me Ed. That's my nickname."

"Sure." Slaight was nervous. You always felt that way

183

when someone older—someone *above you*—told you to be informal.

"So what'd they call you up here for?"

"I found out about the autopsy on the kid. By accident. Soon as they found out I knew, they called."

"Figures." The sergeant major took a long pull on his beer. He looked out the window. Irit and Mrs. Eldridge were going over some of her sketches. Mrs. Eldridge looked interested . . . she laughed. Irit . . . *fit*.

"Lemme tell you something, Ry. I wouldn't have told you this a couple of weeks ago. But you know—got the packers today, movers coming tomorrow. It's the last time, I guess. We're going to Santa Fe, New Mexico. Picked it right off the map. Never been there in my life. We're just going. Feels kind of funny though . . . it's the first time I picked the spot on the map." Sergeant Major Eldridge took another swig, finished the beer, opened the fridge for another.

"In the army, you've got your shitstorms and you've got your shitstorms. Happens all the time. Goddamn command maintenance inspections, stand-downs, division exercises over in Germany . . . and the goddamn war. Now there's one of your all-time shitstorms. *That* one." The sergeant major opened his beer and stared out the window again.

"Yeah," said Slaight, acting like he knew what old Eldridge was talking about. He didn't.

"As I was saying. You've got your shitstorms. This one's so big, you can't even see it. This dead plebe thing. Lemme tell you, Ry, those last couple of weeks up there in 720, it was like being in the eye of a hurricane. Know what that's like? Quiet as hell. Not a whisper of wind. But around you, you know all hell is breaking loose. That's the way it was with the dead plebe. Quiet. Too fucking quiet. It was another one of those situations where not one piece of paperwork got generated. Not a fucking one. Now in the army, anytime the poop-sheets stop flowing, you better sit up and take a look around, son, 'cause something's wrong. Like in Nam. You don't hear nothing,

184

you don't see nothing, you start looking up, up in the trees for snipers. Look up, not down. Same thing with the plebe. I did some asking around." The sergeant major paused and studied Slaight's face. It was a ritual he'd been through a thousand, maybe a million times before. You paused, and you waited for the young trooper to come on.

"I understand," said Slaight, prodding.

"No, you don't," said the sergeant major with finality. "Not this time. Slaight, the lid's down so tight, it took me a week to get a hold of anything. Even then, it was diddlyshit, rumors and such. Another week, just before they retired me"—he sipped his beer—"Just before they retired me, this clerk over in Headquarters comes by and we talk. He was scared. Said a friend of his down at Post HQ told him three MPs got shipped to Korea the week before . . . just like that. Gone in one day. They'd been up at Buckner, working on that dead cadet thing, he said. Then they were gone. He did some sniffing around. Colonel King arranged it . . . the MPs' transfer, I mean. I knew King was up to some shit, because I was watching him come in and out of the office . . . in and out and in and out. . . . That last week, I had lots of free time, and I just wandered around. He was going to see Hedges about twice a day. I figured that's what he was doing, reporting to Hedges, but I didn't know for sure till I seen him." Sergeant Major Eldridge finished his beer.

"Want another?" he asked.

"Sure."

"Well. I knew the lid was on, but goddamn. It's been a long time since I've seen that kind of stuff—used to call it 'midnight levitation,' when they'd take a guy and ship him out overnight, just raise him up and he'd be gone, like magic. So one day the colonel . . . I mean Colonel King . . . he's going over to play tennis right around lunchtime, and he drops off this big pouch on the chair next to my desk on his way out, and he says to me, he says, 'Take care of this for me while I'm gone, will you, Eldridge?' So I figure to myself, okay, I'll take care of it. I went in his office and closed the door and went through the whole pouch . . . anything disappeared, I wanted to know about it, right?" Eldridge grinned widely and swigged his beer.

"Right," said Slaight. Classic sergeant logic.

"CYA. Cover Your Ass. All that good stuff. So I went through the pouch. Took me an hour. It was all the stuff on this plebe, David Hand. Some of it was pretty incredible. They had his whole record, every goddamn thing there was on the kid here at the academy, and some shit that must have come from someplace else . . . intelligence stuff, or something. There were 'red flags,' you know, those little red tabs that mean Top Secret, all over the goddamn place." Eldridge paused again.

"So?" Slaight could barely stand the waiting.

"Well. I can't remember everything I seen, you understand. And I believe if I was ever to be questioned about it . . . I'm not so sure I could even remember what that pouch looked like. I'm getting along in years, you know. And I got this shrapnel wound right here . . ." Eldridge pointed to a scar behind one ear, leaning toward Slaight and turning his head. "I got me this wound right here, and it's been known to affect my . . . uh . . . memory. You understand."

"Sure."

"Slaight. You're a good man. A god *damn* good man. I like ya. And I'm gonna tell you three things that was in that pouch. Three. You listening?"

"You bet, Sergeant Major."

"One. The kid was a homosexual. Confirmed. All over the place. Poop-sheets and poop-sheets and poop-sheets on the kid being queer. Got that?"

"I knew that one."

"Good. Two. There were two . . . that is *two* . . . copies of autopsies in that pouch. Both of 'em typed up. Both of 'em signed by some major over to the hospital. You wannanother beer?" Eldridge crinkled his can and opened the fridge for another.

"No thanks. I'm driving." They laughed.

"Okay. These two autopsies. They were different. Completely different. One of 'em was all about the kid being a fag, semen all over the goddamn place, all that shit. Said suspected murder victim. The other one said nothing about him being a fag. Nothing about a murder. Drowning. Accidental. Water in lungs. You know. Both of 'em signed by this major. Can't recall his name. Now I figured that was a little strange . . . two autopsies, one dead plebe. And with all that other stuff in there—a lot of the red-flagged stuff—about him being a homosexual and all. I don't know what King was doing with two autopsies. Both of them were photocopies. All I know is I seen two of them, for sure."

"Jesus." Slaight whistled, the way Leroy Buck whistled, between his teeth.

"Yeah. Jesus. So I read on, after coming across these two separate autopsies. And we come to number three. Three. One name keeps coming up, all through the pouch. I don't know what the hell this name is doing in there. The name is on the red-flagged poop-sheets. It's on letters. It's on some photocopies of transcriptions of phone conversations. Lemme tell you, Slaight. This name was in that pouch, one end to the other. The name is William Beatty." The sergeant major took a pull on his beer.

"Yeah?" said Slaight, not wanting to appear anxious.

"William Beatty. Number three. Some civilian down in the Department of Defense in the Pentagon. From the looks of it, he knew the kid, David Hand. But the strange thing was . . . this Beatty character, his name crops up in letters from the Pentagon, letters from generals, letters to King, letters to the com, letters from one general to another inside the Pentagon, all kinds of goddamn memos, and letters from Beatty himself to all of these guys. This Beatty . . . he's all *over* the goddamn place, digging in everybody's shit. Looked like he pretty much inserted himself into the thing . . . you know . . . they didn't go looking for him. He came looking for them. For King and Hedges, I mean. As for the rest of them—the Pentagon characters—I don't know. I don't know what this Beatty's story is, but I can tell you one thing about him. He has *got* some friends. It was all *Dear Billy, Dear Tommy, Dear Dave* . . . that fucker was dearing his ass from one end of the Pentagon to the other. And first-naming it with King and Hedges, too. This guy, William Beatty, he's into that dead plebe up to his hindquarters and then some. Deeper. If I was to base my conclusions on poop-sheets alone, I'd say this guy *knows* some stuff. William Beatty, Slaight. That's all I'm gonna tell you."

"Thanks, Sergeant Major." Slaight took a long swig of beer, finishing the can.

"That help you, son?" Eldridge studied Slaight. The kid's mind was churning . . . cranking. He could tell.

"Sure did, Sergeant Major. Beatty. I know him. Know of him, anyway. Jesus. That's the weirdest twist in this thing yet . . . weirder than two autopsies even."

"Well, lemme tell you something, boy. I don't want to *know*. Got that? You keep it to yourself. And if you want a piece of advice, I'd keep my fanny just as far away from *this* shitstorm as my little legs could carry me."

"I've got you, Sergeant Major."

"You're on your leave time, aren't you, Ry?"

"Well . . . if you want to call visiting the com on leave . . . yeah."

"And they just called you up and roused your ass up here, huh?"

"Yeah, they found me. My leave form, up in Regimental Headquarters. They're all on file up there. Easy enough."

"Tell you what, Slaight. I been meaning to drop by old Building 720 before I clear post . . . got a few good-byes to say and all that. Now. Let's see. You'll be back in New York City by tomorrow, if I'm not wrong. That correct?"

"Yeah."

"So you wouldn't know it if somebody yanked your leave form and it just kinda disappeared, would you?" The sergeant major was grinning ear to ear now.

"It's hard to know what's happening up at Woo Poo when you're down in the city, I guess."

"Leave it to me. More important records than god-damn cadet leave forms have been made to vanish for lesser reasons, lemme tell you. And take a piece of advice from an old sergeant, will you?"

"What's that, Sergeant Major?"

"The army only gives you thirty days a goddamn year . . . ." Eldridge nodded his head in the direction of the terrace, where Mrs. Eldridge and Irit sat talking. "Use it." Eldridge laughed and punched Slaight in the stomach affectionately.

"You bet, Sergeant Major."

"Thought I told you to knock that stuff off."

"Yeah . . . but Jesus, Sergeant Major. You're always going to be, well, the *sergeant major* to me . . . to lots of guys. Christ. Just because the army says you're through doesn't mean we have to . . . forget, does it?"

The sergeant major wrapped a beefy, tanned arm around Slaight's shoulders and hugged him tightly. Slaight looked in his eyes, and the sergeant major looked away reflexively.

"I don't guess it does, Ry. I don't guess it does. God *damn*, this is some shit."

"What's that, Sergeant Major?"

"This place. West Point. I been in the army all my god-damn life, and I never seen anything like it. I mean, I've seen it come, and I've seen it go. Hell, I used to know guys, old SODs when I first signed up, thought the army went to hell in a handbasket the day they traded the horse for the tank. I seen some changes in my day, Slaight. By God, I seen some changes. But this place. I'll tell you what. I never seen anything like it in the army till I got here. I served under West Pointers since I was a private, but you'd have told me about this place, I wouldn't have believed you, not in a thousand years, I wouldn't have. The kinds of stuff I've seen here . . . the stuff they *do* to each other . . . makes you wonder, that's what it does. Makes you wonder. I guess retiring is the best thing for me. I'm just an old sergeant. But I'll tell you what. It all seems different to me now. All of it. Now that I've seen

189

West Point up close, I guess my kind is finished in this man's army. I don't belong any more. Know what I mean? I don't *belong.* That's what makes me sad. Learning after all these years that you don't belong. Hell's bells, maybe I never did. Who knows?"

The sergeant major tugged at Slaight's shoulder as they walked out the back door to the terrace.

"You need anything, Slaight, just call Santa Fe information. They'll have me listed in a couple of days. And you tell that Leroy Buck to stay in touch, too. And that John Lugar, too. God *damn,* it's going to be lonely out there without you guys."

Slaight didn't know what to say, so he didn't say anything.

"Irit Dov." The sergeant major embraced her. "Irit Dov. Your daddy's a general, over there in Israel, isn't he? Wasn't I reading about him last year in the papers, during the war?"

"Yes, Sergeant Major."

"Not you, too. Come on. Call me Ed."

"You're not going to get to her either, Sergeant Major," Slaight interrupted. "She's a corporal in the army reserves over there."

"God *damn.* An old man can't win anything any more. Okay, Irit. You take care of this young man, you hear me?"

"Yes, Sergeant Major."

They walked to the Mercedes and got in. They said brief good-byes. It was the way in the army. Sharply. Clean. Leaving was always fast.

From a phone booth in Highland Falls, Slaight called Major Consor and reported on his conversations with General Hedges and the sergeant major. If Consor was disturbed to learn there was not one autopsy, but *two,* of David Hand floating around with his name attached to them, he didn't show it. Consor had unreal control, like the doctors on the television shows. It was like showing emotion was illegal or something. But Consor did ask Slaight to keep the information about the two autopsies

190

to himself and to get in touch if he heard anything else. Slaight promised he would.

They drove back to New York City in fading light. Quietly. Irit watched Slaight. He concentrated on the road and drove well, as he always did. But she knew he was thinking. It was all over his face, wrinkled into a permanent frown, a grimace of distaste. It was impossible for Slaight to hide his emotions, a fact Irit found comforting, for all she had to do was look at him, and she knew what was up.

She didn't ask him anything because she knew if she did, he would snap at her. It was always that way for a day or so after he left the academy. His temper was brittle. She knew if she asked anything, they would have a spat, and later, he'd blame it on West fuckin' Point. That's what he always called it. West fuckin' Point. They'd argue and fight, he'd brood and pout and hide from her—going away, she called it—and when it was all over, he'd blame it on West fuckin' Point.

West Point was his excuse for everything. For all his moods, all his mistakes, all his faults, all his failures . . . and for all his skills, all his talents, for his manners, his sense of right and wrong, his tenderness, his occasional bursts of anger, bitterness, resentment. West Point just sat there on the Hudson and soaked up blame like a sponge. In a way, West Point protected Ry Slaight. West Point protected him from himself—from his true self—and he didn't know it.

When they'd garaged the Mercedes 190-SL and returned to Irit's building, she checked the mail.

"Ry, there's a letter here for you. It was forwarded from West Point," she said.

The envelope was pink, obviously from a girl. He avoided her eyes. They rode the elevator in silence, the floors going by with ringing metallic *clicks*. Upstairs in the penthouse, she disappeared into the kitchen to fix supper. Slaight sat down on one of the sofas, took off his shirt, shoes, and socks, propped his feet, leaned back in his

191

khaki pants bare-chested in the summer night, and opened the letter.

June 20, 1968

152 Chartres St.
New Orleans

Dear Ry,

My brother is dead, an accidental drowning they said. We buried him next to my grandfather in the family tomb, and I cried. For two weeks, I put it out of my mind, but today I couldn't stand it any longer. I got out all the mail I received from him this past year while I was in Paris, and I went through every letter this afternoon. All he could talk about was Ry Slaight this and Ry Slaight that and Ry Slaight did such-and-such and I saw Ry Slaight at the movies and Ry Slaight went somewhere and did something and I heard Ry Slaight said and on and on.

Now he's dead and buried. I don't believe for one minute it was an accident. And I think you had something to do with it. If it's the last thing I do on this earth, I'm going to find out what happened and I'm going to make you pay.

Samantha Hand

Slaight dropped the letter at his side and rested his head on the sofa. Jesus H. fuckin' Christ. Samantha Hand. Today. *This.*

Irit walked in from the kitchen carrying a tray of crackers and cheese, saw Slaight with the letter at his side, sat down across from him, and said:

"Ry? Ry? What is it? Tell me." He handed her the letter. She read it.

"Ry, all day you haven't said a thing about what's going on. I haven't asked you about it because I knew you needed . . . well, I knew you had to go up there to see that man, the commandant. And I knew you needed to talk to the sergeant major. And I knew you needed the time to sort it all out for yourself. But *this,* Ry." She held up the letter.

"What is the meaning of this? I want to know. I have a right to know. This whole thing is destroying you, Ry.

192

And it's destroying us. Tell me. Please. You've got to tell me."

Slaight raised his head and looked at her. She was remarkably beautiful. His hands shook. He put his head between his knees to hide his face. She moved to the sofa next to him and stroked the hairs on the back of his neck.

He was tired and she was right. The whole thing was eating him alive. He was falling apart. He knew he was going to need her. He needed help to see it through.

"Irit, it's a long story. A *long* story. I'm going to tell you all I know. The whole thing. First, I need a drink. I want a glass of bourbon on the rocks, tall. Then I'm gonna start at the beginning, on July 1, 1967, and tell you every goddamn thing I know. Everything I know about this fuckin' ghost, David Hand."

BOOK III

**David Hand
July 1967**

18

Newspapers called it long and hot. In Detroit, Newark, Watts, and New York, there were riots, fire bombings, the helmeted presence of the National Guard. The word "trashing" entered the language to describe wanton aimless violence and destruction mirroring domestically the war still raging in Southeast Asia. In the Middle East another war erupted, flared briefly, and was over. Wishfully, or stupidly, it was known as the Summer of Love.

At West Point, they weren't fooled. All that craziness out in the streets . . . all the screaming and stomping and yelling and burning and demonstrating and music and long hair . . . all of it had *meaning*. Especially the hair. There was something, well, unsettling about long hair. Like rock and roll, long hair was loud, a catcall at America. It was effeminate, a constant reminder of the little black hole in men's hearts which was of the female. That summer, the noise was so loud and the hair so long, it seemed dangerous. It was power derived from appearance. It was dimensionless. It came from nowhere and it went nowhere and it could not be controlled.

This was power in its most subtle form: power in the absence of money. It was power such as only a handful of men understood completely, and in their minds, it was by rights West Point's—the power of the warrior class. Historically, their power was a willingness to wait, to bide one's time in billets at low pay, sometimes as in the 1920s and 1930s, nearly forgotten while the rest of the world went about its business, manufacturing goods and services, achieving status, garnering possessions, land, and money. The warrior class, the West Pointers, eschewed money, they were good at waiting, for at the end of their time on the sidelines, they would go to war and change the shape of the world. Warriors had never been paid very much, so they were said to have served, and what they did was known as *the service*. But it was always more than that. It was a calling, a spirit, a mysterious something not measurable in civilian terms. The power of the warrior class was the power of men willing to kill other men, and who could measure such a willingness in terms of money? In all of recorded history, soldiers had been underpaid and overworked and very, very powerful, and their power had never been effectively challenged, for the willingness to kill or risk being killed had no monetary equal on the battlefield.

In the summer of 1967, their power was challenged, and the effectiveness of the challenge lay in its diversity, decentralization, and almost total lack of money.

The warriors were mired in a war ten thousand miles away which was not changing the shape of the world. And people back home—kids, housewives, students, fathers, congressmen, senators, *citizens*—were saying it couldn't be won and should be ended. *Now*. Guys coming home from the war weren't being met by marching bands and baton twirlers. They were returning to Customs, Greyhound bus stations; three more months of pulling details in some stateside hellhole like Fort Bragg or Fort Polk or Fort Leonard Wood. *Hassles, man*. And outside, "in the world," as the saying went, out there past the gates, in the streets, were increasing numbers of people who weren't interested in possessions, land, or money, who just wouldn't stop chanting *peace*. It was all getting to be too much. Last year, for the first time in the academy's 165-year history, West Point had begun *recruiting*, sending out cadets from the academy to the high schools, competing for graduating students like West Point was just one more college or something. Everywhere, all around the warriors, there were threats. Everywhere, there was *hair*.

Clearly, something had to be done. They had to grab a final symbol to brandish West Point's separateness from the rest of the country, its impregnability. They grabbed the cadet haircut. It made sense. Haircuts were image. They could be extreme, *loud:* white sidewalls, hair so short and bristly around the sides of the head it showed ash-white scalp. Hair so short the head was *shiny*. An inch on top, just beyond burr-head, enough to plaster down with water and grease and barely effect the look of hair. *Hair*. It became an obsession at the United States Military Academy, an obsession propagated by a single man, Brigadier General Charles Sherrill Hedges, the brand-new commandant of cadets freshly minted in Vietnam, a combat hero. He conceived of the cadet haircut as the academy's symbolic *moat*, the thing to be crossed to get to West Point, the belief to be embraced if you wanted to be a cadet. More than anything else during the summer of 1967, short hair would characterize the Military Academy, mark the cadet, *make the man*.

The academy itself was groomed as impeccably as its cadets. It became a military Disneyland, a lush green summer dream, a memory of the way things were. To those boys who traveled from the fifty states and several foreign countries to become cadets, West Point would seem a place Tom Sawyer might have aspired to, even in the hot mist of that hectic summer of 1967.

As the new cadet candidate fresh off the bus from New York passed through the gates of West Point, the academy lay before him frozen in time, so consistent was reality with the images formed in the mind by *The Long Gray Line* on the televison late movie, the yearly spectacle of the Army-Navy football game, the books by Red Reeder he had read in junior high school. To the left was the drill field, lined by the old stables, converted now into warehouses and offices. Above the drill field stood barracks built in the 1920s, long brick buildings with porches and floor-to-ceiling windows, elegant reminders of the "brown-shoe army."

To the right was the Thayer Hotel, perched atop a piece of granite the size of a football field, lobby hung with battle flags, walls lined with regimental crests. And everywhere was granite . . . great boulders and hunks of it exposed on the side of a hill, roads blasted through it, houses nestled among it, granite, granite, and more granite . . . rock . . . *stone*. High above the area of cadet
198

barracks, a mountain of granite, topped by the Cadet Chapel, a building so singularly imposing that in the late afternoon with the sun in the west, it seemed to cast its shadow over the entire academy. The Cadet Chapel was a cathedral of gray stone, walls flowing into the rock so the chapel and its granite mount seemed to be one. At a glance, the chapel looked like a European castle, battlements topping walls, great oak doors giving way to gloomy interiors, the entire structure cold and gray like the rock on which it stood.

Yet there was something oddly gentle about the whole of the academy. The main post was a place of aristocratic stature. Beautiful old brick and wood-frame officers' quarters lined the streets, sitting on huge expanses of well-trimmed lawns at a respectful distance from one another. White wooden signs with neat black stenciled lettering announced the names and ranks of occupants. Many of the old quarters were three stories high, with a fourth containing dormer bedrooms. Sixteen-foot ground-floor ceilings and double parlors with fireplaces, brass doorknobs and cut-glass bathroom fixtures, marble sinks, floors of fine hardwoods or long-leaf yellow pine, screen porches garnished with wicker furniture upholstered in colorful floral prints, oaks and red maples dappling the perfect green lawns with shifting, wind-blown shade . . . the over-all effect was of a past held reverently to the bosom of the academy, a belief in the continuity of things. The buildings and the lawns and the great pieces of granite which surrounded them were like a steady hand upon the shoulder. The feeling was solid. So was the academy. Having stood upon that historic fist of stone for 165 years, its forefinger directing the passage of the Hudson River, the academy provided a solace, a calm no longer enforced outside the gates of the academy.

Inside the gates, solitude was still enforced. There was to the atmosphere of perfect well-being pervading the academy in the summer of 1967 a lesser design and a greater design. The former had to do with getting through the next day, the next week, the next year. *Laying low* seemed the best course. *Wait it out*. The lessons of history, never lost upon warriors, taught that all things would pass, even opposition to the military. West Point would persevere.

The latter design had to do with the reason the Military Academy existed in the first place: to pass a special knowledge of the warrior class to a select group of young men. To *cadets*. The West Point catalogue did not advertise four years of study as a college, though upon graduation a bachelor of science degree was promised. The academy was described as a "way of life." Within the academy's unique notion of itself rested the greater design of West Point: a conservative idealism embracing the ancient ethic by which great ideas, principles, and knowledge were meant to be separated and revealed only to a chosen few. In modern times, this ethic had been distilled elsewhere to a set of rules one followed if one wanted to get ahead. But at West Point, the ethic remained essentially unchanged from 1802, the year the Military Academy was established by an act of Congress at the urging of President Thomas Jefferson.

In the anxiety following the Revolution, men acted in America as men had acted for centuries. In 1797 President George Washington pleaded with the Congress for the establishment of a military academy, noting that the art of making war "in its most improved and perfect state is always of great moment to the security of a nation," and that "an academy where a regular course of instruction is given is . . . an expedient which different nations have successfully employed." Washington and Jefferson would copy the examples of France and England. And the Military Academy copies them even today. The study of military history at the academy has always gone by the course title "Military Art."

And so in the egalitarian vacuum of an infant democracy, an elite would be born to study the military art of making war. In the womb of a system of government consciously shunning royalty, a new kind of royalty would grow. It was a royalty of attitude and achievement rather than of blood, but its intent and effect were to be the same. Those who were chosen for the Military Academy would rise above others. Synthetic elevation was intended, and so it would remain—a great game played on a grand scale, and it would never match the elegant, controlled madness of divine providence. But it would come close. In its way, West Point was from the beginning an embodiment of the American dream. In the eyes of America, West Point would stand forever above even its sister academies. There would always be only one West Point, and to be chosen to go there had no equivalent in American life. The dream was to become a cadet. *Cadet*. The word rang with echoes of the Long Gray Line, tradition so steeped in greatness you could almost smell the sweat and the leather and the steel.

But to become a cadet you had first to become a plebe. In order to turn civilians into plebes, Beast Barracks was necessary—two months of intensive summer training, the academy's equivalent of basic training. Plebes were the fuel upon which the academy ran, and Beast Barracks was the breeder reactor producing plebes, feeding the machine. . . . Plebes were necessary because they were practice dummies for the upper classes. All the things which were unstated at civilian colleges—or in the Ivy League, hidden behind the closed doors of Skull and Bones or the Porcelain Club—were practiced in the open at West Point, encouraged, acted out with a freedom stemming from the academy's total removal from the rest of society like a monastery, a secret cult headquartered on the Hudson behind a stone façade untouched for better than a century and a half.

What it boiled down to was this: In order to become a warrior, you had to understand what it is to be warred upon . . . a process with its antecedents in ancient Greece, certain initiation rites during the Middle Ages. But the thing which fueled the Military Academy goes deeper than that, to man's inhumanity to man, and on a less lofty level, boys' inhumanity to other boys. Beast Barracks was the culture in which this ancient process would thrive. Beast Barracks was the way.

So that summer at West Point, the symbolic trench was dug. Haircuts were stingingly short, trousers immaculately pressed, shirts impeccably starched, shoes shined to mirror perfection. All was made ready. Tradition would reign. Beast Barracks would begin on July 1, 1967, just as Beast Barracks had begun on the first day of July every year. It was important—no, essential—to the interests of the nation that the academy forge inflexibly onward. The generals were determined: The rest of the country might bend—it might crack, hell, might go to the dogs—but West Point would not bleed.

On the last day of June, civilian boys checked into the Hotel Thayer for the last night before they entered The Life. A single word ran through the hotel in a river of apprehension and conjecture.

Cadet.

It was uttered in tones normally reserved for the football huddle and the church confessional. They listened to one another as boys talked themselves into fitful sleep.

Did you see those cadets standing around outside the barracks?

Yeah.

Did you see the looks on their faces, I mean, how serious they were?

Yeah.

Did you see the way they just stood there . . . you know . . . looking at us?

Yeah. Real straight.

Did you hear about all the yelling up in the barracks? A guy was walking by, and he said the cadets were really screaming. Said they were practicing. For tomorrow.

Yeah. I heard.

Silence.

Wow. Whatdaya think?

Silence. They were trying not to think.

I don't know.

Think you'll make it? I mean, through Beast?

I guess so . . . I mean . . . yeah. I'm gonna make it.

Me too. But some of these guys are gonna pussy-out. You can tell.

Yeah. Did you see that guy with his golf clubs and shit? must have got off the bus at the wrong stop.

202

Laughter.

Talk ran through the night like athletic liniment, with the same effect on the tense atmosphere in the Thayer Hotel as balm on a leg muscle. Hot. Full of bluster and ego and fear. Indeed, the Thayer was closer to a locker room than a hotel that night. The boys slept restlessly, like the night before the big game. They knew little of what the next day held. Beast Barracks was a rumor. A secret whispered from bed to bed . . . *pass it on* . . . like word that the camp counselor was making his rounds.

The boys of the summer of 1967 represented a part of the country unsullied by the change outside. They were too young to have been wounded deeply by the death of John F. Kennedy, too young to have remembered the political wasteland of the I-Like-Ike years, too young to have invested themselves deeply in Johnson's peace-preaching in 1964, then been disaffected by the lap-dissolve into a land war in Southeast Asia. They were young, but they weren't innocents. Two years of watching the war on television, observing older boys scurrying through the various passageways of escape from the draft . . . the past two years had hardened them. They had come to West Point in many cases because they had been recruited. They'd been whispered the first clue of the secret. West Point held a promise the rest of the colleges didn't. West Point's promise was integration into an instant elite. All you had to do was make it through Beast.

When the guy tells you to drop your bags, drop them.

Someone, who said his father was a grad, whispered in the darkness. No one could figure out what the hell the voice was talking about, but each boy listened and nodded to himself in silent agreement with the apparent wisdom of the advice.

Yeah. Gotta remember to drop my bags.

Somebody chuckled. Somebody else giggled. If their friends could see them . . . the stories they'd be able to tell, six months from now, when they were first turned loose on Christmas leave. . . . They waited for dawn. They waited for July 1, 1967. They tried not to be afraid. Few were successful.

19

"DROP THOSE BAGS, MISSTAH, DROP 'EM, YOU
HEAH ME, MISSTAH, DRO-O-OP THOSE BAGS,
DROP 'EM WHEN AH TELL YEW TO DROP
THOSE BAGS!"

David Hand lowered two army duffel bags gently to
the cement and raised his head. He was staring into gray
eyes belonging to a tanned thin face, shaded by a gleaming white hat and a mirrorlike black patent-leather visor,
balanced near the tip of his nose. The face grimaced.

"PICK 'EM UP." The words were not yelled so much
as chewed off matter-of-factly, as if *drop those bags* and
pick them up were the most natural thing in the world to
be saying at 9 A.M. on a sunny summer day. The voice
had a coarse, imitation *edge* to it, but not so make-believe
that it wasn't just a bit scary. David Hand reached down
and picked up his bags.

"DROP 'EM."

David Hand laughed. He had just completed a two-
hour process which had divested him of all civilian gear in
his posession, clothed him in a pair of gym shorts and T-
shirt, black plain-toe tie shoes, burdened him with two
fatigue duffel bags stuffed with all the military equipment
and uniforms necessary to get him through the first few
days of Beast Barracks. Hand laughed. Then he looked
into the eyes of the cadet leaning forward only inches
from his face and he realized something was happening to
him he did not completely understand.

This guy was yelling and he was taking the business of
dropping bags and picking them up *seriously*. David Hand
leaned back as the cadet leaned forward until with elbows
locked, pelvis shoved forward, and chin back trying to
avoid the cadet's face, Hand was contorted into a crazy
human question mark.

David Hand wasn't the only one. Central Area was teeming with spastic human question marks, each of whom was being similarly berated, directed to perform odd tasks, bombarded with verbal violence. Hand glanced from side to side. The place was a stone madhouse . . . worse than he'd imagined. Guys were running all over the place, bare knees pumping up and down, gray shorts and white T-shirts darting here and there, stiff black shoes slapping the pavement . . . and screaming! Animals! Growling, snarling, snapping. . . . But they stood there, stiff as cardboard in the crinkly heat, ramrod straight, just like the photos. And the voices—all the screaming and yelling seemed to come from nowhere but everywhere at once! You couldn't see their mouths move! Their faces were shaded by hats, so voices spewed from the shade across the concrete, bouncing off barracks walls, crashing about the ears in a kind of music. The words came in staccato bursts, drum rolls, snapped at the end like cracking whips. It was all somehow handsome and appealing. David Hand could imagine, even in those first few split seconds, becoming just as sharp and quick and sure, just as expertly violent with his tongue, just as mean as they were. He could imagine becoming a *cadet*.

They were like Doberman pinschers, cadets, sleek and gray and vaguely sinister, even when standing in small groups at the end of the area, just watching. They wore gray trousers and white starched cotton shirts and gray epaulets and brass insignia, everything shiny and bright, blinding in the morning sun. They were sneak attack machines whose single purpose was to bring David Hand and other new cadet candidates under control—*total control*—complete domination of one man over the life of another. The first day of Beast Barracks was intended to stun, to leave new cadet candidates nearly senseless wondering what in hell was happening to them, and this was accomplished with a massive injection of order disguised as chaos. It was hard—no, impossible—to tell what was going to happen next. There was only one choice. Listen. *React*. Hand was fascinated, *entranced* by the experience. It was all so perfect.

"AH SAID DROP THOSE BAGS, MISSTAH. YEW HARD A HEAHING?"

Hand dropped the bags. They hit the pavement with a dull thud.

"NOW PICK 'EM UP."

He scrambled for the bags, slung them over his shoulders.

"DROP 'EM."

He let them fall.

"PICK 'EM UP, MISSTAH."

Up over his shoulders went the bags again. Hand was sweating now, salty droplets of water stinging his eyes, wetting his hair, starting down his arms and legs.

"DROP 'EM, AH SAID, DROP THOSE BAGS." The face pitched forward, centimeters between them now, Hand could feel his breath, cadet breath. Startled, he paused.

"DROP THOSE BAGS, MISSTAH. WHEN AH SAY DROP THOSE BAGS YEW DROP 'EM AND YEW DO NOT HESITATE, MISTAH."

Down. Plonk.

"THAT WAS NOT FAST ENOUGH FOR ME, MISTAH. YEW UNNERSTAND THAT, MISSTAH? YEW UNNERSTAND ME, MISSTAH? SPEAK UP, GOD-DAMMIT! AH'M NOT STANDING HERE FOR MY HEALTH, MISSTAH, YEW HEAH ME? NOW . . ."

Hand scrambled for the bags, falling to his knees, anticipating the command. Concrete stung his skin. The voice dropped in pitch, twinged with quiet fury. Hand, on his knees, could feel the cadet's anger, could imagine spittle forming at the edges of his mouth. He did not look up.

"Misstah, Ah did not tell yew to pick up those bags yet. Ah nevah gave that command, misstah, yew unnerstand me? Yew do not move, yew do not even fuckin' *flinch* until Ah give the command. Yew unnerstand me, misstah? Now. DROP 'EM."

Plonk.

Hand, quivering human question mark, sweating profusely, soggy like a wet washcloth. Cadet utterly dry,

206

caressed by an invisible cooling breeze, the voice low, barely tolerant.

"Ah do not like your attitude, misstah, yew unnerstand me? When Ah tell yew to pick up those bags this time, misstah, Ah want to see sparks fly. Ah wanna heah your chest heave, Ah wanna feel you move. Ah want yew to rustle the crease on my trousers in your breeze, yew heah me, misstah? Yew heah me?"

"Yes."

"Speak up."

"I said yes."

"I take it yew mean yesSIR, smackhead."

"Yessir."

"Speak up, goddammit. YEW HEAH ME?"

"YESSIR!"

"PICK 'EM UP, SMACK, PICK UP THOSE BAGS. MOVE . . . MOVE . . . MOVE . . . MOVE!"

Hand moved. The bags heavy on his shoulders. Weigh more each time.

"That is bettah, misstah. Now, yew listen-up, and yew listen-up close. Yew listen-up to me like your little worthless life depended on it. DROP 'EM!"

Drop. Plonk. Sweat. Drip.

"That is the idea, misstah. Yew are one slow smackhead, misstah. Now, yew listen-up, now, you heah? Yew think yew are some kinda hot shit, diddlyboppin' in here outta high school, big hero, goin' to West fuckin' Point. Well, misstah, yew got another think comin', yew heah me?"

"YESSIR!"

"Yew got a brand-new think comin', hey. Yew are gonna be a plebe now, smack. A new cadet. That is what yew are goin' to be later. A new cadet. Right now, today, this minute, yew are a new cadet candidate. Yew got that straight?"

"YESSIR!"

"Ah'm heah to teach yew two things, smack. Two simple things. The position of attention for fourth-classmen, which yew will adopt as your very own way of life.

And your three answers. Now yew listen-up, smackhead. Yew listenin'?"

"YESSIR!" Hand could feel puffs of the cadet's breath as he spat out the words derisively. Sweat rolled off his forehead, down the bridge of his nose, dribbling on his lips, his chin, staining the concrete at his feet. The cadet stepped back a foot. Hand waited.

"SUCK IN THAT OBESE GUT, SMACK! SUCK IT IN, IN IN IN IN IN. NOW ROLL THOSE HIPS BACK AND POINT THOSE THUMBS TO THE GROUND. TO THE GROUND, SMACKHEAD, TO THE GROUND! THE GROUND IS DOWN THERE AT YOUR FEET NOT UP IN THE GODDAMN AIR! RUN THOSE THUMBS ALONG THE SEAMS OF YOUR SHORTS, AND POINT 'EM DOWN. CURL THOSE FINGERS AT THE FIRST KNUCKLE. CURL 'EM! AND SUCK IN THAT GUT, SMACK, SUCK IT IN AND ROLL THOSE HIPS BACK AND STRETCH THOSE SHOULDERS TO THE SKY AND POINT THOSE THUMBS TO THE GROUND!"

The instructions came in a savage rush, and Hand struggled into a body position he imagined fit the description ringing in his ears. He felt like a scarecrow. He looked like a scarecrow. He grinned.

"Wipe that smirk off that dull face of yours, smack-head."

Hand stiffened.

"Now, dullard, yew think this is so funny . . . yew listenin'-up?"

"YESSIR!"

"Yew think it's been a big yuk so far, smack, yew just gonna *love* this next part. Now yew listen-up to me, and yew listen-up close. Ah'm only gonna tell yew this once. Yew take that dull bean of yours, smack, and yew direct your chin skyward."

David Hand had no idea what the cadet was talking about. He blinked and gazed around, trying to see what the other new cadets were doing, hoping he could copy someone. Across the area, he spied another spindly human question mark, gazing in his direction, probably wondering the same thing. He grinned to himself.

"SMACKHEAD!"

Hand wheeled to find the cadet's face only an inch from his. He tried to focus. Beads of sweat flooded his eyes. Under the shade of the cadet's visor, he could see a face. The cadet's eyes were red, bloodshot. Hand flinched, glancing down to avoid the cadet's eyes. For the first time, he noticed the cadet was shorter than he, and had been standing on his tiptoes in order to bring his face close to level with Hand's.

The cadet dropped his voice to a low whisper. He hissed:

"Sssssssmackhead. What is your name, smackhead? Please, be good enough to tell me your name, misstah. Yew think this is all so much fun . . . well, Ah wanna know who's havin' all the fun, misstah." Ridicule dripped from the cadet's voice like sweat from Hand's brow, a steady, slow stream.

"My name is David Hand, sir."

"What did yew say, misstah? Did yew just say something, misstah? I cannot hear yew."

"I said, my name is David Hand, sir. I thought I spoke rather clearly."

"Yew thought yew spoke rather clearly. Isn't that cute. Hey, Leroy! This little bean thinks he speaks rather clearly. Isn't that nice?" The cadet turned to another cadet not far away, his mocking tone announcing to the assembled upperclass cadets that he had a real fish on the line. The cadet called Leroy laughed. They both laughed. A bunch of cadets standing in a group not far away laughed. Everyone laughed. Hand winced, gathered his courage. The cadet was staring at him again. He looked the cadet right in his bloodshot eyes.

"I SAID MY NAME IS DAVID HAND, SIR."

"That's better, misstah. Much better. But Ah still don't believe Ah hear yew properly. Tell me once more. Please. What is your name?"

Hand realized some kind of game was being played, and his mind raced back over the last few moments, an eternity, searching for the answer, the simple phrase he knew would release him from the cadet's counterfeit superiority. He remembered.

"MY NAME IS NEW CADET DAVID HAND, SIR."

The cadet's face moved away, out of Hand's direct vision, and Hand heard him inhaling and exhaling short, expensive bursts. The cadet eased his mouth close to Hand's ear and whispered again, making believe what he said was just between the two of them. Hand knew all the other upperclass cadets were watching and listening.

"Your name, misstah, is not New Cadet David Hand. Your name, misstah, is New Cadet *Candidate* David Hand until yew are told otherwise. Yew got that?"

"YESSIR!"

The cadet stepped in front of Hand and moved back until Hand could see him clearly. A black name plate on the right pocket flap of his starched short-sleeve shirt announced his name in white capital letters.

SLAIGHT.

David Hand would not forget the name Slaight.

"That's better. Yew are beginning to get the big picture, smackhead. Give us a few eons, smackhead, and we may whip yew into shape. But Ah doubt it. Yew are dull, misstah. Dull and ugly. And smelly. Yew are the reason they call this Beast Barracks. Yew are subhuman. Yew are a smackhead, a crot, a dullard, a simple little bean ... in short, smack Hand, yew are a beast. Yew got that smackhead?"

"YESSIR!"

"Now are yew ready to proceed, New Cadet Candidate Hand?" The cadet's voice oozed scorn.

"YESSIR!" Hand screamed reflexively. He was angry.

"Now then. We come to the good part, smack Hand. And yew listen-up to me and listen-up good, smack, cause Ah'm only gonna tell yew once. Yew take that dull bean of yours, and yew direct that chin up. UP, SMACK, UP. SKYWARD, DULLARD. Look up there at the roof of those barracks over my shoulder. Not just your eyes, dullard. Move your whole head. That's better. What do yew see up there, smack?"

"NOTHING, SIR!"

"Well . . . well . . ." the cadet drawled. His accent was a phony, Hand realized. If not phony, at least exaggerated.

"We-e-ell, that's just too goddamn bad, smack, because yew better enjoy the view right now. This is the last time yew are gonna be gazing up in that direction, yew hear me?"

"YESSIR!"

"Listen-up, smack."

Hand looked the cadet in his bloodshot eyes. He was perfect. Down to the last detail, the last thread. Like an expensive toy.

"You roll that chin down. DOWN, SMACK. DOWN, DOWN, DOWN, DOWN, DOWN. That's the big idea. Rest that skinny chin of yours on your skinny neck. Now. Get ready. CRACK THAT CHIN TO THE REAR. TUCK THAT CHIN TIGHT UP ABOVE YOUR ADAM'S APPLE. TUCK IT UP THERE, SMACK. TUCK IT. TIGHT, TIGHT, TIGHT, TIGHT."

David Hand's chin was crammed down against his Adam's apple, like somebody had driven a tenpenny nail up through the base of his skull. The pain at the back of his neck, across his shoulders, was great. He held the position.

"That's a good little bean, Misstah Hand. Yew know what this is, smackhead?"

Hand choked: "NOSIR."

"Yew are assuming the fourth-class position of attention, smackhead, and it is known commonly around here as BRACING, yew unnerstand me, smackhead?"

Hand choked: "YESSIR!"

"Yew will never utter the word bracing, but yew will assume this position at all times, yew unnerstand me? Yew will walk bracing. Yew will run bracing. Yew will eat bracing. In fact, the only time yew will not brace is in your sleep, yew got that, Hand?"

"YESSIR!"

"The only place on the face of this earth yew are permitted to relax from bracing is in your room. But yew do not have a room yet, smackhead. And so yew will brace. Yew will brace everywhere yew go today. Yew will brace unless yew are told to do otherwise, smack. To relax will be known as falling out. But yew will not fall out, smack. Yew will brace. Beginning today, for the next eleven months of your miserable little insignificant life, bracing is your mission, your identity, your fuckin' *destiny*, yew got that, smackhead Hand?"

"YESSIR!"

"NOW, BRACE, MISSTAH. BRACE, GODDAM-MIT! SCREW THAT PUNY CHIN OF YOURS UP AGAINST YOUR BACKBONE AND BRACE! AH WANNA HEAR YOUR NECK CRACK, MISSTAH! AH WANNA HEAR YOUR FUCKIN' BONES RUB-BIN' AGAINST THAT SKINNY CHIN OF YOURS, SMACK! AH WANNA HEAR THE MUSIC OF CHIN MEETING BACKBONE, THE FUCKIN' MUSICAL SOUNDS OF FUCKIN' BRACING, SMACK! BRACE!"

Hand braced. The cadet smiled, thrusting his own chin forward in ridicule, wagging it back and forth in the air between them. Hand braced and swore silently . . . *if I ever get through this day* . . . he didn't have time to complete the vow.

"Now. Yew listen-up again, misstah. Ah'm gonna give yew your three answers. Yew will use them at all times, unless otherwise instructed. Yew are being given exactly three answers, misstah, because it has become abundantly clear that yew are so completely dull, so totally beastly, yew are unable to handle more than three answers. Are you ready, smack?"

"YESSIR!"

"Listen-up. Your three answers are: Yessir. Nosir. No excuse, sir. Yew got that, smack?"

"YESSIR!"

"Okay. Let's have them. What are your three answers, smackhead?"

"YESSIR, NOSIR, AND NO EXCUSE, SIR, SIR!"

"SMACK, THAT'S NO WAY TO ANSWER A QUESTION. GOD *DAMN*. DOES EVERYTHING
212

HAVE TO BE SPELLED OUT TO YEW, BEAN?" The cadet dropped his voice.

"The answer to the question, smack, is as follows: 'Sir, my three answers are: et cetera, et cetera, and et cetera.' Yew got it straight now?"

"YESSIR!"

"Let's hear them now. What are your three answers?"

"SIR, MY THREE ANSWERS ARE: ET CETERA, ET CETERA, AND ET CETERA." Hand could not keep himself from smiling. Two could play the game of semantics, and the cadet had fallen for his own trap. The cadet reddened. Was the cadet going for his throat? The cadet shook his head slowly from side to side in mock resignation. He looked behind himself, then back at Hand.

"Listen-up, you wise-ass smackhead. Yew see that man in the red sash standing over there across the area?"

"YESSIR!"

"We-e-ell, just for the convenience of yew dull, dull beanheads, he will be known for today as the man in the red sash, and yew are going to be seeing a hell of a lot of him, so yew may as well get used to him. When Ah release yew from my presence, which Ah'm gonna do in about one second because Ah cannot stand the sight of yew for another minute, yew will proceed over to the man in the red sash on the double, and yew will report to him, and he will send yew on your next mission. Ah would not advise making any wise-ass cracks to the man in the red sash. Ah doubt yew will find he has the finely honed sense of humor we have shared this morning, smackhead, with all the spinnin' and grinnin' yew been doin'. Yew get my drift, smackhead?"

"YESSIR!"

"Now, Misstah Hand. Let us get ourselves together. What are yew gonna do when Ah tell yew to report to the man in the red sash?"

"SIR, I AM GOING TO REPORT TO THE MAN IN THE RED SASH."

"Do yew know how to report to the man in the red sash, beanhead?"

Hand considered the question. It was loaded.

"NOSIR."

"Smack, yew are so goddamn dull. YEW ARE SO GODDAMN DULL, THEY ARE GONNA HAVE TO OPEN UP A WHOLE NEW CATEGORY OF DULLNESS FOR YEW, A SPECIAL NEW AREA OF DULLNESS, SMACKHEAD, YEW HEAR ME?"

"YESSIR!"

"Now, smack, when Ah tell yew to report to the man in the red sash, yew POST over there, and Ah'm sure if yew stand around long enough, he'll notice your dull bean, and yew can work out reporting procedures with the man in the red sash, yew got that, bean?"

"YESSIR!"

"When Ah tell yew to move out, smack, yew move out ON THE DOUBLE, BECAUSE YEW MOVE OUT ON THE DOUBLE EVERYWHERE YEW GO TODAY AND THE NEXT DAY AND EVERY GODDAMN DAY HEREAFTER, YEW UNNERSTAND THAT?"

"YESSIR!"

"Now, smack. When Ah tell yew to move out, move out. MOVE OUT!"

Hand grabbing for his bags, stumbling, sweat pouring into his eyes, the area a foggy maze of heat and gray and white, bodies, madness, on every side shrieking and cursing and half-naked forms scurrying jerkily everywhere at once, Hand moving in the general direction of the man in the red sash only by concentrating with near catatonia on each successive step he was able to negotiate.

He ended up in a heap of duffel bags and skinned knees and sweat-soaked gym clothes and scuffed shoes somewhere in the general vicinity of the men in the red sash, for in fact there were several nearly identical men in red sashes standing side by side. Each had a clipboard on which he copied the names of the new cadets sent to him alongside a list of tasks to be performed within the next few hours. As tasks were performed by the scurrying new cadets, they were checked off the clipboard chart by the men in the red sash, and a similar check was made on a manila tag pinned to the gym shorts of each new cadet.

The men in the red sash were central control over the entire melee. They ran a rudimentary bookkeeping operation, and by cross-checking gym shorts tag against clipboard, it was possible to ascertain the progress of any new cadet at any time.

The precision of this process, of course, was not clear to the new cadets, who imagined themselves, at the least, victims of unimaginable crime, at the worst, inmates of an insane asylum for which no West Point catalogue or cadet recruiter had prepared them. They rushed from one place to another, on an endless series of missions, each of greater, more pressing import than the last. Moments clicked by like hours. The first day of Beast Barracks would never end. Each new cadet suspected somewhere deep within him this was true. They were trapped. There was no way out and it would never end, and besides, if they ever got out, who would possibly believe them?

From the man in the red sash, who turned out to be a harried but gentle sort, David Hand was sent to the man on the stoop, another upperclassman whose sole function was to teach the proper procedure of reporting to one's superiors. He sent David Hand inside the 11th Division of barracks to report to the company first sergeant. Hand stood in the hallway, waiting his turn, watching other new cadets stumble in and out of the first sergeant's office like wind-up toys, fumbling their reporting over and over again. Finally Hand's turn came.

"SIR, NEW CADET CANDIDATE HAND REPORTS TO THE FIRST SERGEANT OF THE SIXTH NEW CADET COMPANY FOR THE FIRST TIME AS ORDERED." The words tumbled from his mouth in proper order, as much a surprise to the first sergeant as to Hand himself, who stood with his fingers perched above his right brow in close approximation of a salute. Hand was the first new cadet to get the procedure correct the first time all day. He knew it. He tried not to show his satisfaction.

"You think you're pretty goddamn smart, huh, beanhead?" The first sergeant looked up from the paper work on his desk at Hand, still saluting.

215

"NOSIR!"

The first sergeant returned the salute, and Hand dropped his arm to the fourth-class position of attention.

"You got prior service?"

"NOSIR!"

"Your old man a grad?"

"NOSIR!"

"Rotcee?"

"NOSIR!"

"You go to some goddamn toy military prep school, smack?"

"NOSIR!"

"Then what is it with you, smackhead? Why'd you get it right when none of the rest of these fuckers can get their goddamn names straight, much less the whole poop?"

"I was determined to get it right the first time, sir, and I did."

The first sergeant looked up from his paper work again. A haze of icy fury crossed his face.

"That one of your three answers, you worthless arrogant little smack?"

"NOSIR!"

"Then you've learned exactly nothing today, right, smack? Nothing. Nada. Zero. Goose fuckin' egg. Vacuum. Right, smack?"

"I guess not, sir."

"YOU GUESS NOT! SMACKHEAD! GET UP AGAINST MY WALL, SMACK! SCREW THAT NECK TO THE REAR, PULL IT IN, IN, IN, IN, SMACK, IN! I WANNA SEE THAT WALL TREMBLE AS YOUR PUNY BODY VIBRATES, SMACK. BRACE, GODDAMMIT! BRACE UP AGAINST THAT WALL!"

Hand slammed himself against a stretch of institutional green wall and braced. This was it. The real stuff. He smelled it. The first sergeant was genuinely angry. He wasn't playing games. This wasn't make-believe.

"WE DON'T LIKE SMART-ASS PUNKS LIKE YOU AROUND HERE, YOU GOT THAT? WE DON'T

216

LIKE PUNKS WHO THINK THEY'RE SMART SHIT BECAUSE THEY GOT SOME SIMPLE-ASS BULL-SHIT STRAIGHT THE FIRST TIME, YOU GOT THAT? YOU LISTEN TO ME, BEAN. YOU LISTEN-UP GOOD. NOTHING YOU DO IS RIGHT, YOU UN-DERSTAND THAT? NOTHING! YOU ARE A DULLARD. A DULL, DULL SMACKHEAD. YOU ARE NOTHING. YOU ARE LESS THAN NOTHING, SMACK. SO FAR AS I AM CONCERNED, YOU DO NOT EXIST. YOU UNDERSTAND ME?"

"YESSIR!"

"NOW YOU SCREW THAT WORTHLESS BEAN IN, HAND. CRAM IT TO THE REAR. SLAP THE BACK OF YOUR NECK FLAT UP AGAINST MY WALL, BEAN. I WANNA SEE SWEAT COMING OFF YOUR FACE IN A MAJOR RIVER, SMACK-HEAD. I DON'T WANNA SEE ANY DAYLIGHT BE-TWEEN THE BACK OF YOUR NECK AND MY WALL, SCREW. I WANT YOU TO VIBRATE, YOU ARE BRACING SO HARD, SMACKHEAD. I WANNA SEE YOU SHAKE, HAND. SHAKE!"

By this time, the first sergeant was off his chair and leaned forward, both hands on the desk. His face was a wide, impassive mask. He was not angry, he was mean.

A face appeared next to Hand's. He recognized the breathing as that of the first cadet he had encountered at 9 A.M.

Slaight.

"Smack, you know what it means when the first sergeant gets all upset like that?"

"NOSIR!"

"It means he is truly pissed. *Pissed,* you understand? it means he's about ready to boil over that desk of his and clear a space on his wall and invite you to spend the rest of the month up against that space, like you are right now, up against his wall, bracing. You are not interested in becoming a permanent fixture in the first sergeant's room, are you, Hand? You are not interested in becoming part of the first sergeant's furniture, are you, mister?"

"NOSIR!" Hand noticed Slaight had dropped the accent he affected out on the area.

"Then you post out of here, and you rid yourself of that arrogant attitude, you hear me, smackhead?"

"YESSIR!"

"NOW, POST OUT OF HERE."

Hand posted, back to the man in the red sash, who sent him to see the supply sergeant, and from there to the barber, where his head was completely shaved, crew cut, and from there to the mess hall, where he ate a single bologna sandwich he had difficulty swallowing while bracing, having been instructed by the table commandant, the upperclassman in charge of his ten-man mess hall table, that bracing in the mess hall was especially desirable. From the mess hall Hand was sent back to the 11th Division of barracks, to Room 1144, where he was to sort through and inventory the contents of his duffel bags. In Room 1144, he found his roommates. They had already scattered the contents of their duffel bags all over the room and were madly scrambling among the confusing collection of equipment, uniforms, underwear, toilet articles, books, shoes, sheets, pillows, even a box of "Cadet Stationery." The room was an unbelievable mess, and Hand stood in the door, still bracing, his duffel bags at his sides, near tears at the sight of the two subhuman pack rats before him, digging, rooting through their stuff. Suddenly he was struck by the realization he was the same as them . . . he looked the same . . . he had bags of the same stuff . . . he had to sort and inventory it . . . the whole thing was hopeless. He was trapped.

Hand introduced himself to Chauncey Dippel, a tall, skinny, awkward-looking guy from the Bronx, and Lester Woodruff, a slow-moving football player type from some farm town in western Ohio. Except for the shapes of their bodies, the two were almost indistinguishable. Dippel and Woodruff (the new cadets would rarely call each other by their first names . . . there didn't seem to be time) had their heads shaved, and their sweating faces were coated with cut hairs uncleaned by the harried barbers. The two were completely confused by the contents of their duffel bags . . . they didn't know what anything was, where it was supposed to go, what it all *meant*. Which was a hand brush and which was a clothes brush and which was a shoe brush? The toothbrush was easily identified, but eight cross-belts (white cotton), breastplate, waist plate, web belt, shirts (Sierra) and shirts (khaki)? Who knew? Who . . . cared? The three roommates rummaged and guessed and made checks on inventory sheets with a stub of pencil Hand found in a desk drawer.

While Hand stacked the contents of his duffel bags in neat piles on one of the bunks, his roommates scattered stuff from the fireplace to the door and before they knew it, they'd lost track of what was what and whose was whose and they were arguing. Hand could tell. His roommates were . . . well, un-co-ordinated. They didn't have it. And so he kept to himself, sorting and checking and piling and organizing. Before long, he was in what he'd been told was the uniform for the afternoon—gray trousers, black shoes, white cotton shirt with gray epaulets, black web belt, and brass belt buckle. Hand was examining himself in a full-length mirror on the wall when a figure appeared in the door to their room. It was their squad leader, who had walked down the hall from his room, 1141, Rysam Parker Slaight III. Hand saw Slaight and popped to attention, bracing. His roommates didn't notice the presence of an upperclassman.

"You gonna call the room to attention, Hand, or you gonna just stand there with your fuckin' thumb up your ass like some kind of dufus fool?"

"ROOM TENSHUN!" Hand screamed, trying to sound like the upperclassmen he'd heard drilling new cadets on the area that morning. His roommates looked up, startled. They snapped to the brace, quivering at the sight of Slaight.

"So. Smack Hand. Smack Woodruff. Smack Dippel. What a crew. You three better learn to get along. It's gonna be one fuck of a long two months, and you're gonna be spending the better part of it rubbing up against each other like you were fuckin' *married*." Slaight stood in the door, grinning. His three charges braced.

Slaight's grin was forced. The records he'd been handed by the company administrative officer on David Hand showed that he was indeed the brother of Samantha Hand, the girl from Vassar he'd just broken up with, the girl who'd handed him a flower and an antiwar leaflet as he'd walked back to the barracks from the area the last week in May. What in hell was Samantha Hand's brother doing at West Point? And what terminal twist of fate had landed him in Slaight's squad? An appeal to the cadet company commander had failed to dislodge Hand from his squad only a half an hour ago. If one guys gets to change his squad around, Slaight had been told, every guy will want to do the same. No dice. Slaight was stuck.

"Hand, you seem to have your shit relatively well together. Now, you help your roommates here locate their shit, show them how to assemble their uniforms, and the three of you be downstairs in squad formation in five minutes. Get used to it, gentlemen. Co-operate and graduate. Work together. Not one of you little smacks should exit this room for a formation until the three of you are ready to go together. Remember it. Co-operate and graduate. Now, *function.*"

Hand fished around on the floor and helped Dippel and Woodruff get themselves together. When the last epaulet was snapped into place, he checked his watch. Fifteen minutes had passed. They were ten minutes late. They ran downstairs. The rest of the squad was in formation, waiting.

"Drive into Late Ranks, smackheads." Slaight indicated an imaginary line at right angles with the rest of the squad. The occupants of Room 1144 fell in where Slaight pointed.

"This, gentlemen, is Late Ranks. It is where you will stand when you are late to formation. It is not a good place to stand. If you are late occasionally, you will spend your free time decorating my wall with the sweat off your skinny little necks. If you are late repeatedly, you will receive demerits. If you receive too many demerits, you will walk punishment tours on the area during your free time on weekends. You do not want to be late, gentlemen.

Ever." Slaight motioned with his hand for the three to join the rest of the squad. Over and over again, Slaight dismissed the squad and had them form up in the area, running them back and forth up and down the four flights of stairs to the fourth floor at the 11th Division where they lived. He drilled them. Right face. Left face. About face. Forward march. To the rear march. Column right march. Column left march. Hand salute. More dismissals and formations . . . endless yelling and running, sweating and searching, marching and turning and stopping and starting. . . .

The air was peppered with words which would become as familiar as their names: sally port, the arched walkway through the barracks to the mess hall . . . stoops, long covered porches on the first floor of the barracks . . . the 11th Division, the stairwell containing the squad's rooms . . . the sinks, the basement lockers and showers and johns where everyone in the division shaved and bathed. And naturally, smack, bean, crot, smackhead, beanhead, endless variations on unique cadet expletives designed to let the cream of the nation's crop know that they had just arrived at the bottom of the carton, where they would sour for the next eleven months.

All afternoon the upperclassmen prepared the new plebes . . . their uniforms, haircuts, marching, shined shoes, scrubbed faces and necks and hands . . . all of it necessary for the 5 P.M. swearing-in ceremony, to be held in public view on Trophy Point, overlooking the Hudson to the north, and to which the entire class of new cadets would march, organized into squads, platoons, and companies, looking, it was hoped, like a crack regiment of hardened soldiers. Like *cadets*.

It has long been an integral part of West Point tradition that a complete transformation of civilian boy into cadet take place in the space of a single day. The parents of many new cadets remain on academy grounds during the first day of Beast Barracks, and in fact are so encouraged by the academy. Cadet-conducted tours on foot and by bus are offered for parental enjoyment, during which they are carefully instructed in the ways and traditions of the academy. The parents are steered clear of the main area of barracks, of course. What fun would the swearing-in ceremony be if they had spent the day witnessing the creation of a plebe? Blissfully ignorant of what's really going on at West Point on the first day of Beast Barracks, most parents stay for the swearing in. They are assured it will be a truly impressive spectacle.

"But don't expect to recognize your sons," the parents are cautioned by their cadet-guides.

It is the academy's intent that parents are not able to recognize their sons as they march the quarter mile from the barracks to Trophy Point to take the Oath of Allegiance. That so many raw civilian boys are turned, almost magically, into a uniformed, well-disciplined, and handsome military unit is central to an important but nonpublic portion of the mission of the Military Academy, which is to enhance and perpetuate its own image and power at all times. And what better opportunity than the first day of Beast Barracks, an astounding visual success, all those young cadets marching with seeming expert precision down Thayer Road, forming without a hitch around Trophy Point, raising their hands, taking the oath with a single . . . well, older, *man's* voice, booming out over the Hudson and across the academy, a pledge in unison to everything the parents and the army and the academy and the nation stand for. An Oath of Allegiance.

By July 1, 1967, this had been going on for 165 years. The impression given by the first day of Beast Barracks has been as lasting and impressive as the history of the academy itself. In the morning, over a thousand young boys, rank amateurs, walked into West Point, through the portals of those gray stone buildings, from whence they would not emerge until 5 P.M. By then, they had become professionals. The response of parents, press, dignitaries, and tourists would be nothing less than total awe. For if it had been possible to accomplish such a complete transformation—from boy to *cadet*—if it had been possible to accomplish so much in so little time, just think what would happen to their sons over the next four years!

Indeed. Think of it. Samantha Hand considered the

222

fate of her brother as she watched him being sworn in out on Trophy Point. Now he was a cadet. It had been his dream. She had opposed her brother's choice of West Point over a long list of other colleges he had been accepted to. It had nothing to do with her relationship with Ry Slaight, at the time, blooming. The thought of her brother in that gray uniform, the hat, the black shiny shoes—the image made her uneasy. She really couldn't explain her opposition to West Point, so she had little effect on her brother. And once he'd made up his mind and accepted his appointment to the academy, she said no more. Even when she and Ry had their bitter split in May, she's said nothing to her brother. What was his business was his business.

In part as a reaction to her brother's choice of West Point, in part because of her split with Ry Slaight, she had decided to spend her junior year at Vassar abroad, studying art history. On July 2, 1967, she would leave for Paris. She was glad to be leaving . . . her brother, Ry Slaight, West Point, America. In the last year, everything had turned *sour*. Listening to the voices of the young cadets, the Oath of Allegiance, she shuddered. It was all too much.

That night after supper, the new cadets were herded into South Auditorium of Thayer Hall where they signed the official documents making them members of the United States Army with the official rank of "Cadet." This was the real "Oath of Allegiance," a contract promising five years' active duty service in the Regular Army in return for an education at West Point. Confronted with the actual paper work, several members of the class of 1971 walked out of the auditorium and announced to the nearest officer that they wanted to quit. They were the first. More than 10 per cent of the class would drop out for one reason or another before Beast Barracks was over. But not David Hand, not any of the guys in Third Squad, First Platoon, Sixth New Cadet Company—Slaight's squad.

That night studying the records of all his squad members, Slaight resolved he'd do his best to be fair with

David Hand. But he wouldn't go overboard because once he went steady with his sister. And he wouldn't hold his sister's recent behavior against the kid. It ran against Slaight's grain. Among his classmates, he was known as tough but fair. He was proud of the image.

On a single bunk in Room 1144, David Hand lay awake after taps, a thin chain of thoughts tied together the day's experiences for the New Cadet. He knew he was different. Only a few hours in the company of his rather peculiar roommates proved that much. They hardly knew which way was up, and he'd at least figured *that* out. Then there was the deep shit he'd stepped in once or twice that day . . . have to stay out of the way of the first sergeant . . . and Slaight . . . now, here was a guy who was a total mystery, despite his transparent play-acting at times . . . it was tough to know what to expect from a guy like Slaight. Beast Barracks, in short, was going to be a tough grind, much worse than he'd expected . . . but now he, David Hand, was a *cadet*, albeit a "new" cadet. And he was going to make it. He'd show them. He'd show them . . . all of them. David Hand would make himself someone to be reckoned with.

Downstairs, footsteps sounded on the galvanized steel steps of the 11th Division, the officer in charge making his rounds. A dozen yards away, the mess hall purred. Outside the window of Room 1144 facing Central Area, the area clock struck 11 P.M., and moments later, David Hand slept.

20

The days of July 1967 passed for the plebes in Beast Barracks like each step of a reveille run . . . thud . . . thud . . . thud . . . thud . . . a plodding, sluggish motion, pain in the legs and the lungs and the arms, fear somewhere in the back of the mind it would never end, you'd be out there plodding along, beating the pavement, absorbing the pain, *forever*. To say that Beast Barracks was depressing for most plebes would so grossly understate the emotional experience as to render it meaningless. And if there was one thing Beast Barracks had, it was meaning.

The stuff they made you do! Stuff like clothing formations. The whole company is down in the area in front of the barracks, and the company commander gets up there on the stoops, and the plebes are bracing, the upperclassmen all standing around with their arms folded, chuckling, and the company commander shouts so everyone can hear:

"ALL RIGHT, YOU SMACKS, YOU'VE GOT EXACTLY FIVE MINUTES TO GET YOUR FANNIES UP TO YOUR ROOMS AND INTO FULL DRESS GRAY UNDER LONG OVERCOATS UNDER ARMS AND BE BACK DOWN HERE STANDING IN FORMATION . . . NOW, *MOVE OUT!*" He'd yell it all so fast it was hard to understand what he'd said, plebes were scurrying everywhere, whispering to each other as they pound up the stairs at the double time. . . .

What the fuck did he say? Full dress what under what?

They're flipping through the Blue Book, the four-inch-thick three-ring binder of cadet regulations, to find out what in hell *full dress gray under long overcoats under arms* is all about. Finally someone yells in the hallway . . .

Here it is! I found it! It's all that shit they just issued us yesterday, the weird long coats and the new pants and the jackets with the tight black collars and zippers up the front. Says here, we gotta wear our cross-belts and ammo boxes and breastplates and waist plates and carry our goddamn rifles. Jesus! All this shit in five minutes? They think we're supermen or something?

And all the time the upperclassmen are standing around downstairs in the area, lounging on the stoops, drinking Cokes . . . Cokes! Plebes hadn't tasted Cokes in days, weeks! The upperclassmen are lounging around waiting, knowing, just *knowing* that the uniform the company commander yelled out was impossible for the plebes to strap themselves into within five minutes. The plebes were up there in a state of Total Shock, spasing around like a bunch of junior high school boys getting dressed after gym class, afraid they'll be late to English. . . . The upperclassmen are laughing and joking and punching each other in the arm, bored with the whole business by now. Beast Barracks—almost as much of a grind for them as for the plebes, eighteen-hour days, endless formations, sometimes fifteen to twenty formations a day, formation for shots and formations for uniform fittings and formations for drill and formations for classes and formations for poop-sheet signing and formations for new boots and formations for meals and formations for special announcements and formations for bayonet drill and formations for the daily dozen and formations for special lectures after supper and formations for slide shows about Vietnam and formations for more goddamn uniform fittings and formations for more goddamn shots and more formations and more formations and it just seemed like it never ended. So when there was an hour of free time, it made a perverse kind of sense . . . it was funny, when you thought about it . . . to have *clothing formations,* make the plebes run back and forth from the area to their rooms to the area to their rooms to the area, changing from one uniform to another—mixing up the uniforms, like *as for physical education under raincoats under arms* . . . mix up the little fuckers till you had them wondering where they could possibly find another piece of clothing, till their rooms were piled with discarded uniforms, parts and pieces of uniforms, ripped out of their closets and wall lockers, strewn about the room in a huge confusing mess, one guy's shit getting mixed up with another guy's shit so they'd be up all night sorting out the madness . . . then form up the company about three minutes before taps in their drawers, get them standing out there in the night air with nothing on but their baggy old GI shorts and their shower clogs, so guys from other companies are looking out their windows and pointing at this entire company of plebes, formed up neat as you please in ranks of

226

squads and platoons, and none of them wearing anything but their saggy old GI drawers and shower clogs . . . the upperclassmen are holding their sides, they're laughing so hard, it's so goddamn *funny,* they've all been through the same shit themselves and looking back on it, you realize how ridiculous you must have looked, and now you're standing around the area drinking Cokes and waiting for *your* plebes to do what *you* tell them to do so *you* can watch and *you* can laugh at the madness *you've* created . . . and suddenly you realize that what you're really doing is laughing at your fuckin' self, two years ago. . . .

Beast Barracks. It just went on and on and on and on . . . a thing with a life of its own, seemingly apart from the plebes, the upperclassmen, the tactical officers—*a tradition.* That's what it was. A tradition. *The* tradition. Without Beast Barracks, there would be no plebes. Without Beast Barracks, there would be no cadets. Without Beast Barracks, there would be no West Point. Without Beast Barracks the academy would not *run,* it would not function, the academy might as well just dry up and blow away. Beast Barracks was *it.* Beast Barracks was West Point at its most pure. Beast Barracks was West Point in its truest form. Beast Barracks was West Point in its finest hour. Beast Barracks was West Point with everything that made the academy run just hanging out there in the breeze, West Point with its trousers off, West Point stripped down to its goddamn drawers, West Point stripped down to the thing which *created plebes,* down to Beast fuckin' Barracks.

Upperclassmen used to stand around on the stoops at night, drinking Cokes and joking and cursing West Point.

Out in the fuckin' world . . . if they knew what it was, was producing all those bodies they watched on their TV screens every November, marching into that stadium down in Philly for the Navy game . . . out in the fuckin' world if they really knew what goes down up here, if they knew the shit going on during Beast Barracks . . . they'd pull the handle and flush the place right into the Hudson, is what they'd do . . . all those liberal senators and congressmen and do-gooders, they'd die if they knew what

227

was happenin' to the little boys they were appointing to this place every goddamn year . . . they'd have fuckin' heart seizures is what they'd have . . . they see these beans bouncing around here like a bunch of goddamn Ping-Pong balls, fightin' each other for little bits of food at the mess hall table, arguing and punching each other out 'cause one guy steps on the toe of another guy's shoe he'd just spent two hours spit-shinin' . . . fighting and yelling and crying in the night for their mommies 'cause they're lonely and homesick and they miss their little fuckin' girl friends back home in Palookaville . . . waitin' for the goddamn mail every day like it was some kinda holy communion or somethin' . . . and sobbin' and cryin' in their pillows when the letter they were expectin' didn't come . . . comin' to the squad leader's room in the middle of the night all teary-eyed and weepy, wantin' to quit, askin' for special permission to call home so's they could ask their mommies and their daddies if they could quit . . . every one of the little bastards thought about quittin' at least once, most of them a lot more than once . . . rare was the goddamn beanhead who didn't feel the stinging, crippling pain of self-doubt . . . rare was the goddamn beanhead who didn't wonder what in fuck he was doin' at West fuckin' Point, wonder what had possessed him to apply to the goddamn place in the first place, wonder what had made him accept the goddamn appointment from the goddamn congressman, wonder why in fuck he hadn't quit on the first day of Beast when he saw what the fuck was actually going on, wonder why right now—*now*—he didn't just up and take a goddamn walk out the main gate, take a walk downtown and get on a bus and go down to New York and get himself out to the airport and get on the first goddamn plane and get his fuckin' ass home. . . .

The upperclassmen would stand around at night and drink Cokes and listen to the noises the plebes made, those familiar noises of Beast Barracks . . . the pounding of feet up and down the steel stairs as they ran back and forth to the showers, the scratching of pencils and pens on paper as they wrote home to their girl friends, the soft whoosh-whoosh-whoosh of a shoebrush shining shoes, the raised voices of an argument over whose turn it was to sweep up the ghost turds collected under the beds every day like devils, the screamed curse when a can of Brasso fell off a desk and spilled all over somebody's boots, ruining two weeks' work of building up a base of polish necessary for a spit shine, cursing and cursing because the guy knew he'd catch hell in ranks the next day with his improperly shined boots no matter the reason his boots weren't spit-shined . . . Nothing was fair.

The upperclassmen would stand around and listen and joke and down deep inside most of them, they knew what they were doing was listening to and joking about themselves, because they'd all been plebes, not so long ago. In fact, it was the shared experience of having been plebes, just like those guys upstairs, which held them together as upperclassmen . . . which held them to their squads, attached them to the plebes who were theirs, tied them like big brothers to a bunch of kids they'd only known for a few days. They spent eighteen hours a day with those plebes. Sometimes more. They saw them in dress uniform, ready for chapel on Sunday mornings . . . and they saw them naked, down in the showers when each plebe was required to approach his squad leader, supervising shower formations, and report:

"SIR, I HAVE SHOWERED AND SHAVED AND IT HAS BEEN (X) DAYS SINCE MY LAST BOWEL MOVEMENT, SIR!"

They saw the plebes struggling through obstacle courses out in the field, making it over walls they never thought they'd cross, not in a million years. And then listened to the plebes at night, listened to them crying themselves to sleep because they all figured, each one of them, they were the only people on earth who knew the feeling of true pain, what it was to hit bottom, the experience of total failure, the reality, bitter and cruel, to have completely lost your sense of manhood. The upperclassmen knew their plebes, they identified with them, because they had been there. They knew what it was. They'd been plebes. And Beast Barracks . . . hell. This was their second Beast, they liked to joke. The fuckers who didn't draw Beast Detail didn't know what it was all about. Two Beasts . . . Jesus.

Ry Slaight joined in drinking Cokes and joking on the stoops because that's what you did with your nights, and because what was true for the rest of them was true for him. Everything was pretty much of a bell curve at West Point. The squads in Sixth New Cadet Company were all the same. When all was said and done, when all the beans had been divvied up, there was really very little deviation from the norm. Every squad leader had his good guys, his averages, and his fuck-ups. In any squad, it would be three or four good beans, three or four take 'em or leave 'em beans, and a couple of dead-ahead fuck-ups. In yearling math they'd studied statistics and probability, and sure enough, that's the way it broke down, so neat you could predict what you'd get with your slide rule.

And then there was David Hand.

The kid from New Orleans was where it all broke down and fell apart. He was one of your classic Special Cases—Exceptions to the Proverbial Rule. There was nothing in any textbook, no chapter they'd read in Military Psychology and Leadership, no number on the slide rule to explain the phenomenon of David Hand. He simply could not be categorized. He was the closest thing anybody had ever seen to The Perfect Plebe.

David Hand could do everything, and do it better than any new cadet in the company—hell, in the entire Beast Barracks regiment of plebes. At drill, his movements were crisp, precise, executed with an uncanny sense of timing, like a dancer. He could flip an M-14 rifle around like he'd spent four years on a high school ROTC drill team, which he had not. He picked up rifle drill fast and loose, the way he picked up everything else. Bayonet drill . . . he was like a combat vet, hungry and mean. The daily dozen . . . he could do more push-ups, more squat-jumps, more sit-ups, more of any exercise in the army daily dozen than anybody in the company.

Back in the barracks, his shoes, his clothing, his locker, his bed—all were exemplary. He learned Plebe

Knowledge a full two steps ahead of everyone else in the squad. He knew the famous "How is the cow?" poop when the rest of them were still stumbling over their three answers.

"Sir, she walks, she talks, she's full of chalk, the lacteal fluid extracted from the female of the bovine species is highly prolific to the nth degree." The words tumbled from his mouth like dice coming up seven every time, maddeningly perfect.

In the mess hall, he never made a mistake at the squad table. When it was his turn to be cold beverage corporal, the plebe who sat at the end of the table opposite Slaight, table commandant, Hand whipped out the beverages like he'd been born with a pitcher in one hand and a bucket of ice in the other, like a First Avenue singles bar bartender, he was so quick. It was impossible to catch Hand making a mistake because he simply did not make them. He was perfect.

But David Hand was a problem, because he was aloof from his classmates. Despite the frequent warnings of his squad leader, Slaight, who knew of such matters, Hand had an attitude. His attitude was aristocratic, mirrored like the toes of his shoes, shiny perfection. He was better than the rest of them, therefore he needn't stoop to their level. This was not the way of the plebe, and Hand knew it. He flaunted his attitude like an invisible red flag, and upperclassmen charged, only to be repelled by Hand's command of West Point's ways. He had the shit *down*.

Not so his roommates. Dippel and Woodruff were the squad fuck-ups, a pair of dufus beans who were lucky to put on their pants right-side-out in the morning. Nothing they did was right. Their shoes looked like somebody had shined them with a chocolate bar. Their uniforms hung like parachute cloth, billowing at the back, gathered at the ankles, draped in grubby folds from the shoulders. Their beds looked like they'd been made by the help at a cheap motel. When it came to marching, Dippel went one way and Woodruff the other. Marching in step, to the beat of the big bass drum, seemed a near impossibility. They bounced and bobbed against the tide of the company formation. They were out of synch. They were classic fuck-ups.

In any military organization, there is always congenital affection for true fuck-ups. The institution understands that they have to be protected—from themselves, as much as from anyone else. And there is humor. Fuck-ups are funny. They have to be. At bottom, humor is the final survival mechanism. Without a sense of humor, they might as well cash their checks. Hand's roommates fit the pattern. Dippel was so gangling and awkward, watching him get out of bed was like watching a baby bird trying to fly—all legs and wings, flapping around, sheets and blankets flying, everything moving except Dippel's torso, which attached itself to the mattress, refusing to budge until his bed self-destructed, taking with it the better part of his uniform supply, hanging in a neat row along the wall of his alcove next to his bed. By the time Dippel hit the deck, the area of his bunk looked eligible for federal disaster relief.

Woodruff was simply a monster—huge, at 250 pounds, six feet tall, one of those guys with *no neck* . . . his head disappeared into shoulders so huge it took three tailors to fit him for his uniforms, they hovered around him with pins sticking from their mouths, standing on little stepladders, chalking and pinning and muttering to each other. Woodruff's uniforms probably cost double the average cadet's.

He'd been recruited to play football, and though he was an excellent athlete, up in the barracks he was just plain slow. Everything he touched took time. If there was one thing plebes did not have, it was time. So Woodruff was late. Late. And later. He was the kind of guy who found zipping his pants a true challenge, who'd grab his roommate's toothbrush by mistake, and use it to apply polish to the soles of his shoes, then use his Brasso rag to spitshine them, removing another layer of carefully applied polish base with every turn of the cloth until finally it occurred to him that he was rubbing fresh polish on raw leather. . . . But like an athlete, Woodruff had an incredible ability to absorb the blows of Beast Barracks like a huge pillow. He could take it and take it and take it and still come back for more. When the whole squad was down in the dumps, having performed poorly at parade and received a half-hour ass-chewing from an irate squad leader replete with threats of punishment tours and loss of weekend privileges when they finally arrived, Woodruff was the guy who would rally the squad, get them together in his room, and ten minutes before taps, you could hear them. They'd be singing some marching-cadence lyric Woodruff had composed on the spur of the moment, usually at the expense of their nemesis, Slaight:

> *Hey! Hey! Beast Squad three!*
> *Who's the pride of the Infantry!*
> *It ain't Slaight*
> *And it ain't Buck*
> *So it can't be me!*
> *We got wrinkles*
> *We got knocks*
> *We got shoes*
> *That looks like socks!*
> *Take us marchin'*
> *With our guns*
> *This one's for fightin'*
> *This one's for fun!*
> *Hey! Hey! Beast Squad three!*
> *Which is the right end*
> *Of this here M-fourteen?*
> *I don't know*
> *But I been told*
> *That Rysam Slaight*
> *Is growin' old.*
> *Hey! Hey! Beast squad three!*
> *Newest record Slaight got*
> *Is Lewis, Jerry Lee!*

And so on.

Sitting in his room at the other end of the hall, Slaight could not keep himself from laughing as his squad yukked it up down in Room 1144. At moments like those, he could even bring himself to think there must be a worse

233

place on earth to be than West fuckin' Point. Right now, he couldn't think of one.

For the first two weeks of Beast, everything went by the book, or close to it. Then one morning at reveille, Slaight wandered out to formation to find a small but significant change. Dippel and Woodruff were standing in Late Ranks, where they could usually be found along with the rest of the company fuck-ups. This time, Hand, their roommate, wasn't with them. On the surface, it was a minor matter. Hand had left his room, heading out to formation without them. Until that morning, Dippel, Woodruff, and Hand could be found in Late Ranks at nearly every formation. Dippel was so spastic and Woodruff so slow, getting the two of them out to formation on time was a task beyond even the considerable talents of David Hand. And so Hand suffered the ignominious appearance in Late Ranks along with his roommates.

Slaight had been careful not to take Hand to task for his Late Ranks appearances. Clearly, it was not the fault of Hand that Room 1144 was usually late. In fact, Slaight had assigned Crolius, another guy from the squad, to help Dippel and Woodruff achieve the seemingly impossible rewards of being *on time*. It was beginning to work. Already they'd made it to quite a few formations on time, even if they did look a little sloppy. At least they knew it was possible. It was a matter of morale. Slaight wanted the squad to get that rush of togetherness . . . the special feeling he knew they'd have when they were pulling together and it was all working. They were on time. They looked good. They marched well. Nobody fell out of reveille runs. They could be proud. They would be a *unit*.

And now this. Dippel and Woodruff in Late Ranks. Hand in formation. Slaight let it slide. He wanted to see if it was a quirk, a temporary thing the three of them would repair by dinner formation. But all day it happened. Hand on time. Dippel and Woodruff in Late Ranks, looking worse and worse every time. Clearly, Hand had given up on his roommates. His aloofness from his classmates had reached a new high. Slaight told Hand to drive around

234

that night, twenty minutes before taps. It was time for a talking-to—one which Hand had had coming for a long time.

Hand knocked on Slaight's door three times at precisely 9:40 P.M. Slaight told him to enter and grab a piece of wall. Hand stood against the wall next to Slaight's desk, bracing. Slaight lectured about the rules of the game, that old thing about "co-operate and graduate." Hand listened respectfully . . . at least he didn't pipe up with a bunch of lame excuses. If there was one thing Slaight hated, it was a plebe who manufactured excuses for his fuck-ups. That was one of the few good things about Dippel and Woodruff. They didn't make excuses. They just were.

Slaight told Hand he hadn't gotten himself in trouble for helping his classmates. Everyone in the company, including the company commander, knew Hand was perfectly capable of being on time to formations. Hand wasn't running any risks of losing privileges or receiving demerits and landing punishment tours on the area. But Slaight knew there was a key element to that weird thing in the army about institutional affection for fuck-ups. The organization would tolerate them only so long as it sensed the fuck-ups were *trying*. Slaight knew the rest of his squad, similarly mired in the noxious fumes of Beasthood, sensed Dippel and Woodruff were at least trying. What about Hand?

"Nosir. I don't believe they are trying."

"What do you mean, Hand? I put Crolius in there helping you last week, and by last Friday, you two had them down into formation at least half the time. They're not trying? You got to give them a goddamn chance, Hand. That's all."

"I just don't think . . . I don't believe . . . they're trying, sir. If they are . . . well, then, sir, they just don't have it."

"What do you mean, smack, they don't have it? Who are you to determine whether or not they have it, whatever the fuck *it* is?" Slaight was angry, but Hand remained impassive, bracing against his wall.

"Sir, I've spent two weeks down in Late Ranks with
235

Dippel and Woodruff, getting laughed at and hazed by the first-classmen. I've given them as much time as I believe they deserve. If they want to spend the rest of their days in Late Ranks, sir, that's up to them. I am determined to make it my business to be on time from now on."

Slaight was nearly seething with rage. But there was nothing he could do. Ultimately, whether or not Hand helped his roommates get to formation on time affected the performance, thus the morale of his squad. But classmates helping each other was something worked out between classmates. Technically, Slaight could not order Hand to help them. But there was something in the tone of Hand's voice . . . he didn't like the ridicule and abuse he suffered in Late Ranks because Dippel and Woodruff couldn't get their shit together. That was understandable. But something else ate at Hand. Slaight smelled it.

"Hand. What else is going on in your room? What's bothering you about Dippel and Woodruff? I don't think this Late Ranks thing is the whole story. Now give me the rest of the poop."

Hand paused. Slaight knew he'd been right.

"Sir, it's not Woodruff. He's okay. He's just, you know, sir. Slow. But Dippel. It's different with him, sir. I just can't take Dippel any more."

"Come on. Out with it, Hand. This is just between you and me. Close the door." Hand closed it. "Now fall out. Relax. I want to hear it. What you say to me will remain in confidence."

"Sir, Dippel has been buying favors from others guys in the squad in return for fixing them up with dates as soon as privileges start. Last week his mother sent his high school yearbook up from the Bronx, and he's been spreading the word around he'll fix you up with a date, if you'll help him out with stuff. Like guard mount. One guy took his guard mount last week. Another guy has been shining his shoes. Somebody else has been coming into the room before reveille and making his bed while Dippel gets dressed. For all of these guys, he's done this: He takes out his yearbook, and he lets them pick out a girl's picture. Then he writes his mother a letter and asks her to

236

get the guy a blind date with the girl. They all live down in the Bronx, so they're close enough to come up here when weekend privileges start. I just don't like it, sir. It's like he's buying his way through Beast. He's pimping for these guys so he won't take so much gas."

Slaight was stunned. What Hand said made perfect sense. He couldn't blame him. West Pointers were conditioned to despise weakness in those around them, and there was a reason for it, like there was a goddamn reason for everything else at West Point. Weakness was contagious. If you stayed near it long enough, some of it would rub off. In a small military unit like a squad, this was especially true. Hand had suffered the rigors of Late Ranks with Woodruff and Dippel for two weeks, and now here was Dippel, trying to trade blind dates for "favors." The favors were actually the stuff he was supposed to learn how to get done for himself every day. Because Hand had revealed Dippel's seedy practice to Slaight in confidence, there was nothing he could do about it for now; not unless someone else in the squad made a formal, aboveboard complaint about Dippel. Unlikely, so long as they all believed Dippel was the pathway of least resistance where girls were concerned. Slaight remembered what it had been like coming to West Point from Kansas . . . not knowing any girls . . . it had taken months to get fixed up with a date as a plebe. Dippel had quite a scam going.

"Look, Hand. I see your point about Dippel. And I appreciate your candor. But I've got to warn you. You'd better spend some time figuring out how you're going to handle this thing with your roommates. I can't order you to help those guys. What's between classmates is between classmates. But it's like I told you on the first day of Beast, remember? You've got to live with those guys. It's like you're married to the fuckers. And at West Point, it's like the Catholics. They don't recognize divorces here, right? Understand?"

Hand nodded.

"Now post on out of here back to your room. It's almost taps."

Hand saluted and left. Slaight had a new respect for Hand. The kid had principles, he thought. He was aloof, and being aloof was going to get him into trouble—sooner rather than later. But now Slaight knew there was substance behind Hand's style, camouflaged by his aloofness. Or there was something back there, anyway—something Slaight hadn't seen yet. He couldn't be sure. He went back to work on his squad book. In the distance, one of the Hellcats blew taps. It was 10 P.M., and Beast was just about half over for Ry Slaight and the rest of the First Detail July upperclassmen.

21

Almost nightly, the plebes received training on the Honor Code, traditionally, the sacred cornerstone upon which the academy has been said to rest. In fact, the class had been at West Point only a few days when they were introduced to the code formally. Most of them knew about the Honor Code in advance, having read in the West Point catalogue, which had been mailed to all candidates, that "A Cadet does not lie, cheat, or steal." That was the code, lock, stock, and barrel. Or was it?

Omitted from official documents relating to the code was the so-called toleration clause, which required—and still requires—that cadets report any and all violations of the code to which they are witness, or be expelled as an honor violator for having failed to make a report. But knowledge of the toleration clause would come soon. For the time being, the Honor Code seemed simple. The thing which lay behind the code would be explained to them at a lecture delivered by the chairman of the Cadet Honor Committee.

The new cadets attended the lecture at night, after supper, in a huge auditorium. It would soon become known to them as "South Aud." Sweating, wet from the heat outside, they froze within the air-conditioned cavernous hall, located in what was once the old Cadet Riding Hall, Thayer Hall, a place of the 1920s and 1930s, of mandatory equestrian training for cadets, of polo practice and saddle soap and the brown-shoe army. The old Riding Hall, now the main academic building at the academy, was drenched in tradition, with an overpowering air of those who had come before: the Long Gray Line. But who, exactly, was the Long Gray Line? With the exception of a few heroes like Eisenhower, MacArthur, Patton, and Pershing, the new cadets didn't know. But they were in awe. It was the business of plebes to be forever in awe.

A tall, good-looking upperclassman with burred, white-sidewall crew cut, wearing many stripes on the sleeve of his Dress Gray coat, stepped before the class. They nearly gasped. He was the commander of Beast Barracks—the "King of Beasts" they called him, a guy named VanRiper. He was also the Chairman of the Honor Committee, and as he spoke of the code, his voice carried the echoes of the old Riding Hall itself.

"This is *your* code," said VanRiper. "It belongs to *you*." He struck an impressive, cinematic figure in his crisp white trousers and Dress Gray coat. The new cadets listened raptly.

"In the next two months, you will attend many meetings. The workings of the code will be explained to you in detail, by your company honor representative and others. If you have any questions, you should ask them."

VanRiper lectured in general terms on the Honor System, the mechanism by which the code was administered by the cadet upper classes. Then he dropped his voice. In low, serious tones through the PA, he told the new cadets the real reason they were in South Aud this night.

Because the Honor Code belonged to the cadets, they were to talk about it with no one outside the Corps of Cadets. Outsiders had no business with the code. His implication was unavoidable. Upon entering West Point and taking the oath, the new cadets were bound by a trust as solemn as the Oath of Allegiance itself to reveal to no one the most important truths of their lives as cadets. He sug-

239

gested the new cadets not discuss the code even among themselves. They would receive adequate instruction on the code and the Honor System, and if they had any questions or doubts, they should be taken directly to the company honor representative, a first-classman. Discussion of the code among new cadets was dangerous, VanRiper explained. It often led to misinterpretation and misconceptions, either of which could lead further to the dread honor *violation,* the lone penalty for which was expulsion from the Corps.

It was a narrow, dangerous path along which they would move for the next four years. The only way to reach the end was to follow rules. All you had to do was not lie, cheat, or steal, and you were assured passage into that void known as graduation. There was holiness in the Honor Code that was hard to miss. At meetings with company honor reps, pronouncements about the code were delivered in evangelical tones. This was true when the new cadets were counseled to turn in even their best friends or roommates, should they commit an honor violation. The new cadets owed only one higher allegiance, and that was to God. Short of Him, the code was all.

By the third week of Beast, David Hand recognized perfection in a system requiring him to subordinate all emotion, logic, and reason to a higher goal. So much about Beast was petty, worthless, without meaning. The Honor Code could be *used.* Though the code did not remove completely the desirability of establishing deep and lasting friendships with classmates, it did provide an excuse if one was needed. Hand grabbed it. The code put most new cadets on the defensive. The code assumed you were at once cop and criminal, best friend and secret agent. The code was vertical. Every cadet's allegiance was directed upward, to the code. But not David Hand's. He found a more comfortable allegiance, closer to home: himself. He'd play by the rules, all right. The rules protected him. Deftly, Hand had figured the Honor Code's greatest shortcoming and turned it to his advantage.

The Honor System defined the code's strictures along

finite lines, spelling out in detail exactly what was considered lying, cheating, and stealing. Additionally, the Honor System defined the slightest deviation from the code as "quibbling," failure to tell "the whole truth." In delineating the code, however, the Honor System necessarily established those areas which lay outside its scope. The black-and-white Honor Code was surrounded by a gray sea through which one could swim with alacrity. Thus Hand uncovered the secret of the West Point Honor Code only a few understood as well as he. By consciously defining for its young men what they could *not* do, West Point unconsciously established what they *could* do. They could search out the edges of the code and walk them expertly. To David Hand, the West Point Honor Code mirrored the society from which he came. In New Orleans, rules abounded. Finding your way around them was how you got ahead. It was an orderly system with chaos at its core. Mardi Gras alone was evidence that madness was necessary to complete the social equation in New Orleans. At West Point, the equation was more complex—differential instead of algebraic—thus more profound. Plebe year was West Point's Mardi Gras. And the Honor Code provided the masks behind which the academy hid its true identity.

David Hand embraced the Honor Code because it was familiar territory. Its beautiful irony—by identifying evil, the code emboldened cadets to explore and closely acquaint themselves with its cousin, the edge—fascinated Hand, entranced him. The Honor Code offered him a system he accepted unquestioningly. Hand had never taken anything seriously in his life. Examining the code and its myriad nuances, he found he needed it. The Honor Code gave order to his life. The Honor Code epitomized a creature Hand found irresistible: Proud, dignified, taut with military bearing and discipline, dedicated to principles larger than the self, the code's vision of an ideal cadet was ineluctably masculine.

David Hand fell in love with the Honor Code early the third week of Beast Barracks.

Slaight was casting wildly about for a way to flush out Dippel and his crummy little scheme, getting guys to run errands for him, in return for blind dates on weekends. Slaight imagined him, sitting in his room, flipping through the pages of his yearbook, each photo of a pretty girl like money in the goddamn bank. Slaight was pissed. Nobody from the squad was coming forward because they all saw Dippel and his magic yearbook as the only game in town, which indeed it was. But doing a guy a favor was one thing. Pimping for personal profit was something else. In desperation, Slaight decided to call together his squad one night and hold what was known in those days as a "manhood session." He would ask his squad of eleven men, bracing in a semicircle around his desk, who among them was still a virgin. Maybe that would flush out Dippel and put the hammer on his little operation. He called for the squad. When they were positioned, he asked:

"Okay, beans. Who among you is still cherry? We got any virgins in this squad, any of you little bastards not gotten laid by your girl friends back home? Come on. Let's see it."

The new cadets chanced anxious glances at one another, to see if anyone would thrust forward a fist—the cadet equivalent of raising one's hand—the nearly sacrosanct admission he hadn't "gotten any" from his girl friend. There was a moment's pause as they inspected each other. Slaight watched the scene with detached amusement, recalling the exact same moment his plebe year during Beast, the exact same feeling. He'd been the only one in the squad to hold out his fist. Slaight watched the anxiety in the room heat to a cherry glow. For sure, that dufus Dippel, who couldn't get his pecker out without catching it in his zipper, would be the one. David Hand stuck out his fist. Slaight was wrong. His plan backfired. But he had to play it out.

"Ah. Hand. Still cherry, huh?"

"Yessir," Hand answered matter-of-factly.

"Can't hear you, Hand. You saying you haven't gotten any from your girl friend back home?"

"YESSIR," said Hand, his fist still at right angles to his body.

Fuckin' kid's got guts. He surveyed the rest of the squad to see if any of the rest of them would snicker at Hand. This was their chance to get back at the guy who had been lording it over them for the past two weeks, the guy who could do everything better than they could. Slaight pitied Hand when he and his roommates reached their room. Hand would never see the end of this. He remembered his own experience as a plebe, the total humiliation . . . the ribbing and cutting the rest of the guys had done . . . *cherry* . . . *cherry* . . . *cherry*. . . . Slaight regretted he had called the "manhood session." Not only had his Dippel plan failed, but it backfired on Hand, guy who'd pulled Dippel through his first two weeks of Beast. Jesus. There was something about Hand . . . something admirable about his arrogance.

"Stand at attention, Hand," commanded Slaight. He had to do something.

"If I hear any of you fuckers dishing out shit to Hand because he had the balls to admit he's still cherry . . . if I hear one fuckin' *peep* outta you beans, I'll have every last one of you decorating the walls in here until the end of this detail, right up to the minute I go on leave. Is that understood?"

"YESSIR!" The squad chorused the word.

"It just so happens, gentlemen, that my squad leader held a manhood session exactly like this one when I was a beanhead in Beast. And I was the poor fuckin' smack, the only cherry beanhead in the squad, and I was standing there with my fist in the air like some kinda goddamn goon, just like Hand. So I know how it feels. Now, you smacks post back to your rooms and get your fannies ready for bed. And remember. If I hear one goddamn word, that man's gonna wish to hell he'd never dipped his fuckin' wick, I'm going to sweat so much of his neck up against my wall. You got that?"

"YESSIR!"

"Now, POST."

They left on the double.

Over the next few days, Hand grew more distant from his roommates . . . from the whole squad. You could see it. Hand would show up out in the ranks for a formation. He'd be the first one out there, maybe two or three minutes early. And there he'd stand, all alone, until the rest of them would arrive. They'd move in next to him without exchanging secret glances, the way plebes always did, trying to beat the system, get away with breaking little rules like muttering 'heeeeaauh," that seal-honk, the way Slaight and Buck used to do when they were plebes. Leroy Buck was a squad leader in one of the other platoons in Slaight's company, and the two of them stayed up late nights talking about the David Hand situation. It seemed irresoluble. Hand was just as stiff, just as arrogant, just as perfect in his own special way as his classmates, the rest of the squad, were tight-knit as a team. They were like mutually opposing forces, like-poles of two magnets, repelling each other. The truly remarkable thing was that Hand alone appeared to have the strength of the other ten altogether.

Slaight watched them carefully. No one was taunting Hand, at least not out in the open where he could see it. But he could imagine the little diddlyshit that was going on behind closed doors after taps at night, the snide comments, the slippery crap guys pulled on other guys, especially when they were forced to be as close together as a squad in Beast Barracks.

Still, Hand managed to maintain his own. When Woodruff would hold one of his song sessions in Room 1144, Hand would find a reason to be down in the sinks, shaving or taking a shower by himself. He would return to his room precisely at taps, just as the Hellcat began blowing taps, before the cadet in charge of quarters (the CQ) would hit the 11th Division yelling "ALLRIGHT," the old cadet password, echoed by each successive cadet room up the stairwell, from 1111 on up to 1144, signaling that each cadet was present and accounted for at taps, negating the need for a physical inspection of rooms. Hand would make it back to his room before taps, before the Allright, after the rest of the squad had returned to their

244

rooms. He didn't want to have much to do with them, nor they with him.

Morale in the squad bottomed. They *sagged,* the plebes, slogging their way through each day without enthusiasm, without the sense of irony and humor so necessary . . . so necessary to fuckin' *survive.* They weren't surviving. The squad was dying. Slaight began to have premonitions of mass resignations. He felt guilty and helpless. Guilty because it had been he who had forced the issue with Hand. And helpless because Hand was such an ironheaded bastard, as inflexible as the Military Academy itself. There seemed little Slaight could do to bring Hand and the squad back together. He couldn't patch things up. He and Leroy Buck pondered the problem. There just didn't seem to be anything they could do. Hand was such a plucky scrapper of a guy, they both began wondering if he came from Cajun stock down in New Orleans. But there was something else about him, something . . . well . . . *prudish.* That was it. Hand was a goddamn prude. Thinking he was better than the rest of them was conceited, stuffy, morally superior. Slaight began to wonder. He'd never seen anyone quite like Hand before, anyone tied in such a neat, impregnable knot. Slaight wondered if there wasn't something hiding inside Hand's knot. Having no patience for the incompetence and weaknesses of the other guys in the squad was one thing. But Hand really *hated* it. He *hated* weakness. He hated weakness like nobody Slaight had ever seen before. And so Slaight wondered: Why? Why?

He called Hand into his room once or twice for regular counseling sessions—the whole squad got the same counseling so nobody could accuse Hand of receiving special treatment. He told Hand to relax, chatted with him, probed him, tried to figure where all that hate was coming from. Hand wouldn't open up. Not a crack. Slaight learned only one thing in his sessions with Hand, something he would never have suspected without those informal chats. Hand knew nothing—absolutely nothing—about Slaight and his sister, Samantha. It seemed amazing at first, and Slaight probed, tested, talked

245

openly of Vassar and Vassar girls in general, giving Hand every opportunity to let on that he knew Slaight and his sister had gone steady. Finally the conclusion was inescapable. Samantha had told her brother nothing about Ry Slaight. Hand didn't know.

Another day passed without incident. Slaight was getting more and more depressed. If you couldn't lash together a goddamn squad of beanheads, then what the fuck could you do with yourself? Doubt nagged at him like a vulture. He figured any minute the Big Wazoo was gonna come down and call his number, and that was gonna be it, man. It.

At 7 P.M., right after supper, a loud, single knock came on his door.

"Enter."

"Sir, New Cadet Hand requests permission to speak." Hand was in the door, stiffly at attention, impeccable as usual.

"Come on in, Hand. What's on your mind?" It looked like Hand had finally come around to complain that he was getting razzed by his roommates. Then he saw Hand's face. For the first time all week, he looked calm. Content. Hand stood bracing in front of Slaight's desk, eyes riveted on a spot on the wall above Slaight's head.

"Sir, I would like to report a man for an honor violation, and I was wondering, sir. Are you the man to whom I should report?" Slaight grimaced. Here it comes.

"Yeah. What is it? Who is it? Relax, Hand. Sit down. Tell me the whole thing, beginning to end."

Hand sat down in a chair across the desk from Slaight, his back straight, head thrust forward. He spelled out what he had defined for himself as a textbook case of quibbling. It seemed that Crolius, a short, hawk-faced miner's son from the hill country of Kentucky, had confided in Hand that day—after three days of silence on the matter—that he was not a virgin, exactly, but he was "kind of a virgin, you know, if you want to look at it that way," as Hand recalled Crolius' words. Their conversation had taken place that afternoon in the showers. Hand was the last one down in the sinks showering after bayonet drill, and Crolius had remained after the others had gone upstairs. He obviously felt sorry for Hand and the way he'd been treated by the rest of the squad since the manhood session three days ago. So Crolius had decided to confide in Hand, believing Hand would feel better knowing there was another guy in the squad who was . . . well . . . uncertain about his manhood.

"Kind of a virgin, you know, if you want to look at it that way" was a rarefied definition of sexual experience to which eighteen-year-olds were privy in a lonesome way in those days. Crolius was going steady with his high school girl friend back home in Kentucky, and just before he had left for the academy, in a fit of passion, they had gotten into some heavy petting. Once or twice—he couldn't remember exactly—he'd gotten his penis out of his pants, and his girl friend had fondled it. And once he had gotten her pants down, and he poked his penis around "down there," as Crolius told Hand, and he had come. That much was for sure, he said. There had been "one hell of a goddamn mess." But he couldn't be sure he had gotten "inside." Now you could take getting "inside," or you could leave it, so far as Crolius was concerned. The whole thing sure had felt good, he told Hand.

Hand asked him if he was going to tell Slaight that he was still "cherry," and Crolius had said, hell no, far as he was concerned, messing around down there and getting off was "it." David Hand wasn't so sure. In fact, he told Slaight, the more he thought about it during supper, the more he figured Crolius had quibbled when he hadn't stuck out his fist at the manhood session, admitting he was "cherry." He was as much as admitting he quibbled now, explaining his doubt that he had gotten "inside." Hand related his interpretation of the facts with a self-satisfied look on his face.

"Are you serious about this, Hand?" Slaight asked incredulously.

"Yessir. Quite serious. The man quibbled. I want to report him."

Slaight tried to poke holes in Hand's interpretation of the definition of quibbling, pointing out that to Crolius,

247

what he had done had been "it" so far as he was concerned. And when it came to quibbling, the intent to deceive was all-important. How could Crolius have an intent to deceive, when he'd just spelled out to Hand in graphic detail his own sexual experience? Hand stood fast. He had listened to the lectures from the company honor representative with the six senses of a goddamn eagle, and he was convinced he had caught Crolius quibbling. He was going to see Crolius tried before the Honor Committee for not having joined him in sticking out his fist at the manhood session. Slaight was dumbfounded. He stared hard across the desk, fixed Hand's eyes, and held them.

"Hand, you dullard, don't you realize Crolius is the only goddamn friend you've got in this squad? He was the guy who helped you last week with those out-of-control roommates of yours, Dippel and Woodruff. Only when you and Crolius were working together on them did their shit finally start coming together. Crolius didn't have to give you any help. They weren't his goddamn roommates. He did it to help *you* as much as them. He did it to help the squad, dammit. Don't you understand that?"

"Yessir. I understand. His behavior last week in no way obviates the fact that today he quibbled."

"What the fuck are you talking about, Hand? Crolius came to you. He volunteered the information. You didn't catch him hiding anything . . . lying, for crying out loud. He wasn't hiding. It was his way of letting you know that you might still be a virgin, but he identifies with you, Hand. Don't you see that?"

"Yessir. I still say the man quibbled."

"Quibbling. Jesus. You know what a broad fuckin' area quibbling is, Hand? You know how fuckin' broad it is? Lemme tell you. You don't. And what you're going to do if you go the next step with this, which is to the company honor representative, what you're going to do is open up a whole big can of fuckin' worms you know nothing— *nothing*—about, you understand me? You're going to create an enormous amount of trouble for Crolius, who's only trying to be a friend to you, the only decent fucker in the whole damn squad. And you're going to plunge him
248

into deep shit, Hand. He might go up before the Honor Committee. He might not. But it doesn't really matter. The minute you report him to the honor rep, you're going to create doubt in everybody's minds about old Crolius. No matter what happens to him from that time on, his reputation as a cadet will be stained until the day he leaves this goddamn place. You understand what I'm telling you, mister? You understand the gravity of the situation you're creating here? You're fuckin' around with another man's *life,* Hand. Has that thought occurred to you?"

"Yessir."

"And you still figure you're willing to fuck with another man's life because you've got quibbling fuckin' *down,* is that it, Hand?"

"Yessir."

"Well, I knew you were an arrogant little prick, but I guess I just never knew how arrogant. You amaze me, Hand. You really do." Slaight sat there staring at him. Hand stared back, impassive. Emotionless.

"I'll tell you what I'm gonna do, Hand. I'm gonna tell you a little story about old Ry Slaight, just like I told the squad the other day that I had to be the only one to admit I was cherry back in my Beast squad. I'm gonna teach you a fuckin' lesson about quibbling, mister. Then you can make up your mind whether you still want to see the honor rep. Got that?"

"Yessir."

"Now listen-up, Hand. One weekend last year, I was on a trip-section down to New York, and me and a couple of other guys checked into the Statler Hilton in our uniforms, our Dress Gray uniforms. Some chicks noticed us down in the lobby, and in a few minutes, up in our rooms, just as we're changing into civvies and getting ready for a night on the town, there comes this knock at the door. These girls are all from Seton Hall, a Catholic girls' school near here. And they're all in formal gowns. It's their big class ball at the Waldorf Hotel, uptown, seventy-five fuckin' bucks a head. And one of them got stood up by some Princeton preppie fuck-stick. So they asked me and this classmate of mine, John Lugar, if one of us would wear our uniform and take the girl who got stood up to the ball at the Waldorf. She'd shelled out $150, and this stupid shit from Princeton had taken a walk on her, and there she was downstairs in some room crying her little beadies out. So to make a long story short, me and Lugar flipped and I lost. I put my uniform back on, went downstairs to pick her up, and she turns out to be a goddamn fox! At least 2.8 out of 3.0. I mean a looker. So I lucked out—a good-looking chick, tickets to a $150 dinner-dance—what more could I ask, right?"

"Yessir."

"So I take her up to the Waldorf with the rest of these hens and their dates from Princeton and Yale and places like that. I'm in my Dress Gray. And who do I run into up there, but some dufus firstie, who comes up to me, right in front of the girl, and asks me what I'm doing in Dress Gray at a formal ball, where I should be wearing *full* Dress Gray, the formal uniform. I told him how I'd gotten roped into escorting this girl I didn't even know, and he wanders off, and I thought everything was cool. Then I get back here to West Point, and Sunday night, the honor rep comes around to my room and tells me I've been reported for quibbling by some firstie. Said the guy had reported me for an "intent to deceive" because these civilians didn't know the goddamn difference between Dress Gray and full Dress Gray, and he just figured I was trying to pull a fast one on them. Well. I mean, Jesus! I thought I was doing the noble cadet thing, right? And I get reported for fuckin' 'quibbling,' by some half-wit firstie from another company who doesn't know me, never seen me in his life. Man, I was pissed. Anyway, the thing goes to an honor subcommittee, and ends there. I explained to them what the story was, and they killed the charges. The honor rep told me he knew it was a crock of shit, but he had to take it to the subcommittee, because that's the way the system works. You getting what I'm telling you, Hand?"

"Yessir."

"Are you sure, mister?"

"Yessir."

250

"So you understand what I mean about this quibbling thing. It's a can of goddamn worms, Hand. It's like this gigantic gray area in the system. I know they tell you there's no gray areas—there's only black and fuckin' white. But I've been here two years longer than you, Hand, and I've seen the system work, up close. I've seen the Honor Committee come swooping down on a guy, and before you know it, he's gone, and you never even find out what he was supposed to have done. Then you hear about another guy who's done some outrageous shit, and the Honor Committee finds a goddamn loophole in the Honor System, and he's let off the hook. Before the Honor Committee, Hand, there are no rules of evidence, no procedural rights, no right to representation by counsel, no right to confront witnesses against you . . . not a solitary goddamn right you are afforded as a citizen of the United States under the Bill of Rights. The Honor Code is a hell of a good thing, Hand. Nobody can argue with those words, 'A cadet does not lie, cheat, or steal.' But Jesus, the Honor Committee—sometimes they operate like they're wearing black hoods, sometimes they decide the fate of a guy in a matter of seconds, and it's a decision that's going to follow the guy all his life. Nobody's perfect, Hand. These guys who end up as honor reps on the Honor Committee, that doesn't make them any more perfect than you or me or the guys who are charged with honor violations whose cases they've got to hear. Now listen-up to me, Hand. You listening?"

"Yessir."

"I am not sitting here telling you I don't believe in the Honor Code. I believe in the code as much as any other swinging dick around here. But I've got my problems with the Honor System. It seems to me—hell, it's been my *experience*—that there are just too fuckin' many opportunities for abuses within the system, and not enough protections for individuals, which is you and me—and Crolius. Am I making myself clear, Hand?"

"Yessir."

"The single fact that a man cannot confront the witnesses against him just turns my fuckin' stomach,

251

Hand. It makes me sick. Turns a goddamn Honor Board into a kangaroo court, is what it does. And some of these guys I've seen kicked out of here on honor. Jesus. I wish you could see them when they go. It's fuckin' pathetic. They're turned into overnight outcasts. Lepers. So lemme tell you something, Hand. If you go to the honor rep with this thing Crolius told you this afternoon, you are fuckin' with another man's life, and you're fuckin' with it in a very, very serious way. So you better be very, very serious about your convictions. And you better be sure of your motives, mister. You ever heard the old saying 'Discretion is the better part of valor'?"

"Yessir."

"Yeah. Well, around here it could use a little rewording. At West Point, discretion is the better part of honor. And the discretion belongs to you, Hand. *You.* I've told you my experiences, and I've told you my judgment on this. I don't think Crolius was quibbling. I don't think the little fucker is *capable* of quibbling. Don't think it'd even occur to him. Where he comes from, getting it is probably just getting it, any old fuckin' way. Hell, they probably bang sheep in his home county. Who knows? And if you bang a sheep, are you still cherry? Shit, Hand. Crolius was treating you honorably. He was taking you into his confidence. If you report him for quibbling, you better have your shit together, and you better have it together good. Because the whole fuckin' world is liable to come down on that smart-ass head of yours if you don't. Now. You made up your mind?"

"Yessir."

"What are you gonna do, Hand?"

"I am going to report Crolius to the honor representative, sir. The man quibbled. His case belongs before the Honor Committee, not here, between us."

Slaight stood up. Hand stood up.

"I hope you know what you're doing, Hand, because the minute you walk out of this room and head over to the honor rep, your actions are going to follow you and follow you just like a goddamn shadow, and no matter where you go, no matter what you do, no matter the resolution of the case, you're never gonna get away from that shadow, Hand. Never."

"I am sure, sir. Good evening, sir." Hand saluted and departed.

He reported Crolius to the company honor rep that night. The honor rep made his report to the full Honor Committee, which authorized a subcommittee hearing, the Honor System equivalent of a grand jury. The subcommittee decided that the case should go before a full twelve-man Honor Board, the system's equivalent of a trial. All of this happened within a matter of two hours after Hand left Slaight's room.

The next night, the Cadet Honor Board met to hear Crolius' case. He had been given less than twenty-four hours to prepare a "defense." Slaight had never really understood what an accused cadet was permitted to do before a full Honor Board—just sit there silently, defend himself, call witnesses, who knew? The whole business was shrouded in a mystique manufactured into the Honor System by design. The mystique kicked the whole idea of "honor" onto a higher realm . . . a higher realm than, say, the cadet realm. This was, after all, *honor*. And a cadet was only a cadet.

Slaight didn't understand how the system worked, but he knew board hearings were open to upperclassmen, so he decided to attend. Crolius was called. He was first. At a long felt-covered table, twelve first-classmen sat in their Dress Gray coats and peppered Crolius with a rapid-fire series of picky little questions about exactly what words he'd used to tell Hand this and tell Hand that. Crolius, who had been a new cadet exactly nineteen days, was completely intimidated. He got so entangled in his story of sexual experiences, he only served to confuse the board, which interpreted Crolius' frightened behavior as further evidence of quibbling. It was a vicious circle. Crolius was damned if he did and damned if he didn't.

Slaight stood up in the back of the room and asked to volunteer as a witness in Crolius' behalf, since he had been the first person to whom the new cadet's alleged "violation" had been reported. He explained he was Crolius'

253

squad leader, he knew the young man well, and that he thought he could clear up some of the confusion caused by Crolius' obvious misunderstanding of the proceedings.

The chairman of the Honor Board ruled Slaight was out of order, and commanded him to sit down. Crolius turned and looked at Slaight. He knew he was finished, and he didn't know why. Slaight and Crolius were dismissed from the hearing room. A few minutes later, a representative from the Honor Board fetched them from the hallway. The chairman of the Honor Board pronounced the verdict. Guilty. The board had not even bothered to call Hand to testify.

Crolius was served with papers asking that he in good faith and in keeping with the tenets of the Honor Code resign from the academy. The board had no power to officially expel a cadet from the academy. They could only ask him to resign. But all cadets understood. Anybody who didn't resign, who one way or another retained status as a cadet, would be "silenced." No further explanation was necessary. Crolius agreed to resign. It was 11:30 P.M., July 19, 1967. Crolius hadn't been a new cadet for three weeks yet. He hadn't been allowed his first weekend privileges. Only nineteen days had elapsed since the first day of Beast, and already the Cadet Honor Committee was ousting a new cadet for the offense of "quibbling," an offense so broad and so dangerously vague it boggled Slaight's imagination. He was pissed. At himself for having held the manhood session in the first place. At the Honor Committee, for coming on like a bunch of goddamn Nazis, for not giving the kid a chance to explain himself in his slow Kentucky drawl. And he was pissed at David Hand, because Hand had violated Crolius' confidence, he'd stepped on the only guy who had reached out to him. Hand thought he was better than Crolius. Hell, he thought he was better than everybody.

Late that night, Crolius was moved from his room in the 11th Division of barracks to a place called the Boarders' Ward, a no man's land where resignees and others leaving the academy for one reason or another were interred until they could be outprocessed. It was the final

254

humiliation. They were no longer cadets. They were "boarders."

Slaight took David Hand over to the Boarders' Ward the next night. He took him to the room where Crolius sat alone on his bunk, waiting to go back to Kentucky and explain to his parents and his friends and his high school teachers and to the editor of the local paper who had run a front-page story on Crolius congratulating him for being the first town son to be appointed to West Point, and to his girl friend and to her parents—to everybody in his little town in Kentucky—how he had come to resign from the Military Academy so suddenly, where for almost three weeks in the letters he wrote home, he had seemed so happy and so proud. Crolius was sitting there on his bunk in his khakis. It was clear he understood so little about why he was leaving, he was at a loss for words. In his mind, West Point and honor were one. Now he was leaving West Point because of honor, but he didn't understand why. Slaight ordered David Hand into the room and said:

"Hand. You're the man who reported Crolius for what you alleged was quibbling. Now he's got to go home and explain the whole thing to everybody. You sit down here, Hand, and you explain to Crolius why he was found guilty by the Honor Board. You explain to him why he was asked to resign. You explain to him, Hand, why he, Crolius, 'quibbled.' When you're through explaining your extensive understanding of Crolius' fate to him, you report back to my room." Slaight walked out, leaving accuser and accused alone.

Hand reported to Slaight after fifteen minutes with Crolius. He had been unmoved. A violation was a violation. Crolius had quibbled. The Honor Board had found him guilty. He had agreed to resign. The system had worked. What was important to Hand was not Crolius, the man. What was important was the system. Hand had seen Crolius ousted from the academy for "quibbling." He thought he knew how the system worked.

Slaight dismissed Hand. He sat at his desk alone. So Hand thought he knew the system now, huh? Well, he'd give Hand a brand-new view of the system at work, *up*

255

close. He'd take Hand on a journey through the system, through the digestive process which consumed young American boys and produced cadets and eventually, Regular Army officers. It would take time, and it would take thought, and it would take careful, well-planned, and elegantly executed action. But in the end, he'd get inside David Hand and find whatever little worm was in there calling itself a soul and confront the little fucker. Everything up until now, including the Honor Board exercise with Crolius, would seem like so much pitty-pat when Slaight was through with David Hand. Slaight would move on Hand, and he'd move on him for the next twelve days like he was running a goddamn tactical military operation. After all, he reasoned with a certain smile, wasn't that what he'd been trained for?

Taps sounded. Slaight had fucked up, and fucked up but good. Dippel was still running his two-bit operation out of Room 1144. Crolius was gone. Squad morale had ebbed to an all-time low. But Slaight still had twelve days before the end of the First Detail of Beast Barracks. And David Hand remained. He would be dealt with. No doubt about it.

22

It was the way of Beast Barracks. One little mistake, one miserable little slip, one step out of line, just one—*one, goddammit*—and that was it. The whole thing came crashing down around your ears. It was the same for both plebes and upperclassmen, or seemed that way.

If a plebe fucked up, it was like his life came to a screeching halt. Suddenly, nothing he did was right. Everything was wrong. He'd be standing out in the area, look down, and discover that one of his shoes was untied. Just when he figured he'd finally gotten his shit together! What to do? Reach down and tie it, and risk getting caught, making a personal correction in ranks? Or wait for the inevitable arrival of the squad leader, his slow pacing of the squad—he'd notice the untied shoe. You just *knew* he would. He'd look down and see the laces flopping on the ground, and he'd look up, fix the plebe with his eyes, and say something like . . .

Well, well, well, Mr. Dumb Crot. What have we here? A clown act? You tryin' for some kinda award or somethin'? Who you thing you are, anyway? Charlie fuckin' Chaplin? Baggy pants, untied shoes, a goddamn dress-off that looks like somebody inflated a basketball and stuck it up the back of your shirt. You look like a goddamn clown, mister. You don't belong in this squad, you don't belong in this company, you don't belong in Beast Barracks, you don't belong in West Point, you belong in a *goddamn circus.* Now *DRIVE AROUND* to my room tonight at 2130, and I wanna see that uniform of yours sparkle. I wanna see you shine, mister. You hear me? I wanna look up and see you standin' there in the door of my room lookin' so fuckin' good you *sparkle* you hear me talkin'? You're gonna *blind me,* mister, you're gonna put my fuckin' eyes out you're lookin' so . . . *so cool.* . . .

And the plebe is YESSIR—YESSIR—YESSIR—YESSIRing up a storm, the squad leader is standing an inch away yelling in his ear, and the whole world is falling, falling right down around the plebe's ears, the whole thing is gonna stop, the whole goddamn place is gonna *crack*—It's all become too goddamn much, too much to handle.

It could be equally bad for the squad leader, maybe even worse. He's got eleven guys to take care of, eleven goddamn plebes, eleven separate walking duffel bags of problems. This one's got bad teeth, gotta get them fixed. That one can't swim a stroke, he's never been in water in his life, he's gotta be coached and coached so he'll make it through Plebe Orientation Swimming, so he'll make it through Beast and at least get a shot at takin' swimming in Plebe PE during the regular year.

And that one over there, the one with the ears sticking out from the sides of his head like a couple of big oak

257

leaves, the one with the nose, looks like somebody yanked at it with a pair of vice grips, the one whose arms are so long his hands are hanging down around his knees—yeah, *that* one—he's a fuckin' *case,* a textbook case, lemme tell you. You talk about your fuck-ups—well, this kid's created a whole new area of fuckin' up, staked it out all by himself. You know the kid in your high school, always used to carry a brief case to school, wore glasses, always walking down the halls, gazing around, bumping into people, never seemed like he was, you know, *present?* Well, this bean makes a guy like him look like Joe fuckin' Namath, his shit is in such a state of total flap. Tell you what. Don't know where they're digging up these smacks any more. Just don't fuckin' know. They gotta be comin' from someplace, but damned if you can figure where. . . .

The squad leader has a whole squad, eleven plebes, eleven beans, eleven smacks, every one of them different, and yet every one of them the same, because they're all beans when it comes right down to it. Plebes. Sorry-ass excuses for American humanity, a bunch of goddamn accidents looking for a place to happen, and they had to happen *here,* in this squad, all at once, like a human chain-reaction pile-up. . . .

Beast cut through the bullshit, shattering the mirror of cadet narcissism. Beast had a soft underbelly. You ended up learning as much about yourself as you learned about that thing they called *leadership.* Being one of the bad guys for a month taught you that self and other were inversely proportional. Early on, it was clear you had to yield something. Racktime. Movies. Attention to the girl in your life. Usually, it added up to about eighteen hours a day, every goddamn day. And you had to *care* about those eleven plebes. You couldn't fake it. Plebes knew. You knew that they knew, because you'd been a plebe, too. The shared experience brought squad leader and squad close together.

Beast was West Point's most overt usage of one's innate inhumanity to others for the academy's own purposes. Every squad leader was shooting in the dark, and each of them, though they wouldn't admit it, had this feeling he could *kill*—metaphorically, psychologically, even for real—hell, they didn't know, and it didn't really matter. The feeling was what counted. And each of them sure as hell felt the anxiety he'd inherited from a long gray line of hellish, bottomless tradition. So Slaight did what most twenty-one-year-olds would do. He went along, up to a point.

He figured West Point was probably better at "teaching" leadership than anyplace in the nation. After all, the place had been at it with a vengeance since 1802. But Slaight had always held that leadership was at least 50 per cent acting ability—what he called "the John Wayne quotient." There came a time, however, when Slaight learned what it was all about.

The lesson Slaight learned was ironic, for "playing the game," the eternal diversion of most cadets and upon which Slaight looked down with derision, became all-important to him. Slaight was forced to negotiate step by painful step all the traps designed into the "game" in order to come to grips with West Point's special secret. War was indeed the reason the Military Academy existed, and by extension, its purpose was to teach young men to kill. But there was a corollary to the academy's mission, unmentioned by West Point officialdom. You had to be willing to die, not for duty, honor, or country, but for your own men.

That was leadership, the thing West Point had to offer. And there was its secret. The system counted subliminally but necessarily on human imponderables. West Point knew you'd end up loving those whom you were trained to despise and abuse—in this case, your own plebes. The twist was as frightening as it was effective. While the academy supplied you the drum of ego and urged you to beat on it with vigor, ever so subtly was planted a seed of self-sacrifice. Not until he was a squad leader in Beast did "all that gibberish about leadership," as Slaight called it, make sense. Suddenly, it counted. Eleven young men depended on him.

Slaight, lying awake in bed at night, thinking to himself, the only time he's got all to himself, really—when he thinks about it—actually gets down and goddamn *thinks about it*—he loves those beans. Every last sorry-assed one of them. He loves them because they're his. He loves them because they're beans. He loves them because they depend on him, like some kind of father or mother—something anyway. He loves them because down deep, way deep inside, they're him. He was a bean. He was a plebe. He was a fuck-up and a dullard and a crot and a worthless no-good-for-nothin' piece of shit, and goddamn if he doesn't remember what it was like! He remembers what it *felt like*, Beast Barracks, every last one of those hellish days in July and August, and how he loved his goddamn squad leaders, loved them and hated them both. They were always jumping in his shit, coming down on him like goddamn jackhammers, but somehow, when it was all over, he had turned out okay. September came, he got into his regular company, Beast was over, and damned if he didn't discover that he could cope! That was what it had all been about—about coping. A squad leader taught you how to cope. He taught you about life, stuff you'd never forget as long as you lived. When you were finished with Beast, after you'd waded through the muck and the shit they tossed at you, you were a goddamn *cadet*, a regular guy, full-fledged and everything, and you could fuckin' *cope*.

They were a responsibility, those beans, those eleven young American men. One fuck of a big responsibility. And the guy who was directly responsible for them—responsible for whether or not they took their salt pills and wrote home to Mommy and Daddy and took at least a couple of craps each week—the guy who was responsible for every minute of their miserable little lives was the squad leader. All around him, first-classmen and officers, tacs and lieutenant colonels and majors and staff officers and even old Hedges, the Beast C.O., all around him these other guys stood, watching—just watching and waiting. They were waiting for him, for the squad leader, to fuck up, is what they were doing. Waiting to see if one of his guys dropped out of a reveille run. Waiting for Saturday Morning Inspection, to see if his squad was looking Up To Snuff. Waiting for the inevitable, one of the plebes wanting to see the tac, wanting to resign. All those firsties and officers just stood around waiting for the squad leader to fuck up, and just like with the plebes, it took only one, just one little fuck-up, and it was All Over. . . .

Beast Barracks hung together like a fifty-dollar jalopy limping along on retreads, a quart of oil every hundred miles, six out of eight cylinders firing, brakes just *this much* short of needing new drums, the pedal going down within an inch of the floor, everything bucking and jerking and screeching but somehow still rolling—and you knew, just *knew,* if one little piece blew, the whole goddamn thing would grind to a halt and you'd be stuck. It was the way of Beast Barracks.

So David Hand wasn't just a wild card. He was *trouble.* The kid from New Orleans was a plague on the squad, hell, on the whole platoon of forty-four plebes. It was a question of morale. Everybody knew what had happened. Everybody knew Crolius was the only guy who'd eve come close to being a friend of Hand's . . . when Ha turned him in on an honor violation, and they all s Crolius *get it* . . . they all saw him take gas for something they called quibbling, but which looked to the rest of the plebes like a pile of trumped-up crap . . . when they'd seen what happened to Crolius and how Hand just kept lording it over them, beating them at all the diddlyshit stuff plebes were supposed to do every day . . . they cracked, broke wide open, a goddamn wound opened in the squad, in the platoon, a wound that was bleeding and bleeding and bleeding and just would not fuckin' *stop.* . . .

That was when Slaight knew he'd have to do something about Hand. He saw it in the faces of the other plebes. You looked at them, and something in their eyes was pleading, begging, yearning—for what? For release? For help? Slaight didn't know. He wasn't sure. All he knew was, Hand had to be dealt with, and dealt with *now* or the whole goddamn squad was going to up and quit, fall apart, consume itself with self-pity and agony and sorrow

at the memory of poor Crolius. Because they were his responsibility, Slaight knew the whole thing was his fault. But the more he studied the thing, the more he knew—just *knew*—the answer. He'd have to break Hand. Break him open and grind up the worm inside of him, open the smart-ass fucker up so the rest of them could glimpse the truth that Hand was, after all, *human*.

It was the first time in his life Slaight had felt the surge of power, the twinge, the juice that rushed up your backbone once you'd made up your mind you were going to do something, and you knew you were going to do it *right*. No, it was the second time. The first time had been when he'd learned at age fifteen that he could shoot pool—he was a *shooter*, nobody could beat him, he could hustle pool. But this business with Hand was different. Hustling pool was just betting money against skill, when you got right down to it. Dealing with David Hand would be gambling with another man's life. So Slaight set up and he took his shot.

From the start, he complemented an over-all plan with certain tactics of harassment and interdiction. He took command of Hand's time, orchestrating every moment of his day, from the time he awoke in the morning to the instant he climbed into bed at night. Slaight was there. He didn't supervise Hand, he controlled him. Hand wasn't permitted to make a single move which was not in some way directed by Ry Slaight or by Leroy Buck, Slaight's friend and fellow squad leader who had taken a similar interest in "the punk from New Orleans," as Buck called him.

To Leroy Buck, Hand was just an animal. Back home on the farm in Indiana, he'd have gone after such a creature with his .22 rifle or maybe a sixteen-gauge shotgun. Buck's reaction to Hand's special breed of arrogance was not all that far-fetched in the army of 1967. In Basic Training, an army drill sergeant would have simply run Hand ragged, worn him down physically until he either collapsed and was hospitalized or died. To a drill sergeant, it didn't really matter.

As an enlisted man in a regular army unit, Hand would

have been cut out of the platoon and tortured in the vicious, petty ways caged men go at one another. Maybe his platoon mates would have dragged him into the showers and scrubbed him with latrine brushes until his skin bled from head to toe. Maybe they'd have starved him, totally deprived him of food during a lengthy field exercise. Maybe they'd simply take him out in a car late at night, run it up to sixty or seventy miles an hour, and push him out the door. Kill the bastard. When it came to the army, there was no way of telling what men would have done to a guy like David Hand.

But at West Point, the process was elusive, more refined: the ways of Beast Barracks were hidden from the eye and the ear. It wasn't physical, it was psychological, a game played with wits and patience. For always West Pointers had been taught the lessons of bureaucracy, taught to believe that time was on the side of the man willing to do the waiting. Time was an elegant weapon.

So they waited, Slaight and Buck, and they tossed David Hand between them like a badminton birdie. They sent him on little crummy mission after little crummy mission, carrying messages between the two squad leaders' rooms, visiting other upperclassmen of known ugly disposition. Always the results were the same. David Hand was on time. He was neat. He got things straight. He never missed a beat. Every time he reported to either Slaight or Buck, even when he had run halfway across the area of barracks and returned out of breath, he reported expertly, without a single mistake. At first it was maddening, watching this plebe run circles around every design of Slaight and Buck, who figured they could nail Hand in a matter of a few days, it would be only a short time before he cracked. Then they knew. It was going to take time. They settled into a comfortable—for them, anyway—routine.

Hand was kept extremely busy. He had no free time. Zero. He lived his entire life at the behest of Slaight and Buck, who combined their energies expertly. For more than a week, the routine remained the same: Hand running, reporting, delivering, shining, running, reporting, spouting plebe poop, running, shining, running, reporting, bracing against walls, running, more running, more bracing, more reporting, more bracing—and on and on and on, endless variations on the same theme. They thought they'd wear him down. But it wasn't working. Hand was perfect. *Perfect.* It was impossible to make him fuck up. Then one night, three days before the last day of the First Detail of Beast Barracks, three days before Slaight would be out of Hand's life for good, Slaight got an idea. What was the lone weapon he still had in his arsenal? The last goddamn thing he could use on Hand? The only thing he hadn't pulled out and thrown at him so far?

It was 9:35 P.M., the time when plebe mail carriers came to the rooms of upperclassmen to collect mail which would go out early the next morning. Naturally, David Hand was the mail carrier for his squad leader, Slaight. He reported to Slaight's room. Slaight looked up from his desk and signaled for Hand to enter. Hand stood the proper four feet from the front of Slaight's desk and waited, as Slaight finished addressing an envelope. Then he handed the envelope to the plebe. It was addressed to Samantha Hand, Vassar College—Hand's sister. His eyes flared when he saw the name. It was a tiny, fleeting loss of composure. Coming from another plebe, Slaight would have written it off as one more glimmer of emotion in a huge spectrum he had watched his squad go through during the past four weeks—everything from elation, the adrenaline of plebe euphoria when a job had been well done, to utter resignation and defeat, the way they looked right now. With David Hand there had been only one emotion the entire four weeks: superiority. Self-confidence. Ego. Even when Hand had thrust forward his fist, admitting at the manhood session that he hadn't "gotten any" from his girl friend back home, he had done so proudly. Slaight had to admire him for that. The kid had guts.

But now Hand had flickered, ever so slightly, opening the secret door to which Ry Slaight held the key. Slaight just sat there, pretending to go through some papers on his desk. He didn't look up at Hand's face, for he knew

Hand was standing still, staring at the spot on the wall above his head, awaiting further instruction. Slaight glanced at the letter. Hand gripped the envelope so tightly it was crumpled. His hand had unconsciously formed a fist, and the letter was wrinkled like a piece of cloth. This wasn't David Hand, the perfect David Hand who had beaten the Beast Barracks system at its own game. This was a scared kid. Slaight knew he had him.

Slaight continued to shuffle his papers, waiting for Hand to tumble the possibilities around in his mind. He waited, giving Hand the chance to consider every possible scenario. It was quiet in the room. There were twenty-five minutes until taps, until Hand had to return to his room down the hall. Slaight knew he had the time. He told Hand to step around the desk next to the wall, and to relax. They had talked informally before. Now Slaight made it seem like he was giving up, like Hand had won. He asked Hand about New Orleans, about his high school, what it was like down South, what his father did for a living. Hand mumbled unenthusiastic answers.

Slaight pretended not to notice, rambled on about Kansas, about going to high school in Leavenworth, about a girl friend he had back home. He was treating Hand like one of the guys, pulling him *inside.* He explained to Hand the ways of West Point, how lots of guys had a girl friend back home, and another parked somewhere nearby, one of the local colleges maybe, a girl in the city, a stewardess or a secretary, any old girl. He told Hand that's the way he'd worked it. Kept the girl back home happy on leaves, then had all the local skirt he wanted, what a *good deal* it was. Slaight told Hand if he played his cards right, maybe he could work the same kind of deal. Hand nodded, as if to say yes, sir. Slaight babbled on, as if he hadn't noticed the slip in protocol. Then he paused and shuffled through the papers on his desk. He pulled out another envelope, this one addressed to Betty Jane Soah, Fort Leavenworth, Kansas. He gave it to Hand. He winced this time. Slaight leaned back in his chair, let the whole thing sink in. Here was Slaight, telling David Hand all about what a good deal he'd had for the last couple of years . . . a girl friend back home . . . a girl friend somewhere nearby, getting ass in both places. Hand was standing there, holding both envelopes and listening.

He was sweating now, water pouring down his forehead, soaking his shirt collar, pouring down his arms. The knees of his khaki trousers were soaked dark brown with sweat. The envelopes, crinkled in his left hand, were wet. Slaight watched Hand from the corner of his eyes. He was blinking beads of sweat off his eyelashes, water running down his face in a river. Slaight leaned back in his chair, put his hands on his desk, spun slowly around, and looked straight at Hand. It was time.

"You know something, Hand?" Slaight asked. "I've gotten a lot of ass in the last couple of years, but the best piece of ass I ever fucked was your sister."

Hand swiveled on his heel and faced Slaight, sweat pouring from every inch of skin on his body.

"That sister of yours fucks like a goddamn bunny, do it in the fuckin' road, she would. Never seen anyone like her. A regular fuckin' maniac, that goddamn Samantha."

"SIR!" Hand screamed. "YOU ARE TALKING ABOUT MY SISTER!"

"I know I'm talking about your sister, Hand. You're holding a letter I wrote to her tonight in your left hand. In fact, you've ruined the goddamn letter, Hand. Look at it. The fuckin' thing is all wrinkled and soaked with sweat. Give it back to me, mister. What's the matter with you, Hand? Having problems with the idea that I fucked your sister?" Slaight paused. Hand had begun to tremble.

Slaight stood up and walked over to Hand. He turned slowly as Slaight walked. Slaight stood directly in front of him and looked him in the eyes. Sweat was pouring down his face, and his body was vibrating. He was a good three inches taller than Slaight. He was in superb physical condition. Slaight knew if Hand went for him, it was all over. He told Hand to look at him. Hand bent his head forward so their eyes met.

"What the fuck is the matter with you tonight, Hand? You got problems? You didn't seem to have any problems that day Crolius told you about fucking his girl friend. In fact, you seemed real cool about it. You were even cool that night I took you over to the Boarders' Ward to see Crolius, the night before he left the academy. What's the problem now, Hand? I'm just another Crolius. Your sister is just another girl friend. A fuck is a fuck, Hand. What seems to be your problem?"

"SIR, YOU ARE TALKING ABOUT MY SISTER!"

"I know I'm talking about your sister, Hand. So what's the goddamn problem? You don't believe I fucked her? Why don't you run down to the honor representative and turn me in on an honor violation, Hand? Why don't you turn me in the way you turned in Crolius?" Slaight waited. Hand stood there shaking and sweating.

"You are really bothered that I *fucked your sister,* aren't you, Hand? The idea that I *fucked your sister* really gets to you, doesn't it, mister? Well, I *fucked your sister,* Hand. You don't believe me, call her up and ask her. You'll probably surprise the hell out of her, but I'm certain she'll remember me. I *fucked your sister* a whole bunch of times, Hand. She seemed to enjoy it. I know I did." Every time Slaight said *fucked your sister,* he enunciated every syllable, driving the words into Hand like nails. He shuddered.

Slaight stood in front of Hand for several minutes, waiting for him to say something or do something. Slaight considered the idea that Hand might report him for hazing, but he'd told Hand to fall out and relax. He wasn't even bracing. Slaight hadn't touched him. Hand just standing there, shuddering like a cold wind was blowing across his wet khakis. Slaight took a step forward, moving his face to within a couple of inches of Hand's.

"You really hate me, don't you, Hand? I mean, you really, really *hate* me, don't you?" Hand grimaced, closing his eyes.

"YESSIR!"

Slaight stepped back. Slaight knew he had him boxed, but he knew he had to give him a way out so when his collapse came, it would be complete. Total. A real breakdown.

"Well, now's your chance, Hand. It's just you and me

alone in this room, and the door is closed. I told you to relax. No more plebe. No more upperclassman. It's just one man to another man, Hand. Just like you and Crolius. Standing in front of you is the guy who *fucked your sister*, Hand. If you're going to do anything about it, now's your chance. You better take it now, or shut your mouth, get your shit together, and crawl out of here like a good little plebe. You understand that, Hand? I'm giving you your chance. Now take it, or leave it. The choice is yours."

He stood there, vibrating like a human tuning fork, just stood there, his fists clenched, the letter to his sister crumpled into a wrinkled knot. Slaight looked at Hand, and he knew he had him. He stepped close to Hand, stuck his face up next to Hand's left ear, and whispered:

"You're not going to do a damn thing, are you, Hand?" He waited. No answer.

"You're not gonna do one goddamn fuckin' thing, are you, Hand?" Still no answer.

"I cannot hear you, Hand. You are going to have to speak up. I am having trouble hearing you, mister." Then it came.

"NOSIR!" Hand screamed the word. Slaight stood there for a moment, then he stepped back and told Hand to pull out his snotrag and wipe his face. He did. When he was finished, his face all red and swollen, Slaight put his mouth up near Hand's ear and yelled:

"THEN SLAP THAT CHICKENSHIT NECK OF YOURS BACK, SMACKHEAD HAND. CRACK THAT NECK OF YOURS UP AGAINST MY WALL." He flopped back against the wall, sweating and bracing and vibrating. He was finished. Broken.

Slaight stepped away. He felt a strange mixture of guilt and vindication—powerful. Not satisfied. *Powerful*. There was a difference.

"Hand," said Slaight slowly and carefully. "Hand, you drive around to my room tomorrow morning five minutes before reveille, and you drive around every morning at that time until I leave here. You drive around, Hand, and you better be looking good, mister, because I'm gonna be

268

watching you. I'm gonna be watching you, Hand. Remember that. Now, get outta here. Get outta my sight." Hand spun out of the room like a blown tire, out of control.

The next morning he showed up at Slaight's room late. He had completely fallen apart. His shoes weren't shined, his belt buckle was smudged, he hadn't shaved. Hand was broken, and he had nothing to fall back on. No place to go. The amazing thing, Slaight noticed, was that Hand knew exactly what had happened to him. He never asked for any help from his squadmates, and he never asked for a break from Slaight. Even in defeat, he retained a strange dignity. He had played the game his way, and he'd lost, and he would pay the price. One thing about Hand. He knew the goddamn rules.

The morning Slaight left the Beast Detail to go on leave, he called Hand into his room one last time. *Drive around,* he told him. That's what it was all about. Drive around. Control. Do as you're told. *Drive fuckin' around.*

Hand showed up on time. Utter perfection. He knew Slaight was going on leave at noon, and he had pulled himself together one last time. As he stood at attention in Slaight's room, Slaight saw that look on his face again—a look of detachment, like he was only half there. The expression on his face was taunting, arrogant. Slaight saw Hand standing there, a statue, and he dismissed him without a word. His face had said it all.

Slaight had gotten to him, all right. But not completely. There was still a place, somewhere inside him, deep in there, *deep,* that neither Slaight nor Beast Barracks would ever touch. With some incredible strength from that place inside him, Hand had picked himself up, pieced himself together, and he was standing there in Slaight's room telling him; *I'm going to make it, Slaight.* He was saying, *I learned my lesson. I won't make the same mistake twice. I'm going to play the game my way and win.*

Slaight never forgot the look on the kid's face. He never forgot David Hand. The kid had fuckin' guts. You had to say that for him. He'd found an edge, and he'd walked it, and he'd survived. Slaight had no way of know-

269

ing precisely what edge Hand had explored. Nor was he yet well enough acquainted with himself to have realized that David Hand had used him. Hand would emulate his squad leader, Ry Slaight.

Then he'd get killed for it.

BOOK IV

The Kingdom of Steam

23

"Have you told anyone what you have told me tonight, Ry?"

"No." Irit sat next to him, her right hand on the back of his neck. She had been sitting there listening to him for the better part of two hours while he told her about David Hand.

"Why not? I do not see how you can live with all of this inside of you, Ry. I don't see how." Slaight sipped his third bourbon on the rocks.

"I don't know, Irit. I don't know why. I probably wouldn't be telling you, except all this shit with Hedges went down today, and well . . . you're *you,* Irit, you know?"

"No, I do not know, Ry. I do not understand. I can understand the things you have told me tonight. I can understand why they happened. But I do not understand why you have never told anyone. Have you told your parents? Have you told your father, Ry?"

"No."

"Why not, Ry? It would seem to me that your family should be the first to know, if you have . . . problems."

"Problems! What fuckin' problems!" Slaight exploded, nearly spilling his drink, standing up, pacing.

"What fuckin' problems? All this shit I told you tonight was just West Point, Irit, until Hand went and got himself drowned. It was all just West fuckin' Point, what happened up there every day. Who's got problems? All you've got up there is one day after another coming down on your head. You wanna look at it that way, my whole goddamn life up there is a problem, one big goddamn headache. You wanna look at things that way, I probably ought to be put fuckin' *away* for what I've done, Irit. Locked *up.* Jesus! What am I supposed to tell you?"

"But your family, Ry . . ."

"My family! Are you kidding? What the fuck would they know? They're sitting out there in Kansas running goddamn horse stables, is what they're doing. My old man didn't even want me to go to West Point. He and I haven't had a nickel's worth of shit to say to each other in the last three years. I go home, and it's like visiting a goddamn funeral parlor. Eat scrambled eggs for breakfast. Grill steaks for supper. Drink fuckin' beers and stand around and watch the rich kids from Kansas City ride their horses around the riding ring. Drink more beers. Watch the sun go down. Watch TV. Go to bed. It's the same story for everybody I know up there. What are your parents supposed to think? You don't go around telling your parents and friends everything that happens to you at West Point. You *can't*. You can't expect them to understand what it was like to be a goddamn plebe. You can't expect them to understand about Beast. You just can't."

"Then you agree with the—what did you call him?—the chairman of the Honor Committee, the one who gave the lecture to the plebes. You agree with him when he said you were not supposed to tell anyone about your life at West Point. You believe in the need for secrecy. You believe that West Point should remain apart from the rest of the world. You believe that don't you Ry?"

Slaight sipped his drink. He didn't believe it, not for a goddamn minute did he believe it. But he had practiced it, right along with the rest of them. He had practiced it until this very moment, when he sat in his girl friend's living room and told her all he knew about David Hand.

"I don't believe that bullshit, Irit. Christ, if I really believed it, I wouldn't have told you a thing. It's not as simple as . . . either you believe or you don't believe. It's not black and white. I don't believe in that secrecy crap, never have. But I've lived it. I've been caught right in the middle of it because until now, there didn't seem to be any other choice. Even now, it seems like this whole thing was forced into the open. It's like, I *had* to tell you. I

273

didn't have any choice. You already knew too much. Christ. Listen to me. I sound like some World War II spy movie on the TV late movie. You *knew too much, baby, so I hadda tell ya, but now it's all over between us, see?* This is ridiculous."

"It's not ridiculous, Ry. This is very serious. I have the feeling you are admitting to some doubts you never knew you had before now."

"Yeah, I know. You're right. But Jesus, Irit, West Point. What more can I tell you?"

"You can finish telling me *why* you've never told anyone about your experiences there."

"Finish! Irit, don't you understand? I told you about me and David Hand, but that's just, like, the tip of the iceberg or something. How can I make you understand? You go to West Point when you're eighteen. You become a cadet. You do things. You go on leave. You go home for Christmas. You see your folks. You meet a girl. You have a drink in a bar and you talk to the person sitting next to you on a plane. What are you supposed to say to any of them? Listen, yesterday I told this plebe to drive around to my room, and when he came in, he looked like shit. His shoes weren't shined and he needed a dress-off, and he didn't know the movie schedule for the week. So I told him to drive around to my room every morning before reveille for the next month. That'll fix him. Fix *what?* Fix his goddamn dress-off? Nobody even knows what a fuckin' dress-off is. Jesus, what are you supposed to say to anybody? Being a cadet is like . . . being some kind of god. They put you up there and tell you that you're better than everybody else, and at first you know it's all bullshit, but after a while, you've listened to it for so goddamn long, you begin to believe it."

Slaight sipped his drink and paced.

"How the fuck is anybody supposed to understand the shit that goes down up there? Huh? Listen, when I was a plebe, I had this roommate. His name was Danny Gottlieb. He was a Jewish guy from Brooklyn. Father was a tailor. The whole thing. A cliché. Going to West Point was the biggest fuckin' thing ever happened in his family.

So he gets up there, and this guy in the company, a cow by the name of Ryder, he hates Gottlieb. Not because he's a Jew, but because his body is shaped like a pear, you know? He's just . . . like this pear . . . narrow shoulders, wide in the gut and the hips. He's in shape and everything, but he looks like a pear. What can I tell you. So Ryder hates Gottlieb. Every day Gottlieb works on his stuff, getting ready to go out to formation. He works on his stuff until it's all *perfect*. Then he goes out and stands in formation. Down the stairs comes Ryder. You can hear him. He's bullshitting with the other cows. He comes through the door to the barracks and he spies Gottlieb standing in ranks. He walks toward him. He gets ten feet away, and he says, 'Gottlieb, what is that thread doing hanging out of your pocket?' Gottlieb looks down, and sure enough, hanging from his pocket is this tiny little piece of thread, about a half inch long. He says, 'Sir, I do not know.' Ryder tells him to drive around at 2130. So the rest of the day, Gottlieb's whole life is ruined. *Ruined*. Do you understand? Gottlieb can't study, because he's got to work on his shoes, work on his uniform, work on learning all his poop, so he won't catch any shit from Ryder when he drives around at 2130. But he just knows. He fuckin' *knows* he's gonna catch a load of shit when he drives around, because it happens every day. *Every goddamn day*. The same thing. The same way. And me and my other roommate, we need Gottlieb to poop-us-up in math, because he's got the calculus *down*. But Gottlieb hasn't got time to help us, because all he can do is think about driving around to Ryder's room. It went on like that for a fuckin' year. All of plebe year. Nine goddamn months. Every goddamn day. Ryder telling Gottlieb to drive around. And you know what? The next year, Ryder becomes company commander, and he's the best goddamn company commander we ever had. He never gives Gottlieb any shit. They become good friends. How do you figure it, Irit? A total flaming asshole like Ryder becomes a first-rate company commander. Gottlieb, who hated and feared him for a whole year, would cut his arm off for him the next year, because Ryder was always watching
275

out for the company's shit. Always taking care of us. Keeping the tac off our necks. Best goddamn CO we ever had. How do you figure it, Irit?"

"I don't know, Ry."

"I don't know either. And how do you figure this. Gottlieb, who had the most hellish plebe year imaginable, he becomes a regular gray-hog. That's like a super-straight cadet. If anybody had an excuse to slack off yearling year, it was him. But no. Gottlieb digs in, and he's straight-arrow. But these other guys in the company, guys who never had to drive around to Ryder's room once, guys who never had to drive around *period,* who just ghosted through with hardly a plebe year at all, they start resigning like some kind of an epidemic hit, like the last train is pulling out of Woo Poo, and you better get on. *Now.* So the Tactical Department, they watch about twenty guys in the company resign in a row, and they figure something's up. They send this major over from the Department of Military Psychology and Leadership. They're going to do a study. They want to know why so many guys are resigning. So the major is meeting with us twice a week, and he's gotten us broken down into different discussion groups and stuff, and we're all supposed to give him reports on what we think is wrong with West Point. Well. Where do you start? Right? One night we're all sitting down in the sinks meeting with this major, he isn't a grad, and he's a real nice guy. Everybody really likes him. So one night, he just asks for a show of hands. How many are going to resign? A half-dozen guys raise their hands. He starts to ask them why. Guys are saying stuff like, they don't like the educational system, they've decided they don't want to be officers in the army after all, they're disillusioned with this part of the system or that part of the system. Pretty stock answers. You could get the same shit from any half-dozen yearlings at West Point anytime. Hell, you could hear the same shit from any half-dozen college sophomores about any goddamn college in the country. Finally he gets around to this dude Whitford, from Tennessee. Whitford's a real character. He's got an accent so fuckin' thick—Christ, he made Leroy Buck sound like he was from Boston. So he asks Whitford, and old Whitford says—I wish you could have heard him —old Whitford says, 'Suh, suh, Ah'll tell yew what. This here place, Whest Phoint . . . waaalll, suh, Whest Phoint is just lahke this big *coffin*. Yuh come heah on the fust day a Beast, and yuh climbs in the big coffin, and they puts the lid down on yuh. And every day, they drives in another nail, suh. Every day, they drives in another nail.' Old Whitford laid that on the major, and he just called a halt to the whole thing, took the stuff he'd gotten from us back to the Department of Military Psychology and Leadership, and we never heard another thing about it. The study was over. Old Whitford resigned and went back to Tennessee, enrolled in the University of Tennessee, got himself in some fraternity, and he was writing us letters back all the time telling us what a good time he was having and shit. Then one day Leroy Buck, who had been his roommate plebe year, got a letter from Whitford. On a single sheet of paper is written just one line. *Please buy me a Brown Boy and mail it to me, Leroy*. Whitford couldn't get along there without his Brown Boy. So Leroy goes up to Cadet Supply and buys him a Brown Boy and we stuck it in a big box and mailed it down to Whitford at U.T., and we never heard another word from him. I guess he was too embarrassed after that to write to us about what a good time he was having. Because no matter what he'd said, the truth was, he missed West Point. He missed the company. He missed the guys. He was too embarrassed to admit it to us. Asking for a Brown Boy was his way of saying he was kind of sorry he'd resigned. That was one of the weird things. All those guys who resigned . . . you always had the feeling that they regretted resigning on some level . . . like they would always wonder: Did they do the right thing? For the rest of their lives they'd wonder. And they'd wonder: Did they resign because they just couldn't cut it? Christ, I've read these stories in the *Times* about the problems they're having at Ivy League schools with students coping under the strain of academic competition. One story I read said most of the schools have had to open mental health facilities for the students. Man. Competition is one thing. But the shit that goes down at West Point!"

"I know what you mean, Ry. That story about the coffin, it's almost . . ."

"Funny. Yeah, it's almost funny. It *was* funny at the time. We laughed our goddamn asses off over that line. Christ, we'd laugh at anything. I remember one Saturday night that year, yearling year, this goes back two years now. I remember one night I was up in the barracks writing letters, and I heard a ruckus out in the area, so I looked out my window. It was about midnight, and these two firsties from my company were coming back from Snuffy's, the bar where all the firsties went to drink. They were totally drunk. They were doing PLF's . . . you don't know what a PLF is. Okay. A PLF is a 'Parachute Landing Fall,' which they teach you at the Airborne School when you're on the Firstie Trip. You jump off a wall, land on your feet with your knees bent, and roll to absorb the shock of landing. It's a training exercise for Airborne. So these two firsties are doing PLFs off this little wall onto the area. Finally, they both end up on the area, rolling around laughing, and one of them, a little guy who'd spent a lot of hours walking punishment tours—I'm sure he was a Century Man, which means he'd walked over a hundred hours—the little guy starts screaming, 'I love this fucking area! I love this fucking area!' and he starts humping the area. Then the other guy starts humping the area. And they're both screaming, 'I love this fucking area!' and humping, like they're fucking the area. Guys are looking out their windows to see what all the noise is about, and they see these two firsties fucking the area, and they're hooting and hollering out the windows, cheering them on, and the two firsties are humping and humping and screaming, and somebody puts on the Rolling Stones, 'I Can't Get No (Satisfaction),' and turns the speakers out the window into the area, and I swear to you, there was almost a goddamn riot going on. Music and screaming and laughing and these two crazy area-birds fucking the area. Finally somebody calls one of the orderly rooms from the Cadet Guard Room to say the of-

ficer in charge is on his way, because they can hear it all
the way over in Central Area, and the firsties scramble
into the barracks, everybody pulls up their shades and
turns off their lights, and just like *that* . . . it's over. You
believe that?"

"Yes. Of course I believe you, Ry."

"You think they'd understand?"

"I think so."

"Yeah, it all sounds funny in retrospect, when you tell
it like a story, you know? Well, how about this one. There
was this upperclassman and this plebe. The plebe was real
smart. Too smart. He thought he could get away with
playing the game by his rules. The upperclassman decided he wouldn't let him. So the upperclassman broke
him, just busted the little fucker in half, like a water-
melon, cracked him wide open. Saw his insides, the upperclassman did. And you know what? He looked in there
when he got him cracked open, and he didn't understand
what he saw. Isn't that some shit? All that trouble he
went to, breaking the plebe open, and once it was done,
he didn't know what he was looking at. That's West Point
for you. Right there. They teach you all about leadership,
about influencing the behavior of others, they teach all
this shit, and when you put it to use, you don't know
what the fuck is really going on. You're just banging away
in the dark in the general direction of the target. And
West Point stands there and lets it happen. They let it
happen, because they know they control the light switch.
They know it'll stay in the dark. They know it'll never get
out. None of it. You know why, Irit? I mean, you know
why, besides West Point controlling things?"

"Tell me, Ry."

"I'll tell you why. It'll never get out, what goes on up
there, because when it's over, you're too fuckin' embarrassed to admit to yourself that it happened. You're too
fuckin' embarrassed to admit what happened to you when
you were a plebe. You're too fuckin' embarrassed to admit what you did with the power you had when they
made you a squad leader. You're too fuckin' embarrassed
to tell somebody what it was like to stand down there in

279

the sinks and have some goddamn naked plebe come up to you and salute and tell when he took his last crap, and you're sitting there checking between his goddamn toes for athlete's foot, and you're squad leader and mother and father and every other goddamn thing to these guys, and you're only nineteen or twenty years old yourself, and you're coming on like God's right-hand man. You're too fuckin' embarrassed to admit what you learned about what goes on between cadets when they're that close together, because you didn't really understand it all yourself, and what you did think you understood—who would fuckin' believe it, anyway? It all happened inside this goddamn vacuum, this goddamn monastery, and you knew the whole time that West Point wasn't the real world. It wasn't intended to be the real world. You knew it was a giant fantasy, a big goddamn *game*. You knew it was a goddamn game from the first day when that guy told you to drop your bags, and you went ahead and dropped them, and you didn't question it, because you *knew* why. Once you'd dropped your bags, you accepted the goddamn rules and you played the goddamn game. But it was real, too. West Point was fuckin' real. Real enough to hurt. And Christ almighty. Real enough to kill."

Slaight stood there with his empty glass in his hand. He had been pacing back and forth, and he was soaked with sweat, despite the air conditioning in Irit's penthouse. He was sweating and he was tired and he was well on his way to being drunk. He was *killing the fuckin' pain.* Irit listened to him rant and rave for another twenty minutes, and now it was her turn to speak, and Slaight knew it. He flopped down on the sofa next to her.

"Ry, you've got to go to New Orleans, and you've got to tell this girl, Samantha Hand, what you know about her brother. You've got to go, Ry. You've told me. Now you've got to tell her, I don't care how much it hurts. You owe it to her."

"Yeah. I know." Slaight's eyes were closed. He didn't want to think about West Point any more. He didn't want to think about David Hand. He didn't want to face the idea of going to see Samantha Hand. But he knew he had

280

to because Irit was going to make him do it. Good ole Irit. What would he do without Irit? Huh? What would he fuckin' *do*?

"Irit. Let's go to bed. Tomorrow, sweetness. Tomorrow. I'll make all the arrangements tomorrow. I promise you. Right now, all I want to do is climb in bed with you. Right now, all I want to do is climb in bed and feel your body next to mine, Irit. I need you, Irit. You know that?"

"Yes, Ry. I know it."

"You don't mind, do you? I mean, me needing you and all? Is this driving you crazy, Irit? It's about ready to rip my guts out, and I don't want it to hurt you. I don't want West Point to hurt you, Irit. I love you too goddamn much. You know that? I love you. I love you, Irit Dov, and I need you."

"I know, Ry. I love you, too. I love you in some way I don't completely understand. But that doesn't matter for now. Come. Let's get you in the shower, and into bed. Tomorrow, we'll think about New Orleans. Okay?" She looked at the shirtless body next to her. He was already asleep.

24

Two days later, Ry Slaight and Irit Dov stepped off the plane into the kingdom of steam. Heat rose from the streets of New Orleans in vertical ranks of waves, rippling, swirling gas vents from the center of the earth. It was hot in New Orleans, hot and humid. New York was bad in July, but this was unbelievable.

They rented a car and drove to the French Quarter— the Qwa-a-atah, it was called in New Orleans, the old part of the city down on the banks of the Mississippi where the river made a sharp U-shaped turn from south to north. They checked into the Provincial, a small rooming house on Ursulines Street, and spent their first afternoon wandering through the Quarter. Cypress trees lapped up the sun, spread their flat, scalelike foliage in courtyards and alleys between the old buildings of the Quarter like living ceiling fans. Wind off the Mississippi ruffled the cypress leaves, spinning them like tiny green knife blades. Everywhere there were bars and restaurants open to the street, real ceiling fans turning overhead inside, stirring the humid air, sucking cool air from the concrete floors, passing it slowly over the sleepy midday drinkers on its way to the ceiling and out the open store fronts to the street, where the hot sun superheated the cool air and spun it skyward. Slaight had never seen anything like it. The place was like a giant broiler. People didn't live in New Orleans. They just sat there and slowly cooked themselves to death.

Slaight called a classmate who lived in another section of town, and he met them in the Quarter for supper. His name was Nathan Tabor. He was in one of the other companies in the Third Regiment, he and Slaight had had a few classes together over the years. He asked Slaight what he was doing in New Orleans, and Slaight told him "leave." Slaight asked him about the restaurant owned by David Hand's father, a place in the French Quarter called Anthony's.

"Anthony's is *the* restaurant in the Quarter," explained Tabor. "You've got to know somebody to get a table in the place. What I mean is this. The restaurant is really two places—there's the Anthony's that the tourists know about, this famous place in the Quarter, right? You just walk in off the street, and there's this big room and a lot of tables, and you sit down and eat. Then there's Anthony's—a series of back rooms, small private dining rooms upstairs and in connecting buildings, not visible from the street. You have to know one of the back-room waiters to get a table. You call a special number, ask for your waiter by name, and he takes your reservation. When you go, you don't enter by the front door. Just to the left of the front door is a narrow alley between buildings. You walk down that alley, and at the end, you pick up a phone on the wall and ask for your waiter by name.

When he answers, you give your name and the time of your reservation, and you're buzzed into a back room, and escorted to your table. You get a different menu from the tourists, a different kitchen, a whole different scene. There are actually two waiters for your table—your main waiter and his son, who serves as his assistant. Your main waiter takes your order and places your order with the kitchen. Now, the way they work it at Anthony's is like no other restaurant in America. Your waiter is actually a wholesaler to your table. He buys from the kitchen at wholesale, and sells to you at the price marked on the menu, and he pockets the difference. That's his salary. So if you've got a good waiter, he'll watch your food when it comes from the kitchen, and if it doesn't meet his approval, he'll refuse it—send it back for you. He'll make sure what you get is *perfect*. All the time, his son is there at your table, pouring wine, tossing salad, making sure everything is okay. You pay a little extra for this service— not much, really, but you pay. A good waiter at Anthony's can make between five hundred and seven-fifty a week, which he splits by some mutually agreed-upon percentage with his son. The son inherits his job when he retires. Those waiters are really something. They'll cultivate a regular clientele of regulars from New Orleans, and then some big spenders from out of town with the connections to get in. They clean up. The guy who owns the place started out as a waiter, inherited the job from his father. Later, he quit and went into other business, made it, and came back and bought the goddamn place. One of the classic success stories of the Quarter. He's a real power these days. Anybody who's anybody in this town had better be on the good side of William Hand, or he gets stiffed at Anthony's, and if that happens, forget it. In New Orleans, if you're going to make it, you need Anthony's more than Anthony's needs you. This town lives on lunches and dinners at Anthony's and a couple of other places. But Anthony's is the one. Why you ask? You want to eat there? I might be able to fix you up, if you give me a couple of days."

"Yeah, thanks, Tabor. Maybe in a couple of days.

We'll give you a call. We're just trying to get our feet on the ground. This heat is enough to float you away."

"July is not your ideal time to visit New Orleans," said Tabor.

"Yeah. I'm beginning to get that idea."

"What brings you down here this time of year besides leave, anyway?" Tabor was one smart son of a bitch, and Slaight didn't want him digging around.

"Curiosity, man. My girl, Irit, she's never been here, and neither have I. And you only got one leave right? Now or never."

"Sure. Gotcha." They said good night and walked down Royale Street to the rooming house. They spent their first night drinking straight gin on the rocks huddled next to a pathetically inadequate air conditioner hard-pressed to make a dent in the heat, wondering what they'd do to stay cool the next day. They needn't have wondered.

At the ungodly hour—for Slaight, anyway—of 9:30 A.M., Slaight drank two gin and orange juices' worth of courage, turned the corner outside the Provincial, walked the three blocks down to 152 Chartres Street, and rang the buzzer on the cast-iron gate of the fence surrounding a marvelous old Victorian mansion set back from the street by an intricately designed garden, inset with winding brick walks and flower beds and flowering bushes of one kind or another. It was truly an imposing structure, the Hand house, and Slaight expected to be met by a black maid in a white apron when the gate swung open. Instead, a tinny voice sounded over a small speaker mounted on a cast-iron Greek column at the right side of the gate.

"Who is it?" inquired a tinny voice of indeterminate sex.

"It's Ry Slaight. I'm here to see Samantha Hand." There was a pause. Another voice came over the speaker, female.

"Yes. Who is it?"

"It's Ry Slaight, ma'am. I'm here to see Samantha Hand, please."

284

"This is Samantha," the voice crackled from the speaker. "I don't want anything to do with you, Rysam Slaight. Go away. Go away this very moment, or I will call the police and have them arrest you for harassment."

"Samantha, you're not giving me a chance."

"You're damn right I'm not giving you a chance, Slaight. Now, go away."

Slaight gave up when he heard the speaker *click*, signaling that it had been turned off. He walked back to the Provincial, poured himself another gin-and-orange-juice, and announced the grim news to Irit.

"I will go myself," said Irit. "We will not come down here without giving this Samantha person the information which is by rights hers. Wait for me here." Slaight didn't argue. He sipped his drink in the dark silence of the room overlooking Ursulines Street, which had begun to buzz with the commercial truck traffic of the warehouse district through which it passed.

Irit repeated the buzzer process at the gate to 152 Chartres Street. Again the voice:

"Who is it?"

"My name is Irit Dov. I have information about the deceased cadet, David Hand. Let me in, please." Again a pause. The gate buzzed, and opened a crack. Irit pushed her way through. She walked to her left along a brick path. Before she had gone more than a dozen steps, a light-complexioned, extremely thin blond woman who appeared to be in her early twenties stepped suddenly from behind a bush. The two women faced each other in the bright, early morning sun.

"I'm Samantha Hand," stated the blonde flatly. "You've come with Ry, haven't you? I know. My brother mentioned your name in his letters. You're Ry's girl friend. What do you want?"

"You made a grave mistake in your letter to Ry. I read it. And yes, I am here with him. You should not have turned him away. He had nothing to do with the death of your brother, David. But Ry does know how he died. He has come here to tell you everything he knows about your brother and his death. Like you, he believes your brother

285

was murdered. But unlike you, he has the facts. He knows of the autopsy on your brother. He wants to find your brother's murderer. Ry has been drawn into this. not by your letter, but in other, more complicated ways. For reasons which he will have to explain to you himself, the death of your brother hurt him very deeply. You must talk with him. He has not come to defend himself against your letter, for he has no need to. He has come to tell you everything he knows, and you will do yourself and your family a grave disservice if you do not listen."

Irit delivered her well-rehearsed lines in the peculiar lilting English native to Israel. Samantha Hand seemed stunned, speechless. Irit spoke:

"You have reason for concern, Samantha. But you have no reason for fear. Ry cannot hurt you any more than he has already hurt himself. I have listened to him and watched him since he learned of your brother's death in May. It has consumed him. Your letter only served to crystallize what had already become a nearly self-destructive passion. He is determined to find your brother's killer. You can help him. You can refuse to help him. But you must listen to him, you must hear him out. If you do not, I hardly know what to expect from him. I fear for his emotional health, and I fear for his safety. You must give him the benefit of the doubt. You *must* listen, no matter how difficult it is for you. I assure you, this journey has been equally painful for him."

Samantha Hand walked slowly toward Irit and took her by the arm. Her hand seemed frail, bony. Wordlessly they walked to the house. Inside, it was dark and cool, the windows shaded outside by huge oaks, fans stirring the air slowly within the house, drawing cool air from somewhere and circulating it through the rooms on the first floor.

"Where is he?" Samantha asked without emotion. "I'll call." Irit gave her the number, and Samantha dialed the telephone, asking the desk for Slaight's room. He picked up.

"Ry, it's Samantha. I'm sorry. Irit is here, and she has told me. She seems like a wonderful person. I'm glad she came with you. I would never have seen you otherwise.

286

Please. Come over. Have you had breakfast? Come then. We'll eat, and we can talk."

Samantha led the way to a terrace behind the house. The leafy foliage of giant rosebush thickly entwined a latticework gazebo. Samantha told a servant to show Slaight to the terrace when he arrived. The two women drank tea and talked of the weather as they awaited Slaight's arrival. He was there within a few minutes. The former lovers greeted each other awkwardly and sat down across the table from one another. Irit offered to leave, but Ry held her hand, and Samantha asked her to stay. She seemed a steadying influence in a scene that needed one.

It took Ry an hour to outline the events of the past few days, including his knowledge of the real autopsy, the existence of two "official" autopsies, his meetings with Major Consor, the commandant, and the sergeant major. The details were quickly drawn and to the point. David Hand was murdered. The doctor was convinced of it. The sergeant major suspected it. The commandant appeared to be eager to keep it quiet, having offered to buy off Slaight with a battalion command. There was a great deal of intelligence data on the case, the contents of which Slaight did not know. The Pentagon was somehow involved. What, Slaight wanted to know, had the family been told?

"We were told it was an accidental drowning," said Samantha Hand. "We were given no other details. The entire matter was handled very quietly and hurriedly by the authorities at the academy. My father took the superintendent at his word. David was interred without an autopsy here. The academy never informed us that an autopsy had been performed. This is the first I have heard about an official autopsy. Ry . . . I am sorry about my letter. I was distressed. It was just that . . . well . . . it was like I told you in the letter. My brother was obsessed by you. The obsession went back to when you were his squad leader during Beast Barracks. He wrote me in Paris during that time. And it never stopped. I often wondered. What had happened between you two that he would suffer such an obsession? I never told him about you and me. Never. Not before he went to West Point, and never after-

287

ward by mail from Paris. His obsession seemed to come from nowhere."

"It hardly came from nowhere, Samantha. It came from me. That's the other thing I came down here to tell you about. Beast Barracks." Slaight spelled out the story of David Hand during Beast Barracks in equally abrupt, concise detail. Samantha nodded her head once or twice, as if to agree, or to acknowledge something she already knew. When Slaight was finished, she sighed deeply.

"I didn't know all of it . . . not like that . . . but it sounds so much like him. Like what he would do. He was that way in high school. Headstrong. Impossible in many ways. My father was desperately opposed to his going to West Point. He is on the Board of Trustees at Tulane, and he wanted David to follow in his footsteps. David wouldn't listen. My mother, on the other hand, was completely romanced by the idea of the academy. It appealed to her sense of patriotism, all those young men in their uniforms with their stiff white trousers and their full, proud chests. I guess, being from the South, she envisioned scenes of lawn parties with great tents spread over acres and acres of grass, girls in long flowing gowns moving soundlessly about, the tinkling of ice in crystal cups filled with punch, the sounds of a band playing a fox trot somewhere at the edge of the crowds of cadets. . . . They were at such complete odds with one another over David and West Point, I didn't know what to do. I of course knew that West Point was nothing like my mother envisioned it . . . nothing like David envisioned it, for that matter. But my mother had violently opposed my going North to Vassar. She wanted me to attend a local girls' school—a finishing school more than a college. And it was my father who gave his approval to Vassar. So I could not bring myself to come between them. I felt I had only one choice, and that was to stay out of the whole thing and let David make up his own mind. For whatever reasons of his own, he chose West Point. I never really understood why. I never asked. I accompanied him to West Point for the first day of Beast. I watched them march out to Trophy Point that afternoon to take the oath. I watched them march back to the barracks. The next day, I left by air for Paris. A week later, I learned you were his squad leader. You can imagine my shock!"

"Well, you can't imagine mine. One chance out of thirteen hundred, and I got him."

"Yes. And you 'broke him,' as you say. That must explain why he continued to follow you around the academy. He did, you know. He reported to me your every move. Everything."

"I didn't know that. I never saw him again, after that last morning in Beast. Never heard anything about him, either. Not until that day on the area, when I was told he was . . . dead."

"David made it sound in his letters as if you two had become friends . . . of a rather distant sort. He made it sound like you confided in him from time to time. He always knew what you were up to. I found out about Irit within a week of your return to West Point in September of 1967. By Christmas, I felt as if I knew her. David must have spent half his free time spying on you, Ry. It's all very strange. Very, very strange."

"Yeah."

"But he always lived in a fantasy world. He loved books and movies. In high school, he was completely wrapped up in the Thespians, and after school hours, with one of the local little theater groups. He was always dreaming. I think becoming a cadet . . . the army . . . it was just one more of his dreams. But the dream was bigger than he could have known this time. He was just a child. He had no way of knowing. . . ."

"He was more than just a child, Samantha."

"What do you mean by that?"

"It's the last thing I came down here to tell you. I wouldn't tell you, but I'm convinced—and so is Dr. Consor—that this had something to do with his murder. I'm really sorry, Samantha . . ."

"Ry. What is it?"

"Did you know that your brother was a homosexual?"

"That's a lie! A despicable lie!"

"It was part of the doctor's findings in the autopsy, Samantha. I don't want to go into the details, but the doctor found that your brother had had sex immediately before death. He had sex with another man."

"No."

"Samantha. I'm not lying to you. I've told you everything I know about your brother. Everything that went down between me and him. Now I've got to tell you this, because the doctor is certain, and I am certain, that the man with whom your brother had sex murdered him. He's the guy we're looking for. That's what it comes down to, grim as it is. But it's the truth."

Samantha stared blankly across the garden for a few moments before speaking. When she finally spoke, her voice was measured, firmly in control.

"You are a contemptible whore, Ry Slaight. I knew the moment I agreed to see you that you would do nothing but cause more grief, more suffering. What is it about you? Why must you prey on me and my family like this?"

"I didn't come down here to . . . prey, Samantha. I knew I would cause grief. It wasn't easy for me. If you won't believe me, ask Irit."

Samantha Hand turned slowly and faced Irit. Tears dribbled down her cheeks. Their eyes met, and Irit simply nodded. Samantha faced Slaight.

"It's none of your fucking business, Ry." She spoke rapidly, and the words came from deep within her chest, a rumble of anger and frustration.

"I know, but. . . ."

"You're always saying, 'I know.' Well, fuck you and all you know."

"Samantha . . ."

"It isn't doing me, or my family, or even you any good, all this you say you 'know.' " She spat the word at him.

"Goddammit, I didn't come down here to do you or anybody else any good." Slaight stood up from the table, pacing the concrete deck of the gazebo.

"You wrote me a letter. You figured your brother was murdered. You said I had something to do with it. You told me I had something to do with the fucking war in Vietnam one day, too. Remember?" He glared at her, leaning forward, hands on the table, his face a foot from hers.

"Remember that day? Well, fuck you and all you 'know' about that war, Samantha Hand. You and that bunch of overfed cunts from Vassar can take your bullshit about the war someplace else. Why don't you demonstrate over at Yale? Ever think about that? Shit. A flower and a leaflet will get you laid at Yale. Those fuckin' guys will end up buying and selling slots in line units in Nam, sister. One year from now, they'll be trading stocks down on Wall Street. They'll be trading blood stocks. They won't have to watch the war on TV. They'll see it everyday on the broad tape, in numbers. All the companies that are feeding off that fucking war like a bunch of pigs at a trough. So fuck you and your uppity crap about me and West Point and the army and Vietnam. I don't need it."

"Ry . . ."

"Fuck you."

"Ry . . ."

"I said fuck you."

"Ry. Wait." The voice was Irit's. Slaight stopped at the bottom of the steps to the gazebo. Samantha was standing, her head erect and proud. Irit stood next to her. Samantha spoke.

"I didn't mean to . . ."

"You didn't mean shit. You say you wanna know who killed your brother. So do I. You got your reasons. I got mine. I didn't come down here to haunt you, or harass you. I came down because I need your help. You help me, and we'll nail the son of a bitch who killed your brother. You take a walk now, and those fuckers at West Point will bury your brother but good. They're runnin' scared, Samantha. I don't know from what, or why, but they're runnin'. And they're coverin' their tracks as they go. You wanna help me nail your brother's killer, talk. If not, we'll be on our way."

The three of them stood for a moment like cast-iron statues in the heat. Then Samantha sat down, Irit with her. Slaight returned to his chair and sipped his drink.

"Okay, Ry." Samantha stared across the garden. Her

291

eyes were glazed. Her face was thin, drawn tight, brittle, like expensive porcelain.

"You have no business knowing this, Ry." She looked him in the eye for the first time all morning. "But you know everything else. You may as well know David the way I knew him."

Slowly at first, with the cultured broad-A tones spoken by natives of New Orleans, she talked about her brother, her family, and the city of New Orleans. They seemed tightly entwined, like the vine covering the gazebo. Slaight found the story fascinating. Irit found it chilling, uniquely American, like the late movies he always wanted to watch on television.

David Hand had been valedictorian of his high school class. He was captain of the debate team, a contender for the state debate championship, president of the school's Honor Society. He was president of the Key Club, the high school adjunct to the local Kiwanis. He often traveled to small towns near New Orleans to address Kiwanis luncheons.

"He was popular, Ry," said Samantha, hoping the word meant as much where Slaight came from as it did in New Orleans. It did. "David seemed to float through high school in an air-conditioned sphere of adulation and quick, easy fame. There was only one thing more beautiful, more perfect than the whole social scene we came from. David. And he knew it. He was like Troy Donahue in *A Summer Place*. Nobody noticed life wasn't a movie. No one cared. He was too perfect, and they cherished him for it. They used him like a mirror. They all wanted to see something of themselves in him, and he knew it. He must have used you the same way, Ry. That would explain his letters, the way he followed you, watching you, admiring you."

"Yeah, I guess," said Slaight, waiting for Samantha to continue. She spoke haltingly at first, picking up speed as her memory poured out, a catharsis interrupted only by the insistent buzzing of bees around the gazebo. Slaight listened quietly. Irit gripped his hand beneath the table.

The town fathers were proud of young David Hand.

When they lunched at Anthony's they clapped the senior Hand on the back and told him the town, hell, the whole nation had a future leader in young David. He was a youngster they could all be proud of. When they learned he was going to West Point, not to Tulane, his father's alma mater, the news failed to dim enthusiasm for David Hand. He would bring honor to New Orleans no matter where he went to school.

Samantha explained that her father had remained deeply perturbed by David's unexpected decision to go North to West Point. His displeasure had nothing to do with his politics, which were sufficiently conservative that beating the commies over in Vietnam seemed one hell of a good idea. He just didn't want his boy David becoming a statistic before he had a chance to . . . make his mark. The very idea of the Military Academy displeased the elder Hand. It was almost like entering the seminary. You were locked up for a long time, four years, and when they let you out, the army still had you for five years' active duty. An eighteen-year-old boy making a commitment like that! By the time his son had completed his obligation, he'd be married with a couple of kids, William Hand decided. An army career would be almost irresistible under those conditions. Even the prospect of inheriting Anthony's, the finest restaurant in the French Quarter, would probably fail to lure his son from the army. He was too damn headstrong. Once he made up his mind, he'd never change it.

William Hand had spent his whole life changing. He'd come up the hard way. His father had been a waiter at Anthony's. The job had provided the family enough money to own a house, and to send William to Tulane, the university across town, across Canal Street, over near Audubon Park lazily scattered among the trees and grass and wide boulevards that didn't exist in the Quarter. Tulane was to have been William Hand's way out, and it was. He took a job with a bank downtown and rose to assistant manager. With a keen eye, he watched the real estate market. One day he withdrew all his savings and invested in a big piece of swampland not far outside town,

293

a place no one figured would ever go anyplace. William Hand knew better.

New Orleans reached the edges of its natural boundaries—the river to the south, west, and east, Lake Pontchartrain to the north. The peninsula of delta landfill which for two hundred years had contained the city of New Orleans was full. The city needed a place to spread. It needed suburbs. Those suburbs would become known as Fat City, the place people moved to when they left the Quarter, and the grubby low-rent districts bordering the river. Fat City was William Hand's swampland. He cleaned up. At thirty-five, in 1945, he bought Anthony's where his father still waited tables. His father retired to a house in Fat City. In 1946 William Hand married Rosemary Bonaparte, the daughter of one of the wealthiest oilmen on the Mississippi Delta.

Such a marriage was not socially out of order in New Orleans, Samantha explained. The city took the lavish spectacle of the son of an Anthony's waiter marrying the daughter of Francis E. Bonaparte in its stride. It was part of Louisiana history, part of state pride, that the blood of disparate families mixed like silt in the waters of the Mississippi. Everybody knew the silt was there in the river, because it was deposited daily on the constantly shifting islands and backwaters and sloughs which were the Mississippi delta. But in the water, Mississippi silt was invisible. The water was muddy, and so were the histories of the families which had settled the only state in the Union with civil codes based in French law, instead of British law, like the other forty-nine. In New Orleans it seemed everyone was related in one way or another. The city rested, William Hand often told his daughter when she was old enough to understand, not on landfill, but on a quicksand of family ties which depended on a peculiar gentlemanly form of blackmail for cohesion. In New Orleans you collected information on your fellows the way you deposited your money in a bank. You were what you knew.

William Hand wanted his son to inherit Anthony's. It was a matter of family pride. Samantha knew from the

294

time she was a little girl that restaurants in New Orleans were a man's business. Food was taken too seriously to be left to women. Because of the machismo surrounding her life in New Orleans, which naturally included the restaurant she knew she would never inherit, Samantha decided to go North to Vassar. She didn't want to become another of the frail New Orleans blossoms that passed for girls in her high school class. Like her mother had been brought up, they were being trained for a different kind of success. In New Orleans women didn't inherit businesses, they inherited men. Samantha didn't want any part of it. She left in 1965 for Vassar.

Her father could never figure out his own son. The boy was smart. That much had been confirmed many times over. He was headstrong, too . . . headstrong like his mother, a woman who masked a considerable will behind the floral flounce of New Orleans femininity. Samantha knew—or sensed, really—it depressed her father that everything about her brother had come from her mother's side of the family. He had her handsome yet soft facial features, skin that looked so moist it seemed to be thinly coated with honey. He had his mother's soft pale blue eyes, and her wispy, chocolate brown hair. When David spoke, you could hear the elegant, leisurely tones of his mother's voice in the ebb and flow of his words. He talked the way the Mississippi moved, with an inexorable certainty, slowly, self-confidently, as if speech had been not a gift of God but a right, something which ran in his blood at birth.

Samantha said David wasn't just impressive in high school. He was downright precocious. Once, when she was home from Vassar for Christmas, her father had gotten drunk and told her late at night, *the boy is possessed*.

"It was eerie, Ry," Samantha explained. "My father isn't an excitable man. He can't be, to run the most important restaurant in New Orleans, all the other family investments he's made over the years. But the next day, I had lunch with him at the restaurant. David came in. I saw him, coming through the doors of the restaurant with all these Kiwanis men. They followed him. They followed him like he was the Pied Piper, and his tongue was his flute. He was talking, talking, and you could see it. They felt caressed by his voice. Father was right. David was ... frightening."

Samantha stared at Slaight, waiting for his reaction.

"Yeah. I know what you mean," he said.

"No, you don't, Ry. You don't know what it was like, because you weren't his sister. You'll never know."

"No, I guess I won't," he agreed. They were silent, each of them staring at a plate or spoon on the table before them. The maid began clearing the table, asked if anyone wanted anything else. Slaight asked for a gin and orange juice. The maid glanced at Samantha, and she nodded her assent.

"You still drink too much, don't you, Ry?"

"Yeah, I guess so," he said.

"You seem different, though. Quieter. Less the wild man you were when I knew you."

"Yeah." Irit gripped his hand under the table.

"Is it over now, Ry? What you've come for? Have you told me everything you've come to tell me? Is there anything left I can tell you?" Samantha seemed drained, empty of feeling. Slaight hated to press her for more. But he had to.

"I know this has been hellish for you, Sam," he began, calling her by her nickname accidentally. She blushed. "But I need one last thing. I want the name of your brother's best friend in high school. I want to talk to him."

25

Billy Patou agreed to meet Slaight the following night in a little bar on St. Charles Street in the Quarter. It was a typical French Quarter spot—wide doors folded back, the dimly lit interior of the bar open to the snarling bumper-to-bumper tourist traffic of the street. He said he'd be dressed in blue, and he was. From head to toe, Baby blue. Sneakers. Socks. Jeans. T-shirt. He was about Hand's age, nineteen, and skinny, it was hard to figure how somebody could weigh so little and still live. Even his face was skinny, about as wide as his neck. He had hair the color of the wicker bar stool he was sitting on, sipping some white frothy concoction that looked like a gin fizz. When Slaight sat down next to him, he turned his head slowly to face Slaight. Bill Patou's face was deeply pock-marked by acne scars. Slaight took one look and thought: Billy Patou had been David Hand's horse-holder, an old army term describing somebody who just followed another person around, catering to his every whim. Without saying anything, Billy Patou stood up—he was about 5′9″, Slaight's height—and led the way back to a courtyard behind the bar. He sat down at an old round oak table and signaled a waiter. Billy Patou knew his way around. But he was nervous. Slaight saw it. His eyes flicked from side to side, and his long slender fingers drummed the table in a quick tattoo. The waiter came.

"I'll have another one of these," said Billy Patou, holding his glass. He looked over at Slaight.

"I want a Dixie," said Slaight, referring to the local beer, at twenty-five cents a bottle, the kind of bargain that could turn you into an alcoholic.

"You didn't bring anyone with you?" asked Billy, glancing back toward the bar.

"No," said Slaight. "You asked me to come alone. I did."

"You said you wanted to talk about David," said Billy, draining the last of his gin fizz, with a slurp. "I don't want to talk about David. He's dead. He's gone now. He was my friend."

"I know he was your friend. Listen, man, let me introduce myself. I'm . . ."

"I don't want to know who you are!"

"Okay. If that's the way you want it. But Hand's sister told you who I am, didn't she?"

"All she told me was, you were David's friend. That's all I want to know. You were his friend, weren't you?"

"Let's put it this way. I knew him. He was in my squad at West Point. Upperclassmen and plebes aren't friends. But I knew him. Pretty well."

"Okay. So what do you want to talk about? Samantha said you have some questions to ask me. I don't want to answer questions about David. He's gone now . . . a tragic accident. I never thought he would *drown*! He was a good swimmer. The best."

"It wasn't an accident, Billy."

"Wasn't an accident! What do you mean? That's what they said. That's what the priest said at the funeral. It was an accident!"

"Look, Billy . . ."

"Don't call me Billy! Call me . . . Ray. Call me Ray. That's my name down here."

"You're not from here? From the Quarter?"

"No. I live in the Garden District. If my parents knew I was down here . . . I'm not supposed to come down here, is all. So call me Ray."

"Okay. Ray. Look, your friend David didn't die accidentally. He drowned. That much was true. But not accidentally. He was murdered."

"Murdered! You've got to be kidding! This must be some kind of sick . . . joke. I'm leaving." He stood up.

"Look, Ray or Billy or whateverthefuck your name is. Sit down. Samantha told you to talk to me, didn't she? She's David's sister, right? You can trust her, right? Come on, goddammit, answer me."

"Yeah. Samantha. She said you were . . . all right."

"So sit down and listen to what I have to say." He sat down, drumming his fingers. Slaight could feel his knees bouncing under the table.

"Settle down, kid. I don't bite, you hear? I came here to meet you tonight to tell you one thing, and that's already done. David Hand was murdered. Now, I want to ask you something. And I want you to think hard. I'm trying to find who murdered David Hand. I'm gonna find the guy who killed him, and I'm gonna bring him up on charges in the army and see him hang for it. You understand me, now? You see what I'm driving at?"

"I guess so," said Billy/Ray. "But why you? Why hasn't there been some kind of official army investigation, if what you say is true?"

The waiter brought the drink and the beer. The courtyard was ten degrees cooler than the street outside, and potted palms hung over sparsely scattered tables. Nobody else was in the courtyard. The kid might be scared, but he wasn't stupid.

"I can't answer that," said Slaight, sipping his Dixie from the frosted bottle. "I can't answer you, because I just don't know the answer. I don't know what the army is doing, or if they're doing anything, or why. All I know is this. I want to find the guy who killed Hand. And I need your help."

"Me? Why me?"

"I thought you might remember something—something from when you two were in high school. Hand was killed at West Point. The best guess is, he was killed by another cadet. Now, *think*. Did David Hand ever talk to you about any cadets he might have been, you know, friends with? Any cadets he was especially tight with?"

"When he came home from West Point for Christmas, he talked a lot about one guy. I think his name was . . . Slaight somebody . . . I can't remember exactly."

"That's me. My name is Slaight. Ry Slaight."

"Well! He certainly admired you! He went on and on about what a . . . neat guy you were. He thought you were quite the ideal cadet. *His* ideal, in any case."

"Yeah. So? Anybody else?"

"I never heard him talk much about anybody else at Christmastime. There was one cadet, though. Before David went to West Point. He came down here and visited our high school . . . let me see . . . in the fall of 1966. He was on a recruiting trip or something. He gave an address to the entire senior class, in his uniform and everything. He was quite something to see. David was really taken by this cadet. I think he was the reason David decided to go to West Point. Before that cadet visited our high school, I don't think David had given it much thought. He had applied to several colleges, some of the Ivy League schools, Tulane, Duke, a few others. But that cadet . . . I think he made up David's mind for him. He never stopped talking about West Point after that. Never."

Hand had been recruited! Jesus! Slaight's mind raced.

"Look, ah, Ray, I want you to think about this cadet. Can you remember his name?"

The kid's face twitched wildly, his fingers drumming. He was giving himself away. The cadet recruiter was a sensitive memory.

"I . . . don't . . . remember. How am I supposed to remember? That was almost two years ago! Goodness! Do you think I have total recall or something!" Nervously, the kid fumbled for a cigarette and lit it with one of those expensive thin gold lighters you saw advertised in *The New Yorker*.

"Listen to me, Ray. I want to tell you something. I know David Hand was a homosexual. He had sex with a man immediately before he was murdered. Let me put it bluntly. Whoever fucked him killed him. Understand?"

"Well!" The kid blew a long breath of smoke across the table. He crossed his legs. His fingers stopped drumming.

"I'm not as fuckin' straight as I look, kid," said Slaight, bluffing, acting like he knew more than he actually did.

"Who said you were? You don't have to get testy . . ."

"I'm not getting testy Ray, or Billy or whateverthefuck your name is. I just want answers. What about this cadet recruiter. You remember his name or not?"

"I *told you*. I can't remember *everything!*"

Slaight sipped his beer. Kid's definitely a screamer. Definite.

"Okay then. Let me put it to you this way. Did Hand have a thing with the cadet? Back in 1966, I mean."

"My. You are putting it to me, aren't you?" The kid blew smoke across the table again, straight in the face of Slaight.

"Don't get cute with me, Patou. I didn't come down
300

here to play fuckin' games. I came down here for information. Facts. Now, *give*."

"And if I don't? What are you going to do? Take me in the alley and fuck me in the ass? Huh? Is that what you really want? Is that why you're so eager to find David's killer? You make it with David, too?"

Slaight reached across the table and grabbed the kid by the T-shirt. He yanked him down, slamming his face on the table. The kid didn't make a squeak. Didn't even drop his cigarette. Slaight held him there and whispered:

"I didn't make it with David Hand, kid, but I want to know who did. And you're the man who can tell me. Now, when I let you go, you sit up like nothing happened, and you start talking, and no more faggot wisecracks. You understand what I'm saying?"

"Yes." Slaight released his grip on the kid's T-shirt. He sat up and took a drag on his cigarette, calm as you please.

"Talk."

"You *are* serious, aren't you?"

"You bet."

"I should have known. Samantha said . . . well. That doesn't matter."

"What exactly did Samantha say?"

"She said not to play games with you. She said you meant business. But I didn't know that you . . . knew."

"So now you know that I know. What about Hand?"

"What's going to happen to me? If what you say is true, this guy has already killed once. And if anything gets out . . ."

"If anything gets out, what?"

"My parents . . ."

"You're in the closet. I shoulda known."

"I'm not in the closet. I'm in the fucking attic!"

"Okay. Nothing will get out. This will be Top Secret. Between you and me. You've got my word."

"Isn't that quaint! With your word and a quarter, Mr. Slaight. I can buy myself a Dixie beer."

"Look, Patou, if I tell you what goes down at this table will remain a confidence, that's what I mean, you hear me? You think I'm down here in this goddamn hellhole on leave time for my health? Huh? You think this is just one big lark for me? A goddamn game? Well, you got another think coming, Patou. It's not. The shit's getting so deep around the death of David Hand, it's going to take a rowboat and oars to get out pretty soon. And I'm caught in it, dead in the middle of the shit, through no goddamn fault of my own, for reasons that need not be explained to you. I want to know what you know. You talk, and everything is cool. You just sit there and play dumb, which you are not, and everything may not be so cool. Got it?"

"Okay. *Okay.* Just don't raise your voice like that again, please. *Please.* I want another drink."

"So order yourself one." The kid signaled the waiter with his glass. Slaight raised his beer bottle. The waiter acknowledged the gestures with a nod.

"Where do you want me to start?"

"With the cadet who came to your high school in '66. That's as good a place as any."

"Okay. You probably already suspect it. David had an affair with the cadet while he was here."

"What do you mean, an affair?"

"I mean David Hand fucked him in the ass, that's what I mean." The kid lit another cigarette.

"So."

"They got drunk. The cadet was here for three days. He came to our high school the second day. David hung around after the lecture, asking questions. I guess they went out to dinner together. David could be quite persuasive. He was a real *charmer.* Anyway, he told me about it later. They went drinking around the Quarter. The cadet wanted to see one of the TV shows on Bourbon Street. David took him."

"TV shows?"

"Transvestites. Female impersonators. Strictly tourist shit. Bourbon Street isn't part of our gay scene. But David said the cadet was really getting off on the TVs. They went to his hotel room afterward. They were pretty drunk. The cadet was still in his uniform, so the first thing he did was strip to his shorts. David told me later that's what cadets do all the time. Get out of their uniforms. But then, David didn't know. He took it as a signal. He started coming on to the cadet. The cadet got really mad, hit him, split David's lip. He was bleeding. It scared the cadet. He was all over David, with cold washcloths. You know. Then David noticed. The cadet had a bone. He was turned on. So David starts cooing. Let me tell you something. David could *coo*. Meanwhile, they're still drinking. The cadet is staggering drunk. David is high, but not drunk. So he does his number."

"His number?"

"He goes down on the cadet. Suddenly, the cadet is all turned on. David thought the guy was straight at first, then he wasn't sure. Anyway, David goes to the bathroom to check his lip, and he sees a tube of K-Y in the cadet's bag, his little toilet kit, along with some rubbers. He thinks, at least he goes both ways. So David walks out of the bathroom with the K-Y, and the cadet is passed out on the bed. He just climbed on, and before the cadet knew what was happening, David was doing it. That was his thing. He really dug getting off on straight guys. I bet he fucked half the Kiwanis leaders in town by the time he graduated."

"Yeah?" The kid sipped his drink, as the waiter served Slaight another Dixie.

"Straights were his thing. It was all ego with David. He wasn't satisfied making it with gays. He wanted the feeling . . . I don't know how to explain it to you, because I never really understood it myself. I guess David wanted the feeling of changing someone. Did he ever come on to you?"

"No."

"There. That explains why he never stopped talking about you this past Christmas. He obviously wanted you. Badly. But he was afraid of you."

"He told you that?"

"No. But I could tell."

"How?"

"I was his *friend*. Don't you understand that, yet? He was the only real friend I ever had." The kid puffed on

303

his cigarette, looking away. It was the first emotion he'd shown, other than nervousness. Slaight sipped his beer, giving the kid time to recover.

"So what about the cadet? You remember his name?"

"I told you already! That was two years ago! I'm supposed to remember every one of David Hand's goddamn fucks! Give me a break!"

"Okay. Okay. You remember what class he was in? Did David tell you?"

"He was an upperclassman."

"I know that much. They don't send plebes on recruiting trips."

"All I remember was, he was an upperclassman."

"Well, let me ask you this. Did David see the cadet when he got to West Point? Was he still a cadet when David was a plebe?"

"Yes."

"Did Hand still have a thing going with him at West Point? Did he mention anything in letters, or when he was home on leave?"

"He saw the cadet at West Point. Yes. But he never said much about it. I had the impression he didn't see him very regularly. But I couldn't be sure. David just didn't talk about him much. That was his way. Once he'd made it with someone, the thrill was gone. It was like it was over. He would brag and brag when he'd fuck some guy for the first time, especially if he was straight. Or he'd talk endlessly about somebody he wanted to fuck. But once the . . . ah . . . deed was done, as they say, you didn't hear much about the person again. That was David. When he came home for Christmas, he was always humming this little tune. Once I asked him what it was, and he sang the words. I couldn't believe it."

"What were the words?"

"I'll never forget them. He sang: 'I'm gonna be an Airborne-Ranger. I'm gonna live a life of danger.' I think that's the way he really saw himself. He got off on the danger. I guess he was really very masochistic."

"What makes you say that?"

"Because what he really wanted, I think, was to be
304

making some guy, some straight dude, and have the guy get ripping mad and beat the shit out of him. He loved that edge. He used to say fucking wasn't fun unless you didn't know if you were going to make it. He used to say that, then . . . then he'd laugh."

"He'd laugh?"

"Yes. He'd laugh. He was laughing at me."

Slaight sipped his beer. The kid stared across the courtyard. This trip to New Orleans was turning out to be more than he'd bargained for. He had the feeling he was taking the kid's confession or something. Funny thing was, the feeling was familiar. He remembered. It was like Beast, when a plebe would come to you with problems, and you'd sit there and listen to him, and the kid would be pouring it all out and you'd be listening and wondering what in *hell* to do with it all, all of the gush, all the emotion, that big space inside the kid between today—*right now*—and back when. . . .

"Do you want anything else from me? My blood type? My sign? I'm a Pisces. Does that help?" The kid was blowing smoke again, tapping his fingers.

"I want you to think about the cadet. You're sure you can't remember his name?"

"Certain."

"Do you remember what he looked like?"

"He was . . . handsome. Good-looking. And tall. About David's height. Trim. Fit. You know. Military."

"You remember the color of his hair?"

"Come *on*. Next you're going to ask me if he had bad breath."

"No. Next I'm going to ask you if you could pick his picture out of a yearbook. Could you?"

The kid paused, smoking. He was scared. He'd probably already told more than he ever intended to tell. Slaight waited.

"I . . . don't know. Maybe. But *listen*. That was two years ago! How many times do I have to remind you? People . . . change. Times change. And David is dead. Gone. What difference could it possibly make? Who's to

305

say this guy killed David? You're just . . . shooting in the dark. That's all you're doing."

"I'm shooting in the dark, Patou. You're right. But now I've got a target. And you've got a flashlight."

"Maybe you've got more than one target, Slaight. I forgot to tell you. There were several cadets at our high school that day. Three of them, as I recall. Each of them gave lectures to different groups."

"And your group was?"

"All the seniors who had lunch at the first sitting. I remember now. The lecture was just after lunch. Some seniors heard another cadet earlier. Some heard another lecture after ours. I can't remember which cadet addressed which group. It was all mixed up. They spoke to the junior class, too. That's why there were three of them at school that day. Ours was the biggest high school in town. Over four thousand students. More than one thousand seniors alone. That's why they had to break us up into groups. The auditorium would seat only five hundred at a time."

"Jesus. So there were three cadets in your school recruiting that day, and Hand made it with one of them, huh?"

"That's it."

"Did you see all three of them?"

"I saw cadets in the halls between classes. I don't know if I saw all three. They all looked the same to me."

"Do you remember if any of them had stripes on their sleeves, you know, like this." Slaight outlined a chevron on the table with his forefinger.

"I think so. I can't be sure. I don't remember if David's cadet had stripes or not, if that's what you're getting at."

"That's what I'm getting at."

"Well, I don't remember."

"But you might be able to pick this guy out of a yearbook. Is that correct?"

"I honestly don't know. Are the photos in uniform, those gray jackets?"

"Yes."

"Well, they all look the same to me. My goodness. I
306

hardly recognized David at Christmas in his uniform. They make you look so . . . stiff."

"Yeah. Know what you mean."

"Are you finished now? Can I go?"

"Just one more minute. I need to know how I can get in touch with you. Maybe later this month. Maybe in September, when school starts again. I might want to let you have a go at the yearbook, see if you recognize anybody."

"Not through my parents! I don't want them involved . . . well . . . you understand, don't you?"

"Yeah. I understand. How about Samantha? Is it okay to have her call you?"

"Yes. That would be all right."

"Where do you go to college, Billy? Down here? Tulane?"

"No. Yale. I went North to . . . be close to David. But I never heard from him. I never saw him. Not until Christmas. Even then, things were . . . different. You know?"

"I think so."

"What is it about that place, West Point? David seemed so . . . changed. It wasn't just the uniform or the haircut. He seemed . . . like a different person. What do they do to you at West Point? Is everyone changed like that . . . I mean . . . so their own best friends hardly recognize them?"

Slaight finished his beer and looked at the kid. He was leaning on his elbows, peering through the semidarkness across the table. His face was earnest. He really wanted to know.

"I'll tell you what, Billy. I've been there three years, and I'm damned if I know. I guess you'd have to ask my best friend, back home. I guess we're all a little different after being at West Point. It's that kind of place. It does . . . it does change you, I guess."

"And where is back home for you?"

"Kansas."

"Kansas! Phew!"

"Yeah. Phew."

307

"So you won't call my parents, and you won't tell anyone . . . what I've told you tonight. Is that right?"

"I didn't say that."

"Then what did you say?"

"I said nothing would get out about you. I won't tell anyone I've spoken to you. The only other person who knows your identity is Samantha, and she won't talk. You know you can count on her."

"Yes. I know that."

"But you've got to understand. I'm going to make use of what you've told me tonight. I've got to, if I'm going to figure out who killed your friend Hand. But I won't tell anybody where I got the information. So far as I'm concerned, I went out for a drink tonight and talked with a guy by the name of Ray. Right?"

"I have your . . . word?"

"You've got my word, man. You can count on it. Far as I'm concerned, you're just some dude in a bar. Satisfied?"

"Yes. I guess so. It's just that . . . well . . . I really . . ."

"You really what?"

"I didn't really plan on telling you any of this. I thought it was none of your business."

"You're right. It's not my business. It's the business of the men who run West Point, but they're sitting on their fannies waiting for the smoke to clear. Before it does, I'm gonna figure out who killed Hand, and I'm gonna make them get off their asses and nail him." Slaight signaled for the waiter to bring the check, scribbling on an imaginary scrap of paper in the air with his hands.

"Why?" Patou stared at Slaight across the table.

"Why what?"

"Why are you doing this?"

"I don't know. It bothers me. That's as good a reason as any."

"That's interesting. David told me last Christmas he did something that bothered you, and you really gave him hell for it. He called you a 'take charge guy,' that was the phrase he used. Take charge. The way he said it, I could tell he admired you."

"Yeah." Slaight stared at the check, digging in his wallet. Patou was making him nervous, and Slaight was doing his best not to show it.

"Hand ever tell you why he went to West Point?" Slaight asked the question defensively, to break the sticky, hot silence.

"I don't think he ever said it out loud." Patou stirred his drink, thinking. "But I always kind of knew why he wanted to go to West Point. It's funny. We never talked about it—him going to West Point, me going to Yale—because we didn't have to."

"Yeah? Why not?"

"I told you. We were friends. I *knew* him. I guess you . . . wouldn't understand."

"Try me."

"I knew he'd go to West Point the day that cadet came to our high school. David watched him. He just followed him around and watched him. If you could have seen his eyes . . . sometimes, he'd get this look. It was like he was looking at himself in the mirror, only different. I don't know how to explain it. You'd have to see it."

"I did."

"That's right. You were his commander or something, right?"

"Yeah."

"So you know what I mean . . . about the look in his eyes."

"I think so. But I'm not sure I understood it, not completely. That's why I asked you if Hand ever told you why he wanted to go to West Point. I could never figure it. I didn't know he was homosexual, but somehow, I knew he was different. He didn't fit."

"The way David talked about you, I'm surprised you didn't know he was gay. I would have thought . . ."

"Look. I didn't know he was a fag until the day he died." Slaight bristled, glaring at Patou, then shifting his gaze quickly to the side. He looked through an arched doorway at the bar. It was late, but business was brisk. New Orleans. Jesus.

309

"I know what it was!" Patou brightened, waving his arms, nearly spilling his drink.

"You know what?"

"That look in his eyes. David's. The look he got watching the cadet. It was like singing in the showers, after gym class. We used to do it all the time. You know how your voice always sounds better in the shower, more resonant, fuller? Then you walk back to the lockers, still singing, and it's just your same old voice again? That's the way it was, the look in David's eyes, watching that cadet. It was like he was admiring himself in the mirror, only better. He was watching an image he knew would disappear when the cadet left. There was always sadness in his eyes, too. I could see it. With the cadet, it was worse. I knew he'd fuck that guy when I saw the way he watched him. I just knew it."

"What are you saying, Patou? You're talking in circles."

"You really don't understand, do you?" Patou peered at Slaight through the dim, smoky air.

"Hey, if I understood all this shit, you think I'd be here in this hellhole feeding questions into you like nickels in a juke box? Come on, man. Give me a break."

"Incredible." Patou sipped the last of his drink with an abrupt slurp.

"What?"

"You're so *straight*. I mean . . . you don't see it, because you're the answer to your own question."

"Damn straight I'm straight, Patou." The kid looked up, and they both laughed.

"Okay," said Patou, signaling the waiter for another drink. "Okay. I get the message. I mean . . . it was always so clear to me, I guess I never stated it out loud. David went to West Point because West Point was the straightest place on the face of the earth. That cadet, in high school, he was straightness personified. David fell in love with West Point because he wanted to become it. It was always that way with David. Image. The straight guys he used to fuck, he was never satisfied because they never

310

lived up to their own image. Once he'd fucked them, they weren't straight any more. You see what I mean?"

"I think so."

"West Point . . . David's image of West Point was like the final edge of maleness, beyond anything he'd ever encountered—oil rig roughnecks, Cajun longshoremen, cowboys in the movies. Beyond John Wayne. Sure. He fucked that cadet when he was here recruiting. But West Point was different. I think David thought West Point would . . . change him. Is that what West Point does? Does West Point have that kind of power?"

"In some ways. Yeah. It's got power. A special kind of power."

"What kind?"

"Shit, man, if I could answer that one, I'd have my own academic department up there." Patou laughed. Slaight sipped the beer Patou had ordered.

"Is West Point as straight as David thought it was?" The question was loaded, and Slaight knew it. He sipped his beer. Patou was asking questions now.

"Yeah, I guess so. Hand's image of the place was correct. He couldn't have missed it with his eyes closed. They work on that image of West Point, shine it till it gleams. They've got it down. They should. They've been polishing the West Point image for a hundred sixty-five years now. If Hand fell for the image, he wasn't the only one. There's plenty of others, me included."

"And the cadets? Are they as straight as they seem?"

"Yeah. Christ. Getting laid at West Point is like a requirement for graduation. Women are part of the currency, traded for goods and services. And status. The guys are straight, all right."

"But David wasn't. Nor was the cadet he fucked, the one you think killed him."

"Yeah. I know."

"Are there any other gay cadets?"

Slaight stared straight ahead.

"Did you ever know one?"

"Yeah. Sort of."

"What do you mean, 'sort of'?"

311

"This guy in my class, from another regiment, a guy I don't really know, he stopped by my room one day to bullshit. I'd seen him around. He was one of the smart guys, up there near the top of the class. We both worked on the cadet magazine, *The Pointer*. So he stops by, we're talking about the next issue, and he asks me what I'm doing over summer leave. I tell him. Then he tells me he's spending his summer leave working as stage manager for one of the off-off Broadway theaters in the Village. Tells me it'll be his third summer working there."

"So?"

"So I knew what the scene was with off-off Broadway theater. I wrote a story for *The Pointer* about two plays I'd seen down there the year before. He knew I knew. He never came right out and said it, but he was telling me he was homosexual."

"And you didn't turn him in?"

"Turn him in? For what? One of the incredible ironies about West Point is the fact there's no regulation against homosexual behavior, but there are a slew of them proscribing relations with women, saying what you can and can't do and when and where. Shit. You wouldn't believe it. Anyway, that's not why I didn't turn the guy in. It was obvious he needed to tell somebody, I mean, he had to let it out in the open, and he figured I would understand, and I did. It was just one of those things. Everybody needs to talk to somebody about something really private, you know? I did, too, when I was a plebe. When I needed someone, there was a guy I knew I could go to, and depend on, and be there when I needed him. Same with this classmate. You could think of it as an unwritten rule. You don't rat on a guy when his own personal hammer comes down on him like that."

"But this unwritten rule—is it West Point's?"

"No. It's the cadets', as much a part of the system as the uniform. But there's one crucial difference. What belongs to the cadets does not necessarily belong to, or have the approval of, the academy. Often the two are at odds, as different as . . . you and me."

312

"I know what you mean. At Yale, it's not the same, but there are parallels, I guess you could call them."

Slaight shifted nervously in his seat. He enjoyed talking to the kid. Patou was smart. But it was getting late, and he wanted to go back to the rooming house, back to Irit. Here he was, sitting in a bar in New Orleans, talking to this screaming faggot as if . . . The glow of Patou's white palm caught Slaight's attention and interrupted him. Patou was waving at him.

"I don't want to keep you, but . . ."

"No, man, that's okay. Go ahead."

"You never really answered my question. About West Point. You said it lived up to David's image of how straight he thought it was. But you never said whether or not West Point was *really* straight. Inside the image, what's it like? What is it about West Point that gives it the 'special power' you said it has?"

Slaight twirled the bottle of Dixie beer in his hand, pondering the question. Patou was driving at the core of something Slaight himself had always avoided, and he was coming at it from an angle no one, *not a single person*, had attempted, at least not in Slaight's experience. Quickly, Slaight added up what he knew: the murder, Hand a secret fag, the cover-up, Hedges and the rest of them running scared from something Slaight couldn't figure. He didn't buy the commie demonstrator angle, Hand's murder affecting national security. Hedges didn't buy it either. Hedges was using that bullshit in the all-us-men-together manner, welcoming Slaight into the insiders' covey, a special center rarely opened, promising everything. Guys he had known during his three years at West Point had eaten each other alive trying to get there. Slaight's instincts told him Hedges promised more than he would deliver. His father had a phrase for it, one he remembered from years ago when they were showing horses at the county fair. "Carney blow," his father called it, as they walked down the midway. "They say it costs a quarter. So does five songs on the juke box. So does a one-armed bandit. You get what you pay for." Slaight had been down plenty of midways since that hot summer

313

afternoon fifteen years ago. He had trouble recalling their various "attractions," but he remembered his father's cynical advice, word for word.

Now Slaight had new information. Pursued properly, it might force the identity of Hand's killer. And he finally understood something about the engine which had driven Hand with such inhuman energy through Beast Barracks. Hand didn't go to West Point to get laid, to fuck cadets. David Hand went to West Point to test himself, to see if he could live up to West Point's definition of manhood. What had long perplexed Slaight now made a perverse kind of sense. *Beast. Crolius.* Hand's stubborn refusal to listen to reason, to play by the rules. Having tested cadets and found them, like other humans beings, weak, Hand began testing the system.

Hand wanted to fuck West Point.

"Jesus, Patou. You're asking me to explain West Point. I'm no expert, man." Slaight was trying to wiggle out. Patou pressed him.

"But you know something. I can tell."

"Okay. Okay. I'll tell you what I know. You read *God and Man at Yale?*"

"Yes, I've read it."

"You think you understand what Buckley was saying?"

"Well. *These days,*" Patou glazed the words with derision, "Buckley is considered something on the order of Cro-Magnon man. I guess he basically took issue with Yale's philosophy that all sides of any question can be presented with complete impartiality. He thinks a university should propound a more unified point of view, if not an actual ideology. Events seem to have passed Mr. Buckley without his notice."

"I'd say that was a fair reading of the book. Consider this: Buckley would be happy as a pig in shit at West Point. The academy is everything he wants Yale to be. It has a single mission. To produce soldiers. It has its own prepackaged set of values, the West Point values. The academy presents the point of view it wants to present, on the questions it wants to raise. There are no other questions, no other points of view, no other values, no other

314

mission. An illustration. At the moment, we are fighting a war against forces led by one Ho Chi Minh. In the three years I've been there, West Point has not seen fit to tell me anything about Mr. Minh, other than the fact he is the enemy, and perhaps incidentally, their leader. We are taught nothing of his politics, his mission, his values, in short, those forces which may motivate him and his legions to wage war against our army. Up at West Point, only one thing counts. West Point. Answer your question?"

"Yes. Sounds pretty conservative."

"That isn't the word for it." The two stood up, facing each other across the table.

"Then what is it?" Patou asked.

"It's like a laboratory, or a zoo. Everything is out in the open, flourishing. Outside the gates, there is democracy. Inside, there is West Point. Going to West Point, you learn how men work, the way they fit together. This may sound strange, but it's West Point's way of preparing you to lead our army, which serves a democratic society."

"Yeah, I see what you mean. It's almost exactly the opposite of what Yale tries to do."

"There's only one West Point, man. It's a unique experience. Can't get it anyplace else. Hand must have known it, or sensed it, anyway."

"He did. You're right. But you still haven't answered my question. Is West Point as straight as David thought it was?"

"Christ! You're fuckin' obsessed with how fuckin' straight West Point is! I told you the place isn't overrun with fags."

"I know, but you're still avoiding my question. Why? Does it frighten you?" Patou stared earnestly at Slaight. He wasn't teasing. He really wanted to know, in the same way Slaight had become obsessed with figuring out what was going on behind the cover-up of Hand's murder. They began walking slowly out of the bar's garden.

"I guess I just don't know the answer, Patou. You're asking me something I don't know much about."

Patou nodded as if he understood.

"If what you say about Hand's image of West Point is right, then he at least had a handle on it. West Point is all men. It was conceived of by men, it's run by men, only men are admitted as cadets. There are all these god-damn men in one place at one time, and there's no way, *no way, man,* you can get away from it. It's like this, Patou. While you're at West Point, the men who run the academy have total control over your life. Total. Everything you do is controlled and measured by them. It lasts four years, four long fuckin' years. During that time, you go from being controlled to being one of the controllers. It's like driving through a small town late at night. If you blink, you miss it. The passage is that quick. Know what I mean?"

"I think so."

"No, you don't, Patou. You've got no idea whatsoever. Know why? You haven't *been there,* man. You haven't been a cadet."

"That's ridiculous. You're saying you can't learn about something without experiencing it."

"That's right. Exactly."

"Then what about books? What about education? West Point is supposed to be a college, isn't it?"

"Forget education, Patou. West Point is a way of life. That's the way the academy describes itself, literally. A way of life. Quit thinking of West Point as a place, and think of it as being alive, like an animal or a human being. West Point propagates its own species. They're called graduates, West Pointers. They're different from you and me. They're special. They're *better*. And they're all men."

"Sounds like fascism to me."

"Fascism, smashism. Who gives a damn? You wanted to know what it was like. I told you."

"How did it feel, like you said, being controlled all that time, then becoming one of the controllers? It must have been something of a shock." Patou smiled nervously. "Like getting drunk for the first time and waking up with a hangover." Slaight laughed.

"I don't know what it felt like, Patou. I never thought about it. I told you. It just happened. Fast."

"Do you think David knew about West Point? I mean, by the time he died. The way you told me about it just now."

They were walking out of the bar, and Slaight stopped. He faced Patou in the glare of the streetlight. The kid's blue outfit glowed. He was dressed for the street.

"That's the best goddamn question you asked me all night, Patou." Slaight stared past him, across the street. Even late at night, you could see heat rise from the streets of New Orleans.

"You know what I think? I think David Hand knew more about West Point than I'll ever know. I'm not sure how, and I'm not sure why. But inside, I know it. I knew it back in Beast, when I was his squad leader. He had West Point figured. He knew about fuckin' control, man. He *knew*." Slaight stepped from the curb in the direction of Ursulines Street. He was tired, and he needed to talk to Irit before he slept. His conversation with Billy Patou bothered him. The kid had raised as many questions as he'd answered. Maybe Irit had some ideas. Maybe, hell. She always did.

"You remind me so much of David . . ." said Billy Patou. Slaight heard him, but he kept walking and did not respond. He couldn't.

BOOK V

Duty, Honor, Country, Self

26

Slaight was hanging up his uniforms in the closet of Room 226, New South Barracks, making trip after trip up and down the stairs, back and forth to the company trunk room, moving his books and shoes and boots and file cabinets and stuff back into his old room in Company D-3. It was August 27, 1968, the first day of Reorganization Week, the seven days immediately preceding Labor Day weekend. From the four corners of the globe, cadets were returning to West Point to prepare for the new academic year. Slaight had spent August at Fort Leonard Wood, Missouri, as a "third lieutenant" on the Academy's Army Orientation Program. He was the executive officer of an Infantry Basic Training Company. Thirty days of hell. Another Beast Barracks, army style. He was glad to be back in his old room.

The sign on his door said his roommate was going to be John Lugar, a tall, rangy redhead from San Bruno, California. Lugar, as usual, was late. Slaight was glad to have him for a roommate. Leroy Buck, now the company first sergeant, had not only given him back his old room, he'd put him in with Lugar, a good guy. Slaight was straightening his stuff, filling drawers, making his bunk, aligning his books. Then he saw the note. It was Scotch-taped to the shade on his desk-lamp.

The handwriting was tiny, hard to read. He bent over.

> *Slaight: Grimshaw wants to see you up at*
> *Bldg 720, ASAP. Today.—CQ*

The note had been left there by some dimbo yearling. They'd been back from Buckner for several days. Beast was over at midweek. Now it was Friday. When in hell was "today"? He leaned out his door.

"Hey. Cee Que! Get up here. Room 226." He heard footsteps on the stairs, two at a time. A freshly mown yearling in khakis appeared in his door.

"Yessir."

"I'm not sir to you any more, Ridgeway, you dullard. You're a yearling now, remember? You got recognized last June. My name's Ry. You first name is . . ."

"Barry."

"Yeah. Barry. Okay, Barry, I got this note here. What-thefuck is it supposed to mean? When, may I ask, is 'today'?"

"Grimshaw came by first thing this morning. I guess he knew you were due back today. He told me to leave a note for you to come up and report to him as soon as you got back. He said to tell you that you'd better be looking good, too. He was . . ."

"He was being fuckin' Grimshaw, is what he was."

"Yeah."

"So I'm supposed to drive around to see Grimshaw, huh? He say what it was about?"

"Nope. Just said to leave the note."

"Well. From now on, Barry, when you leave a note, you leave it out where a guy can fuckin' see it. I've been in and out of this room a half-dozen times and never saw this damn thing. Grimshaw's probably going to chew me a new one, because I couldn't see this microscopic excuse for a goddamn note."

"I'm sorry. I must have . . ."

"You fucked up."

"Yeah."

"Well, do me a favor, will you? Scare up a couple of beans and get them to haul the rest of my stuff up here to my room. And tell them to carry Lugar's up here, too."

"Ry?"

"Yeah. What is it?"

"They said we can't use plebes to carry upperclass gear during re-orgy week this year."

"Yeah? Well, who is 'they'?"

"The cadet regimental staff. They put out the word this morning."

321

"You seen anything in writing?"

"No . . ."

"Get the beans together and organize them and get that shit up here, before some poop-sheet comes down. Far as I'm concerned, what I just heard is a goddamn rumor. Right?"

"If you say so."

"I say so. Now move, man. Move! I got to get myself together for my audience with Grimshaw." Ridgeway ran down the hall, calling out unfamiliar names. Jesus. A whole new set of plebes to get used to. And now Grimshaw. This could not be good. Slaight thought for sure when he talked to Hedges that day in June . . . he thought for sure Grimshaw would be shitcanned. Slaight pulled on his khakis and wondered what was going on. Only one way to find out. Building 720. Grimshaw's office.

Bang! Bang!

"Enter."

"Sir, Mr. Slaight reports to the company tactical officer as ordered."

"Ah. Slaight. Good of you to come. What time is it?"

"Sixteen hundred, sir."

"Sixteen hundred. You just coming off leave?"

"Nosir. AOT. Fort Leonard Wood."

"What took you so long to get up here?"

"I didn't get the note until a few moments ago, sir. The charge of quarters left it in my room as you told him, sir. I just didn't see it."

"You didn't see it."

"Nosir."

"Are you having trouble with your eyesight, Mr. Slaight?"

"Nosir."

"Look down at your shoes, Mr. Slaight. What do you see?"

"Shoes, sir."

"Shoes in need of a good spit-shine. Am I correct, mister?"

"Yessir."

322

"I'll ask you again, then. Are you having problems with your eyesight?"

"Nosir."

"Look in the mirror on my door, mister." Slaight did an about-face and looked in the mirror. This game had been played before. He about-faced again.

"What did you see, Mr. Slaight?"

"I saw myself, sir."

"You notice your haircut, mister?"

"Yessir."

"Two inches on top, mister?"

"About that, sir."

"About that!"

"I'd say it was close to two inches, sir, without taking out a ruler and measuring."

"You getting smart with me, mister?"

"Nosir."

"You planning on starting off this year the way you finished last year, Slaight?"

"Nosir."

"Then I suggest you get yourself back down to the barracks and deport yourself like a soldier, mister. Do I make myself clear?"

"Yessir."

"If that means getting fitted for eyeglasses, Mr. Slaight, perhaps you'd like to pay a visit to sick call. Your eyesight seems to be ailing, mister. Would you like some help filling out a sick slip, Slaight? I've got a stack of them right here on my desk for you. Special. Like me to fill one out for you, Slaight?"

"Nosir." Slaight's temper was barely . . . just barely under control. Grimshaw had been laying for him ever since that business with Major Consor.

"Well, mister. I want you to avail yourself of sick-call privileges at least once each week. And every Saturday morning, during barracks inspection, I want a report on the status of your health, signed by a medical doctor, displayed in a manila folder on your bunk, mister. I want it out there where I can see it. And you know what I want stenciled on that manila folder, mister?"

"Nosir."

"I want that folder to read, in letters one inch high, 'Slaight's Sick-Call Report.' Is that understood?"

"I'm not certain, sir. Let me get this straight. Are you ordering me to go on sick call every week?"

"Let's put it this way, Slaight. If you know what's good for you, you'll do as you've been told. Understood?"

"Nosir. What if I have no need for sick call, sir? What if I have no need for sick call, but I do have need to attend my first academic class in the morning, sir? What if I'm scheduled for a test each morning of the week, first period, and I am required by the Academic Department to take those tests unless I am sick, sir, a valid, academic requirement. And what if all five days in a row, sir, I am not sick. Thus I have no legal or moral reason to take sick call and miss a test. What then, sir? What is good for me then, sir? I'd like some guidance here, sir. I really would."

Grimshaw fidgeted in his chair, never taking his eyes off the cadet standing before him at the position of attention. Oh, how he wished Slaight would utter the least little insubordination! How he'd like to nail that squealing little bastard to the wall, put him out there on the area where he belonged.

"Mr. Slaight. I believe I've made myself quite clear. I want this report—'Slaight's Sick-Call Report'—displayed on your bunk every Saturday morning until I tell you otherwise. I don't care if you have to go on sick call during your free time on Saturday afternoons. I don't give a goddamn what you do to get that report every week, do you understand me? I want to see it displayed, I want the manila folder lettered as I told you, and I want to see the signature of a medical doctor every week, Slaight. Every week. Is that understood?"

"That is understood, sir."

"Now. I suggest you drive yourself down to the barracks and get yourself looking strac, mister, because the commandant wants to see you at 1745, in his office. Now get out of my sight, Slaight, before I pull out my two-dash-ones and quill you into the middle of next week. Get out of here!"

The cheeks of Grimshaw's thin, childlike face were quivering he was so mad. Slaight paused one beat . . . two, watched him shake. He saluted.

"Good afternoon, sir," he said. Grimshaw returned the salute, and Slaight left.

He went straight to Buck's room and told him about Grimshaw.

"What are you going to do, man?"

"I'm gonna do what I should have done last fuckin' year. I'm gonna call that lawyer, Captain T. Clifford Bassett, and I'm going to see him before I report to Hedges. I have been back here exactly five hours, Buck. Five fuckin' hours. The shit's up around my goddamn knees. I can feel it getting deeper. Hey. Keep an eye out for Lugar for me, will you? Tell him if I know Grimshaw, he'll be down in the company area tonight, and he'll pay a special visit to our room. And do me a favor. Keep an eye on those beans the CQ put on my room. Make sure they get our shit in there in some kinda order. I figure we're going to have about an hour after supper before Grimshaw is bopping around, making his presence felt."

"Okay, Slaight. I'll take care of it for you."

"Jesus. Re-orgy week was never like this. What a hell of a note. And wait till you hear what I've got for you on the Hand thing. I'll tell you at supper. Hey. Put me on your table, will you?"

"Already have. Me and you and Lugar and Kenny Towne, a couple of decent cows, the yearlings who are doing my company clerking for me, and the two best fuckin' beans I could find."

"See you at supper formation, Buck."

"Heeeeeaauh!"

"Yeah. Heeeeeeaauh. Fuckin'-A."

27

Slaight picked up the phone in the D-3 orderly room and dialed the number for the Department of Law.

"Captain Bassett, please. Mr. Slaight calling."

"Just one moment, please." A secretary.

"Captain Bassett."

"Sir, it's Mr. Slaight. Rysam Slaight. I had you for law a couple of times last year."

"Yes. Of course! Slaight. What's on your mind?"

"I've got to see you, sir. Today. Right now. Have you got, I don't know . . . an hour?"

"Sure. Come on over. You know where we are . . . basement of Thayer Hall, down here with the heat ducts and the boilers. . . . Can I ask you what this is about?"

"I'd rather discuss it when I get over there, sir."

"Sure. Come on down. I'm in Room 408. You'll see my name on the door."

"Yessir. Good-bye, sir."

Slaight ran up to his room, changed into his Class A shoes, ran a shine-rag over his belt buckle, dabbed some Brylcreem on stray hairs. He ran over to Thayer Hall. No time to lose. Com at 5:45. It was 4:30 now.

He found Captain T. Clifford Bassett buried in a closet-size room so full of paperwork it looked ready to burst.

"Claims. They've got me pulling post claims officer. You would not believe what people lose when they move. And every item, every description of every little doodad has to go through me. If I see another van lines company name, another shipping firm, another air-freight outfit, I'm going to turn in my JAG Corps branch insignia and tell them to make me a Spec-4 and put me in the Infantry. Anything's got to be better than *this*." Bassett laughed in that squinty-eyed way, his wide face smiling from one side to the other. His ample frame was doing little to lessen the crowded conditions of his office. Over in the Tactical Department, they would call Bassett a "typical goddamn P—overweight, indifferent, probably subversive." Slaight knew better. T. Clifford Bassett had been editor of the *Law Review* at Harvard Law, and had spent three years with Sullivan and Cromwell on Wall Street before getting drafted, opting to serve four years as an army lawyer, a captain, rather than two years as an enlisted man. Around the Law Department he was considered eccentric. But he was respected. He was by a full head and shoulders the best lawyer in the department, and everyone including the colonel, the tenured professor of the department, knew it.

Bassett signaled for Slaight to be seated. He spread a small hole in the poop-sheets on his desk, withdrew a yellow legal pad from some secret stash, pulled out a black army pen, and peered over the top edge of his army-issue glasses, perched on the end of his nose, used only for reading.

"So. Mr. Slaight. I never thought I'd see you again. What seems to be the hurry?"

"I've got to go see the com today at five forty-five. I'm going to need some legal advice. One way or another, I've gotten myself neck-deep in shit, if you don't mind my saying so, sir."

"I don't mind."

"I'm going to have to give it to you quick, sir, and you're going to have to keep what I tell you to yourself. In total confidence."

"You want this to be an official legal counseling session then?"

"Official?"

"Yes. In that way, it's covered by lawyer-client privilege. I am bound by law not to divulge anything you tell me, not even before a court of law, not even under the orders of the general himself."

"That's good enough."

"Now, what's this about, Slaight?"

"The cadet they found drowned up in Popolopen last May, Captain Bassett, kid by the name of David Hand."

"Ah yes. I saw the report when it came through here. An accidental drowning, as I recall."

"It wasn't any accidental drowning. The kid was murdered. By another cadet. The kid, David Hand, was a homosexual. He got himself fucked in the ass just before he drowned. The guy who fucked him killed him. I have very good reason to believe the murderer was another cadet. I've done some pretty extensive research on the death of David Hand, sir. I've got it narrowed down. It was one of three cadets . . . perhaps one of six . . . who were on a recruiting trip to New Orleans in 1966. Hand was recruited by one of the cadets. He had an affair with the cadet at that time. The affair continued here at the academy. I'm pretty sure the guy Hand made it with in New Orleans was the guy who killed him up at Popolopen."

"Yes. Indeed. But one of three—maybe six—cadet recruiters . . . that's still a rather broad area of suspects, isn't it? And isn't there a chance that it could have been another cadet entirely?"

"There's always a chance, sir. But it gets narrower. I've got a guy I think can identify the cadet Hand had the affair with. If we can link Hand directly to one guy, one cadet, I think we've got him. Even if the odds are against us, and it's not him, I think the pressure will be great enough that the guy will come clean. He'll help flush out the murderer. Any way you cut it, Hand was murdered. It wouldn't take much police work to figure out who did it. But the thing is . . . nothing is happening. Nothing is being done. The commandant knows Hand was killed. But he hasn't done a goddamn thing. He called me off leave in June to talk to me about it. I tried to come see you then, but you were on leave, too."

"Yes. I got a note from my secretary that you'd called."

"Well, here's the thing. The com tried to make a deal with me. Keep quiet, and he'd make me a battalion commander. Now, sir. I stand dead in the middle fifth of the class in Aptitude, about six hundred in General Order of

Merit. I'm about as much of a battalion commander as you are Infantry." Bassett laughed. "He knows it, and I know it. But when I left his office in June, the offer still stood. Now, today, in about an hour, I've got to go see him again. And I want to know what I should do. I want to know my legal obligations, insofar as having knowledge of the commission of a felony is concerned. And I want to know my rights—what protection I have under the UCMJ, whatever USMA regulations are involved. Basically, I want total legal advice, as fast and complete as you can give it to me."

"Hmmmmmm." Bassett leaned back in his chair, stuck the pen in his mouth, and chewed quietly. "You *have* got yourself a problem here. Open the door, will you?" Slaight opened the door behind him.

"Adrian? Adrian?" Bassett's secretary looked up from her typing. "You can go home now. I won't be needing you any more today."

"Thanks, Captain," the secretary said. She stood up, preparing to leave.

"Close the door, Slaight. Now. I want you to start at the beginning." Bassett had a smile on his face. It was an odd smile, and with his big nose and glasses perched there, his eyes squinting, his big eyebrows dancing on his forehead like a couple of caterpillars, he looked owlish. Slaight liked Bassett. He knew Bassett was going to enjoy this. He was going to fuckin' *eat it up*.

"I want you to give me the whole story, Slaight. All the information you've got. Every last single solitary scrap. Every tiny detail. You may not know what's important. You let *me* decide what's important, and what's not, okay?"

"Yessir."

"And stop calling me sir. I want all the information on this Hand matter you've got, and I want to know where you got it. In what form—written, verbal, firsthand, secondhand. I want to know the names of the people you've talked to, so I can get some idea of their veracity. As closely, and as quickly as you can, I want you to reconstruct your entire involvement in this matter. I want to know what transpired between you and the commandant in June. *Exactly.* And I want to know by what miracle or act of God you think you've narrowed down the list of people, or cadets, who may have murdered this young man, Hand, to three, or six. And why. I want to know your reasoning behind every last thing you tell me."

Bassett rocked forward in his chair, took pen in hand, and peered over his glasses. The smile was gone.

"Now. Give it to me straight. We haven't got much time."

Slaight ran it down, the whole thing, from the first day he saw Hand in Beast back in '67, right through his conversation with the kid in blue in New Orleans, through his phone calls to the sergeant major out in Santa Fe. The sergeant major had touched a friend in the Registrar's Office for the names of the cadets who had made the recruiting trip to New Orleans in 1966: two firsties, '67; two cows, '68; two yearlings, '69. Slaight's class. Three of them, the sergeant major learned, had been scheduled to speak at Hand's school—one cow and two yearlings. The two firsties had spent that day with local civic groups. But there were no records on file at the academy listing who actually made the appearance at Hand's school that day. The records showed the schedule, but there had been no after-action report, army lingo for a record of what actually happened. So there it was. Slaight gave Bassett the names, he had them memorized. Bassett nodded and scribbled, nodded and scribbled, stopping only to push his glasses back up on his nose.

Only once during the entire course of Slaight's story did Bassett stop writing, looking startled:

"William Beatty, huh?" he asked, obviously recognizing the name from somewhere. "I wonder what in hell *he's* doing in on all this?" He scribbled Beatty's name, put a circle around it, and nodded for Slaight to go on.

Slaight spat out the story rapidly, reflexively. To his surprise, he found himself tiring of the subject. It seemed so long ago that day on the area back in May. In June he had a file going. By the time he left New Orleans, the file had turned into files. Now, after a month at Fort Leonard

Wood, pondering the facts, making phone calls, filling in the gaps, staying up late at night thinking and drinking and talking to Irit on the phone, the files filled a one-cubic-foot-square Sears and Roebuck file box. Page after page after page of notes, nearly verbatim transcripts of phone calls, ideas jotted down, things which he recollected, sitting bolt upright in the middle of the night. The facts. A separate file folder for each person involved. Another folder for each fact unattachable to a specific person. A folder containing notes on each significant meeting—Hedges, the sergeant major, the kid in blue. And a crude cross-referencing system, annotating people, places, conversations, facts, ideas, conjecture, conclusions. The Sears and Roebuck box weighed thirty pounds now. He knew. They weighed it at the St. Louis airport when he flew back to New York.

Yes, he was tired of the whole thing, as he rattled off the details from memory, tired, but still determined. Now, after his confrontation with Grimshaw, whom he'd expected to have vanished into thin air, or perhaps another tour in Vietnam, coming back to West Point and finding Grimshaw still riding herd over D-3 after listening to Hedges castigate him for "weakness," Slaight didn't know what to think. He didn't know what to expect. He was scared. The summer was over. They had him back at West Point now. Grimshaw—all that diddlyshit crap about the sick-call report and haircut and shine—Jesus! The meeting with Grimshaw meant nothing had changed. They were playing for keeps.

As he recounted the details of the Hand case to Bassett, the whole business seemed like a war story or something. Listening to himself talk was like sitting around the mess hall out in Leonard Wood, listening to a bunch of dufus sergeants talking about what it was like "back in Nam . . . in the bush," thinking up detail after detail, day after day, contact after contact, killin' fuckin' gooks, man, that's where it's fuckin' at. You ain't *been there* till you seen them fuckin' dinks, man, dinks coming out of the woodline, coming atchew through the wire, man, trip flares going off all over the fuckin' place, man, whole fuckin' night lit up like Times fuckin' Square, man, tracers and mo-gas and shit going off all around you, and dinks, fuckin' dinks. . . .

They were never the enemy. Always "dinks" or "gooks" or "Charlie," like the war wasn't being fought against an enemy as much as it was being fought against an idea—something none of them could *grasp,* so they pulled names out of their asses and threw them around trying to describe the undescribable. Sitting there in Bassett's office, Slaight felt the same way, helpless, like he was trying to overcome some huge doubt with a flood, a goddamn *torrent* of details, facts, names—throwing all this shit at Bassett, just sitting there in that tiny office throwing everything he knew at Bassett like a desperate fool, so strung out, there was nothing left to do but talk. Talk. Talk. Hoping somebody would fuckin' *understand.* Now he knew what they meant when they said *been there.* How could you describe what it was like to have *been there* to somebody who hadn't *been there?*

Slaight spewed data, checking the time, and slowly he began to realize why his old man had always refused to talk about the war when he'd been growing up. As a kid, he knew his father had fought in the war—World War II—because his mother told him. She'd let it out every once in a while. That was when "your father was gone." *Gone.* The word she used to describe it, the war. *Gone.* And Slaight would ask his father about the war, from when he was just a little kid, maybe he'd been to the Saturday matinee, and maybe he'd seen *To Hell and Back,* or some other glory-hole war movie, and he'd come home and ask his father about the war, and always it was the same. His father would say: I'll tell you about it, son, when you're old enough. When's that, Dad? he'd ask. When you're old enough to understand, son, his father would say, sitting on the screen porch, drinking his martinis. When you're old enough to understand. Slaight never got old enough to understand.

He left for West Point in June of 1965 with his mother's blessing and his father's unspoken disapproval. Now he knew why. Sitting there in Bassett's office, talking about his own version of *been there, man,* he knew why. His father had entertained the hope of all fathers—that somehow things would be better for their sons and daughters, somehow the world would become a better place, a place where you didn't need to understand, because there just wasn't anything that was necessary to understand in the way you had to understand a war, understand the reasons men went out and killed other men. His father had known if Slaight went to West Point, the day would come when he'd have to understand. The notion so saddened him, so depressed him, that he couldn't have made the world a better place or something—a bottomless fatherly depression. . . . He almost hated his son for going to West Point. Consciously or unconsciously, it didn't really matter. The fact remained the same. His son would understand. He'd become one of them. Slaight could almost see his father in his mind's eye, sitting there on the porch in the late afternoon, sipping his martinis and smoking his cigarettes with his back to the boy. He wouldn't—or couldn't—face him, because he was helpless.

When he was finished, Captain T. Clifford Bassett leaned back in his chair, let his glasses slip down to the tip of his nose, stuck the end of the army pen back in his mouth.

"Well," he said. "As you said. Deep shit. And getting deeper. When are you scheduled to see Hedges?"

"Five forty-five."

"Ten minutes. Okay. Legally—let me emphasize this—*legally* this is where you stand. You have no firsthand knowledge of the commission of a felony. You certainly have reason to believe a felony was committed, but you do not have firsthand knowledge. Therefore, you are under no legal obligation to report anything to the authorities. You see?"

"Yeah, I think so."

"Okay. Morally. You can do as you damn well please. You can spill your guts to Hedges, if it will make you feel any better. You can keep your mouth shut if that would make a difference. Morally, it's open field running, Slaight. You go in any direction you want. Just between

333

you and me, however, between lawyer and client. I would not advise telling Hedges any more than you have to. From what you've told me, he has not exactly shown himself to be eager to roll back the rock. If you ask me, Hedges would just as soon see you going out with the tide. You represent, shall we say, a threat."

"A threat?"

"Indeed, Slaight. There was never an Article 32 investigation run on this Hand thing. You recall the Article 32 investigation from your Military Law studies with me, no doubt—the military equivalent of a grand jury. An investigation to determine whether or not, in fact, a crime has been committed. If there had been an Article 32, I'd know about it. They all come through the Post JAG office, and at West Point, the Department of Law is the Post JAG office. No Article 32. No crime. Except for you, Slaight. You and your knowledge of the autopsy. Hedges doesn't know anything else, does he?"

"No. All he knows is, I talked to Consor."

"Good. Keep it that way. Now. How to handle Hedges today? I'd go in there and keep my trap shut, if I were you. But don't forget. You are bound by the Honor Code, which puts you in a, shall we say, class apart, insofar as the UCMJ is concerned. In other words, Hedges has the Honor Code as an extra little cannon in his arsenal. And don't put it past him to use it, Slaight."

"Don't worry about that, sir. I've heard all the stories."

"Indeed. Then you see what I'm driving at. If he asks you a question, you are honor-bound to answer the question truthfully. If you don't, he'll bounce you out of here on an honor violation, which is probably exactly what he'd like to do with you. Get rid of you. ASAP. So answer his questions, and answer them truthfully. To the letter, and not beyond. The trick is, of course, to divert him—keep him from asking questions, as much as that's possible. Having never met the man, I am uncertain as to how you should proceed in that direction, Slaight. My advice is . . . watch your step."

Slaight was just sitting there, listening to him, this

round little captain, sitting in his tiny office, boiling it all down.

"Captain Bassett, I really appreciate this. I mean, I really appreciate what you're doing for me, giving me all this advice. I've been looking for advice like this for weeks. But I've got to ask you something. What the fuck is *going on?*"

Bassett sat there looking at Slaight.

"Mr. Slaight. You'd better get yourself over to the commandant's office. You've got only—let me see—four minutes."

"But, sir, I wanna know. What's *going on?* I wanna know."

"Slaight. On your feet. Out. You've got only a couple of minutes before you see the com. I'll wait for you here in my office. Come on over when you're finished seeing the com. We'll talk. I want to hear what he has to say."

Slaight standing up and grabbing his cap, mumbling thanks, feeling for the doorknob, heading down the hall and up the stairs, back across Thayer Road, into the area of barracks, up to the com's office. Old Bassett. What a guy! He just sat there in that little office of his and took it all in. Then he just boils it right down. It's all so logical. You go in, and you see the com. You step here. You don't step there. You *watch your step.* It's all so fuckin' *logical.* Jesus. You go to West Point, and they pump you full of logic, you study law, you study math, higher math, higher and higher math until finally you're up there with integral calculus and differential equations, statistics and probability, sliding into applied sciences and engineering . . . they've given you *the key,* the goddamn language of logic, and what they're telling you is . . . take this logic, kid, and apply it. Use it. Believe it. Logic as science. Logic as The Answer. Logic with all its logical ends to mysteries of life. Logic as religion. You get down in there so deep, so deep in the math and the science and law and tactics and shit, and finally you're *inside the logic.* You look around, and there are all these facts, all this information, all these formulas and ways to deal with information, ways to filter it, ways to make information work for you.

335

But between you and the logic is empty space. *You're in a hole,* nothing around you really, just space, air . . . no map, no boundaries, no *edge to the logic.* The logic is a dream, one of those quick ones, thirty-minute nap, a whole week goes by in thirty minutes, but when you wake up, you can remember only the last five minutes of the week, and man, they *sucked.* . . .

That's where Slaight was now, taking the stairs to the com's office two at a time, cap in his left hand, khakis slapping, slapping . . . *slap* . . . *slap* . . . *slap* . . . wetly against his calves with every step. He was inside the logic, inside the hole, and he didn't know what in hell was *going on.*

28

The door was open.

"Slaight. Good to see you, young man. Come on in." Brigadier General Charles Sherrill Hedges was down at the end of his office, seated behind his desk, waving at Slaight with his left hand. Slaight assumed the position.

"Sir, Mr. Slaight reports to the commandant of cadets as ordered."

Hedges returned the salute, indicated the chair next to his desk.

"Sit down. Sit down! God *damn!* Good to see you. How was your summer? Get your fill?" The general chuckled. He was sitting sideways, one leg crossed, hands behind head. A carbon. Slaight in the same chair. Exactly the same as that day in June.

"Fine, sir. My summer was fine."

"I heard you did a hell of a job out there at Leonard Wood. One *hell* of a job. Your battalion commander called me the other day to say so. You were the only cadet on AOT in that training brigade, weren't you?"

"Yessir."

"Well, mister, you left one hell of an impression on those people out there. You were a credit to the Corps, Slaight. A credit. Your battalion C.O.—a colonel . . . whatshisname?"

"Perdue, sir."

"Yes. Colonel Perdue. He said you taught all the battalion classes. That true?"

"Yessir."

"How many hours in all? He told me. I can't recall."

"Seventy-seven, sir."

"Seventy-seven! In thirty days. God *damn*, Slaight. You did a fine job. Outstanding, young man. Outstanding." Hedges rocked back and forth on his tilting chair. He gazed across the area. Slaight hadn't been called in six hours after his return to the academy to be congratulated for his performance on AOT. Chummy. Hedges was being chummy. Slaight waited.

"Slaight, I haven't got much time this afternoon—got to be over at the supe's office in, let me see, twelve minutes. But I called you in this afternoon to let you know that my offer—the one we spoke about in June— the offer still stands. A battalion, Slaight. Your own battalion. You still interested?"

"I'm not sure I understand, sir."

"The battalion, Slaight. You recall we spoke about making you a battalion commander."

"Yessir. And I also recall that we spoke about the fact that I'm in the middle of the class in Aptitude, and that I stand about six hundred in General Order of Merit."

"Fuck the G.O.M. And fuck Aptitude! Your performance out there at Leonard Wood on AOT is all I need, young man. You know that?"

"I guess so, sir."

"You guess! You did a damn fine job, an outstanding job for that battalion, and you know it, Slaight. Come on, mister. Buck up."

"Yessir."

Hedges dropped his foot and rocked forward in his chair. He placed his hands on the desk. His nails were immaculately manicured—pale glowing moons against the light tan of his fingers.

"There remains only one other matter for us to discuss then. The accidental drowning of Cadet David Hand."

Slaight looked at Hedges. *Accidental drowning.* He wasn't wasting any time.

"It has come to my attention that your interest in the Hand matter has . . . ah . . . continued. Is this correct?"

"Yessir."

"Your opinions about the Hand drowning—are they the same as they were when last we spoke on this subject?"

"They are, sir."

"You believe he was murdered, then."

"Yessir. I do."

"Have you . . . ah . . . taken any action, as regards the Hand matter?"

"Action, sir?"

"Official. Have you taken any action . . . official action. Have you done anything in a . . . ah . . . legal sense, Slaight?"

"Nosir. Nothing official."

"Have you formed any opinions as to who might have committed this murder you believe took place? You still believe the official disposition of the case was . . . incorrect?"

"Yessir."

"Yessir, what?"

"I mean, yessir. I have some opinions. And yessir, I believe the official disposition of the case was incorrect. I believe the man was killed."

Hedges stiffened. He ran his thumbs along his belt line, taking the wrinkles out of the front of his khaki shirt. With his left thumb, he brushed his Airborne wings.

"You have names, Slaight?"

"Yessir."

"How many?"

"Six, sir."

"You believe he was murdered by six people?"

"Nosir."

338

"What do you believe, mister?"

"I believe one of the six men whose names I have may have murdered him, sir."

"I see."

Suddenly it was clear. Hedges had sucked him in! He'd been so busy watching his step, he'd missed it completely. Hedges acted as if Slaight had stated definitively in June that he believed Hand was murdered, when, in fact, all he had done was acknowledge he'd spoken with Consor. It was Consor who figured Hand was murdered. The opinion had not been Slaight's, it was Consor's! Hedges had slipped one past him. He'd gotten Slaight to *commit*. He was on record as believing Hand was murdered now. No turning back.

"These six names, Slaight. Do you have them with you?"

"Yessir." What to do? There was something in there . . . something Hedges said. Something logical. Think, goddammit. *Think. Logic.* How the fuck did Hedges lead into it? The battalion . . . Hand . . . any official action . . . that was it. *Official.* Fuck.

"Sir. May I say something."

"What is it, mister? Make it quick. I've got to be at the supe's in a couple of minutes."

"Sir, I'd like to make an official report. You are the commandant of cadets, sir. You are the commander, sir. I'd like to make an official report to you, sir, in your capacity as commandant of cadets. I'm going to give you the six names, sir." Slaight reached into his pants pocket and pulled out a piece of folded yellow legal paper. He withdrew a pen from his shirt pocket, carefully buttoning the flap. He began writing the names on the yellow legal paper.

"The six names, sir, are names of cadets or graduates, sir—officers, sir. I have strong reason to believe that one of these men is the man who murdered David Hand, sir." He continued writing. Hedges stared at him. If Hedges could make an assumption and operate from that position, so could Slaight. What could be more obvious—more *logical*—than making an official report? Doing his duty. That's what he was doing. His duty. He handed the sheet of paper with the six names to Hedges. He glanced at his watch. It was 5:57. He was banking that Hedges had to see the supe at six. . . .

"This comes as . . . something of a shock . . . mister," said Hedges, taking the sheet of paper from Slaight.

"You asked me if I had taken any official action, sir. I hadn't. Not until now. You have the names now, sir. All six of them. If you want to know how I got these names, sir . . ."

"Mr. Slaight. I have to be going . . ."

"If you want to know how I got these names, sir, I can tell you quickly. David Hand was recruited. One of these six men recruited him, on a trip to New Orleans, part of the cadet recruiting program. And that man is, if my reckoning is correct, the man you're looking for, sir." Hedges held the sheet of paper and stood up slowly. Two can play this game. Hedges was standing now, holding the piece of paper in front of him like it was poisoned. Slaight stood up.

"Mister. You let me handle this from now on, you understand me? You got that?" Hedges glared at Slaight. It was the first time Slaight had seen him show anger. Real anger. Hedges was pissed, and he wasn't taking the time—he didn't have the time—to hide it.

"I've got your six goddamn names. Now, you let me handle this thing. You hear me, Slaight? You obviously didn't take the advice I gave you last summer. This case is hands off. You understand that, mister. *Hands off.* You let me handle this. If I hear that you . . ." Hedges' lips quivered. "If I hear that you have anything more to do on this Hand thing, Slaight, I'll rip you a new asshole. You understand me?"

"Yessir."

"You won't know what hit you, got that, Slaight?"

"Yessir."

"Now, post out of here, and don't let me hear another goddamn word about you. You got that, Slaight? Not one fucking word."

"Yessir. Good afternoon, sir." Slaight saluted and left.

Hedges was still standing there, holding the sheet of paper. Slaight could see him from the area, through the big windows of the commandant's office. Hedges and Slaight's six names. God *damn.*

Captain Bassett was puffing on a pipe when Slaight knocked on his door. Bassett nodded in the direction of a metal-frame U.S. government issue office chair and sat down. He told Bassett everything that had happened up in Hedges' office. Bassett chuckled, sending little puffs of acrid smoke out his dime-size nostrils, when Slaight told him about making an "official report," about Hedges standing there with the sheet of paper with the six names on it, just standing there, holding the paper . . . how pissed he got. Bassett chuckled and nodded. Then he pulled his pipe out of his mouth and said:

"You know what my advice is right now, Mr. Slaight? I advise you, as your lawyer, to do just as the commandant said. Sit back and let him handle it. You've done your duty. Lay low. Don't give him the tiniest reason to notice you . . . not the least reason to come down on you. My advice to you is disappear." Slaight nodded his assent. But the question he'd asked Bassett earlier still nagged him.

"Sir, you didn't seem too shocked when I told you the whole story this afternoon. You just took it all down. Now I want to know what's *going* on. For the life of me, I can't figure it. This stuff is beginning to drive me crazy. What have we got here at West Point, anyway? A nest of faggots? This kid Hand isn't just some kind of freak. I want to know what's *going on.* The whole thing has me . . . I don't know what to believe any more."

"Well, Mr. Slaight, I've been here two years. There have been instances in the past . . ." Bassett puffed on his pipe, tamping it with the eraser end of a pencil.

"What goddamn instances? When?"

"Last year. An officer and a cadet were caught *flagrante delicto* down in North Auditorium one night after taps. The cadet was medically discharged. I don't know what happened to the officer. Two other cadets

341

were medically discharged for homosexuality . . . that was over a year ago, I believe."

"Jesus. I didn't know about any of this."

"They don't exactly issue press releases every time they get rid of someone, Slaight."

"Yeah. I know what you mean."

"I'm sure you have heard about the cadet 'flashers,' the exhibitionists."

"I've heard about them. We had one in our company two years ago. The one they called the 'Phantom.' He got away with dropping trou for six months before they caught him one night, down at the bottom of the ramp leading up to New South Area."

"Ah, yes. The 'Phantom.' I recall the case. He was medically discharged."

"They medical-discharge all these guys?"

"Not much choice. Any other type of discharge requires too much paperwork. Hearings. A medical can be expedited. They get one of the exhibitionists on the bus and out the gate in a couple of days."

"Christ. I didn't know that."

"Indeed. Now. Getting back to your question, as to whether or not there's a 'nest' here . . . I just don't know, Slaight. The psychiatrist, over at the hospital, his wife is friendly with my wife. We live on the same block up in Cornwall. She's told my wife quite a few stories. The shrink never sees any of the officers stationed here, of course. My God, think how that would look on your record! April 4. Major So-and-So visited the post psychiatrist. Diagnosis: mild anxiety. Prescription: five milligram Librium. Can you imagine?" Bassett laughed.

"Yeah. They'd love that down at the Pentagon."

"Sure. The promotion boards would have a field day with a prescription for Librium. So. The shrink doesn't see any of the officers, but he sees plenty of their wives. His wife and my wife have discussed his—shall we say—practice over a few cups of coffee. Let's put it this way. Here at West Point, there are certain problems among the officer corps. I wouldn't imagine that they are any different in nature than those on any army post. But the atmosphere at the academy exacerbates the problems. To put it bluntly, the main problems are alcoholism and impotence. There are quite a few unhappy wives on this post. I don't know what the divorce rate is. I doubt that it would differ significantly from, say, that of a major American corporation. But here, problems are forced beneath the surface of things and held there. By the time an officer gets to be a major, by the time he's got ten or twelve years service, the last thing he wants is to make even a ripple on the surface of the pond. The *last* thing."

"I see what you mean."

"Now, this David Hand business. My guess is that it's an isolated incident. If all that you say is true, and I have no doubt that it is, Hand looks to me like a—shall we say—exceptional figure. If he's as intelligent as you say he was . . ."

"Oh, he was smart, all right. You better believe that."

"Yes. Well, if he was as smart as you say, there may have been a touch of blackmail involved. If not blackmail, then paranoia. The man who killed Hand may have feared that Hand was going to expose him in some way. Hand sounds to me like the type who would excite, let us say, a reasonable fear that he might *do* something. You've been here three years, haven't you, Slaight?"

"Three years. Three long goddamn years."

"Then you no doubt have noticed that this place— West Point, I mean—fairly bubbles along a little current of fear. It's like . . . fuel. It's what makes the place go. Easy to find. Nonperishable. And invisible."

"I don't guess I've ever thought about things that way, Captain. Jesus. Does that apply when it comes to my tac, Major Grimshaw."

"Grimshaw? He's your tac?"

"Yeah. A real winner. He had me up in his office this afternoon, chewing my ass because the com found out he kept me on the area last May when Major Consor, the doctor, wanted to medically excuse me from the area for my feet. They were really fucked up."

"What do you mean?"

"I mean Grimshaw put out the word that nobody in
343

our company could take a medical excuse from area formation. He said he'd double our hours if we did. So I had to walk . . . everybody had to walk . . . no matter what was wrong with you. We had guys on the area last winter who had the goddamn flu, sick, puking, everything. It was ridiculous."

"You're wrong, Slaight. It was criminal."

"I guess that's one way of looking at it. Yeah."

"You said he was chewing you out today?"

"Yeah. He's making me go on sick call every week now. Wants me to put a manila folder on my bunk every Saturday morning for inspection, containing my sick slips. He told me to stencil 'Slaight's Sick-Call Report' on the folder. Christ. He's really out for my ass. He's gonna do everything he can to put me back on the area."

"I'll tell you, Mr. Slaight. What this Major Grimshaw has told you to do is a violation of army regulations. No commander can humiliate his subordinate because he has gone on sick call. This goes back to the incident in World War II—the Patton thing. There's a clause in the 600–200 series . . . I'll find it for you, if you want."

"I'll take your word for it."

"Anyway, there is a specific clause, intended to prevent just such behavior. You would be fully within your rights if you chose to simply ignore Grimshaw's order that you display a sick-call report. I've had my eye on this Grimshaw character for a while now. It looks to me like he's going too far, this time."

"What do you mean, this time?"

"We had one of the kids from your company down here last year, looking for some advice about his bank account. It seems that the bank computer said he overdrew his account, when actually he did not. The computer made an error in the hundreds column, indicated a huge overdraft. Grimshaw wrote the kid up, gave him a fifteen and twenty. The kid wrote an 'Explanation of Report,' and then a 'Reconsideration of Award,' both of them showing his checkbook figures, proving that he hadn't overdrawn his account. Grimshaw ignored him. The kid walked off the fifteen and twenty. Then he received a letter from the bank, apologizing for the computer error. The kid had already walked off his hours. He came down to see us—me, actually—wanting to know if there was anything he could do to get the fifteen demerits rescinded. I helped him draft another 'Reconsideration of Award,' appending the letter from the bank. He sent it up, and Grimshaw rifled it right back to the kid, called him up to his office and threatened him, told him if he took the 'Reconsideration' any higher, he'd get him. Scared the pants off the kid. I tried to get him to go to the wall with Grimshaw, but the kid was too scared. If I had known he was pulling that crap about sick call—not permitting his men to receive proper medical attention—I'd have brought him up on charges myself."

"What do you think I ought to do? If I just disobey his order, what happens to your 'lay low' strategy? That goes out the window, doesn't it?"

"Good point. Tell you what. You make up the manila folder like he told you. Then, if you feel like going on sick call, go. If you don't, then don't go. Leave the damn thing empty. See what he does. If he so much as utters a word to you about it, let me know. I'll dig up the regulation, and I'll pay him a personal visit. I've got enough on Grimshaw right now, with what you've told me, to put the son of a bitch in Leavenworth. There's nothing I'd like better than to nail him. These bastards in the Tactical Department think they're . . . *gods*. My, my. You have got me excited about this." Bassett knocked his pipe on the heel of his shoe and began reloading it.

"I think there's some kind of connection between Hedges and Grimshaw, sir," said Slaight. "Hedges told me last summer he was going to put Grimshaw away for that business with the area and my feet, and I get back today, and there he is, big as fuckin' life."

"I don't care if Grimshaw has a direct pipeline to the President. The law is the law, and it's about time that lesson was learned around here."

"Yeah. I've thought about that once or twice myself. Mandatory chapel ought to go down the drain, too. But Jesus. You know what Hedges said last year? Some guy

345

asked him about chapel one afternoon, when he was giving a talk to our regiment. He said—I think I can quote him almost exact—he said: 'If mandatory chapel goes, then the next thing that's going to happen is they're going to let women in here. Then the next thing that's going to happen is they're going to allow cadets to marry. Then you know what we've got? We haven't got West Point any more. All we've got is a goddamn college.' "

Bassett relit his pipe and chuckled.

"I never said Hedges was a dummy," he said. "He's right, you know. Tradition is like a high wire. The tighter you pull it, the harder it is to walk. West Point had been walking the high wire for a long time now. Things are getting tighter and tighter. Some day, Slaight. Some day, this place is going to change. It won't happen while you and I are here, but we'll see it in our lifetime. You can count on that."

Bassett stood, shoving papers, seemingly at random, into an old leather brief case.

"Now I've got to be getting home. You talk about chewing out. My wife is going to be grinding her teeth by the time I get home. You keep in touch, Slaight. Let me know what happens with Grimshaw. And remember what I said. Keep your nose clean, and lay low. Don't do anything stupid, like drink in the barracks, or miss a class or a formation. Don't give them any excuse to nail you. Hedges has the ball now. Let's see what he does with it."

"Yessir."

"And stop calling me sir. My name is Clifford. You can make plans now to come over for dinner, the first week in September. You and anybody else from your company whom you want to bring. Okay?"

"Yeah. Sure. That'd be great."

"See you then."

"Okay. Thanks, Captain. You really put me back on the track today. I was really flapping there for a while."

They walked upstairs together, Bassett turning north, heading for the parking lot out past the baseball field, Slaight walking west, past the library, back to the barracks.

346

That night, Grimshaw visited Company D-3. At 10:15, he banged on the door of Room 226. Slaight and John Lugar snapped to attention. Grimshaw strode around the room, looking things over. When he reached the sink, he stopped. He pulled a pad of two-dash-ones from his uniform pocket, scribbled on the pad, tore off the slip of paper, and laid it on the counter next to the sink. He turned and looked at Slaight.

"Have the company commander send this up tomorrow morning with the company logbook, mister." He walked out. Slaight walked over to the sink. He picked up the two-dash-one.

SLAIGHT, RYSAM PARKER III   Co. D-3

Room in disarray, i.e.: dusty floor; improperly made beds; cluttered desktop; uniforms improperly aligned; dusty bookshelves; spots in sink.

> Grimshaw, N.E.
> Maj/Inf
> Tac/D-3

Firstie year had begun.

29

It was that way. Bam. You were back. Back at West Point. Back in The Life. It never let up. *Hit. React. Hit. React.* You laughed it off, punching each other in the arm, joking, oof-goofing-and-half-stepping in the hallways, popping towels in the shower, acting like a bunch of high school football players on an "away" football trip, But it never let up. Never. West Point wouldn't let you forget you had been a smack. A bean. A crot. A dullard. They were all around you. New smacks. New beans. New crots. New dullards. West Point never let you forget the past, because the past was *you*.

Slaight and Buck and Lugar and the rest of the guys in D3 shook it off. Coped. By firstie year, for some damn reason, the bullshit made sense. It never ended and it never let up, and you didn't really want it to. If everything went smoothly, without a hitch, if everything were somehow *easy*, it would have invalidated everything that had gone before. And everything that had gone before was *you*.

The attitude was . . . I've sucked shit this long, why not another goddamn year? Why shouldn't these new beans suck the same shit?

Indeed. Why not? Tradition was a seductive trap, and everybody fell for it.

The attitude made about as much sense as anything else about West Point, not much sense at all. You dropped your bags, and you took the place at face value. West Point was gray, you were gray, by the time you graduated, your hair might as well be gray, too, and for more than a few guys, it would be. Gray faces and gray hair and gray uniforms and gray barracks, with the leaves falling off the trees, the wind howling up the Hudson, snaking along the river at water level, hitting the sides of the cliffs, clinging to the stone like gas coming off dry ice, following the contours of the academy, sweeping across the gray concrete area, down your gray wool overcoat collar, sneaking down there under your T-shirt, gray, too, after three years at the cadet laundry, as gray as your notebooks and your blanket and the tiles on the floor of your room in the barracks, and the tiles in the showers and the marble partitions between the johns . . . gray wind, whistling through a gray place in a gray time, under doors through window jambs, turning the air you breathed gray, your teeth gray . . . it was a wonder, the guys in D-3 used to joke, that they didn't find a way to issue gray toothpaste in gray tubes, so you could brush your gray teeth with a gray toothbrush out of a gray toothbrush case, all of which were displayed on the gray shelves of your gray medicine cabinet, mounted on your gray walls. It was a joke, but like everything else about The Life, it was real too. Real enough so you had to laugh at it to get by. John Lugar used to say that Lenny Bruce would have had met his match at West Point. Only the United States Military Academy could absorb his penetrating, razor-edge paranoia without showing a wound. Lenny Bruce, Lugar said, could successfully needle the Catholic Church, because the goddamn Catholic Church didn't know what to do. West Point did. They'd just put him in an auditorium full of cadets and let those stony gray faces eat him alive.

Guys got a lot of rack. Sleep. Rack was like women. You went at it with a vengeance, greed. You wanted to sleep the way you wanted to fuck. You could never get enough. In D-3 they coined code words for the sleep they coveted every day. Night was just plain rack. Then starting in the morning, there was ABR: after breakfast rack. MPR: mid-period rack, between classes. BDR: before dinner rack. ADR: after dinner rack. PMR: afternoon rack. BSR: before supper rack. ASR: after supper rack. Guys would stay up bullshitting and studying until 1 or 2 A.M. then spend the next day napping, sleeping every loose minute. Guys could lay down on their bunks and be asleep in two minutes, one minute. There were levels of rack. Deep rack. Ultra-deep rack. And deepest of all, something called self-destructive rack, sleep so deep, guys would wake up with a nosebleed. It happened all the time. Nobody could explain it. Nobody tried. They just grabbed a hand towel, soaked it in water, and stopped the bleeding. John Lugar used to say it was the body getting off.

"Hey, Leroy, your brain's having an orgasm," he'd say, when Buck would wake up with a nosebleed.

"Fuck you, Lugar," Leroy would say, mopping up the mess.

Slaight would laugh. Everybody would laugh. Blood all over the goddamn place, blood on the pillow, blood on the floor, blood all over the sink and the counter, blood on your T-shirt . . . everybody would laugh. It was self-destructive rack. It was the way.

September went by. Guys settled in.

October came. Grimshaw kept out of the way. Some kind of general orders came down from Brigade that tacs were supposed to let the firsties run things. Grimshaw didn't even inspect the company Saturday mornings. Slaight's sick-call report just sat there, untouched. The five demerits he picked up that first night disappeared in the muck of digging in. Booking it. Weekends, they went down to Snuffy's and got drunk, or up to a place outside Newburg called the Ideal Nite Club, a country and western bar where you could dance and drink beers for a quarter. Sometimes they took off for New York City, ran around, got drunk, stayed at some cheap hotel, shacked up with girls, got laid, and showed up in ranks on Sunday night smelling like beer and pussy. They were firsties. They were hot shit.

Slaight spent most of his time with Irit Dov. He had the feeling he was hiding. It didn't sit well with him, hiding, but it was better than walking the goddamn area. T. Clifford Bassett checked in with him every week. Anything happening? Nope. Okay. Keep your nose clean. Sure thing. There goes another week, gone like the wind up the Hudson, gone gray and cold like the winter, creeping up on the academy . . . visibly. West Point was the only place in the world where you could *see* temperature. You looked out your window at a little flag hanging from a flagpole at the end of the area, and there, for everyone to see, was the "uniform Flag" for the day. It told you which one of your overcoats you should wear, which hat, the little flag even told you when to wear your goddamn raincoat. It could be pouring rain outside, you'd look out there, and if the little flag didn't say "wear your raincoat," you didn't wear your raincoat. You wore what the little flag told you to wear, and you didn't ask questions. Everybody knew what happened when you asked questions, when you didn't follow the flag. Two-Dash Hedges made sure of that. He wrote a guy up for not obeying the flag early on, put the poor bastard on the area for two months, gross disrespect and heavy discredit or some such shit, but everybody knew. Rain or no rain, cold or no cold, you did what the little uniform flag told you to do, or you paid. It was the way.

One morning at 10:30 Slaight returned to his room from his first two classes and found a big note taped to his door. It was from the CQ and it said to report to Grimshaw, ASAP, as soon as possible. It was October 21, seven weeks into the year. Slaight put a gloss on his shoes, shined his belt buckle, straightened his tie, checked the uniform flag, donned the appropriate outer gear, checked himself one last time in the mirror, and headed up to Building 720. The note had come as a surprise. He was curious. What could Grimshaw have up his sleeve? Nothing was happening. Nothing. On an impulse, he stopped in the orderly room and called Bassett to tell him he was going to see Grimshaw. Bassett said to come over to his office when he was finished. Slaight said okay. Then he walked out of the barracks, under the stoops, and up the back stairs to Building 720. He knocked on Grimshaw's door. He heard the familiar voice. *Enter.* Grimshaw was on the phone when he walked in, talking to somebody. It was all radio talk, Grimshaw on the phone . . . *roger* this . . . *roger* that . . . *over* . . . *six* . . . *roger that* . . . *six-out.* "Six" was radio lingo for a commander. Grimshaw hung up the phone, took Slaight's report, returned the salute, indicated a chair. Slaight sat down. Grimshaw was smiling.

"The little woman," he said, pointing at the phone. "Finest little chunk-a-fanny this side of the Hudson. Wants me home for lunch." Grimshaw, grinning, pointing at the phone . . .

Six . . . roger that . . . *Jesus!* Right then it stung him, deep in the spine, down the back of his neck heading south. This dimbo major's sitting there talking radio baby talk to his old lady on the phone, expecting me to sit here listening . . . listening to that shit like it's all . . . normal . . . *logical* . . . like every goddamn major sits in his office talking radio talk to his wife like that. He knew it. The shit's coming down. Slaight just *knew.*

"Mr. Slaight, you know why I've called you up here today?"

"Nosir."

"It's my duty, mister, to inform you that Aptitude proceedings have begun against you."

"Aptitude proceedings?"

"That's right." Grimshaw picked up a familiar file. Slaight's Aptitude file.

"We're in the process of . . . ah . . . preparing paper work to . . . ah . . . convene an Aptitude Board to . . . ah . . . hear your case."

"When do I get to see this paper work, sir?"

"You don't, mister."

"Then when is the board, sir?"

"You'll be informed in due time, mister. Any other questions?"

"Yessir. Do you have my standing . . . I mean my class Aptitude standing in my file?"

"I don't know what your standing is, Slaight. All I know is, there's going to be an Aptitude Board, and it's going to hear your case."

"I'll tell you what my Aptitude standing is, sir, since you don't seem to know. I stand in the middle fifth of the class. Now I've got a question. If you're going to run an Aptitude Board on me, what about the firsties in the bottom two fifths of the class? What about them? You going to run some kind of an assembly-line Aptitude Board, sir?"

"Don't get smart with me, mister. I'll quill your ass in a minute."

"I'm not getting smart, sir. I asked you a valid question."

"And I don't have to answer your questions, Slaight. Not a fucking one of them. You ask entirely too many questions around here, mister. Too many for your own fucking good. Got that?"

"Yessir."

"Now, I've been keeping track of the 'Slaight Sick-Call Report.' We're in the seventh week of the academic year, correct?"

"Yessir."

"And there are no sick slips in the folder you've been

352

displaying on your bunk every Saturday morning, correct?"

"That's right, sir."

"Then you disobeyed my orders, didn't you, Slaight?"

"Nosir."

"Then how do you explain the empty folder, mister?"

"I didn't go on sick call, sir. I wasn't sick."

"I gave you specific instructions, mister. I told you to go on sick call every week and display your sick slips in that folder."

"You told me to do what I thought was best for me, sir. I didn't get sick. I didn't go on sick call. I figured what was best for me. I followed your instructions to the letter. I did what I thought best."

"You're verging on insubordination, mister."

"Sir, I am discussing with you a situation which obviously has bearing on this Aptitude Board you've told me about, which obviously has bearing on whether or not I'm going to remain a cadet here at West Point, since Aptitude Boards are not empaneled to reward cadets for their exemplary behavior. I'm not being insubordinate, sir. I just want to get the facts straight."

"The facts *are* straight, mister, and they're all right here in this folder."

"When do I get to see them, sir?"

"You don't. You'll hear them. From the board."

"Yessir."

"Now, drive your ass back down in the barracks. And if I were you, mister, I'd go on sick call first thing tomorrow morning."

"Sir?"

"Yeah."

"I'm not going on sick call. Good morning, sir." Slaight saluted and left.

At the end of the hall, he stopped at a secretary's desk and asked to use the phone. He dialed Bassett's number. Bassett picked up.

"It's Slaight. It's happening. Right now."

"What? Slow down, man. What's happening right now?"

"You gonna be at your office for a while?"

"Yes. Until lunch."

"I'll be over before lunch. We'd better talk."

"Good. I'll take you to lunch at the Officers' Club."

"I'm not sure you'll want to, when you hear what I've got to say."

"Come now, Mr. Slaight, it'll be *fun.*"

"Sure. See you."

Slaight ran down to the barracks, into Leroy Buck's room to give the news.

"Slaight. You seen this?" He held up a sheet of paper. Slaight took it. The paper listed the names of cadets excused from class for three days the following week to take part in SCUSA, the Student Conference on United States Affairs, held annually at the academy, attended by students from two hundred colleges around the country. Slaight had spent the last three years working on the committee which was in charge of setting up SCUSA—all the administrative and technical garbage necessary to put together four hundred civilian students and about one hundred cadets, break them down in discussion groups, where they would spend three days on "world affairs." This year, 1968, with campus SDS chapters expected to pack quite a few of the college delegations, SCUSA promised to be interesting for a change. The *Times* was due to cover the melee. Slaight checked the list. He looked for the committee he now controlled, Committee Chairman Slaight. His name wasn't on the list.

"What the fuck?"

"You believe that shit?" asked Buck.

"Where in hell is my name?"

"Ten to one it's Hedges. Ten to one, Slaight. You better get over to the Social Science Department and see the officer in charge of your committee. Ask him what the fuck is up."

"Yeah." Slaight spun out of the room, down the stairs, double-timing across Thayer Road, heading for his OIC's office. He didn't bother knocking. Walked past the secretary, stood by the major's desk. In his left hand he held the excused-from-class list.

"Have you seen . . . this . . . Major?" He was still panting.

"Yes, I've seen it, Slaight."

"You gonna do anything about it, sir? I mean, how am I supposed to run my committee . . . how am I supposed to put together SCUSA for you, if I'm not free from classes?"

The major looked up from his desk.

"Close the door, will you?" Slaight reached around and closed it.

"Have a seat. I know about the list, Slaight. All I can say is, I'm sorry. But please. Please don't ask me to do anything about it. Please."

Slaight looked at the major.

"It's that heavy, huh, sir?"

"Please don't ask me to do anything, Slaight. That's all I can say."

"Well, let me ask you one thing, sir. Just one thing. You don't have to answer verbally, so if anybody asks, I can tell them you didn't say a thing to me. All you have to do is nod your head yes, or nod your head no. I just want to know one thing, Major. One little thing. Who's responsible for this? For me not being on the list. Grimshaw?"

The major shook his head no.

"Hedges?"

The major nodded his head. Yes. Slaight just sat there, staring at him.

"Please, Mr. Slaight. Don't ask me . . . I've got a wife and kids. My career . . ."

"Yessir. I got you. The committee, sir. I got a good cow for a deputy. I'll send him down here to see you this afternoon. Now I gotta go."

Slaight bounced downstairs to the Law Department two at a time. He walked into Room 408. Captain T. Clifford Bassett started clearing a hole in the pile of papers on his desk.

"So?"

"So it's happening. This morning. All at once. Grimshaw calls me in. They're convening an Aptitude Board. I asked him why. He wouldn't say. Asked him to see the papers. Wouldn't show me. All he did was ream me for not having any sick slips in my folder on Saturday mornings. Then I get back to the barracks, and the excused-from-class list is down for SCUSA. I'm head of the committee that runs the show administratively. My name isn't on it. I just got back from the OIC for my committee. Asked him who was responsible. He was fuckin' pathetic. Pleading about his career, Jesus. He wouldn't say anything, but I got him to nod his head. It was Hedges. Captain Bassett, it looks like the shit is coming down. Now. All at once."

"Settle yourself, Slaight. Settle down. There's nothing to worry about. Yet. Let's give this thing some thought. The list for SCUSA we won't concern ourselves with. That's just a slap in the face, and a stupid one at that. He's showing his hand, showing it too early in my considered opinion. But the Aptitude Board. Did Grimshaw say anything about when it would happen?"

"He said I'd hear in 'due time.' That's all."

"Excellent. Excellent. Grimshaw is just the crack in the door. Regulations require that any Aptitude proceedings originate with the company tactical officer. So that means it's just starting. And you've got to remember. They feel time is on *their* side. They'll keep you dangling for a while. Tension. They love to play with the tension. While they think you're dangling, we'll be getting your ducks lined up. We can use time, too. I'll keep track of your board with a friend in the Department of Military Psychology and Leadership. MP&L officers sit on the boards. In the meantime, we'll begin a few delaying tactics of our own. A request for representation by counsel before the board, for example. There's a neat one. They'll need an opinion from the judge advocate general before they can turn you down. It'll take at least a week to grind that opinion out of this office. I'll see to that. Then we can put in requests for witnesses on your behalf. One at a time. One each day. We've got plenty of time, Slaight. Don't worry about that."

"I'm not worried about time, sir. I'm worried about this

356

goddamn Aptitude Board. I've seen those things in action. I got called as a witness by a guy in my company they were boarding back in 1966. They asked me a couple of questions, he called a few more witnesses, and that was it. He was in the Boarders' Ward the next day."

"Yes. I know all about Aptitude Boards. Not exactly your paradigm of procedural rights. But don't let that bother you. We know what's behind this thing. The murder of David Hand. Slaight, you hold a lot of cards. Our only problem now is to figure out when to begin playing them. And in what order. Now, are you ready to lunch at the club? I think it would make good politics for those in the Tactical Department to observe us lunching together. Let them know where things stand. Don't you?"

"Yeah." Slaight grinned. Bassett was prepping to go to the wall.

They lunched at the O Club, as it was called. Slaight had a steak sandwich. Grimshaw watched him chew every bite from a table across the room. The little woman hadn't gotten him home for lunch, after all.

30

"Ry, I want to know what's happening to you. What's going on? Something is *wrong*." Irit was angry, and the tone of her voice on the phone caught Slaight off guard. He took her call in the company orderly room. It was Thursday night, around 11:30, October 24. Three days had passed since he learned about the Aptitude Board. He hadn't told Irit about it, not wanting to upset her unnecessarily. Bassett seemed to have things fairly well under control. His draft of Slaight's request for counsel before the Aptitude Board had gone up the chain of command today.

"Irit, what's up? What are you doing calling me at this hour? It's after taps."

"I want to know what's going on, Ry. There is something you are not telling me. There is something *wrong*."

"What do you mean, something wrong?"

"I'm being watched, Ry. It's been going on for several days now."

"Watched? By whom?"

"I don't know. All I know is, I am being watched."

"Irit, call me back on another number, will you?" asked Slaight, giving her the number for the phone in Leroy Buck's room.

Slaight took the stairs two at a time, hit Buck's door, and flopped on his bunk. A Marty Robbins album was playing softly on the stereo. Buck was working on some damn computer program he had designed to predict the outcome of the presidential election, based on a sampling of cadet opinion, via computer-card straw poll. Buck had run the program several times and had a sample of about 750 cadet votes by now. Nixon was ahead, Wallace second, Humphrey a close third. The phone rang. Slaight picked up.

"Irit?"

"Yes. Ry?"

"S'me. I'm up in Buck's room. We can talk now. Tell me about this again, slowly. You're being *watched?*" Buck's head swiveled like a snake's.

"Yes, Ry. I'm positive. It's an around-the-clock surveillance on my shop and my apartment. I waited to call you after I had made sure."

"You *made sure?* How? What is this, anyway, some kind of paranoid New Left gibberish? I feel like I'm talking to . . . Mark Rudd or one of those Columbia idiots or something. Come on, Irit. Get serious. You're talking to 'nothin'-but-the-facts' Slaight." Buck laughed aloud.

"Ry, this is no joke," said Irit, her voice level, words like stainless steel. She heard Buck's laugh, Slaight's chuckle.

"Are you sure the phone you are speaking from is secure?" she asked.

"Secure?"

"Yes. Secure. Are you sure the phone is not bugged?"

358

"Jesus, Irit. First you're being watched, now there's bugs in the phones. What gives?"

"I'm calling you from my grandfather's, Ry. I have been watched for the past three days . . . maybe more. Maybe a week. It's hard to tell for sure. I did not start keeping track of the surveillance until three days ago. Today I had my grandfather check with friends in the government in Israel. I am not under surveillance by Israeli intelligence. My grandfather assures me of this. I have told you before, Ry. In my country, this is no joke. We are accustomed to intelligence activities. I have friends who are Israeli agents . . . here . . . elsewhere. We must live constantly with terrorism, so we must live constantly with intelligence activities. Surveillance, the tapping of telephones—this happens all the time in my country. It happens here. I know. I have more than one Israeli friend in the business world here in America who is in reality one of our intelligence agents. Believe me, Ry. I am not joking. I am being watched, but not by Israelis. These men are professionals. I have the feeling, Ry. It has something to do with you."

Slaight leaned against the pillow on Leroy Buck's bed in a state of near catatonia. She was dead serious. He remembered talking with Irit about the Israeli equivalent of the American CIA—how in Israel the whole business was just taken for granted, because it was so goddamn necessary. Once they'd had dinner in New York with a friend of Irit's from Israel, and afterward, after they'd spent a leisurely evening discussing the Middle East and the news business—for her friend was a reporter—Irit told him her friend was also an intelligence agent. He was stationed in New York to keep an eye on Arab business activities in the United States. His job covering Wall Street for Reuters provided an ideal "in," she explained. Slaight had been intrigued—and horrified. Knowledge of *foreign agents*—the very words evoked images of Hitchcock films and paperback novels—no matter what country they were from, operating in the United States, *his* country, disturbed Slaight. The idea of espionage ran counter to his essentially democratic conservative instincts.

359

He recalled arguing with her—*what right have they to* and on and on—then the cold, harsh realization that she wasn't talking about rights, she was talking about what had to be done. She was talking about survival.

Now here was Irit laying it on him again about intelligence agents . . . they were American, and moreover, they were probably watching her because of him. Ry Slaight. *Jesus.*

"Irit, I don't know what to say," he stuttered.

"You don't have to *say* anything, Ry. Just answer my question. Is there anything wrong, anything you haven't told me?"

"Yeah."

"Do you think your phone is secure . . . it is not tapped?"

"I don't really care, Irit. It's all out in the open now. I put off telling you until this weekend, because I didn't want to spoil your week for you. Yeah. I'm in trouble. Big trouble. They're running an Aptitude Board on me sometime soon. I don't know when. And I'm catching shit from the tac again. Something is up, Irit. It started Monday."

"That was when I first noticed them. Monday. I kept track of them Tuesday and Wednesday. That night I visited my grandfather and asked him to contact his friends in Israel. We just received word tonight. They are not Israeli. Who could they be, Ry?"

"Jesus, Irit. I don't know. I can't think of why they'd want to be keeping on eye on you, unless . . ."

"Unless what, Ry?"

"Unless something big has happened in the David Hand case that I don't know about, which might explain why they're eager to bounce me out of here, and they just might by trying to cop some dirt on you to use against me at this Aptitude Board. Christ. Enough people up here know that I've been going out with a foreigner now. Who can tell?"

"Ry, I can't tell you the reason, but I can tell you they're watching me twenty-four hours a day. Three shifts. The shifts are irregular, so there is no pattern. I never see the same face in the same location twice. In Israel, when they put physical surveillance on you, it means they've already tapped your phones. So I am afraid for my phones now. I will not talk to you from home or from the shop."

"Well, goddammit. This is ridiculous. I'm not doing anything wrong. You're not doing anything wrong. We've got nothing to hide."

"This is true, Ry, but you never want to give them anything they can use. *Anything*."

"Well, goddammit. This shit is going to stop. I'll take weekend tomorrow and come down and check these fuckers out. Grades came down this week. I'm 2.3 or above in all my subjects for the first time all year! I can take leaves on Friday afternoons, now."

"Well, good for you!" She sounded genuinely excited. Then her voice dropped again, steely. "But what do you propose to do, Mr. Big Shot? Do you think you can walk out and make them go away—*pooof!*—just like magic? It does not work this way in Israel. I am sure it does not work this way here."

"Let me give it some thought. I'll let you know before I come down tomorrow."

"Not on the telephone, Ry Slaight."

"Goddamn. Forgot. Okay, you'll be at your shop tomorrow afternoon, Right?"

"Yes, until six."

"I'll get word to you, Irit. Just don't leave the shop until you hear from me tomorrow."

"Okay, Ry . . . Ry? I hope you know how serious this could be."

"I do, Irit. Believe it. I do."

They said their good-byes, and Slaight told Leroy Buck the latest news.

"Goddamn-goddamn," said Buck. "What you gonna do, Slaight?"

"You got a 2.3 in all your subjects, Leroy?"

"Yeah."

"So has Lugar. Maybe it's about time the three of us took an old-fashioned weekend leave in New York City, stayed at the Van Rensselaer, just like the old days, huh?"

"You thinkin' what I think you're thinkin', Slaight, goddammit?"

"I don't know, Leroy. Haven't done much thinking yet. Get one of those bean runners of yours in here, and get him to wake up Lugar and tell him to get over here."

Buck banged his fist on the wall next to his desk twice, and within seconds, a bathrobe-clad plebe was standing at attention in the door.

"Get over to 226 and tell Mr. Lugar I wanna see him," commanded Buck.

"Yessir," said the plebe, about-facing and double-timing down to Lugar and Slaight's room. Buck walked over to the stereo and changed the record. Tammy Wynette. By the time she was singing the "V" of "D-I-V-O-R-C-E," a sleepy John Lugar was scratching his red hair and wondering what the fuck was up, that he had to be roused out of the rack by some goddamn plebe to see the goddamn company first sergeant.

"That girl friend of yours, Josie Irene, she still a reporter for the Bergen *Record?*" asked Slaight.

"Yeah. Ole Severns been moved to the city desk now. They took her off night rewrite. Good deal."

Slaight suggested that the three of them repair to the shower room, where two banks of six shower heads going full blast would drown out their conversation. Paranoia, he was discovering, had its own twisted logic.

It didn't take long for the three of them to work out a feasible plan. Convinced of the accuracy of Irit's assessment of her surveillance—for John Lugar had long been an admirer of Irit Dov—he insisted on drawing up a set of plans. Into his extensive file of maps dove Lugar, and up he came with the best street map of New York he could find.

"Even shows the directions of the one-way streets, and every alley in the Village," he boasted. He and Josie Severns had used it many times to find obscure off-off Broadway theaters.

Leroy Buck insisted on renting the car.

"If we're gonna figure out what the fuck is really going on, we gotta be mobile," said Buck.

"Not bad, for a farm boy," laughed Lugar. The three were standing naked in the corner of the shower room, all twelve shower heads blasting hot water, turning the place into a steam room. They were joking, dancing through the hot showers, gathering around Lugar's now-soggy map, spread on one of the wood benches running down the middle of the shower room. They had no idea who the intelligence agents were, of course . . . or if in fact they were intelligence agents at all. Nor did they know where they were to be found, for Irit's description of the situation had carefully avoided details. But they were confident they'd come up with something. Hell, what had they spent three and a half years at the Military Academy for, if it wasn't to have a bit of self-confidence when it came to matters of tactics and strategy?

Friday afternoon, October 25, the three drove to New York City and parked several blocks from Irit's boutique on Madison Avenue. Slaight waited on the street until a young kid happened by. For two dollars, he got the kid to deliver a message to Irit: Meet them in the back room of a bar across the street from where they were parked on Seventy-eighth Street in ten minutes. She showed up on time.

Slaight outlined the plan. Irit would return to the shop, business as usual until closing. Once she had locked up, instead of going back to her apartment, she would walk a few blocks up Madison, grab a cab, and take it in a big ten-square-block circle back to the same bar on Seventy-eighth. The "agents," she explained, had stationed themselves in a drugstore across from her boutique, one of the last on Madison that still had a fountain. They plugged dimes in a meter for a nondescript Chevy at curbside all day. Chevy today, Ford yesterday, Buick the day before that. They weren't dummies, these guys. Somehow, they always found a parking place on her block at night for whatever car they were using. By morning, the car was gone, and a new one would show up in front of the drugstore. She had gone on a walk around the block one night. Nobody was sitting in the car. She had the feeling they were still around, but she didn't know where.

"That's why you're taking your long cab ride to the bar here, Irit," said Lugar. "I've watched enough spy movies to figure they'll put one guy on you on foot, and one in the car. If we're lucky . . . well, let's see."

Irit went back to her shop. At ten minutes to six, Lugar and Slaight walked up Madison. Buck hopped in the rental car, drove around the corner, and pulled into a standing zone a block away from the drugstore.

At 6:05, Irit backed out of her shop, locking the door and the electronic burglar alarm. She walked briskly up Madison Avenue. A man in a charcoal London Fog raincoat followed, a half block behind her on the opposite side of the street. Two blocks ahead, John Lugar waited at the corner of Eighty-fifth Street, an unlit cigarette in his hand. Slaight stayed back at Eighty-first and Madison, just inside the entryway to an antique store, his eyes riveted on Irit, moving now two, now three blocks away across the street and up Madison.

She reached the corner of Eighty-fifth Street. Stopped. Moved a half block up the street into a bus stop zone and waited. The man in the charcoal London Fog reached the corner of Eighty-fifth Street, and did some disinterested window-shopping. Irit spied a cab. She raised her hand.

Slaight signaled Leroy Buck. He pulled out from the curb, heading up Madison, passing the Chevy just as it was starting its engine. Irit's cab arrived. She opened the door. The man in the charcoal London Fog stepped to the curb. John Lugar made his move.

"Hey, mister, can I bother you for a light," he said, dangling his unlit cigarette in front of the guy's face. Lugar stood between the man and the curb, blocking his way. The man fumbled in his pockets for matches. Irit climbed in her cab, shut the door, and signaled the driver to take off. He did.

"Thanks, mister," said Lugar, puffing on his cigarette in the cold fall air. The man started to move away, but Lugar cut him off again.

"Say, I wonder if you could help me . . ." Just then, Leroy Buck drove up, heading north on Madison, slowly, the nondescript Chevy behind him. The man in the charcoal London Fog made a move toward the Chevy. Leroy Buck stopped, threw the rental car in reverse, and made-believe he was backing into a parking slot cutting off the Chevy. Irit's cab was disappearing up Madison in traffic. John Lugar was pestering the man in the charcoal London Fog about the Whitney Museum. Suddenly the man waved his right arm wildly, and the nondescript Chevy pulled around Leroy Buck and raced up Madison after Irit's cab.

They'd done it. They'd separated the pursuers. Buck followed the nondescript Chevy, following Irit on her wild-goose chase. John Lugar thanked the man in the charcoal London Fog for the light, and walked downtown. Slaight moved to a better storefront. He watched the man in the charcoal London Fog. What would he do? Where would he go, now that he'd lost his partner in the car? Back to the drugstore? Slaight was banking . . . *no*. Slaight was banking he'd go to a place where he could establish secure communication with his partner in the Chevy. He was banking he'd go where they were holed up. The man in the charcoal London Fog headed back down Madison, crossed to the east side of the street at Eighty-third, turned left on Eighty-second, walked past the entrance to a luxury high-rise, past a couple of brownstones, and turned onto an old double-wide tenement, which had been gutted and "renovated" with tiny overpriced studio apartments, catering to the quick-turnover stewardess and secretary trade. John Lugar had moved to Irit's apartment lobby. He watched the man enter the building. Slaight stayed out of sight on Madison.

About 6:15 a light came on in the apartment, second from the top, left. Slaight headed for the bar on Seventy-eighth Street. When Irit walked in, he dropped a dime in the pay phone and dialed the phone in Irit's building's lobby. Lugar picked up.

"I'm going to turn her loose now," said Slaight.

"Okay, I'll hold the line," said Lugar.

Irit walked back up Madison, the four blocks to Eighty-second Street, turned into her lobby, and headed for the elevator. The nondescript Chevy turned the corner not long afterward.

"Chevy here," said Lugar.

"Thought so," said Slaight.

"Lights out in apartment," reported Lugar. "And now venetian blinds are going up . . . face visible in apartment window, just a shadow, but it's a guy. It's *the* guy. He's standing up, taking off the overcoat," said Lugar with satisfaction. "Chevy parked . . . goddamn, I think they've got that space reserved, you know, with one of those little white cardboard parade permit things . . . man getting out of Chevy, heading for same apartment, going in. He's there."

"Okay. Come on down. Leroy's here," said Slaight from the pay phone in the bar. Lugar took a couple of minutes to reach the bar.

"So Irit's tucked away for the night," Lugar announced. "I think you better keep your fanny out of there, Slaight. They've got a full view of everyone going in and out of that building, and you may be the one they're waiting for."

"Yeah. I know. Let's hop in the car and get downtown, get some supper at the Puglia. Tomorrow comes the fun part. Josie in town yet?"

"She's down at the Van Rensselaer right now, waiting. Already got our rooms."

"Gentlemen, let us leave our friends to exercise their night vision, drive downtown, and get our shit together for tomorrow." They did.

Saturday morning, 11:30, October 26, the three cadets and the woman reporter for the Bergen *Record* loaded into the rental car and drove uptown. It was a simple plan, hatched by John Lugar, eagerly agreed to by his girl friend, Josie Irene Severns, who at twenty-three had cut her teeth as a newspaper reporter covering political corruption in Hudson County, New Jersey, with the exception of Mayor Daley's Cook County, probably one of the largest political sludge-heaps in the nation. In a year fraught with the spectacle of the Democratic National Convention fracas, demonstrations and political dissidence of every conceivable sort, a story on domestic intelligence gathering seemed to Josie Irene Severns one of national importance, and one hell of a lot of fun. Like most cadet girl friends, she held little truck with the demonstrators. But again like most cadet girl friends, issues about the war raised by Bobby Kennedy and Eugene McCarthy had made their mark. The girls were none too keen on the war their boyfriends were doubtlessly going to fight.

Leroy Buck pulled the rental car to a stop a block from Irit's boutique. Josie hopped out and headed for the boutique, just another customer. Once inside, Irit stood behind a rack of clothes and pointed out today's watchers. Josie checked her purse. All was ready. Irit tied a red scarf around the neck of one of her mannequins in her window—a prearranged signal. Buck, Lugar, and Slaight jumped out of the car and moved to the corner of Eighty-first and Madison. Josie walked out of the shop and directly across the street to the drugstore.

Two men sat in a booth near the window, nursing cups of coffee, toying with stale English muffins. Josie took a counter seat near them, ordered coffee, turned her back, and pulled out John Lugar's Nikon. Without warning, she wheeled the counter stool and snapped six photos of the men in the booth, seated about eight feet away. She placed the camera on the counter, produced a note pad and her wallet, and approached the booth. The men were stunned.

"Gentlemen, my name is Josie Severns, and as you can see by my police department press badge, I represent the Bergen *Record*." She slid into the booth next to one of the men.

"Now. I would like to ask you a few questions about intelligence activities. We may as well start with what agency you gentleman represent. CIA? FBI? Military Intelligence? Defense Intelligence Agency?" She looked eagerly in their eyes, and she knew they were wondering *what in fuck* is going on?

367

"Come now, gentlemen, don't be shy. I've been watching you for a few days. You and your friends are getting to be regulars here. Now, let's cut the crap and get down to basics. Who are you with, and why are you watching the woman who runs the store across the street?" Again she watched them. She knew she had them. They were making the same mistake the New Jersey pols made. They thought if they just ignored a "girl reporter" long enough, she'd go away.

Bad mistake with Josie Irene Severns. She could wait out the stoniest Hudson County courthouse stare-down. And there she was, sitting in the booth with these two spooks, still holding her main question. On an educated guess—based upon research into the career of Brigadier General Charles Sherrill Hedges, gleaned from a bio in *Assembly*, the West Point alumni magazine—John Lugar figured the surveillance was the work of the Defense Intelligence Agency. The FBI had no reason to muddle in the army's affairs. Military Intelligence agents spent most of their time running background checks on guys who were being put in for security clearances. Best of all, General Hedges had served for two years, after his first tour in Vietnam, as a liaison officer on the staff of the Secretary of Defense between the CIA and the DIA. Since he worked for the Secretary of Defense, Hedges had been the DIA's man. He probably still had good contacts there, reasoned Lugar. Josie sprung the question, standing up, thrusting her notebook back in her purse:

"Well, then, gentlemen, if we don't get anywhere this way, perhaps we'll get somewhere when I get this film developed this afternoon, print it in tomorrow's paper, and send a clip down to the director of the Defense Intelligence Agency, inquiring about what his noble employees were doing on a coffee break during their surveillance of Irit Dov's boutique. What do you think, gentlemen? Do you think that will produce some answers to my questions?"

"Let's have that film," stated one of the men flatly. He was wearing a navy blue suit and tie, and his face looked like a pane of glass, his skin was so shiny.

Josie grabbed her camera and her purse, tossing two quarters on the counter. Just then, Buck, Lugar, and Slaight walked in.

"Nothing doing," she said.

"I said I want the film," said the man. "This is official business. You are interfering with government business. Now, give me that film, miss."

Buck, Lugar, and Slaight stood next to her silently.

"I've spent my whole career interfering with official government business, mister, most of it rather unsavory. You two remind me of poolroom stiffs I know in Hoboken. Only there, they've got something constructive to do with their time. They watch people shooting pool. What are you guys watching? To see if the knees on Irit's stockings sag by the end of her day?"

"That will be enough of your wisecracks, miss. Now give us the film."

Lugar grabbed the camera and slung it over his shoulder. Slaight stepped forward. He decided to play the scene to the hilt. If he was going to go, may as well be in style.

"It's my understanding that you two dipsticks, and the two you replaced last night, are denizens of something called the Defense Intelligence Agency. Is that right?"

Nothing.

"Well, I'm Ry Slaight, the guy you've probably been waiting for. I'm here for two reasons. One, to ask you— no, to *tell* you—to get off my girl friend's back. If you don't pack up your shit and shut down this crummy little stake-out, I'm going to notify the ACLU and have a team of lawyers up here serving you with every kind of goddamn civil writ they can crank out. Two. I'm going over to see my girl friend in her shop, and from there, to her house. My friends here are going to photograph everything you do while I walk over to her shop, and while we walk up to her house. Then they're going to hop in cars and drive downtown and make sworn statements as to what they have seen today and last night."

Slaight waited for the men to say something. They said nothing.

"We know where you're staying. We know where you

go every day. We know when you change shifts and cars. Look at that hunk of shit you've got out there now! What is that, some kind of practical joke? A goddamn Falcon!"

The men didn't say anything. They weren't taking the bait. Slaight was hoping for some sort of confrontation Lugar could photograph, but it wasn't coming. He reached in his pocket and withdrew two envelopes. Each contained a carbon of a letter to the director of the Defense Intelligence Agency, outlining the "moves" of Rysam Parker Slaight III and Irit Dov on Saturday, October 26, 1968. He handed them to the men at the table.

"There is your report, guys. File the fucker. I already sent it special delivery to Washington last night. Your boss has probably already gotten it." To Slaight's great surprise, the men took their envelopes and pocketed them. *Fingerprints.* The men left money on the table, stood up, and left wordlessly.

"Weird," said Lugar. "You gave those two enough reason to kick your ass from here to Philly, and they didn't do nothin'."

"Yeah? Well, fuck them and their marching orders," said Slaight. He was feeling good, better than he'd felt in months, in fact. They all walked over to Irit's shop, she told her assistant to run things for the rest of the day, and the group headed for her place. They drank, cooked, talked, and joked all afternoon and into the night. Three cadets and a lady reporter, putting the arm on a couple of spooks from God-only-knows-where! Think of it! Think of the report old Hedges would get up at Woo fuckin' Poo! Wait'll he puts an eyeball on the bottom of the report Slaight handed the men in the drugstore. Sketched at the bottom of the page, about three inches high, was a replica of the clenched fists which emblazoned T-shirts, flags, banners, and placards at every demonstration photographed and filmed for the past year! Not just any fist, but *the* fist! Wouldn't that give old Hedges something to train his binoculars on!

They laughed and laughed but never so hard as they laughed at Leroy Buck. He was taking a course in advanced Ordnance Engineering, and just yesterday, his small five-man section had been given a secret lecture on military weaponry. One of the two majors who taught them held up a Plexiglas model of an artillery shell, a 105-mm howitzer round. But this howitzer round was full of wires and transistors and little round balls and weird shit, inside the Plexiglas casing of the shell's warhead. The instructor told them the model howitzer round was still in the early stages of development, that he was holding a dream, really. He hinted broadly that the model howitzer round represented the furthest reaches of tactical nuclear weaponry development. Then he got so excited, holding the model howitzer round, fondling it, gazing into its multicolored interior, he just burst out with it:

"Gentlemen," he said, "this puts tactical nuclear weapons down where they belong, at the company level. With this round a company commander will be able to knock out an entire enemy company with a single round. Imagine that! One call on the radio, and zap! And it'll be clean, gentlemen, the company commander will be able to move his men through that area within a matter of hours. This is tac-nuke of the future, gentlemen. Maybe by the time you're company commanders you'll have the privilege and the pleasure of deploying this little baby!"

Leroy Buck told the story perfectly, imitating the major's authoritarian inflection, uncannily accurate, even through his thick southern drawl.

"Next thing you know," he went on, "they'll pull us down there in the goddamn basement of Thayer Hall, and they'll hold up a little Plexiglas sphere, and say, this here, gentlemen, is the *nuclear grenade*. Now this little bugger puts tac-nukes down where they really belong, in the hand of the lowly infantryman. With one pitch, even the dullest PFC'll be able to knock out a whole enemy *squad*, the little tac-nuke just makin' the neatest little mushroom cloud you ever did see. A fuckin' nuclear grenade! That's gonna be the next goddamn thing!"

They all guffawed, even Irit, Leroy Buck's imitation of the major was so perfect, the twisted extension of logic of the nuclear grenade was so—well—so goddamn *funny!* What else could you do but laugh your ass off at the

371

concept of the nuclear grenade after a day like today—
hell, after the last goddamn three and a half years!

The more grim the joke, the harder they laughed, the
more they drank, the *funnier* it all was. It was the way.

31

Charlie Napier, a clean-sleeve firstie with whom Slaight
had walked the area many times, came to the table the
next night, Sunday night, October 27, 1968. Napier had
gotten slugged cow year, 66 demerits, 132 punishment
tours, and six months' confinement to his room, for that
unique cadet "offense," PDA—public display of affection.
PDA effectively speaking made it illegal for a cadet to
touch a girl in public. Public was defined as anywhere—
literally, anywhere, on or off academy grounds. Affection
was defined as touching with the hand, and went onward
and upward past the kiss on the cheek to the nether
regions of the embrace, and finally, as in the case of
Charlie Napier, to the act of intercourse itself. In Napier's
case, it was *suspected* intercourse, but it was PDA just the
same.

What had Napier done to justify the stiffest punishment
meted out at West Point, short of expulsion? He and his
girl friend had checked into a motel one Saturday night.
The motel keeper, a local Highland Falls cadet-hater, had
sought to report him for PDA, but the room was regis-
tered in the girl's name. So the motel keeper had gone to
the West Point library and leafed through company photographs—some 3,200 cadets in all—in the *Howitzer*, the
cadet yearbook, until he found Napier's face. He found
his name. He reported Napier to his company tactical officer. The tac in turn reported Napier on a two-dash-one.
The tac had thought Napier ought to get some kind of
slap on the hand, and 8 & 8 for being dull enough to use
a local motel if nothing else. But when the form came

372

back from old Two-Dash Hedges, Napier's "offense" had been reworded:

"Gross lack of judgment, so as to bring discredit on himself, the Corps of Cadets, the United States Military Academy, the United States Army, and the Nation, i.e.: sharing a motel room with a member of the opposite sex on or about April 15, 1968."

The announcement of Napier's offense, made by the brigade adjutant at lunch in the mess hall one day in early May, had been a clear warning to others who might be entertaining similarly licentious thoughts about girls and motel rooms. The reading of the "offense" over the booming PA left the mess hall hushed, stunned. Hell, everyone knew what went on behind closed doors, especially the closed doors of motel rooms. But the word was already around the mess hall. In Napier's case, there had been no evidence. He could have slept in the tub, he could have napped in a chair. The motel keeper, Two-Dash Hedges, *nobody* knew what went on between Napier and his girl friend, because a motel room was not public. The message was clear. Hedges had decided to make an example of Napier. Not only was touching a girl on academy grounds illegal, so was the presumption of sex—not sex itself, merely the *presumption* of sex—even off the grounds of the academy, even in a motel room.

Eventually, the cadets laughed it off, as they laughed off everything else that made no goddamn sense at all. They went about their business of fucking anything wearing a skirt—cautiously, is all. Just about everyone, that is. John Lugar, Slaight's roommate, had spent three and a half years in the cadet library, combing its stacks, its collections of rare academy memorabilia, its unclassified "papers," in a futile search for the man he called "the sick motherfucker who conceived of PDA." If he ever found the man's name, he said he was going to plaster it all over every company bulletin board in the Corps, a total slander of the bastard, let everybody know who had first decreed cadets could only look at girls—unless, of course, you could get off-post and into a motel room with a girl, and now with the Napier slug, old Two-Dash Hedges had

373

attempted to proscribe even that normal, healthy, male sexual activity.

So when clean-sleeve Charlie Napier, by this time something of a hero—or at least a public figure in the Corps—showed up at the Buck/Lugar/Slaight table on Sunday night, his presence was especially ominous. Slaight had just finished flaunting the fact that he was going to spend the night with Irit Dov in front of two intelligence agents of some sort, and if that couldn't be defined as public display of affection, what could? But Napier's visit brought still grimmer news.

"Slaight," he said slowly, for Charlie Napier was not one of your fast talkers, residing as he had for the past three years in the bottom ten in the class in General Order of Merit (considered a likely contender for Goat).

"Slaight, I've got some . . . ah . . . bad news for you. While you was away on weekend, your tac, Major Grimshaw . . . he was officer in charge. . . ."

"Grimshaw was OC?" Slaight interrupted. "He wasn't scheduled to be OC this weekend."

"I know . . . he . . . ah . . . volunteered, I guess you could say. Anyways, I was pulling guard, like I usually do on Saturdays, because I'm slugged and all, you know, and Grimshaw comes in and says he wants me to take him on an inspection of your company. You know the regs . . . the OC has to take a cadet guard with him wherever he goes. So I figured he's an asshole, like everybody says, and he just wants to rape his own company, you know? But uh-uh. He didn't do nothing of the sort. He just goes on over to New South, straight up to your room, and he went through every one of your files. I know. I had to stand there and watch him do it. He must have spent two hours in your room . . . this was about, you know, two A.M. Saturday night, er, Sunday morning, you know. So I'm standing there, just sleepy as hell, and he went through all your files in your cabinets. I don't know what he was looking for, but he kept muttering to himself he'd find it somehow, so I don't guess he found whatever it was he was after, you know?"

"Yeah," said Slaight.

374

"Slaight, you know about this, man?" asked Buck.

"Hell no. Haven't looked in my files. I just came back, jumped in my Dress Gray and out to formation at the last minute. Jesus. This is some shit."

"Yeah," said Napier. "But that ain't half of it, Slaight. I mean, going through your shit and all. That was something. I had to tell him I didn't think it was right, what he was doing. He told me I was being insubordinate and to shut my goddamn mouth, or he'd shut it for good. So I stayed quiet and just stood there and watched. He read everything, Slaight. Every goddamn thing. The funny thing was, he kept saying something about this one guy."

"Which guy? Who?"

"He kept saying, real low like to himself, 'Beatty said it'd be in here someplace . . . Beatty said it'd be right here in his room.' Anyways, he mutters that a bunch of times, but he didn't take anything. So he's leaving the room, right? And you know that little stick he carries, with an AK-47 bullet for a tip, and an AK shell at the end? You know the stick?" Everybody in D-3 knew about Grimshaw's war-souvenier stick made from the ammunition of a Russian-made Kalachnikov submachine gun.

"Well, he takes his little stick and he points it at your picture on your card, next to the door, and he says loud enough so's I can hear, he says, 'You little communist cunt. You little communist fag whore. We're going to get you.' Then he turns around, and sees that I heard him, and he says to me that I may as well forget about you being a classmate much longer, because you already got one foot out the gate, then he says, 'He's got one foot out the gate, we got his cock on the block, mister, and when we chop it off, his other foot'll go, too.' Well, Slaight, you and me's walked some goddamn hours together, but I never knew you was in so deep, man. I didn't know. I had to come over and tell you about this man, because no matter what you done, it don't deserve that kind of shit."

Buck invited Charlie Napier to sit down for a cup of coffee, but he had to get back to his room for confinement. Slaight barely managed to mutter thanks as Napier shuffled off.

"Slaight, what are you gonna do?" asked Buck.

"I'm going back to the room, I'm going to check my files, see if anything is missing, see if he took anything when somebody else was on guard, maybe not as decent as Charlie, then I'm gonna sit back and wait. Grimshaw will be around either tonight or early tomorrow, depending on whether or not he had a chance to report to King, or whoever he's reporting to, or if he's reporting at all."

"You don't think he did that on his own initiative, do you?"

"He could have. He knows I'm in deep shit. He just might figure, if he can come up with the crowning blow, it'll make his career. Guys have been known to do a lot less to advance their careers. But that doesn't fit with what Napier was saying about him muttering about Beatty."

"Beatty?"

"Yeah. The guy down in the Pentagon, the civilian fucker. He was all through the stuff in the pouch, remember?"

"Yeah. I remember now."

"Jesus. I wonder who Grimshaw's talking to: King, Hedges, or Beatty? Hard to figure."

"What do you think he was after?"

"Come on, man. Take a fat guess."

"Your Hand files."

"Man wins the big purple teddy bear."

"If he didn't find them, they weren't there. So where are they, Slaight?"

"You do not want to know. That is one piece of information you do not want to know."

Slaight called Captain Bassett from Buck's phone as soon as he returned to the barracks, relaying the word he'd gotten from Charlie Napier. Bassett said Grimshaw's search of his room had been illegal right down the line: no shake-down of entire company, no probable cause, and no criminal investigation to justify search and seizure.

"You've got to be suspected of having committed a crime for *any* kind of search of your effects to be legally conducted, Slaight. Even if there is reason to suspect you committed a crime, there must also be reasonable cause to believe that illegal items of potential evidence were in your possession. Since Grimshaw left your room empty-handed, obviously any probable cause he had was a figment of someone's imagination—probably his. So don't worry."

"But what do I do if he comes around to my room?"

"First you ask him what you're being charged with. Then you ask him if he's shaking down the company, in essence, force him into admitting that he's not shaking down, that he has no probable cause. Then, once you've got the upper hand, you do what he tells you. Answer all his questions truthfully. Remember, there's no Fifth Amendment with the Honor Code. If he wants to confiscate something, ask him to describe the article or piece of paper exactly, then ask him if he's giving you a direct verbal order. If he is, produce what he wants, if it's in your possession or capability to do so. Oh. Goodness. Almost forgot. Make sure you've got witnesses. Make sure there are a couple of your classmates in there for the whole thing."

"But Captain Bassett, with him muttering about Beatty, we both know what he's after."

"Indeed we do. However, you haven't got those files. I don't have those files. I entrusted those files to a third party, who shall remain nameless, and from there, I don't know where they went. So I don't know where the files are, you don't know where they are, you can produce no files. You have no ability to produce those files. In fact, I would say that you have *no legal authority* to produce those files at this point."

"It's gone that far, huh?"

"You have no legal authority, Slaight. Those files could be used as evidence. Let us just say, in terms you can understand, those files are being held in escrow—though escrow is hardly a criminal term. But in this case, it applies. They are in safekeeping. In reserve. To you, they are as good as gone, so you can tell Grimshaw that. Gone. There's your word. *Gone.*"

Grimshaw was waiting for Slaight in Room 226 at 9:15

Monday morning, October 28, 1968, when Slaight, Buck, and Lugar returned from their first class, History of the Military Art. They hadn't slept much the night before, awoke at 6 A.M., the class started at 7:45 A.M. and ran until 9:05 A.M. Slaight was tired. He was not in the mood for Grimshaw, who stood, legs apart, in the middle of the room like he owned the place. Perhaps, as tactical officer of Company D-3, he *did* own the place. The prerogatives of command, and all that. But Grimshaw's stance, and the surly, bitter look on his face, plunged whatever semblance there was of commander and commanded into the septic tank of mutual disrespect, barely contained.

Slaight called the room to attention. Grimshaw indicated with his AK-47 stick that Slaight should be seated at his desk, and with a sweep of the stick, all others should leave the room.

"Sir, I respectfully request that these men be allowed to stay in this room. I know what happened here on Saturday night, Sunday morning, and I believe we are going to have some disagreements. My attorney has advised me that I should have witnesses present for whatever happens today."

"And if I order these dullards from the room, Mr. Slaight? What then?"

"I will phone my attorney, ask him to drop whatever he is doing, and come over here to act as my counsel in this matter."

"Mr. Slaight. The matters we have to discuss are of no concern to either these men or your *attorney*, as you call him." Grimshaw sneered the word, like Bassett was some kind of subhuman species hardly worthy of recognition by Higher Beings . . . Higher Beings, of course, comprising that select minority of army officers who were, in the following order: West Pointers, Infantrymen, combat veterans, Airborne and Ranger Qualified . . . recipients of Silver Stars, Bronze Stars, Air Medals, and anything else they could get their hands on in Vietnam. Captain T. Clifford Bassett was not a Higher Being.

"Sir, I beg to differ," said Slaight, who had taken his seat, as indicated. The rest of the guys stood around uncertainly. "Everything you and I will discuss this morning has been discussed with these men. Everything you and I will discuss has been discussed with my attorney. So go ahead, sir. You went through my files. What is it you want to ask me?"

Grimshaw was enraged, but contained it nicely. He slapped his thigh once or twice with the black leather gloves held in his left hand. He gazed about the room as if looking to write some quill, just to get things off on the right—or was it left?—foot. He leveled his gaze at Slaight.

"Stand at attention, young man." Slaight jumped to his feet.

"I want everything in your possession relating to Mr. William Beatty. *Everything*, Slaight, and I want it now."

"William Beatty, sir?"

"You know who I mean, goddammit."

"I don't have any materials in my possession relating to a Mr. William Beatty."

"I know that, Slaight. I've been through this room. . . ." He cut himself off with a sharp intake of breath and the snap! of his teeth cracking together. "You've got it somewhere else. Where is it?"

"Sir, I don't know what you're talking about. I've never had materials in my possession relating to this William Beatty, whom I do not know. I don't know what your connection is to Mr. Beatty, sir, but I've nothing relating to Beatty."

"Then what have you done with it, goddammit?"

"Done with it, sir? I don't have 'it,' whatever 'it' might be."

"You mean to tell me you have nothing, *nothing* to do with Beatty in your possession at all?"

"That's right, sir." May as well drop the bomb. "I have heard his name once or twice, sir, if that does you any good. But of course . . . I've heard quite a few cadets know this Mr. Beatty. I am only sorry that I haven't made his acquaintance. Had I the pleasure, maybe I could help you, sir."

"Don't get smart with me, Slaight."

"I'm not getting smart, sir. I am volunteering information I thought might be of use or interest to you. Mr. Beatty seems to have quite a following among certain cadets. It so happens I am not one of them. I am sorry, sir." Slaight paused, waiting.

"Sir, may I ask a question?"

"Go ahead."

"Is the nature of your inquiry here this morning official in any capacity, sir? I mean, are you conducting a shakedown of the company for data on this Mr. Beatty? Or have you singled out my room?"

"This is no shake-down, and yes I've come directly here. That is self-evident. Now, don't you go trying to play barracks lawyer with me, Slaight, because I'll guarantee you'll lose."

"Yessir. One more question. Are the nature of your requests for my supposed materials on Mr. Beatty direct verbal orders, sir?"

"You damn well fucking better believe they are, mister. And if I find you've disobeyed me, I'll rip skin off your buttocks with pliers, goddammit. If I find out you've lied, you are *out*, Slaight. You understand that? *Finished*."

"Yessir. One last question, sir, I simply forgot. When do I hear about my Aptitude Board?"

"You'll hear when we're goddamn good and ready to tell you, Slaight. And not a moment before. And if you think you're going to get legal representation before that board, mister, you'd better think again, because you're not."

"I've been thinking about it a lot, sir. I simply want some time to prepare. I'd like to know the nature of the charges against me."

"You'll find out, Slaight. Soon enough." With that, Grimshaw tipped his black gloves to his hat brim and stalked from the room.

The cadets settled on the bunks. Somebody went for Cokes. Buck played an album by Waylon Jennings, which seemed to take the ugly edge off things.

"What do you think, Slaight?" asked Lugar.

380

"I don't know. How 'bout you?" Lugar shrugged in reply.

"Goddamn-goddamn," said Leroy Buck. "We could have a million fuckin' ideas, and I don't think we oughta go talking about them around here. I'm beginning to think these goddamn walls have ears. I wanna get me some MPR. Mid-period rack's always best. No telling when the next shitstorm's gonna hit. Could be today. Could be tomorrow. Who fuckin' knows? When in doubt, fellas, follow the example of ole Leroy. Get rack."

They did.

32

Slaight was asleep when two loud knocks sounded on his door at 11:15 that Monday night. The company and battalion honor representatives entered without invitation. They were in Dress Gray, unusual after taps in the barracks. Slaight looked up. The lights went on. He was still half asleep, but he knew they were on honor business. He'd been charged with an honor violation. The questions crammed his mind: When? By whom? For what?

"I think you know why we're here," said the battalion honor rep ominously. He was a stubby little guy who'd been an all-state football player in West Virginia in high school. He came to West Point as a football recruit. He never got over it when he discovered that at 175 pounds dripping wet, he couldn't cut it in college ball. The D-3 company honor rep was from Arkansas, slow-talking, fast-witted dude who played lead guitar in the cadet rock and roll band, "B. Arnold and the Traitors." He was handsome, loose, hip, a cadet rock and roll star. Slaight could tell by the look on his face this after-taps honor visit didn't sit well with him.

"Get dressed. Dress Gray," commanded Dudley, the

battalion honor rep. "You're going before a subcommittee tonight."

"Tonight? What the fuck is this all about? It's past taps, man. What is this, anyway? Selma, Alabama?" Slaight was pulling on his trousers, and he was good and pissed.

"Come on, Ry. Just co-operate. Let's get it over with," said Sam Kip, the company honor rep. "The less you say, the better."

"I wanna make a phone call," said Slaight as he zipped up his dress coat.

"No phone calls," said Dudley. "Let's go. The subcommittee is waiting up in Building 720 right now."

"At least tell me the charges," said Slaight, stopping in front of his mirror to check his hair.

"You find out soon enough," said Dudley. "Let's go. We want to get this over with by 2400 hours."

They walked single file, Slaight between the two honor reps, up to a conference room in Building 720. It was the same room they used when they boarded out Crolius. Out the window, he could see the Cadet Chapel, its stony presence outlined against the moonlit sky. Slaight was told to take a seat. Six of his classmates sat in a semicircle in front of him. They weren't guys he knew. His company and battalion honor reps were not permitted to sit on the subcommittee, but they stayed in the room as observers. One cadet, a five-striper, probably a battalion commander, spoke:

"You have been charged with an honor violation, and this subcommittee has been convened to determine if there is sufficient evidence to warrant a full Honor Board. Do you understand?"

"Yeah. What's the charge?"

"The charge is that you lied to an officer, in that you told the officer you would not divulge certain information to others, and then you went and divulged said information."

"What officer? When? What information? How in hell do you expect me to answer this charge when you don't give me any details?"

The cadets on the subcommittee glanced at each other. They didn't have the details, either. Slaight leaped into the gap.

"Who brought the charges in the first place? Let's start there."

The cadets drew their heads close together in a huddle and conferred.

"The charges were originally brought by Major Grimshaw, your tactical officer, who spoke to your company honor rep, Sam Kip, late this afternoon."

"Yeah? What did he say?"

"He said basically that you'd lied, just as we outlined."

"Well, that's the sketchiest fuckin' outline I've ever heard in my goddamn life. You guys yank me out of bed up here and pull together a subcommittee to tell me Grimshaw says I lied, and you don't even know what I'm supposed to have lied about? Jesus fuckin' H. Christ. Who's running this Honor Code show? You guys or Grimshaw?"

Sam Kip stepped forward.

"Maybe I'd better call Major Grimshaw and get him to elaborate."

"Do it," said the five-striper.

Kip disappeared. Slaight could hear a phone being dialed in the office next door, the muffled sounds of a conversation. Kip was gone for five minutes.

"We've got to wait for him to call back," he announced to the subcommittee, when he returned to the board room.

"So who's Grimshaw got to call?" asked Slaight, taking a shot in the dark.

"I don't know." Slaight studied Kip's face. He didn't know.

The phone rang in the office next door. Kip left to answer it. Another five-minute conversation. He returned. Slaight was told to leave the room. He walked out in the hall, stood there for a moment, and figured: If they can do it, so can I. He walked in the next office, picked up the phone, and dialed Buck's number. Buck picked up.

"Leroy, they got me in the conference room up in 720,

383

holding a goddamn honor subcommittee. Get Lugar and come on up here. The Honor System booklet says these things are supposed to be open to the upper classes, but they yanked me up here so fast, I didn't get a chance to tell anybody."

"On our way," said Buck. Slaight returned to the hall, pacing. The door open, and Sam Kip signaled for him to return. He took his seat. The five-striper spoke again:

"Major Grimshaw did not bring the charges. He relayed charges brought by the commandant of cadets. The facts, as Grimshaw outlined them, are these: You told General Hedges twice—once last summer and once in August, during re-orgy week—that you would not discuss certain matters with others. This morning you told Major Grimshaw you had discussed these matters with cadets and someone you referred to as your attorney. That is the charge. You lied to the commandant in that you promised you would not divulge certain information, then today, you admitted to Major Grimshaw you had."

At that moment, Buck and Lugar strode into the room.

"What are you two doing here?" asked the five-striper.

"More to the point, what are *you* doing here?" asked John Lugar, a smile plastered across his red freckled face.

"We're holding an honor subcommittee, and you are not permitted . . ."

"Says here we are," said Lugar, opening a small book with a light blue jacket. "Says right here in the Honor System pamphlet that all honor committee hearings are open to the upper classes. Here. Wanna see?" Lugar held out the small blue pamphlet.

"Where'd you get that?" asked the five-striper.

"In the library. I checked it out. Found it under 'standards and traditions.'" The five-striper examined the pamphlet.

"This is last year's. Doesn't apply."

"What do you honor reps do? Change the Honor System every year and not tell anybody about it? What is this shit?" Slaight stared the five-striper in the eye.

"Last year's Honor System pamphlet does not apply here. These two must leave."

384

"Okay," said Lugar. "You show me in this year's pamphlet where it says we've got to go. Show me the exact paragraph. Every honor meeting I've attended for the last three and a half years, the honor rep said all upperclassmen could attend Honor Committee functions. Now show me the System pamphlet that says we've got to leave."

"I don't have it with me," said the five-striper lamely.

"Then we stay. Go ahead with your business," said Lugar.

"But this is different. Even if I had the pamphlet, Major Grimshaw said this was . . . sensitive."

"Major Grimshaw!" Slaight spat his name like a piece of bad meat. "What the fuck does Grimshaw have to do with this? He runs the Honor Code now? Who's in charge here, anyway? You or Grimshaw? Come on. Is it all just a bunch of rhetoric, a bunch of shit—'the code belongs to the Corps'? Or are you going to abide by Honor Code custom and let them stay?"

The five-striper looked nervous. A neat stack of cadet chevrons had not prepared him to *make decisions*.

"Okay. You guys can stay. Sit down over there." He indicated folding chairs along one wall. Lugar and Buck sat down. Buck unzipped his dress coat and withdrew a yellow legal pad of paper and a pen and prepared to take notes.

"No notes!" screamed the five-striper.

"Whatssamatter? You ashamed of what's goin' on here?" asked Buck.

"No. . . ."

"Then you won't mind if I note the proceedings—for the edification of my colleagues back in the barracks, of course, who have an equal right to be present at this hearing." The five-striper sat mute.

"Okay, guys, let's get back to it," said Slaight, energized by the presence of his friends. "Question: What information did I promise the com I wouldn't divulge?"

"I don't know," said the five-striper.

"Any of the rest of you know?" asked Slaight. Heads shook, no.

"Question: How can it be determined if I divulged this

385

so-called certain information if we don't know what in hell it is?"

Blank stares.

"Major Grimshaw said you told everything to the guys who were in your room this morning and to your attorney," said one of the subcommittee reps.

"Everything? Everything about what?"

"I don't know," said the five-striper.

"For the record: The guys in my room this morning were Buck and Lugar, sitting right over there," said Slaight, looking slowly around the semicircle sitting before him. "My attorney's name is Captain T. Clifford Bassett. I've told all three of them lots of stuff. Now it appears to me that we can handle this thing two ways." Slaight paused.

"Go ahead," said Sam Kip, the D-3 honor rep, breaking the silence.

"Okay, Sam. Thanks. Method One: We can deal with these so-called charges of Grimshaw's about so-called certain information with raw technicalities, itty-bitty rule by itty-bitty rule. Method Two: We can deal with the facts. Which will it be?"

The honor subcommittee huddled.

"Let's hear your reading of the technicalities," said the five-striper.

"Okay. Grimshaw says I lied to the com. The alleged lie involved the mysterious certain information. You don't have the certain information, thus you can make no determination as to whether or not I divulged the certain information. All you've got is Grimshaw telling you I told him I told Lugar, Buck, and the lawyer everything. Everything about what? Everything could be the schedule of my bowel movements. You don't know. So you can make no determination as to whether there are enough facts to warrant an Honor Board, because you have no facts. Zero facts. Nothing."

The subcommittee huddled again.

"I see what you mean," said the five-striper.

"Now. You want to know what went down between me and the com? I'll tell you what went down. The com

386

called me in twice and offered to make me a battalion commander—me! a battalion C.O.!—if I'd keep my mouth shut about what you call certain information. That is, if I would shut up and forget certain things, I'd be wearing stripes. Observe my sleeve, guys. You see any stripes? I'm a file-closer, a cadet sergeant. I made no deal with the com. I promised him nothing. So Grimshaw's bullcrap about me promising I wouldn't divulge the mystical certain information is just that. So much bullcrap. I will say this. The com told me not to go talking to anyone about this certain information, and I went ahead and talked about it. So I disobeyed his order. Disobedience is a violation of regulations, guys. Not honor. If the com wants to write me up for it, he can. In fact, they're calling an Aptitude Board on me pretty soon, so I'd imagine it'll all come out then. But this shit Grimshaw came off with to Sam Kip—it's no honor violation, guys. You've got nothing on me."

"I guess not," said the five-striper. "But Hedges . . . he's not going to be happy about this."

"Hedges!" It was Lugar, walking over from his seat by the window. "What the fuck does Hedges have to do with this?"

"We've got to file a report, showing the minutes of the subcommittee, our finding, and the reasons for our finding."

"Show me in this goddamn Honor System pamphlet where it says you've got to report to the com," said Lugar, enraged.

"It doesn't. I know. Hedges put out the word informally last year, when he first became com. We've got to report everything to him, whether a subcommittee finds for a full Honor Board or not and whether the full board finds a guy guilty of a violation or innocent. We report everything to him."

"In writing?"

"Yes. He even had a special form printed up for us."

"So no matter what happens after an honor charge has been made, a guy will still have written records in his file about it, huh?"

"I guess so. I don't know what happens to the reports we give Hedges."

"You don't know!" Lugar was seething now. "You don't know! Jesus, what are you running here? An Honor Code or an inquisition?"

"Don't get uptight, John," Sam Kip stepped in. "What's the finding of the subcommittee?"

They huddled briefly.

"No evidence. No Honor Board. You can go now," said the five-striper.

"What are you going to say in your report to Hedges?" asked Slaight.

"I don't know. We'll think of something. This kind of thing has happened before. We'll cope. Don't be surprised if we have to run another subcommittee on you later this week, if they come up with some evidence. We'll let you know."

"Give me some notice next time, huh, guys?" said Slaight over his shoulder, as he, Buck, and Lugar walked out. "This is the essence of cool . . . the midnight honor patrol."

"You think you're the essence of cool, Slaight," said Arthur Dudley, the battalion honor rep. Slaight wheeled. He felt the tug of Buck's hand on his left sleeve.

"Don't say anything, Ry," said John Lugar.

Slaight gritted his teeth, turned, and left. Things were bad, Arthur Dudley was doing his damnedest to make them worse, but at this point, Lugar was right. Dudley didn't count. The three friends walked back down the stairs to New South Area. It was quiet, a few windows lighted dimly by desk lamps aiding the "hives," the cadets who really dug in and *studied*, maybe the late-night letter writers, the guys who in the wee hours felt the bottom edges of cadet loneliness and reached out with pen and paper for girl friends near and far.

D-3 had a guy like that, Jay Bloomingburg, from some small town in northern Washington State, of Canadian-American stock. He was always writing to girls, *always*, late at night, alone at his desk while his roommate slept. It was like writing a girl was something he could only do

alone. Sometimes, if his roommate stayed up late studying, you could find him in the shower room, sitting on one
of the wooden benches writing his letters on a clipboard.
He was a gentle guy and deeply religious—to the point of
seeming simple-minded at times, though he was actually
an intelligent, engaging person when you got right down
to it. He sang in the chapel choir, taught Sunday school,
and attended daily prayer services every morning when
other guys were getting ABR, precious after breakfast
rack. Though it wasn't talked about openly around the
company, it was known that Bloomingburg was still a virgin. Despite all his letter writing, he'd never been laid. He
didn't want to be. He was going to wait until he married,
he was that old-fashioned.

Bloomingburg was waiting in the hall outside Room
226 when they returned from Building 720. The CQ had
told him that a bunch of firsties had disappeared in the
direction of 720 in Dress Gray, and Bloomingburg wanted
to know what happened. He was concerned. John Lugar
used to tease him that his middle name was "Sincere," but
it didn't bother Bloomingburg. He knew it was true.

When Lugar, Buck, and Slaight reached Room 226,
Bloomingburg followed them in. He saw their Dress Gray
uniforms, checked his watch. It was 1:30 A.M. He smelled
honor.

"What happened, guys?" he asked in all innocence.

"None of your fuckin' business, man," snapped Slaight.

"Hey, Ry. I just wondered. I was worried when I
heard . . ."

"Yeah? Well, you hear too fuckin' much, and you
worry too fuckin' much, and you oughtta go back to writing your fuckin' letters, man, and leave us alone."

"Ry, I'm sorry, I didn't mean to . . ."

"You didn't mean . . . *shit*. Why don't you go dig out
your fuckin' Bible and say us all a prayer. That's what
we could really use. A fuckin' prayer." Slaight sneered at
the word prayer. Bloomingburg left, and in a moment, returned with his Bible.

"Aw, fuck, put an eyeball on this, guys," laughed
Slaight, pointing derisively at Bloomingburg.

"Hey, Ry, knock it off," said Lugar, who openly professed atheism, but admitted he would buckle under to a Catholic wedding to his girl friend, Josie Irene Severns, when the time came. Bloomingburg sat down on Lugar's bunk and started flipping through his Bible.

"When you gonna come down off the God act, man?" asked Slaight.

"Come on, Ry. Cut the shit," said Leroy Buck, a Southern Baptist from a congregation of about thirty back in Burning Tree, Indiana.

"Hey! What fuckin' good is God gonna do up against an SOB like Hedges, huh? What the fuck you think you're gonna find in that goddamn book, anyway? Blue-prints for happiness? A goddamn map through the West fuckin' Point mine field? Think you gonna find you a piece of ass in there, Jay, huh?"

Lugar grabbed Slaight by the T-shirt and hauled him up from his desk chair. Lugar outweighed him maybe ten pounds, but it was all muscle. He coached the company intramural boxing team and had fought his way into Brigade Finals, West Point's version of the Golden Gloves, every year but one, his plebe year. He was walking the area that year and couldn't train properly.

"One more word out of you, Slaight, one more god-damn word and I'm gonna check you into the hospital myself. Only you're not gonna like the way I put you there." Slaight peered into Lugar's eyes. They were bloodshot with fatigue.

"I know you've had some trouble, Ry. I just thought I might be able to help," said Jay Bloomingburg. He had his Bible open now, and in a low voice he began reading from the 23rd Psalm—*Yea, though I walk*—and Slaight was in shock, *trite, trite,* I *don't believe this.* . . .

Slaight's folks made him go to Sunday school downtown until he was fourteen. Fourteen! Nobody went to Sunday school when they were fourteen. But Ry Slaight did, in his black tie-shoes and his black suit with the little speckles in the fabric, a 1950s special that had been bought from Sears three sizes too large so he could wear it all the way through junior high. Bloomingburg was reading the 23rd Psalm, his voice a steady drone. They made him memorize the damn 23rd Psalm, just like they made him memorize everything else. And none of it amounted to a hill of shit. None of it. Not until his dog died.

His folks had bought the dog, a dachshund, when he was born, so he'd have a companion, somebody to grow up with out on the farm twenty miles outside Leavenworth where his father ran his riding stables, Wild Acres. Since he had no brothers or sisters, the dog, Rags, so named because all his life his little dog nest had been a pile of old dishcloths and rags, old Rags had been the guy he grew up with. He died at sixteen, an elegant old creature with a gray muzzle and gray eyebrows where once light tan hair had offset his sleek black coat. When Rags died, Slaight was crushed. He came home from school to find the dog laid out on a piece of plywood next to the house, and he just knelt there. His mother, Jill Ritter Slaight, didn't know what to do to help the boy, so she went in the house and brought out the family Bible. Its satin bookmark unfolded the 23rd Psalm, so she stood there in the spring Kansas sun, birds chirping in the trees around the house, squirrels chattering like they knew their foremost adversary had fallen, Slaight's mother stood there in the sun and read the 23rd Psalm aloud. The sun hit the back of Slaight's neck, his tears stung his cheeks, he'd just begun to shave, and his dog lay dead.

The words he heard, the words his mother was reading, hit him for the first time. It went beyond jarring his memory of a passage he had to memorize six years before. It went beyond all that talk in Sunday school, endless discussions of the true meaning of things. His mother's voice went way beyond and landed somewhere deep in what he would come to know as his subconscious, some invisible place inside himself where he hid secrets—secrets he and Rags had shared growing up, secrets he shared with no one, secrets he didn't even share with himself. He listened to his mother, listened to her finish reading the Psalm. He stood up straight, embraced his mother and said: Ma, let's go bury Rags, and they did. He knew strength that day at sixteen, the strength that comes from knowing death and moving on, the strength that was in his mother's voice—he'd known about it for years, but never *focused* on it so clearly—and the strength in her words, in the words of the 23rd Psalm. He didn't understand the strength, didn't know where it came from, where it was going, or what to do with it. He just *felt* it.

Now in Room 226, New South Barracks, Jay Bloomingburg's high-pitched voice carried those words again. The four of them—Slaight, Buck, Lugar, Bloomingburg—sat in the room in their drawers, as cadets always did at night in the barracks. Bloomingburg read, and they felt drawn together, Slaight perhaps more than the others with his memory of his dog Rags, Slaight, cynical, logical old Slaight, at twenty-one, ready to bite poor Bloomingburg's head off because all he wanted to do was reach into his little bag, pull out the tools at his disposal, and *help*.

Irit said it all the weekend before, that night they blew away the physical surveillance that someone had been running on Irit. They were drunk in bed, and it was dark except for the glow of the clock radio at bedside. Out in the living room, they could hear Leroy Buck settling in for the night on the sofa. Lugar and his girl friend had left for the hotel. All of them were blasted out of their skulls, laughing at Buck and his accent and his stories, reveling in the glow of their "victory." She lay next to him, spooning, he could feel her bosoms pressing against his bare back, and she whispered in the darkness. . . .

Ry, don't you know you're becoming the thing you're fighting, the thing you hate? You behaved the same way I would expect those men to behave, plotting your elaborate plans, going through your rehearsals. You are driven, Ry. Driven. Why? Why go on? What do you expect to accomplish?

He lay next to her and wondered. Why? She was right, of course. He was driven like a crazy man. But didn't she understand? Could she understand?

I want to find out what's going on, Irit. Can you under-

stand that? What's going on. You know how I'm always telling you about those officers up at West Point coming back from Vietnam, those sergeants I met at Leonard Wood, how they're always talking about that feeling, that feeling of being there? Well, I think I'm getting close, Irit. I think I'm almost there. I'm going to find out how it feels, how it feels to have been there. I'm going to figure out what's going on, Irit, if it's the last goddamn thing I do.

She nodded silently in the dark, holding him tightly, as if she didn't hold him he would up and go away.

Bloomingburg finished reading the 23rd Psalm and some other passage in the Bible he said was a favorite, folded the black book, and looked up. Slaight was sitting at his desk with tears streaming down his cheeks, a great flood of tears, not just a sprinkle but a thunderstorm, dribbling down his cheeks, down his neck, soaking the neck of his T-shirt. He was sobbing openly, gulping air like a lawn mower engine running rough, gasping, sucking air through soggy nostrils, hands atop his head, elbows askew, knees jiggling, big bloodshot brown eyes pouring water like the old double faucets down in the sinks of Central Area. Slaight gasping, gasping, skirting hyperventilation only by bending at the waist, putting his head between his knees, squeezing air from the lungs, slowing the frantic pumping of the diaphragm, his heaving, quivering rib cage.

Lugar and Buck looked on, not knowing quite what to do. Bloomingburg got up from the bunk, walked over to Slaight's desk, wrapped his thin arms around Slaight's back, and held him, Slaight's wet face tight against Bloomingburg's stomach. He held Slaight, Each time he felt the sobbing cadet start to gasp, struggling for air, he held him tighter, matching his breathing with Slaight's, slowing down, slowing, slowing, until finally Slaight was just sitting there at his desk, wrapped in the thin drawers-and-T-shirt-clad body of Jay Bloomingburg. He wasn't crying any more. He felt empty and selfish. He knew he was drawing strength from this guy, this super-straight-religious nut he had considered a mark. A sucker. The fall guy in a thousand little intercompany practical jokes.

Bloomingburg's problem was that he was a true believer. Anybody could con Bloomingburg out of anything. Even the notorious Billy Dickey, the well-bred dude scam artist from Raleigh, North Carolina, a classmate over in the other battalion, old scamster Dickey could touch Jay Bloomingburg on something as basic as a chain letter, he could sell him chances on cadet lotteries nobody ever seemed to win. Bloomingburg as a firstie was as gullible as a plebe. Most of the firsties in the company owed him money borrowed for weekends long gone and forgotten. Bloomingburg could not say no. Slaight—all of them, really—had always written him off as a kind of quaint, gentle weakling, a nineteenth-century gentleman caught by accident in a poorhouse crammed with louts and fools.

Yet there was Bloomingburg, and there was Slaight in his arms. Chancing upon the scene who could indentify the strong from the weak? Who knew what lay within those secret places inside each cadet? Not Slaight. Not Buck. Not Lugar.

Did Jay Bloomingburg?

Slaight mustered up synthetic courage . . . he found it easier than he had supposed . . . perhaps the courage wasn't so synthetic . . . raised his head and looked at the face above him. Bloomingburg was moving his lips in silent prayer! None of the other guys could see him, for his back was turned to them, but Slaight could. Slaight held still and let Bloomingburg finish his prayer. He looked down at Slaight and smiled.

"You're okay, Ry. I know what you're going through. You'll be okay. Everything will turn out all right."

Slaight looked at the guy's face—he knew nothing of what had been going on for the past six months—*and he believed him*. Jesus. That was weird. Believing old Bloomingburg—about anything, much less *this* . . . all the shit flying around his head. . . . But Bloomingburg had this look, some look on his face Slaight had never seen before, and it said he knew. He fuckin' *knew*.

"Thanks, man," said Slaight coarsely, coughing. "I guess I kinda lost it there for a minute. I'm sorry I laid that stuff on you, man. I didn't mean it. But this middle-

394

of-the-night Honor Code stuff . . . man. They ought to just issue those guys white robes and get the whole thing out in the open."

Bloomingburg walked over to the bunk, picked up his Bible, neither agreeing nor disagreeing with what Slaight said.

"Anything I can do for you, Jay. . . ." Slaight's words trailed off.

"Hey!" Bloomingburg turned, all smiles. "You can help me with my poly sci paper next week. You know how I always pick topics that are too broad, and end up with fifty books and five footnotes and go Dee," meaning Deficient, flunking, 1.9 or less out of 3.0. "Well, you can help me pick a topic and poop me up on how you do those papers. I've seen you. You spend about an hour in the library taking notes, an hour in the periodicals room, check out four books, and they hand you a 2.8 or a 2.9 like you *deserved* it or something."

"Well. You said it yourself. I do." Slaight laughed. They all laughed. It was pushing 3 A.M., and the atmosphere in the room was like the last three hours had never happened. Buck checked the TV movie listings in the *Times*.

"Goddamn-goddamn," he announced, drawing everyone's attention. "*Thunder Road* is playing the late-late show on Channel 5 in ten minutes. Anybody wanna go downstairs and get a Coke and watch it? Gotta watch fuckin' *Thunder Road*, man. Music alone's worth staying up."

"Can I come?" asked Bloomingburg. He had never joined their late-late show craziness before. Ever.

"Sure," said Buck. "Bring your Brown Boy. Gets cold down there in the basement."

"You might miss chapel tomorrow morning, Jay," teased Lugar.

Bloomingburg blushed.

"Shit, Lugar. I don't think God'll mind this once," said Slaight.

"Don't guess He will," said Buck. "Come on."

They watched Robert Mitchum drive fast cars for fast money and die young, and they climbed in the rack at 5

A.M., an hour before reveille. Company D-3 wouldn't see much of them the next day. They were too busy catching up on lost racktime.

33

Noon, Thursday, October 31, 1968. The plebe mail carrier delivered a letter to Room 226. It was a blue envelope, addressed to Slaight, and it looked familiar. He stuffed the letter in the pocket of his short overcoat and walked out to ranks. The regiment marched off to lunch. As they rounded the corner onto Brewerton Road, they could smell it. Whole companies of cadets moaned in unison as they made the turn. Veal cutlets. Brussels sprouts. Mashed potatoes. The odor was like last night's leftovers had been left to rot on the tables. The high mustard cabbage stench of the sprouts was mixing with cheap veal, frying in what was probably reconstituted french-fry oil . . . moans could be heard in Central Area, in Old South, everywhere the mess hall could be smelled.

Seated at the table in the south wing of the mess hall, Slaight tore open the envelope. It was from Samantha. Her handwriting was crisp, real longhand, not the phony-preppy rounded t's, p's and g's a lot of other girls affected. She wanted to know what had been going on with her brother's case. She mentioned Vassar, where her studies were as challenging as the life-style was tedious . . . five days of tough academics, then two days dating around the Ivy League schools. That was why Slaight referred to Vassar as the West Point of the Seven Sisters. Vassar girls couldn't wait for weekends, to get away. They were just like cadets.

At the bottom of her letter, she mentioned she had gone through her brother's letters a second time. It had taken her this long to summon the inner strength to face them. She discovered David Hand had a second, less obvious obsession, other than Ry Slaight: someone called "William Beatty." She enclosed a Xerox of the first letter she received from Hand mentioning Beatty.

I met this real gentleman from Washington last week, just by chance. I was out walking around the Plain on Saturday, and he pulled up in a car and asked if I wanted a ride. I climbed in, just to get warm. It was one of those really cold December days. Anyway, his name is William Beatty, and he is some kind of deputy Secretary of Defense down in the Pentagon. He comes up to West Point all the time, knows lots of cadets and officers. He asked me if I wanted to have dinner with him at the Thayer that night, and I said yes, of course! What a good deal! It was a nice dinner, and he asked me if I would escort him to chapel Sunday morning. Another good deal! I got to go to late services, instead of going early at 0800! We had brunch in the mess hall together. He was really impressive—very intelligent, and of course incredibly well versed on military matters. The strange thing was, he seemed to know everybody Sunday morning at brunch, and most of the guys who came up to talk with him were really high-ranking firsties, and all of them who weren't in my regiment recognized me! (Plebes can't be recognized by guys in their own regiment until June Week, *or else*.) He told me he's coming up here again after Christmas, so I guess I'll see him then. Oh yes. The other thing was that he told me to be sure to join the Military Affairs Club this year, so I can get two trips to the Pentagon every year, starting next year. He said he would show me around personally. He's the most impressive man I've met so far as a cadet, Sam, and he's not even an officer. Isn't that something?

Slaight read the Beatty Xerox a second time, then passed it to Lugar and Buck. On his way to class after lunch, he dropped the letter off with lawyer Bassett. Hand's description of his weekend with William Beatty had been uncannily perceptive. It fit precisely everything Slaight had heard about him. Beatty pulled a kind of . . . power seduction . . . that was it! . . . power seduction . . . impress the hell out of them with Pentagon gossip

397

and offers of introductions to men in power. Beatty made it abundantly clear, Slaight had learned, that he invited cadets down to the Pentagon for very good reasons. If a firstie was going into the Infantry, Beatty would arrange a lunch with the colonel in charge of Infantry Branch personnel . . . the man in charge of assignments to choice command slots in choice posts around the globe. If a firstie showed unusual interest in his Ordnance Engineering course, which was essentially a course in the study of the science of weaponry, Beatty would arrange to escort him out to the research and development command at Fort Belvoir. The only piece that didn't fit was David Hand himself. What was Beatty doing impressing a lowly plebe? His normal protégés were first-classmen. Plebes . . . well, they had three years to go before Pentagon contacts and trips to research centers would do them any good.

When Slaight returned from his two afternoon classes at 3:15 P.M., the D-3 CQ had two messages for him: See Bassett today. See the commandant, 1730, 5:30 P.M., Friday, November 1, 1968. Tomorrow.

Bassett wanted to shoot the breeze. The request for legal counsel before the Aptitude Board was still neatly lodged in legal wrangling, so everything was going as planned on that front. Slaight told him about the abortive honor violation charges Hedges had lodged against him on Monday. Bassett packed his pipe and nodded, lit it, filling his windowless office with smoke which disappeared into the ceiling, through an exhaust fan, hidden behind an egg-crate plastic false ceiling with concealed fluorescent lighting, heating and air conditioning ducts, electric wiring, sundry untidiness. All classrooms in Thayer Hall were like that: windowless, lit by fluorescence. Bright colors and small, fifteen-to-sixteen-man classes made the place tolerable. Just barely. Not Bassett's closet. Nearly waist-deep in organized chaos, the only way to survive, obviously, was to stay stoned on coffee and this strange, bitter mix of pipe tobacco.

Bassett didn't seem surprised at the honor subcommittee . . . he never seemed particularly surprised at *anything*, having concluded, apparently, at West Point the totally bizarre was perfectly normal. You got the impression if Bassett learned a day had passed without incident, he'd get really upset. *Too quiet*, he'd mutter. *Better keep our antenna out.* Once Bassett chuckled and used a slogan Slaight had seen on the bumper of VW buses outfitted for hippiedom on the highways: "Paranoia is its own reward."

Slaight was adjusting to the confines of Bassett's cubbyhole when the lawyer cleared a hole in the papers on his desk, and produced three typescript documents. One was an official paper documenting that Hedges had ordered Slaight's name withdrawn from the list of cadets excused from class for SCUSA. No longer did they need the word of the frightened major who had been OIC of Slaight's committee.

The second was a copy of the report of the cadet honor subcommittee to the commandant on the disposition of charges against Rysam Parker Slaight III.

"Recommend no further action be taken," was the last line of the report.

"Recommend!" yelled Slaight, coughing. "Who the hell are they recommending to, anyway? Hedges or the chairman of the Honor Committee?"

"Rather clear, don't you think?" Bassett held up the cover letter on the report. It was addressed to, and initialed by, Brigadier General Charles Sherrill Hedges, Commandant of Cadets.

"That kind of puts the lie to the old 'cadets run the code' myth, doesn't it?"

"Indeed it does," said Bassett, bouncing his eyebrows gleefully. "How do you think I came to possess this little item? Divine intervention?"

"No. How?"

"One of your classmates. Certain of your classmates have made the same conclusion you've just made and are taking the situation into their own hands—principally in the Fourth Regiment, I might add. I am not at liberty to disclose to you the identity of the man who passed this document to me—lawyer-client privilege, you know—but he gave his permission that you be allowed to see it.

You've got more friends than you know, over in the happy Fourth. I would guess—roughly, this is—about a hundred of them. They've got the neatest little cheating system you've ever seen."

"And you got the report to Hedges from one of them? That thing could only have come from—from an honor rep. Christ!" Bassett grinned and puffed.

"Lawyer-client privilege. Cannot disclose." Slaight had hit the nail on the head. There was at least one honor rep involved in a cheating ring in the Fourth Regiment. Phew! Hot stuff.

"Take a look at this," said Bassett, peering over his glasses. His red nose looked like a small plum.

Slaight read the poop-sheet. It was a deposition, or sworn statement, telexed from somewhere. All identifying marks had been taped out with white tape before Xeroxing. Slaight skimmed the telex. His eyes stopped skimming when he hit the part about the second-class epaulet found at the scene of the crime.

"A cow epaulet was found up there at Popolopen, where Hand was floating?"

"Not where he was floating. Read on. It was found beneath his neatly folded uniform. The young man was nude when fished out of the lake, if you'll recall."

Slaight kept reading, closer now. The telex was a copy of a sworn statement taken from one of the military policemen who had been on the scene the morning Hand's body was discovered. Other than Hand's uniform—complete with personal effects, shoes and all—the only thing found on the scene was a cow epaulet, an epaulet belonging to one of Slaight's classmates, for they had been cows back in May when Hand drowned. The epaulet disappeared and was never seen again by the MP. Two days later, he found himself on his way to Korea, where the sworn statement had been taken. Slaight handed the poop-sheet back to Bassett with a quizzical look on his face.

"A Harvard Law classmate of mine, not quite so fortunate as myself, is boring himself to death in Seoul these days. I got on the army long-distance system one night,

400

patched myself through the main Pentagon switchboard, and tracked him down. He found the MP and took the statement." Bassett knocked his pipe on the heel of his shoe, pausing to reload and relight.

"As you can see, this telex appears to narrow our prospective suspects drastically—your classmates who were scheduled to speak at Hand's high school along with the man from '68."

"Jesus. That is a help."

"Not so fast, Slaight. Don't jump to conclusions. Creep up on them, slowly, so they don't see you coming." Bassett grinned. His wide round face was infectious, the delight he took, rooting around in the academy's dirty laundry.

"I stayed late at the office early this week and made some calls to Mr. Hand's alma mater, his high school. The guidance counselor who arranged the cadet recruiter lectures confirmed who actually spoke that day. The same three who were scheduled to speak by the academy. We should have known. Cadets are so marvelously responsible . . . *predictable.*"

"Yeah. Don't I know it," said Slaight.

"The same guidance counselor, who was quite eager to be of help actually, provided me with three interesting bits of information. Follow me closely: One of your classmates was from New Orleans and spent all his free time at home. Your other classmate was from the same company—they were roommates—and he stayed with the same family. Their time in New Orleans is entirely accountable. The guidance counselor reserved a room in one of the larger French Quarter hotels for the man from the class of 1968. The same guidance counselor was David Hand's guidance counselor and was instrumental in his decision on the Military Academy. The same guidance counselor introduced Hand to the cadet from the class of 1968. Later she said, Hand had referred to the cadet when discussing his decision to attend West Point. She was unbridled in her opinion that our man from '68 had had what she called 'quite profound effect on David,' Little did she know."

"She remember his name?"

"Of course. Her memory matches exactly the name we have from the Registrar's Office. She even recalled that young David had written her not long after entering West Point, complaining. She was careful to point out almost all college freshmen complain. No college ever lives up to its reputation, she said. Anyway, she said she received a letter from young Hand while he was in Beast Barracks complaining that his squad leader did not live up to the image he had of cadets from his acquaintanceship with our man from '68." Bassett chuckled, pipe smoke seeming to emerge from his ears, his shirt collar, everywhere at once.

"You were not exactly David Hand's catalogue cadet, Slaight. In other words, he was telling his guidance counselor he wasn't getting what he'd ordered through the mails. 'Oldest story in the book,' she said. Feisty old babe."

"Then it looks like we've got our man," said Slaight, his voice having lost its edge of excitement. There was something of a letdown when you sensed that things were coming to an end.

"Not so fast, young buck. This still leaves us the other three cadets in New Orleans at the same time. Now I'll admit. According to your interview with the Boy in Blue, the chances are strong, *very* strong that he's our man. If you can get a positive physical identification from a photograph, I'd say we're coming close to a case. Opportunity ... motive ..."

"What about the cow epaulet?"

"Throwing the dogs off the scent. He probably thought there'd be a real investigation. What better way to draw attention from himself than to point all signs at your class, the year the murderer graduated and left West Point for good. Classic ploy. I could cite criminal cases ... let me see ..."

"Come on, Clifford, enough with the cases. Try them out on your cow students this year. Right now, I'm interested in this case, the David Hand case, and how we can nail this SOB. I've got to go see Hedges tomorrow at five-thirty again. No telling what's going to happen, his honor charges failing and all. I need total legal advice. What strategy do you suggest for Halloween, lawyer Bassett? Trick or treat?"

They laughed. Bassett called his secretary for coffee.

"Two things," said Bassett, puffing up a storm. He always puffed away and said *two things* or *three things* when he was getting ready to unload what he called his "heavy artillery."

"One: I have been told not to give legal advice to you, Rysam Parker Slaight III, from this day forth."

"What the fuck?"

"The colonel called me in this morning—the department head, the tenured professor of law—and he told me not to counsel you any more. He said if you needed legal counsel, you'd be assigned counsel. I explained to him that I was the counsel of your choice, and that army regulations stipulate a soldier is entitled to counsel of choice unless the military situation dictates that provision of such counsel is impossible or impractical. Or too expensive. I've got plenty of time on my hands, and most of these claims from all the summer moves have been filed and are now out of my hands, believe it or not." Slaight looked at Bassett's cluttered office. It was hard to believe.

"My teaching duties take up minimal time. I have only one or two other cadet clients. I gave the colonel every reason in the book I should remain your lawyer. Finally, he told me to do as I was told and to get out. Before leaving, I asked him if he was giving me a direct verbal order to that effect. His words were—I have them copied down here somewhere—here: 'Bassett, if you counsel that little prick Slaight on this Hand business again, I'll personally see you get twelve months in Vietnam to contemplate your actions.' That was precisely what I had waited for. I hurriedly copied down the colonel's words, in his presence, dated the sheet of paper and signed it, ran out to his secretary and had her notarize the signature, time, and date. Then I walked back into his office with my copy of his threat in hand, and I told the colonel if he even picked up the phone to get me on orders for Vietnam, I'd have a federal district court restraining order on his desk before he could get the JAG branch in the Pentagon to call back. That pissed him off, but he didn't say anything more about counseling you, so I am operating on the assumption that our lawyer-client relationship is intact."

"Jesus. They're really uncorking on you, too, huh?"

"Indeed. But in so doing, they tipped their hand. I made no secret of the fact I am in possession of this telex. They're willing to threaten me with Vietnam to back me off. I have a theory, Slaight. You know me well enough to know how I deplore theories and speculation. Well, this one is just too obvious to pass up. I think they know who killed David Hand. I think they know we're close to identifying the killer. They're willing to try almost anything to stop us. This would explain the threat of Vietnam duty by the colonel, the surveillance of your girl friend, the illegal search of your files, the phony honor charges, and of course, the Aptitude Board. Army officers are like surgeons, Slaight. They like to cut. They *like* it. When they see something wrong, their first instinct is, cut it off. Worry about the rest of the body later. There has been enough cutting in this David Hand case that I've begun to fathom its style. I believe the style is that of William Beatty, my favorite character in our amateur soap opera. We know this much: He was, shall we say, friendly with David Hand. According to what the sergeant major told you, he was up to his neck in Pentagon machinations behind the David Hand case. And Beatty fits this in another, more interesting way."

"What's that?"

"He is a colleague of Colonel Addison Thompson," said Bassett gravely. He stared at notes he had scribbled on a sheet of paper in front of him, like he wished an answer would leap from the page and squirt him in the eye. The name of the head of West Point's Department of Social Sciences was never taken lightly. Now it was being linked, through Beatty, to David Hand.

"As you probably know, Colonel Thompson is about the closest thing we've got around here to an honest-to-God academician. He has his master's, his Ph.D., and honorary degrees from Lord only knows how many distinguished colleges and universities, including most of the Ivy League. He is the man credited with having 'liberalized' education at West Point, pushing for more elective subjects, more concentration in specific areas, if not actual majors, and less of the broadbrush-stroke approach West Point has pursued for so long. For many people in this country, Colonel Thompson *is* the modern Military Academy. He helped establish the Air Force Academy. He spends fully a third of his year down in the Pentagon, consulting on matters relating to national security. He is the army's professor emeritus to the rest of the world, and the rest of the world *loves* him."

"So?"

"So that's just the surface of Colonel Thompson. What is less known publicly, but appreciated privately in government and big business, is the rest of his career. During World War II, he was a key aide to General George C. Marshall, the Army Chief of Staff. There are those military historians—and they are not few in number—who credit Thompson with authorship of the 'Marshall Plan,' the economic blueprint for European recovery from the war. It is known, in certain circles, that Colonel Thompson was one of the authors of the National Security Act of 1947, the law passed by the Congress establishing the CIA. Thompson has served as an adviser to every director of Central Intelligence since Dulles. He is tight with such public and not-so-public power brokers as the Editorial Board of the *Times*, major bankers and brokers on Wall Street, and most of the Council on Foreign Relations. The truly astounding thing about a man like Thompson is that he is able to continue his influence . . . no. Let me correct that. He is able to make his influence *grow* despite any political ties to either party, Democrat or Republican. He is recognized by both sides as a patriot, a statesman, a scholar, and a gentleman. That he is also an army officer has hardly mattered. But by far the most frightening of the five hats he wears—if we can call them that—is the hat patriot. There is nothing more pernicious than a patriot without identifiable politics. One has only to recall Hitler of the 1930s to reacquaint oneself with that lesson of history."

"Jesus. So you're saying Colonel Thompson is a lot more than the head of the Social Science Department."

"Yes. And a lot less. According to certain friends of mine at Harvard with an interest in international relations, Thompson's politics haven't changed much since the days of Joe McCarthy. His image as the Great White Liberal of the Service Academies is a wonder of modern public relations. It's easy to be a liberal, Ry, when your liberalism is contained neatly within this tight, beautiful ghetto called West Point. Outside the academy, I am told, our Colonel Thompson is something less than liberal in his views of domestic and international affairs."

"The war?"

"He has been known to advocate the bomb-them-back-to-the-stone-age approach to war in Southeast Asia."

"So William Beatty is a colleague of Colonel Thompson's, huh?"

"Well, both a colleague and a protégé. You see, it was Thompson who put him where he is in the Pentagon, so he owes his career to the man. But Beatty's job is now of such a nature that they operate in the same circles, see the same people, attend the same parties, socialize with the same defense industrialists and bankers and Wall Streeters, so in a sense they have become colleagues. But everyone knows where they stand with Colonel Thompson. He probably has more debts outstanding in Washington, D.C., than the President himself, because he's simply been at it longer than the President. He was there at the beginning of everything. Everyone owes him something. I know William Beatty does." Bassett relit his pipe.

"So. I think Beatty is some kind of key to this thing, and I think the key leads directly through Thompson, but for the life of me, I cannot figure out *how*. Much of this material on Thompson is so old, it either doesn't hold water any more, or all the water has evaporated. So there are one hell of a lot of dry wells surrounding the man.

But for every dry well, let me assure you, he has sunk ten new ones, and they *produce*."

"So how does David Hand fit in with William Beatty, and how do they fit in with Colonel Addison Thompson?"

"If I could answer that question, Slaight, we could fold up shop."

"Yeah."

"So when you go in to see Hedges, if you get a chance—the barest opening—probe him about Beatty a little. See what kind of reaction you get. I've done some asking around. It seems our friend Hedges, as a cadet, was one of Colonel Thompson's first 'boys,' after he left Washington and took his permanent professorship here at the academy. Their relationship doubtlessly continued while Hedges was liaison in the Secretary of Defense's office between the DIA and the CIA. Thompson has cronies up to here"—Bassett slapped the bottom of his chin with the back of his hand—"in both intelligence agencies. I think it's safe to say Hedges and Thompson are not strangers to one another."

"Christ. This thing just gets deeper and deeper, doesn't it?"

"Yes, Ry, it does. If you'd applied yourself while studying law under me, you would have noticed the same thing about the law. It just gets deeper and deeper. You follow the cases further and further back, looking and looking for that one decision that gives you an 'in,' some little kernel of information or legal interpretation which you can cull out and apply to the present and attempt to affect the outcome of things as they stand today. But you were . . . ah . . . one of my sterling 2.3 students, right, Slaight? Just high enough for long weekends, not high enough to show you were really *trying*."

"Yeah. Nothing personal, but law wasn't exactly my favorite subject."

"What was your favorite, Ry? I'd really like to know."

"Mechanics, believe it or not. I carried about a 2.8 in both solids and fluids."

"Mechanics?" Bassett removed his pipe and exhaled incredulously.

407

"Yeah. There was something so . . . *neat* about mechanics. It all added up. They called it 'resolution of forces.' I always liked that phrase."

"I do see what you mean," said Bassett, leaning back, propping unshined shoes on his paper-strewn desk.

"Captain? Thanks for standing up for me with the professor of law like you did. With my 2.3 average under you, I know I don't deserve it." They laughed.

"Forget it, Slaight. If they ever do send me to Vietnam, I'll end up in some air-conditioned trailer in a base camp, processing claims just like I'm doing here. Boring myself to death. At least here at the academy, things are *happening*. Listen. I want to see you tomorrow after your confab with Hedges."

"Here? In your office?"

Bassett puffed on his pipe for a moment, his eyes glistening.

"No," he said. "Come over to the Officers' Club and meet me in the bar. Tomorrow night is 'Happy Hour.' There are always lots of Tactical Department types present for duty at Happy Hour. Let's rub it in their noses a little. Give them something to gossip about." Bassett chuckled at the plan, his round face beaming, eyes darting around, looking over the top of his glasses.

"Happy Hour. Jesus."

"Yes, Mr. Slaight. Happy Hour."

"See you then." Slaight was gone, on the run. He had work to do. Calls to make. His meeting with Hedges was twenty-four hours away.

34

Friday, November 1, 1968, 1730 hours.

"Sir, Mr. Slaight reports to the commandant as ordered."

"Have a seat, mister."

Slaight sat down. Things seemed different . . . almost casual. The commandant was seated behind his desk with his uniform jacket open, his short collar unbuttoned, his tie askew. He busied himself finishing some paperwork. Slaight waited.

"I've called you in today, Mr. Slaight, to let you know that this business with the plebe, David Hand, has been resolved. You've got nothing to worry about now. You can go back down to the barracks and enjoy your first-class year. How should I put this? You have . . . ah . . . pointed out certain matters, and they have been resolved. Any questions?" Hedges stared intently at Slaight's face.

"Resolved, sir? How do you mean, resolved?"

"The situation is over, Slaight. Finished. You are to stop your meddling, get down to the barracks, and start acting like a cadet again, instead of a cheap private eye."

"I still don't understand, sir. Hand was murdered. I want to know who killed him and what's being done about it."

"You are right, Slaight," said Hedges, chewing his words like tough steak. "The little fag was killed. And the man who killed him . . . he took the only honorable way out. He volunteered for Vietnam. He's over there right now, a platoon leader in the Big Red One. A combat leader."

"Honorable? *Honorable*?" Slaight's voice raised an involuntary octave. "General Hedges, are you kidding me? You mean you know who killed Hand, and you're saying Vietnam is his honorable way out?"

"That's right, son. The man's in Nam right now. This minute. Combat. Volunteered for Long Range Reconnaissance Patrols, the Lurps. Honorable duty. *Necessary*. Same thing."

Slaight sat there in Hedges' office so stunned he couldn't speak. Finally the words came. He would call Hedges "General" from now on, a subtle gesture, but one to which a man like Hedges would be attuned. It meant he'd never again hear the word "Sir" from Slaight's lips.

"General, can I ask the man's name, the man who killed Hand?"

Hedges stopped his poop-sheet shuffling and looked at Slaight.

"You already know, don't you, mister?"

"Yes, General, I do."

"Julian VanRiper, '68. Damn fine man when he was here. Doing a fine job with the Big Red One Lurps, I'm told."

VanRiper. He'd been C.O. of Beast and then Fourth Regimental commander, a strait-laced SOB with a reputation for writing up his own classmates, an almost unheard-of practice in the co-operate-and-graduate atmosphere of the academy in the 1960s. No wonder he and Hand had a thing going! Neither one of them gave one half a shit about anyone but himself. Theirs must have been a shared, insular paranoia. In the end, what they had mistaken for emotion had consumed one of them. Hand. At least the West Point co-operate-and-graduate philosophy had that much figured out. To do otherwise was to cannibalize your fellows, living off their energy, their blood, their lust for The Life. At West Point, you either joined-up or you died. Slaight wondered if the same thing held true for other bureaucracies, other colleges, big civilian multinational corporations. He wondered if the cannibalism represented by the homosexual murder of David Hand was endemic to the military, to West Point. He'd been at it for six months, and he still didn't know what in hell was *going on*. He was beginning to conclude he'd never understand it when Hedges interrupted.

"There's no use in your going any further with this thing, Slaight. As I said, everything has been taken care of. There will be no charges preferred against VanRiper. You may as well forget the provost marshal, Slaight. You have no evidence. Only conjecture, son. And your kind of conjecture won't stand up in a court-martial. All it will do is get you deeper in trouble. If you know what's good for you, mister, you'll forget you ever heard of David Hand. You'll forget the whole thing."

"If I knew what's good for me, General, I'd never be in here with you in the first place."

410

"That's correct, mister. You wouldn't."

"So I guess I don't know what's good for me, General."

"No, Slaight, you don't. And that's been your whole problem, right from the start. You'd better start learning the rules around here, mister, and you'd better start playing by those rules. Or you're *out*. You hear me?"

"General, I already know the rules. West Point's rules. The army's rules. Your rules. *All* the rules. I guess I just haven't been playing the game by those rules, General. Any of them."

"Mister, you think you know the way the game is played around here. I am here to tell you that you *do not*. Am I understood?"

"Yes, General."

"Now. Let's come to an agreement here. Are you going to start playing by the rules, Slaight?"

"General, if you mean by that, am I going to keep my mouth shut about the David Hand case, the answer is no, General. No."

Hedges' face turned burgundy red, and his head seemed to sink into the lapels of his uniform jacket. A transformation began to take place. Slowly, his gaze never leaving the cadet sitting in front of him, Hedges buttoned his ribbon-bedecked uniform jacket. He buttoned his shirt collar and straightened his tie. Over and over again, he ran his left hand along the bottom of his jacket, ensuring the left flap covered the right. Standing up, he jerked his arms, exposing his cuffs. An informal, friendly figure when Slaight first walked into his office, Hedges was now standing erect, the very essence of military bearing. He walked around the edge of his desk and stood a few feet away, rocking slowly back and forth, heel-to-toe, heel-to-toe. His tongue ran from one cheek to the other across his teeth. Slaight could see it. Hedges was thinking. He was rehearsing his lines.

"I am going to see you out of here, Slaight. If it takes me my full tour of duty as commandant, I am going to see you out of here, mister. I am going to stand at the main gate next to the MP shack, and I am going to personally supervise your departure. I am going to get you, mister. When I am through, you're going to have no place left to hide. You will not know which way is up. Lurp patrols in Nam are going to look like a good deal, compared to the state you'll be in, Slaight. Just wait and see."

"If that's the way you want to play the game, General, then I guess that's the way we'll play it."

Silence. Hedges ground his teeth. Slaight could see his jaws working. He walked forward and stood two feet from the chair in which Slaight was still seated. Slaight took the signal, and stood.

"You'd better have your ducks lined up, mister. You'd better know what you're doing if you decide to go up against Charles Sherrill Hedges."

Slaight stared at Hedges. He still refused to lock eyes.

"Have I made myself understood, mister?"

"Perfectly, General. Perfectly."

"Then you drive your goddamn communist ass out of my office, Slaight. The next time I see you, Slaight, it's going to be from the rear, when your ass is on its way out that gate."

Slaight grabbed his hat and saluted.

"Good afternoon, General," he said. At the door, he glanced over his shoulder. Hedges had clenched his right fist and was shaking it in the air after him.

In the hall outside the commandant's office, Slaight passed the cadet first captain, the brigade commander, the highest ranking cadet. Pete Locke, from an army family. His father was retired and lived in Arlington, Virginia. Slaight and Locke exchanged nods. They didn't know each other. Locke was on his way in. Slaight presumed it was their daily meeting, the com and the first captain, getting together for a few minutes before supper to discuss tomorrow's business. He was looking forward to meeting Captain Bassett at the O Club bar. He presumed wrong.

"Have a seat, Locke," said Hedges, indicating the chair Slaight had just vacated.

"Pete, I want that kid out of here. I don't care what it takes. I want him out."

"I'm not sure I understand you, sir," said the first captain.

"I said I want Slaight *out*, goddammit! Do I have to spell the word for you? That Aptitude Board we're running on him probably won't work. He moved from the middle fifth of the class to the second fifth because of the damned efficiency report his battalion C.O. filed on him for AOT this summer. But I want him out, Pete. Demerits, honor . . . I don't give a damn what it takes. I want him out, and I want him out by Christmas. Now get cracking."

First Captain Locke saluted and left. He had known the com was out for Slaight's ass, but *this*. Never had an officer told him, in so many words, to "get" another cadet on honor, which is exactly what Hedges had just done. He paused in the com's outer office. He saw one of the buttons light up on Hedges' secretary's phone . . . she had been dismissed for the day, as had his aide. Behind the closed door to the com's office, Locke heard Hedges dial the phone. He counted the digits. It was a long-distance call. Then he heard Hedges' muffled voice:

"Bill Beatty, please. General Hedges calling."

So! He was calling that guy in the Pentagon again! Locke walked downstairs, wondering what to do. The com had put him in a difficult—no, an impossible—situation. If he tried to "get" Slaight on an honor violation, that in itself could be interpreted as an honor violation. On the other hand, if he didn't he would be disobeying an order from the commandant. He decided he'd better pay a visit to this guy Ry Slaight over in the Third Regiment and see what was up.

Inside, tie loosened and feet resting atop his desk, Hedges talked long-distance to William Beatty in Washington.

"Bill, everything is go. You can start the ball rolling on Rylander next week. I've got Slaight scared stiff, and if we don't get him with this Aptitude Board, we'll drive his ass out of here some other way. Let me assure you. We'll have him in greens with PFC stripes on his sleeves by the first of next year. Then he's in your court. I'm sure you know what to do with him. A passing acquaintanceship

413

with our friend Charlie over in Southeast Asia probably wouldn't hurt." Chuckling merriment danced across the long-distance wires between West Point and the Pentagon. Matters were firmly in hand. Soon, Hedges could take the steps necessary for his final move: across the street, through the courtyard, and up the stairs and into the supe's office. To stay.

First Captain Peter Locke surprised Slaight when he walked into Room 226, New South Barracks, just after supper. Lugar looked up, and at the sight of the tall, good-looking six-striper, almost snapped to attention. It took supreme concentration to treat a guy like Lock as . . . classmate, an equal. He had one of those young Gregory Peck faces, the dark handsome good looks of a born general. It had always seemed there was an unwritten requirement that first captains and other high-ranking cadets be attractive . . . not just good-looking, but . . . idols. Statues to the American idea of *cadet*. Pete Locke filled the bill. At 6'1", 185 pounds, a letter man in soccer and lacrosse, he was the ideal first captain. There was a certain awkwardness—intimidation—in his presence. Slaight couldn't recall ever having laid eyes on Peter Locke, except standing in formation way out in front of the Corps of Cadets with his brigade staff . . . and that afternoon, on his way in to see the com. Locke walked in and introduced himself.

"Maybe we should go somewhere and talk," he began.

"Forget it, man," said Slaight. "Anything you've got to say to me, you can say to him." He nodded his head at Lugar. Leroy Buck wandered in, wearing his gray cadet bathrobe. "Him, too," said Slaight.

"Well, I don't know what kind of trouble you've got yourself in with the com, but today, it just got too deep for me," said Locke.

"How so?" asked Slaight.

"The com told me—I guess he *ordered* me—to 'get' you today. He said he wants you out by Christmas. He told me he didn't care how I did it. He mentioned demerits and . . ." Locke paused, gazing at the toes of his shoes, gleaming black mirrors under the overhead lights.

"And?"

"And he mentioned honor. That's what got me. He was telling me to get you on an honor violation, and he didn't care how. I decided then and there, I had to come over and tell you about it. Nobody . . . *nobody* has ever come to me and talked about 'getting' someone on honor. Least of all, the com."

"Jesus. Thanks, man," said Slaight. He offered Locke a Coke from a garbage can full of ice glommed from the mess hall after supper. Locke accepted and sat down.

"Look, Slaight, I don't know what you've done, but nothing in my experience warrants the kind of thing the com was talking about today. I mean, I've seen him go to some lengths to make examples of guys . . . Charlie Napier is a good case. Six months for shacking up. You wouldn't believe what I went through over that."

"I'd believe you," said Slaight, studying Locke's face. He was tired . . . all firsties looked permanently tired . . . but Locke's face showed a deeper dimension of fatigue, lines, like a pair of firstie's winter uniform gloves, ragged out, resewn, and ragged out again.

"Anyway, you sure manage to take up a lot of his time. I have to report to the com twice a day, you know. Once before lunch, and once just before supper. For the past couple of months, it seems like every time I report, he's muttering something about you, or talking to some guy in the Pentagon on the phone."

"What guy?" Slaight tried unsuccessfully to contain his eagerness.

"He was on the phone to him again today when I left. Somebody called William Beatty. I've heard of him. I know we've got classmates who are friends with this Beatty. But I have no idea why he's always talking to Beatty on the phone about you."

"What makes you think the subject is me?" asked Slaight.

"I've been in his office when he took calls from Beatty. Every single time, they talked about you. It was all very

415

circumspect, naturally. I could never fathom the real nature of their conversations, and to tell the truth, never really tried. Being first captain, you learn one thing real quickly. Sometimes, the less you know, the better off you are."

"Know exactly what you mean," said Slaight.

"Do you feel like telling me what this is all about?" asked Locke.

"This is one of those areas with a big sign outside, and it says, 'you don't want to know,' " said Slaight.

"Can I ask you this? Does it involve honor?"

"No way," said Slaight. "You know Hedges charged me with a violation not long ago, don't you?"

"Yes. I saw the report of the subcommittee."

"He shot his wad with that one. What's going on between me and Hedges now is personal. I guess that's the best way to describe it. Personal. Pisses me off that he tried to drag you in on it."

"Well, all I can tell you is this. I've never seen anyone, last year or this year, go up against Hedges and win."

"That's okay," said Slaight. "I'm not sure winning is the point any more."

"If it isn't winning, then what is the point? Why don't you just knuckle under and get Hedges off your back?"

"I'm not sure what the point is. But I'm way past knuckling under, straightening up, and flying right . . . all that shit."

"I see," said Locke. "Well, I'll tell you what. You'd better keep your nose clean. He's going to have every tac in town watching every move you make. If you sneeze at a parade, he might call it 'gross disrespect,' and put you on the area. Once he's got you walking the area, it's all over for you. He'll get you on demerits, for sure."

"Thanks for the warning, man." Slaight stood up. Locke's brawny lacrosse attack-man shoulders almost filled the door.

"Hey," said Slaight. "Anything I can do for you . . . ask."

"Sure thing," said the first captain, disappearing around the corner downstairs.

Slaight grabbed one of the phone booths and called the news to lawyer Bassett.

"Take a weekend leave and get yourself out of there for a while," said Bassett.

"Now? This weekend? We've got stuff to do."

"You wanted total legal advice. I'm your lawyer. There it is. Get out of here. See you Monday."

35

Slaight spent the weekend with Irit in New York. Saturday afternoon, they browsed the galleries along Madison Avenue near her boutique and stopped off at Parke Bernet to see some antique jewelry on display, due to be auctioned in a few weeks. That night, she talked him into doing something she'd been working on for weeks: She got Slaight to call his father.

From Irit's penthouse, Slaight told his father the whole story, from beginning to end, right up to the visit from the first captain. His father asked a few questions, but mostly he uh-huhed, uh-huhed, and grunted yeses and noes as Slaight plowed the same old ground, the same recitation of people, places, facts, the questions, the unresolved answers. When he was finished, his father surprised him.

"I find it all hard to believe, son, but I believe you. And I'll stand behind you, all the way, whatever you do. I'll do anything I can to help you."

Slaight didn't know what to say. It had been so long since he and his father had done more than exchange good mornings over the breakfast table when he was home on leave . . . well, he just didn't know what to do. His father broke the silence.

"What are you going to do now, son?"

"I don't know, Dad. But I'll tell you one thing. Hedges isn't going to run me out of here. I'll walk the area till my

417

feet wear off, I'll drive around to his office every day till I graduate, but he's not going to get me."

"Do you have a plan, son?"

"Not really. But I'll follow the advice of my lawyer, Captain Bassett. And I've got a few other sources to touch. We're not finished yet. If it comes down to it, and I think it will when they convene that Aptitude Board, I've got some dirt to throw at them they don't know about yet."

"Son?"

"Yeah, Dad."

"Don't go throwing dirt around like you're saying. Your grandpa always used to say it ends up getting all over the guy doing the throwing, no matter how smart he figures he is."

"I'll remember that. Hey, Dad, can I ask you one last question before we hang up?"

"Sure, son. What is it?"

"All this time . . . I mean, I've been at West Point over three years now, and I'm twenty-one years old . . . all this time, how come you never told me about the war? How come?"

"I never figure you'd . . . *understand*, son. That's all. I didn't want you growing up with a bunch of romantic notions about war, and I thought if I told you what I'd done, you'd want to be like me, do the things I did, act the way I acted. No man in his right mind is proud about going to war, son. You're sad. I didn't want you to grow up, I guess. I didn't want you to end up sad. You understand what I am saying to you?"

Slaight could hear the plaintive tone in his father's voice.

"Yeah, Dad. I understand."

"I see you do, son. Talking to you tonight . . . I can see that all I did was make you more curious." His father paused, and Slaight could hear him lighting a cigarette, the top of his Zippo lighter snapping shut, an exhalation of breath.

"Listening to what you had to say tonight, son, I see that you know more about what men are capable of doing

418

to each other than I knew when I was twice your age. I knew about war, I knew about killing with rifles and artillery and the rest of it. But I didn't know this *other stuff. . . .*" His father coughed. "I didn't know this other stuff. There are all kinds of war, son. All kinds of violence. You're learning that now. It took your mother, bless her, to teach me about people, the things they do to each other, violence, the little everyday wars people fight."

In his mind's eye, Slaight could see his father at home, sitting in the big overstuffed chair near the fireplace. He was glad Irit talked him into calling his dad.

"What do you mean, Dad? What did Ma teach you?"

"Well, she let me know about those people from Kansas City who stabled their horses with us. She finally made me understand what they really stood for. All those years we stabled their horses and trained their kids, and I organized their hunts and the jumping every spring . . . and I never knew. I was never really one of them, but because of riding and our stables out at Wild Acres, they took me . . . us . . . in. They made me believe I was one of them. Finally your mother made me realize the truth. We were just tolerated, was all. It's a quiet violence, that social stuff. Son, I hope you're able to cope with what you learn about those men up at West Point, because I'll tell you the truth. Wouldn't have been for your mother, I never would have coped." His father paused again, and Slaight waited.

"No matter what happens, son, try to understand those men and what they're doing to you. If you can do that, you're halfway home. Whatever you do, try to keep in mind they're only human. God made them. God made you. Don't let your hatred for them and what they're doing consume you. Don't let them get to you, son, because if they do, you'll end up like them. Please. For your old dad. Try not to hate. Try your damnedest. Someday, you'll be thankful you didn't."

"Okay, Dad. I'll try."

"Whelp." His father always said "whelp," instead of "well." "Whelp, better be going. You take care of yourself. And take care of your girl friend. She seems like an awfully good woman."

They said good-bye.

Monday morning, Slaight found lawyer Bassett deep in the bowels of Thayer Hall. He looked up from his desk, glasses falling to the tip of his nose.

"What are you here for? Wanna know about life insurance? Great idea. Get some." They laughed. Old Bassett had a sense of humor that cut through the bullshit at its thickest.

"Any news?"

"Yeah. Your Aptitude Board is one week from today. Got official notice this morning Something's up, Slaight. Hedges is too confident. He's been sitting on something for a long time. I can *feel* it. You know that long dead period between your meeting with him during re-orgy week and your next meeting in late October? And now he's willing to give you a full seven days' advance warning, seven days to line up your ducks for the Aptitude Board. He's got something big going, Ry. Something bigger than the Hand thing. I just feel it, that's all. When I was working down on Wall Street, sometimes you could feel an opposing attorney getting ready to make an unexpected move. They'd get . . . cocky . . . Hedges is cocky. They always make some little mistake that tips you off. Well, I've been watching Hedges for quite a while now. This seven-day warning is it. He's getting ready to move. Move fast. Move heavy. I don't know for sure, but I think he's got more going here than the David Hand murder."

"So what do we do?"

"*We* don't do anything. *You* get on the phone to your friend the sergeant major out in Santa Fe. Have him hit the NCO grapevine in the Pentagon. See what's going on. Hedges has his hands tied up here. He's committed on your Aptitude Board, and he committed when he told the first captain to get you on honor. But all his options are still open down in the Pentagon. I can't be sure . . . but if he's moving, it's down there. Tell the sergeant major to pull out all the stops. We need a handle on what's going

420

on at Department of the Army level. We need it by mid-week. There's more at stake here than the death of one cadet, Slaight, and we need to know what it is."

Wednesday afternoon, November 6, 1968, at 3:20, the message was waiting for Slaight, taped to his door by the CQ.

SLAIGHT—CALL SGT MAJ ELDRIDGE ASAP

Slaight dropped a dime, dialed the 505 area code, and the local number for the sergeant major's house.

"Sarenmager, sir." It was the way sergeant majors always referred to themselves and to each other—*Sarenmager*, a wedding of the two words.

"Sergeant Major, it's Ry Slaight. What have you got for me?"

"You on a clean phone?"

"I'm in another company area, in a phone booth. That heavy, huh?"

"You better believe it. Slaight. I had to put my soul in hock to the supply sergeant for this poop."

The sergeant major chuckled to himself at his old army lingo. Slaight chuckled, too. It was impossible not to love a good army sergeant major. If they had them in civilian life, John Lugar once said, executives would have to hire consultants, who'd have to go to linguistics experts to try to come up with something to call them. The attempt would be an expensive failure, Lugar said, because there just wasn't a civilian word to describe the function and worth of a good sergeant major.

"Shoot. I'm taking notes," said Slaight, leaning against the wood side of the phone booth.

"That guy Beatty—William Beatty—he flew up to West Point this morning on a special Department of the Army plane. I couldn't get a complete line on what he's up to, but he was scheduled to meet with Hedges first thing this morning. And word is, he'll be up there for a week, maybe a week and a half."

"So what do you figure is going on?"

"I can't tell you much, Slaight. My sources are not the

best, and my information is incomplete. But I know this. More than one of my buddies down in the Pentagon told me our boy Beatty has been cranking up something big for the past couple of weeks. Something so big, he imported a special staff of typists and clerks to do his work for him. Everybody was told they were free-lance office workers, like Kelly Girls. But one guy looked into it, and the clerks and typists all came from Associated Electronics, one of those new computer/weapons/R & D companies with their fingers in every defense pie but hairpie." Again the chuckle. Slaight stifled a laugh.

"Fast as they were there, they were gone. The clerks and jerks from outside, I mean. Then Beatty schedules this visit to West Point. Your man Bassett was right. Something's going on. I got a line on the Pentagon switchboard. Him and Hedges have been on the phone, five, maybe six times a day for the past couple of weeks. And that guy Thompson, he's been talking to Beatty every day, too. I don't know what's happening, Slaight, but you touched a nerve with this thing. One of my guys down there says this is the hottest he's ever seen it. *Ever*. He said not even the Tet Offensive generated this much heat. I don't know how this kid David Hand plugs into the action, but he does. One of my guys put an eyeball on some poop in Beatty's outer office one day, and it was stuff on Hand. He couldn't tell what it was, but he saw the name. You touched a fuckin' nerve, Slaight."

"Jesus. Sounds like it."

"You want some advice from an old retired sergeant major?"

"That's why I'm talking to you, Sergeant Major. You know that."

"It's time you had a one-on-one with this guy Beatty. He's your man. If I was you, I'd get him alone. Bluff him. Sprinkle David Hand's name all over the damn place. Let him know that you're onto his involvement in the David Hand thing. Watch him close. If he starts to squirm, push him. Make him think you're right on the verge of doing something really rash, like going to the papers. But don't be specific. Just let him believe you're cracking, and you're making your move this weekend. When you've got him really sweating, walk out without saying a word, like you're heading off to do whatever it is he thinks you're going to do. If I'm not wrong, this guy Beatty's the kind who believes in ghosts. He's got to, sitting where he's sitting. Give that SOB something to be afraid of, and he'll pull every string there is, he'll do anything to protect his anonymity. He's a back-room fucker. He'll want to stay that way. You get him to think you're gonna expose him, and it'll be all over. That's the way I figure it, anyways."

"Thanks, Sergeant Major."

"Don't mention it. Hey. Ry. Lemme know how things go, huh?"

"Sure."

Slaight hung up and dialed Bassett, relaying his notes from the conversation with Sergeant Major Eldridge.

"Do it," was all Bassett said. "Do it."

Slaight dropped another dime and called a cadet in the First Regiment whom he knew was close to Beatty. Unsuspecting, the cadet told him Beatty was staying in the Eisenhower Suite of the Hotel Thayer and would probably be there the rest of the afternoon. The cadet had just talked to him. He was to "escort" Beatty to supper in the mess hall that evening, at six.

It was four o'clock. Slaight had two hours.

36

William Beatty was sitting behind a huge desk at the far end of the Eisenhower Suite. Slaight recognized him from photos in *Assembly* magazine, photos from awards ceremonies at the Pentagon, visits to various army posts, speeches at Founders Day Dinners.

"Can I help you, young man?" he asked, smiling. He removed his glasses. Even from a distance, Slaight could see his face was unlined, smooth, fleshy like a baby's. An

423

extra chin dangled beneath a dim, five o'clock shadow. Slaight closed the door to the suite behind him. The room was a memorial to things West Point. Everywhere were the colors, black-gray-gold, the motto, "Duty, Honor, Country." Slaight didn't pause to examine the plaques, mementos, flags, and photographs of famous occupants of the suite. He walked straight for Beatty's desk.

"My name is Ry Slaight," he announced as he reached the middle of the room.

"I know who you are," answered Beatty.

"And I've come to talk about the murder of David Hand."

Slaight halted, hat gripped tightly in his left hand, the stiff collar of his Dress Gray coat rubbing his chin. Beatty's smile dissolved into terminal weariness, arid, so dry and scaly you knew even his sweat glands were tired, tiny facial ducts and pores shriveled, empty, finished. Beatty fumbled in his jacket pocket, withdrew a vial of pills, and popped two in his mouth, swallowing.

"I have this . . . condition . . ." he stuttered.

"I don't care what condition you have, Mr. Beatty. I'm here to talk about a young man, David Hand, who seems to have passed away quietly, with no official fanfare, and very, very little sympathy. And you two were *such good friends.*" Slaight enunciated slowly, watching Beatty. His face sagged, like a sponge, oozing up just a bit, then down, reacting to forces unseen beneath the surface.

"Sit down, Mr. Slaight," said Beatty weakly. Slaight remained standing.

"I guess I've known this day would come for a long time now," said Beatty, looking out the window, past the barren leafless trees, at the Hudson.

"What are you going to say to me, Mr. Slaight? Go ahead. Say it."

Slaight started pacing, back and forth across the carpet in front of Beatty's desk.

"Look. This kid was murdered. I know it. The commandant, Hedges, he knows it. You know it. And we all know who killed him, don't we, Mr. Beatty? Don't we?"

Beatty nodded, still staring out the window.

424

"VanRiper. He was one of your boys, wasn't he, Mr. Beatty? Wasn't he one of the guys in your crowd last year, one of the guys you're always taking down to the Pentagon and introducing around? Wasn't VanRiper one of your sterling crew . . . a general-in-the-making? Wasn't he?"

Beatty nodded.

"Well, goddammit, everybody knows he killed Hand, and nothing's being done about it. *Nothing*. There has been no Article 32 investigation, no charges, no court-martial, no nothing. The guy who murdered Hand killed him in cold blood, grabbed the poor bastard and held him underwater till he drowned . . . he's free as a bird right now. That wouldn't have anything to do with the fact he's a homosexual, would it, Mr. Beatty?"

Beatty turned and faced Slaight.

"What about it, Mr. Beatty? Hand was a fag. VanRiper was a fag. A murder was committed, and nothing is happening. I want answers. I want to know why VanRiper is over in Vietnam right now, bopping around, a free man."

"You're wrong there, Mr. Slaight. He was killed on patrol two days ago. I received word of his death yesterday."

"So that's why you're up here at the academy! You know who killed Hand, and now that he's dead, too, you've got nothing left to investigate and all that's left is tying off a few loose ends. Well! I've got a file on the David Hand murder that will choke the goddamn New York *Times*, as well as any congressional committee looking to throw its weight around. I'm one loose end you're not going to tie off, Mr. Beatty. You're in this thing up to your neck. . . ."

Beatty stood, and Slaight, startled, stopped pacing and faced him.

"And so are you, Mr. Slaight. And so are you." Beatty leaned forward, his hands resting on the green desk blotter before him. "We've got a file on you, too, Slaight. A nice fat file full of details about you and your . . . shall we say . . . *relationship* with the late Mr. Hand. We know all about you and your supposed 'counseling' sessions with

Hand, those many hours he spent in your room, the two of you alone, behind closed doors. We know about the times you two were spotted together in the sinks, when you held Hand downstairs for 'special inspection' just before taps. Beast Barracks was, well, conducive to certain freedoms as well as discipline, was it not, Mr. Slaight?" Beatty stared at Slaight through squinty eyes.

"You haven't got jack-shit on me, Mr. Beatty," said Slaight, staring levelly across the desk. "And this bluff you're running is losing air so quick, I can hear it hiss."

"Oh, Mr. Slaight! Such bluster!"

Slaight stuttered in anger.

"Page after page, Mr. Slaight. An entire log, hour by hour, clocking the time you spent alone with Hand. Firsthand accounts. Affidavits from individuals in your squad, from your fellow squad leaders, from upperclassmen. An impressive collection, Mr. Slaight. Equal in every way to the circumstantial so-called evidence you have, I'd bet."

"And what does it add up to, Mr. Beatty? Tell me. Where in your Beast Barracks catalogue about Hand and me is the grenade you can pull the pin on? What are you trying to say? Me and Hand got it on? You got a tape of pillow-talk from sweet thing David, bragging that he fucked his squad leader during Beast? Come on, Beatty. The shit's been deep too goddamn long, and I'm getting tired of the stink. Put up or shut up."

"We've got it, Mr. Slaight. Believe it."

Slaight paused. Beatty wasn't just bluffing. He probably had a stack of affidavits, he might even have listened to Hand blowing smoke about Beast, making up a bunch of shit to counter the crippling breakdown he suffered when Slaight hit him with all that stuff about his sister. If Beatty was bluffing, it was at least formidable. He had obviously planned for a frontal assault by Slaight well in advance. Slaight considered his position. It wasn't good. Beatty was calling him a fag, in effect; it was more than a bluff, it was a dare. Slaight felt quickly for his options and found only one: retaliate in force, but scout him, feel him out first.

426

"I'll believe it when I see it, Mr. Beatty. That's what I'm here for. Haul out the shit and show it to me. So far, all I've seen is talk. You want me off this Hand thing, you're going to have to scrape me off with data. Now give."

Beatty reached in the pocket of his suit jacket for a pair of glasses, and opening his briefcase, withdrew a thick manila envelope. He squeezed open a metal clasp and spilled its contents onto the blotter. Slaight glanced at the tier of paper work. A glance was enough. It had the aroma: *official*.

"Let me see," said Beatty, fitting his glasses over his slightly protruding ears. "There's so much here. . . ." He continued to flip through the papers. "And it's all so . . . *interesting*." He enunciated the word with the precision of a lawyer giving his final arguments to a friendly jury. Confidently. A smile passed his lips as he withdrew a legal-length document, at least twenty pages thick, holding it before him, Joe McCarthy-style, so Slaight could see only the blank side of its last page.

"Here we have it, Mr. Slaight," said Beatty, his smile widening into a darting grin, an odd rapid succession of twitches hovering somewhere this side of euphoria. He flipped through the pages of the document, saying nothing. After a moment reviewing its contents, Beatty closed the document, gripping its sides tightly. Slaight stood there, studying the man. Then he noticed. Beatty's hand had formed fists. With an abrupt slam, Beatty brought the twenty-odd pages hard atop the desk, scattering the rest of the paper work. He looked up at Slaight, removing his glasses with his left hand. The smile was gone.

"What we have here, my boy, is a simple case of adolescent obsession. Understandable. Ordinary. Even admirable, from at least one angle."

"And that angle, Mr. Beatty?" Slaight scouted.

"Your . . . ah . . . *interest* in the death of David Hand . . ." Again Beatty spoke the word with spooky authority. "Your . . . *interest* as you have made abundantly clear, has far exceeded normal bounds and reflects nothing but jealousy on your part, Mr. Slaight. Raw jealousy."

"Jealousy? Of what?"

"You had your problems with his sister, Samantha—David said she could be quite the bitch—and you took out your hostility on David. And so, Mr. Slaight, you found yourself . . . your *true* self . . . but you lost David. He was a pretty boy, and his loss must have been expensive. *For you*." Beatty smiled evenly, his squinty eyes opening slightly to take in Slaight's barest reaction. All the cards were out now. The bluffing was over, and Beatty was calling.

Slaight was just beginning to drift, that same . . . *so this is the way it happens* . . . drift, when the notion seized him. Thank God for Military Art, he muttered inwardly. Scouts in. Now. Retaliate. In force. No other choice. The instinct came from deep inside him, down there for Lord only knows how long . . . the streets back home, the old man and his way with horses, Ma, her poundcake wisdom uttered in her slow Kansas drawl after supper as she washed and he dried . . . *retaliate*. And Ma, she always had the same parting words, no matter the problem, or its solution.

Take care, son.

She was right, every time, Slaight recalled, his skidding memory racing across his past and coming to a halt right here, now, at West Point, Beatty standing in front of him waiting to see if he'd fold or move. Slaight smiled to himself. They even taught it in Tactics at West Point. The word was discretion, only he'd always like Ma's better: *take care.* Nodding his head slowly up and down, as if to signal yes, Slaight slumped into an overstuffed chair at the side of the desk in mock resignation. He sighed audibly, folding his hands in his lap across the zipper of his Dress Gray jacket.

"Christ, Mr. Beatty, this is really something," said Slaight, staring at the spit-shined toes of his shoes. Beatty's shoulders sagged, relaxing, and a smiled crossed his face. Slaight crossed his legs and tapped the toe of his right foot in the air soundlessly.

"I mean, you've got this file, you've got this mystery document I still haven't seen, I mean, all I'm hearing is words, and still . . ." Slaight lingered, as though he was

428

uncertain as to what he should say next. Beatty eased himself onto his chair. Now the two faced each other across the pile of scattered documents, paper work, the connective tissue of organizations large and small, the blood of bureaucracy. Poop-sheets. They made Slaight feel comfortable. Words on paper. And he hadn't been shown a single one.

"What I'm trying to say, Mr. Beatty, is . . . it's all so fuckin' *ordinary*." He let the word hang. Beatty didn't react, waiting. Slaight looked up from the toe of his shoe and fixed Beatty with a stare.

"So fuckin' ordinary, man. Everything I've heard about you, I expected you'd come loaded to do some real business, and here you sit behind this pile of crap, and all you're doing is saying, Slaight, you're either a closet queen or a faggot, you fell for Hand like the rest of us, and that's what drove you to crank this thing until you're sitting in a room with a deputy Secretary of Defense. Jealousy. For crying out loud, Beatty. Is that all you can come up with? Jealousy is the cheapest, two-bit human twist, man, the kind of jealousy you're pushin' could be satisfied with the back of my hand or a tongue-lashing over two martinis. Christ, man, your act is so full of shit I can hear your asshole puckering." Slaight glared at Beatty, drilling him, not at all sure his ploy would work. Beatty stared back silently. Smart. The level was verbal, spoken words, and so long as it remained that way, Slaight figured Beatty had the upper hand. It frightened him, scared the shit out of him, but he knew he'd have to act, *move*, if he was going to nail Beatty.

"What's the matter with these poop-sheets? How come you haven't handed me the piece that's going to send me back to the barracks with my thumb in my ear, looking for a place to hide?"

"Unnecessary," said Beatty. "You know the facts at least as well as I."

"THE FUCK I DO," yelled Slaight, swinging his right foot across the top of the desk, scattering papers into Beatty's lap, against the wall, carrying academy knick-

429

knacks like army mules and replicas of Civil War cannons with them. Beatty leapt to his feet, his face crimson.

"I'll see you in Leavenworth for that, mister!" he screamed in a high-pitched whine. "That's assault! I'll have you court martialed, you insubordinate little . . ." his voice sputtered off into a series of wheezes and gasps for air. Slaight remained sitting, recrossing his legs.

"You haven't got diddlyshit in that pile, Beatty. If you did, you would have tacked me one tack at a time to the top of this desk, poop-sheet by poop-sheet. You're smart, Mr. Beatty. But you forgot something. If you're gonna bring guns, you'd better be ready to use them. You didn't. Elemental tactical error. They teach it plebe year. Feints don't work when you got nothing to back them up with. Your shit is in the wind, Beatty. Sit down."

Beatty reached for the phone, dialing, still sputtering. Before he hit the third digit, Slaight reached across the desk and hit the cradle buttons, and the line went dead. He leaned closer to Beatty.

"This is how it shakes down. You're calling me a faggot. You wanna call names?" Slaight stood up, reaching for his cap. "Let's go. Right now. Out that door. Let's go public, Mr. Beatty. No sense name-calling behind closed doors. Let's go public. You lay out your garbage, and I'll lay out mine, the networks and the papers will be up here in battalion force, and we'll see who comes out on top. You wanna call me a faggot? Okay by me. But you do it out there where people can hear you, because in here, it don't fuckin' *count*." Slaight was standing by the door, hat in left hand, beckoning with his right. It was a gamble, a dangerous gamble, and a shitstorm waited outside if Beatty moved. But it was all Slaight had. He waited.

Beatty didn't move. He sat down, staring at the cluttered desk, picking a cuticle on his left hand with his right forefinger.

"It's all over, Mr. Beatty. You know why? I've got enough bad shit in my files on the David Hand murder to crack the granite this place sits on. You'll feel the tremors from West Point all the way down in your office in the Pentagon, Mr. Beatty. You'll feel the tremors right there

430

in the office of the Secretary of Defense. And if my information is correct, a lot of other big dudes down there will feel the same tremors when the David Hand murder case breaks open. You know the old term 'knee-level wind,' Mr. Beatty?"

Beatty shook his head no.

"That's what happens when knees start shaking. Knee-level wind. You better get used to it, Mr. Beatty. You better invest in some paperweights for your desk, because there's gonna be a goddamn hurricane of knee-level wind when I'm finished, Mr. Beatty. When I unlock that file of mine showing the butt-fucking and cock-sucking that went on, when I'm finished showing how Hand was killed, and *why* . . . Well. I leave it to your imagination. Where do you think the chopping will start? With you? Somebody else? One of the generals you wrote letters to concerning Hand? Hedges? Thompson? Where will the ax fall first, Mr. Beatty? You'd better start figuring."

Slaight paused, stopped pacing, and glared at William Beatty. He would get no answer. He didn't need one. The answer to his question was all over Beatty's face, a soft, doughy confection of every deal he'd ever made, every string he'd ever pulled, every connection he'd ever touched, every bureaucratic ploy he'd ever executed, every career he'd either helped or destroyed. Slaight stared at the man before him.

"I'll be going now, Mr. Beatty. I see we've got nothing to say to each other at this point. Maybe next week, when the fur begins to fly. Just remember this, Mr. Beatty. Your good friend David Hand . . . his death came cheap. Just like every other poor SOB who gets fucked in the ass, one way or another, up here at West Point every day. But from this moment on, Mr. Beatty, it's going to cost you. Hand was a bright, charming, pretty boy, like you said. The way you two got along . . . he deserves better, don't you think?"

Slaight walked out of the Eisenhower Suite, out of the hotel, headed north, toward the barracks.

William Beatty picked up the telephone and made several telephone calls, three to the Pentagon, and two local: Hedges and Thompson. His conversations were brief. There was no time for elaboration. It was over.

The deputy Secretary of Defense started packing his bags. He would fly back to Washington that night. The next few days were going to be rough. There were so many pieces to be picked up, so many moves to be made, so many debts to be called in. And now they were maneuvering defensively. They had to move fast.

Somehow, Hedges had miscalculated. Slaight *knew*. Beatty didn't know how, and at this point, it didn't really matter. Slaight *knew*.

37

Slaight talked to lawyer Bassett, the sergeant major, Dr. Consor, his father. Over the weekend, he talked to Irit, and he made up his mind. Sunday night, Bassett outlined a plan. The next morning, Slaight would make his move.

On November 11, 1968, at 9:15 A.M., Cadet Slaight reported to the superintendent of the United States Military Academy. He carried a brown metal Sears and Roebuck file box. The supe was "extremely busy," according to his aide. But when he was informed of the nature of Slaight's visit, entry was easily gained.

The superintendent had been stunned earlier to learn that over the weekend, his commandant, General Hedges, and the head of his Social Science Department, Colonel Thompson, had departed West Point on special orders. Thompson had taken a high-level position on the National Security Council, and Hedges was scheduled to work for something called the Office of Emergency Preparedness. No explanations were given for their sudden reassignments to powerful posts in the federal government.

But a much greater shock awaited the superintendent in a pile of paper work that had appeared mysteriously on his desk sometime over the weekend, when his office was

432

closed. The death of a cadet sometime last May . . . he barely remembered the name . . . an accidental drowning as he recalled . . . but the paper work, Xeroxed and organized into neat categories, alleged that the cadet had been *murdered*, and that he, the superintendent, had covered up the murder. It was all done in a very gentlemanly fashion. No formal charges. No allegation of criminal acts. Just a request from Department of the Army for his resignation, undated. Rylander was dumbstruck.

When Slaight unlocked his metal box and began laying out his files, recounting the events of the past six months with calm, almost icy precision, the superintendent just sat there and listened. It all made sense now—the whole story. That SOB Hedges had been gunning for him all this time, and he'd been too slow, too *old*, to have seen what was going on behind his back. The story of the cadet's murder was complex and ugly. The superintendent listened with grim fascination.

It was the way things were these days, the general concluded. You falsified your body counts, and you awarded yourself medals for imaginary valor in an imaginary war. If you could do that, you could do anything. And this was it. This was the war in Vietnam brought home on the shoulders of the men who fought it. This was Hedges' personal little war. The superintendent had simply fallen behind, caught in the dust of men like Hedges, who would weld together from the junk pile of their careers the army of the future. For the sake of the country, the superintendent hoped it would run.

When Slaight had finished the story of the murder of David Hand and the elaborate cover-up which followed, Rylander stood, motioning for Slaight to follow. They walked through the outer office, into the hall, and climbed a set of stairs growing more and more narrow the higher they climbed. The superintendent pushed open a door, and they were outside, atop a small parapet, the roof of a tower dominating the Academic Building Headquarters.

"This is where I come to do my thinking," said the supe. "Like it?"

Slaight looked around. You could see everything from
433

up there . . . all the way down the Hudson to the Bear Mountain Bridge, upriver to Cold Spring, the cadet barracks, the Chapel, the Plain—everything.

"You did the right thing, Slaight," the superintendent said. "Don't worry about an Aptitude Board or anything else. I'll take care of everything before I go."

"Before you go, sir? You're not going to take the fall for Hedges! Not after what I've told you!"

"No. I'm not caving in on this Hedges business. They already have some young buck picked to replace me next month. I've known about it for some time. He's a big Vietnam hero, biggest hero they've got right now. Commands something called the American Division. Racked up the biggest body count in the war. They're bringing him here, so you cadets can see what a real Vietnam hero looks like up close. He'll be cracked up to look like Christ in a green beret when he arrives for the change-of-command."

"I didn't know anything about that, sir."

"Neither did Hedges, apparently, or he wouldn't have bothered with this damn-fool scheme to pin the cover-up of that murder on me. Hedges. He's one to watch. He's going places."

"You're not going to nail him, sir? For what he did? He committed at least three felony violations of military law that I know of."

"Nail Hedges? With him down there on the staff of the OEP? If I tried that, the White House would get involved, and the whole business would come out. We can't allow that to happen. Not to the academy."

Slaight stood atop the parapet watching the Hudson go by. The supe wouldn't go down in flames, but he'd go quietly, just so the academy wouldn't get hurt, so the good name of the academy wouldn't be dragged through the mud. *The academy.* Jesus.

"What are you going to do now, son?" The supe looked at him. The cold November wind ruffled the lapel of his uniform jacket. "This army needs men like you, Slaight. What you did here—it took guts. We need your kind."

434

"What I did had nothing to do with guts, sir."

The superintendent looked at the cadet, studied his face. The boy's eyes were empty pools of hatred and fear. He'd gone too far, too fast. He'd paid for it. He'd seen the look before.

"What am I going to do, sir? I want out. I've had enough. The academy will never be the same for me, sir. Not after this. You can do what you want to protect the good name of West Point, sir, but I'm not so damn sure there's anything left worth protecting any more."

The superintendent stared across the Hudson, his back to the cadet.

"You're not going to . . . go public . . . with all the information you've got? If you give it to the newspapers, they'll use it against us. They'll smear us. The army's got enough trouble with the demonstrators and the war and everybody against us. Don't give them *this*."

Slaight thought fast. He'd learned his lesson. He'd paid his dues. The time had come for him to be the one making the deal. He held all the cards.

"I won't go public with this stuff on Hedges and Beatty and Thompson and David Hand if you get me out of here free and clear, sir. I want to be discharged from the service. I don't want to graduate from West Point. I don't want to be an army officer. And I don't want to go the resignation route. I'd have to serve four years as an enlisted man that way, sir, and they'd get me. You know they would."

The superintendent studied the cadet. He was right. Even if Slaight graduated and was commissioned a second lieutenant, Hedges and his crew would figure a way to get him. Hell. When you set out to get the superintendent of the United States Military Academy, the life of a second lieutenant is small potatoes indeed.

"All right. I'll take care of it. But give me a few days. It's going to take me awhile to get the paper work through without tipping off Beatty or Hedges, any of their allies."

"In the meantime, sir, I want to go on leave. I'm finished with West Point. *Finished*."

"Done. I'll sign the leave papers myself. Now. About your files . . ."

"You can take my file box, sir. It's yours. But I must tell you I'm keeping copies of everything for my own protection. You'll have to take my word that I won't give them to the newspapers."

"I'll accept that."

The superintendent and the cadet walked down the stairs from the tower. Slaight picked up his short overcoat and hat, heading back to the barracks. It was almost 10:30. The guys in the company would be back from class.

They were waiting in his room when he got there, Lugar and Buck and Towne and even Bloomingburg. All the guys who knew what was happening. Kip, the company honor representative, walked in. They had their class shirts off. Somebody put a Buck Owens record on. Out in the hallway, plebes could be heard delivering the mail, collecting the laundry. Somebody called one of them a dullard, and there was a resounding *crack* as the plebe snapped his heels together and hit the wall. Another plebe spouted the menu for lunch: meat loaf, lima beans, mashed potatoes, sir. Things were returning to normal.

The guys said it was all over the Corps that morning about Hedges and Thompson leaving on special orders. Even Grimshaw and Regimental Commander King were gone, back to the Big Red One in Nam. Their departures were greeted with typical cadet enthusiasm. Having Grimshaw and King out of the way was a "good deal."

Slaight told the guys in his room about meeting with the superintendent. He told them how Hedges had tried to pin the cover-up on the supe, how the supe figured Hedges had been out for his job. He told them everything. Then he said he was leaving. No one spoke. Leroy Buck picked up the *Times*, turning to the financial pages. Lugar pulled his Brown Boy around his shoulders. It was like they expected Slaight to announce he was resigning, and if they waited long enough, the notion would pass—he'd

436

forget it, pick up a book, and they'd all settle back into being firsties again.

The whole room looked up in unison when First Captain Pete Locke walked in and broke the silence.

"The supe tells me you're resigning, Slaight. I've just come from his office. He told me everything. Listen, man. You can't do that. You can't resign *now*. Not after everything that's happened. We need you, Slaight. You're like a symbol that the . . . ah . . . system works. You know?"

"Yeah," said Slaight. "I know what you mean."

"I've got real problems with our classmates over in the Fourth Regiment. I've been told you know about them."

"Yeah."

"Well? You gonna stay? Those guys over there look up to you, Slaight. Guys you don't even know. They've been watching you—watching to see what happened to you. And these guys, the guys in your company. Your friends. This thing is bigger than you, especially now."

"Yeah." It was John Lugar. He was standing, facing Slaight. "If you leave now, it's like . . . it's like saying they beat you, Slaight. It's like giving up. You *won*, man. Don't you see that? You've got to stay. What good is everything that happened to you, that happened to us, man, if you take a walk?"

Slaight was sitting behind his desk, toying with a row of pencils, moving one over the other in hopscotch fashion, avoiding the eyes around him. Leroy Buck put aside the *Times*, flipping a lock of blond hair out of his eyes. The motion of his head caught Slaight's attention.

"Slaight, you fuckstick. Look around this here room." Buck's southern accent warmed the air. He pointed soundlessly to the file cabinets and stacks of poop-sheets and magazines and newspapers. The room was truly a headquarters, Slaight its natural commander. The presence of the first captain, Pete Locke, was testimony to that.

"You just gonna up and leave this shit, Slaight? You lazy, no-good-for-nothin' dimbo. Dontcha see there's still shit to do? C'mon, man. You leave now, and ole Hedges won. He said he'd see your ass out of here, and leavin' like this . . . goddamn-goddamn . . . you're lettin' him *win*, Slaight. You can't do that."

Slaight looked around the room. They were all watching him, and they were right. He was copping out. He was a leader, a natural-born leader. The day he decided to get to the bottom of the David Hand case, he had created an issue. It was like he'd held aloft a guidon, and they had followed him. Now that he'd gotten to the bottom of it, he was telling them that it hadn't been worth it. And he was telling them something else, a secret he'd kept from them and from himself the whole time. Without saying it aloud, he was hinting at his ambivalence about his ability to lead. He was afraid of it at the same time it turned him on. The death of David Hand had caused him to catch a glimpse of his strength, his inbred ability to wield power. For a long time, he had derived an enormous satisfaction from his ability to influence others. He thought he knew most of its components, all of its dimensions. He'd tested himself. But now he knew something about his abilities he hadn't known before, and he knew he had to tell his friends about it. He didn't know what to say, where to begin.

"The thing was never winning or losing, Buck. Not really. The thing was . . . Jesus . . . to test the system. Did the fuckin' system work? It was part of playing the game, Leroy. Thing was, we decided to play the game right to the hilt. We took the system at its word. We played by their rules. Hell, you play by their rules the day you walk in here and drop your fuckin' bags when the man tells you to drop 'em."

"What the fuck does dropping your goddamn bags have to do with the price of eggs?" asked Buck angrily.

"Gimme a break, man. What I'm sayin' is, we accepted the terms. So you've got to measure the results in their terms. Did the system work? Yeah. Hedges is gone. Thompson is gone. Grimshaw is gone. They're all fuckin' gone. They never got me, man. I'm leaving, but I'm leaving on *my* terms. I made the deal. You understand that? I'm keeping my mouth shut, and the supe is fixing it so

438

I'm discharged from the army. It's my decision, and my deal. Nobody is forcing me."

"So what?" Lugar was on his feet. "You wouldn't make a deal with Hedges, but now you're making a deal with the supe. What's the fuckin' difference, Slaight? Ends up the same, no matter who makes the deal. The whole thing is hushed up. Nobody'll ever know what happened. You're full of shit, Slaight. You just saw a good deal, and you took it." Lugar was mad as hell, and his face blazed more red than his hair.

"Hey, fuck you, Lugar. You wanna blow the whistle on Hedges and the rest of them? Go ahead. You guys know everything I know, including you, Locke. You guys could call the New York *Times*. Any one of you. You don't need me to put Hedges up against the wall. You got your own minds to make up about that. I'm not going to help you." No one spoke. Slaight was challenging them, and his voice had a tired, angry edge on it.

"Okay, Ry. You made your point." It was Kip, the honor rep. "But what about the point Lugar raised? To me, it makes a difference, who makes the deal, and what the deal is." Kip's calm voice eased the tension in the room.

"Okay. Lugar's right. You wanna accuse me of taking the better of two deals, getting out when the getting is good? You've got me. I've got no excuse. I'm doing it. But we all know how much the old West Point 'No excuse, sir' line is worth. It's supposed to work for plebes, but hell, it didn't even work back then." Leroy Buck chuckled, then everyone laughed, recalling some private plebe experience, when 'no excuse' had proved itself inadequate as an excuse. A plebe materialized at the door with a dozen Cokes. Somebody gave him a couple dollars, and he left. Guys slurped thirstily from paper cups.

"You guys have got to understand that it wasn't easy for me to decide to leave West Point." The room fell silent. Straws stood at attention in half-empty cups.

"Breaking that commitment, the commitment you make the first day of Beast . . . it was tough. But when you come right down to it, the issue was never who was gonna

439

win, who was gonna lose. The issue wasn't even David Hand. The issue was West Point. I had to make up my mind about West Point, and I did. I don't belong here. I guess I never did belong here. But it took all this shit comin' down for me to figure it out. I owe West Point one hell of a big debt. This place taught me I wasn't cut out to be an army officer. Know what I mean?" Slaight glanced around the room. There was no reaction, only the same stunned silence. Then Leroy Buck spoke.

"But you're a fuckin' leader, Slaight. That's what it's all supposed to be about, bein' a leader You always had it knocked. Fuck, I remember back when we was plebes . . ." Slaight interrupted him.

"Look. The system says, way down deep, either you join up or you die. That's the nut of truth inside the fuckin' combat example they're always talking about. Well, the way I figure it, Hand never joined up, and he died. The thing I learned these past few months is that I never really joined up, either. And I don't want to die. What I'm saying is this: The system works. West Point is *right.*"

John Lugar walked across the room and stood in front of Slaight. His powerfully built boxer's body bulged beneath his laundry-wracked tattered T-shirt.

"What are you saying, Slaight? You're saying Hedges and the rest of them were right. You're too fuckin' smart to try and pass that gas. And you're no chickenshit. Every guy in this room knows that. So what do you mean, the system works? You're not making any sense, at least not to me." Heads around the room nodded assent. Slaight had known it was going to be difficult to make his friends understand what was inside him, that it might be impossible. He stopped fiddling with the row of pencils and stood up. Walking around John Lugar, he began pacing the length of the room. Sweat poured from his armpits, and his head ached.

"The thing was always West Point, guys. You're asking me what I mean, the system works. Okay. West Point will survive. That's what I mean. The institution will survive, that's what I mean when I say it works. It's the nature, the fuckin' *job*, of places like West Point to survive, to go forward. We use the word 'system' too loosely. You've got to stop thinking of West Point as a machine, and start thinking of it as a living thing, *alive*. Living things reproduce themselves. That's the way they survive. Fuckin' amoebae reproduce themselves. If they didn't, they'd be extinct. There'd be no fuckin' amoeba. Same with West Point. This place survives the same way amoebae do. The system works because we're the system, man. We used to be kids, civilians. Now we're cadets. In June, we'll be officers . . . I mean, you'll be officers. Grads. West Pointers. In July, it'll start all over again. Another bunch of beans, another Beast Barracks, another year, another class of grads. It works. It's alive."

Bloomingburg, whom Slaight noticed was for once without his Bible, spoke:

"I understand what you mean, Ry." His voice crept just above a whisper, but everyone heard him.

"I figured you would, Jay."

"Me, too." It was Leroy Buck, standing at the stereo, turning the record over.

"So West Point will survive, and maybe it's right that West Point should survive this shit. I mean, look at the fuckers who were involved. Hedges. A goddamn psychopath. Grimshaw. A paranoid. Thompson. A secret Nazi. Beatty. A mystery man with connections in the highest levels of the military and civilian establishments of this country. West Point was right, the system worked, because Hedges and his crew didn't count on guys like us, guys like Captain Bassett, Sergeant Major Eldridge, guys who were willing to pay the price. You wanna believe in something, man, you don't just sit back and watch, waitin' to see if it works. You jump in there and make it work. Hedges wasn't willing to pay that price, man, and he isn't com any more. Same with the rest of them. They took it all for granted. They had power, and they'd had it so long they forgot power is earned. You work for it. Those fuckers . . . they made the fatal mistake. It's a mistake that was just sitting there waiting for them, like a pothole in a road. One of the oldest in the book. They forgot power is a privilege, bestowed upon those who earn it, and began thinking of power as a *right*."

"What about David Hand?" It was Pete Locke, first captain, standing over near the door, arms folded across the breast of his Dress Gray jacket. "How does he fit in? And how about VanRiper? Hell, he was a regimental commander. He was going to be a general. Everybody talked about him that way "

"VanRiper believed in ghosts. He thought Hand was going to blackmail him, come back and haunt him some day. I know enough about Hand now to know VanRiper was wrong. Hand wouldn't have done it. Hand was too . . . vulnerable to have attempted blackmail. So the ghosts weren't real. They were in VanRiper's head. But he imagined them, believed the ghosts to be real enough he killed Hand to erase them from his mind. He murdered. It was the West Point way. Hand the enemy. Trouble was, VanRiper was a fag, too. He was killing the part of himself he hated, the faggot in him. West Point does not allow for the possibility that the enemy is you."

The record changer clicked, and a Marty Robbins album plonked onto the turntable. Nashville crooning eased gently from the speakers in the corners, taking the edge from Slaight's tirade. He stopped pacing the room, realizing that he had begun talking to his classmates and had ended up lecturing them. He felt foolish. He was omitting what he'd really wanted to tell them, the part that hurt, the part about himself.

"How 'bout Hand, Slaight?" Leroy Buck asked. "You still ain't said nothing 'bout Hand."

"Yeah, I know. Hand is . . . well, he's more complicated, and I'm not sure I understand David Hand, even after all the shit that's gone down. One thing I'm pretty sure about: West Point was right when it came to David Hand. The system said: Check your bullshit adolescent arrogance at the door, and watch your step, mister. David Hand ignored those rules, and now he's dead. I'm not sure his death is evidence that he couldn't have gotten away with ignoring the rules, if VanRiper hadn't killed him. Guys get away with breaking and ignoring rules every day around here. Some of them make a career out of the practice." Lugar and a few others chuckled. Pete Locke smiled.

"In Hand, though, the drive ran deeper. Hand was such a good cadet . . . you know, he just had it *down* . . . he got bored with the challenge of becoming a cadet, the challenge of plebe year, and he began testing the system. I have an idea Hand was such a good plebe because"—Slaight stared out the window—"because he was a fag. He was already a plebe, before he got here, if you get what I mean. That's why he had it knocked."

"Are you saying fags make better plebes, Slaight? Or that being a plebe is faggy?" John Lugar asked the question. He was genuinely curious. The rest of the guys appeared to be studying the bottoms of their empty Coke cups with unusual interest.

"All I'm saying is, Hand understood something about what goes on here at West Point that we didn't understand. At least, I certainly didn't understand it when I was his squad leader in Beast, and I'm not so goddamn sure I understand it now, either. One thing about him, however, is clear. Hand bucked the system, and he enjoyed it. He thrived on it. He loved it."

Leroy Buck looked up. "Yeah," he drawled. "You could fuckin'-A say that again." The room fell silent. Marty Robbins was singing about trains and love gone wrong, an embrace of musical subject matter only country and western singers had the balls, or bad taste, to assault. Slaight had no idea why, but it worked.

"Well, I did, too, goddammit," said Slaight. Every head in the room turned to face him. He was standing by the window, leaning against a file cabinet.

"I've bucked the system one way or another for three and a half years, but it wasn't until this Hand thing that I discovered how much I liked it. I fuckin' *loved* it, just like Hand. Me and him were the same that way. I knew it back in Beast last year, but I'd never admit it to myself. But I fuckin' know it now."

Leroy Buck put a Tammy Wynette record on the

stereo, "Stand By Your Man." He sat down on the bed and whistled that soft whistle of his, through his teeth.

"The thing that got to me . . . Christ, this is tough to explain. It bothered me when I knew, down deep, how much Hand and I were alike. But the thing that really got me was the more I fought the system—Hedges and the rest of them—the more I became like them. The process was absorptive. You couldn't get away from it, because after a while, it surrounded you, and you were inside it. You become the thing you're struggling against. I saw it first in Hand, when I began to find out more and more about him. At first, I thought he didn't fit in. Then I realized he did. I mean, look where he fit! Beatty . . . Thompson, they were thick with Hand. When he got killed, paper work flew like you wouldn't believe, Hedges and upward, Lord only knows how high. But it was invisible. Let me ask you something. You think if Hand wasn't a fag things would have been handled differently? You damn straight they would have! Christ, the flood of poop-sheets and snoops and MPs and investigators that hit this place would have blinded us. But Hand—not a flutter. He was in there, guys. Deep. I'm not sure, but with Hand, it might not have been a case of becoming the thing you're fighting. To us, Hand appeared to buck the system. I think it's possible Hand was part of the system the whole time."

Guys were studying their fingernails, playing with their shoelaces, polishing their belt buckles with their shirttails. They were listening, but they consciously avoided Slaight's gaze. Everyone except John Lugar. He spoke, his voice low, tinged with carbon-steel acuity.

"Enough of this shit about Hand and West Point and the system, Slaight. What about you? If you've got all this stuff figured, and looks to me like you do, how come you're taking a walk?"

"I made up my mind to resign quite awhile ago. When I figured I was getting my kicks the same way as Hand was, I decided it was time to cash my check. I never told you guys, I never told anybody, because . . ." Slaight stopped and looked around the room. He'd known it would come

444

to this. "Because if I did, I'd have to tell you why. I didn't want you guys knowing the real reason I was so obsessed by the death of David Hand. I just wanted you to help me nail the son of a bitch who killed him. I couldn't tell you how much of myself I'd seen in Hand. I didn't want you guys knowing I was comparing myself to a fag."

Lugar gave Slaight a look that said he knew there was something Slaight was holding back. It was instinctive among cadets. You knew you had to respond.

"There's something else, too," said Slaight, choosing his words carefully. "You guys all know me. I've always been kind of an underground leader, a force just beneath the surface of things here at West Point. I've enjoyed the combative feel of it, staying just out of sight, out of reach, but still whipping it on 'em anytime I felt the urge. Then this Hand thing forced me out in the open, and I was tested, really tested, for the first time. I found out I was good. Better than I thought I was. At a certain point, last summer, I knew I had them. I can't explain how or why. I just knew. And it made me nervous . . . scared the shit out of me." Lugar looked up, startled.

"How come?"

"Because I knew then I believed the bullshit. You know. We're always joking around. Who believes this bullshit, anyway, the party line crap they're continually feeding us? Punching each other in the arm during lectures, when some air corps major gets up there on the stage, and he's having an orgasm about his gun ship, his fuckin' mini-guns and his recon-by-fire and all that shit. It's a gas right?" Lugar nodded and a couple of guys chuckled at the memory. There had been so many lectures like that. . . .

"But there's a bottom line to the bullshit, and the bottom line says we're better than the rest of them. We're special. We're being let in on The Secret. I found my own private version of that bottom line and explored it, and discovered they're right. I am special. I am better. That bothered me. But it isn't what scared me."

Slaight had captured their attention again, every one of them, as he usually did when he turned it on, clipped an edge on his voice, widened his eyes and lit a tiny fire in them, moved his hands expertly, like a pianist's, touching the keys of control. He had them now, and he kept it up. He wanted them to remember every syllable he uttered. He knew they would. He had the power, and one last time, he'd exercise it, touch them with invisible brush strokes of color . . . *change them.* . . .

"Hell, believing the bullshit is okay. Every goddamn place pushes one version of it or another. Up at Harvard, they think an MBA is a master key to the vault in the Chase Manhattan Bank. Fuck. The secrets of clubs at Yale like Skull and Bones are darker then the cracks inside King Tut's tomb." Laughter. They were rolling. Time to pull in the reins.

"Once I'd accepted the fact I believed the bullshit, I started testing it, from both ends. I tested the bullshit itself: Are we in fact better? And I tested my belief in it. Fuckin'-A if the equation didn't balance!" More laughter. After three years of engineering, their humor was calculable.

"That's when I got scared. Once the fucker balanced, I kept testing and it didn't tilt one way or the other. I ran out of parameters. I had nothing left to test with. I started crowding the edge. Down near the end, I was just whipping it on, firing blind, running amok. And it was working, clicking, like it was coming straight out of a field manual. But it wasn't. It was coming out of me, and that's when I knew something West Point never prepared me for. I was using power that was coming from a place I didn't know about, some place outside of me. I had no idea where it was coming from. I didn't understand it, thus I couldn't control it. Everything here at West Point is so goddamn rational, you get used to it. You depend on it. And this feeling of power that came from nowhere, it was crazy, I guess the feeling was, it controlled me. The only time I ever felt anything like it was last year in Beast, when Hand was in my squad. I don't know what you call it. Strength. Power. Magic. Spirit. But he had it. You could fuckin' *see* it." Their eyes remained fixed on Slaight as he wound down, striking them with the name

446

Hand like an uppercut to the solar plexus, leaving the room winded, a vacuum sucking air.

"Goddamn-goddamn," said Leroy Buck, breaking the silence, attesting the veracity of Slaight's description of Hand. He changed the record. Johnny Cash sang "Orangeblossom Special." Buck whistled along with the tune through his teeth.

"West fuckin' Point," said Buck. He blew that soft whistle of his: "Slaight, you know somethin'? You as gray as the fuckin' area out there. You go on down to New York City, and you shack up with Irit Dov, and you go ahead and be a goddamn civilian, and you'll still be a gray son of a bitch, Slaight, just as gray as them fuckin' trou you wearin', gray as your T-shirt, gray as fuckin' Dress Gray, Slaight."

"And you're an arrogant fucker, man," said John Lugar, laughing. The room cracked with laughter, the tension broken. Pete Locke, the first captain, shook hands with Slaight and excused himself, asking Slaight to stop by before he left. One by one they stood up and shuffled out the door, mumbling stuff like *See you later, man*, and *Let's get together in the city sometime*. Slaight was nodding and saying, *Yeah, sure*. Finally there remained Slaight and Buck and Lugar. John Lugar stretched out on his bunk and pulled his Brown Boy around his shoulders. Leroy Buck walked to the door, stopped, and turned.

"Gonna get me some rack, Slaight. See you at dinner formation." He shuffled down the hall. As he turned the corner, Slaight heard him:

"Heeeaaauh," came the seal honk. "Fuckin'-A, Slaight."

"Heeeaaauh," answered Slaight, exchanging primitive noises of cadet sanction. He walked down the hall to the phone booth, dialed a number in the 212 area code. When he heard the voice on the other end, he said:

"Irit, it's me. Drive up and get me this afternoon, will you?" She said okay, and he hung up. On his way back to his room, Slaight collared a plebe and issued him a wake-up time and method, two knocks, crack the door, and whisper. Then he crawled under his Brown Boy and got some rack before lunch.

MASTER NOVELISTS

CHESAPEAKE   CB 24163 $3.95
by James A. Michener

An enthralling historical saga. It gives the account of different generations and races of American families who struggled, invented, endured and triumphed on Maryland's Chesapeake Bay. It is the first work of fiction in ten years to be first on *The New York Times Best Seller List.*

THE BEST PLACE TO BE   PB 04024 $2.50
by Helen Van Slyke

Sheila Callaghan's husband suddenly died, her children are grown, independent and troubled, the men she meets expect an easy kind of woman. Is there a place of comfort? a place for strength against an aching void? A novel for every woman who has ever loved.

ONE FEARFUL YELLOW EYE   GB 14146 $1.95
by John D. MacDonald

Dr. Fortner Geis relinquishes $600,000 to someone that no one knows. Who knows his reasons? There is a history of threats which Travis McGee exposes. But why does the full explanation live behind the eerie yellow eye of a mutilated corpse?

8002

Buy them at your local bookstore or use this handy coupon for ordering.

This offer expires 9/30/80